How to Represent a Ghost

How to Represent a
GHOST
A Kate Williams Mystery

Becky A. Bartness

iUniverse, Inc.
Bloomington

How to Represent a Ghost

iUniverse books may be ordered through booksellers or by contacting:

iUniverse
1663 Liberty Drive
Bloomington, IN 47403
www.iuniverse.com
1-800-Authors (1-800-288-4677)

ISBN: 978-1-4620-1846-8 (sc)
ISBN: 978-1-4620-1847-5 (e)

Printed in the United States of America

iUniverse rev. date: 06/09/2011

Prologue

She lost count of the number of days she'd been there. At first, she could tell night from day by the change in the intensity of the heat; at night the temperatures fell a few degrees but never enough to provide much relief. Now, she no longer cared to make the distinction. The passage of time was unmarked and relentless.

She no longer cried out or banged and scratched at the floorboards above her. She didn't have the energy, and even if she did, no one would hear her. No one would care.

She knew she was dying. As she drifted in and out of consciousness, the lines between past and present, memory and immediacy, blurred. She seemed to float outside her body, observing her imminent death detachedly.

She didn't know who her biological mother and father were. She'd been in the state's foster care system since birth. Her mother was a heroin addict who had shared her heroin-laced blood with her fetus; the baby girl was born an addict and spent the first three months of her life in withdrawal. Most adopting parents don't want heroin babies, so, over the years, she had been passed from one foster home to another. She didn't mind; she had never known any other kind of life.

She'd never understood the big deal about parents. Some of the foster families were nice. One foster mother had given her a plastic baby doll she was now too old for. But still she clutched it at her side—even now. Other foster parents were not so nice. She formed no special attachments with the former and bore no grudge against the latter. She judged relationships according to usefulness and adjusted her behavior to the extent and in the manner necessary to serve her purposes, survival being foremost among them.

Her current foster mother wanted her to sit quietly in her room, and she only seemed to fuss over her when *he* was coming over. She hated the clothes her foster mother made her wear before *his* visits: stupid little baby doll dresses that made her look five instead of ten. That's what she was wearing now. She had been waiting in her room for *him* when her foster mother had changed her mind and told her to pack.

Her foster mother had slammed drawers and stuffed clothes into an old suitcase, shouting, "Hurry. We need to get out of here before he gets here."

The little girl had assumed that she was moving to another house. That happened a lot.

Then they heard the car outside.

Chapter 1

The pounding and drilling were getting on my nerves. Stu Napolitano, the slowest contractor in the world, had decided to show up at my office on a Saturday to catch up on his imaginary work schedule. The most I could determine was that The Schedule, as Stu reverently referred to it, consisted of whatever time was convenient for Stu. If it weren't for the fact that he was the only contractor in town that I could afford, I would have booted him off the job months ago.

During my sixteen years of legal practice, I have developed the habit of coming into the office on Saturdays to work without the weekday interruptions of telephone calls, client appointments, court appearances, and staff meetings. I wasn't counting on Stu and his loud equipment ruining my business-Zen. But I was conflicted. I could tell Stu to pack up and come back during the work week when things were already so chaotic that the additional noise and confusion would barely be noticeable. But then remodeling my circa-1920s bungalow-turned-office (of which only the kitchen and reception area were complete) would suffer yet another delay, and Stu would be part of my life even longer.

My office (formerly the master bedroom) and the offices occupied by MJ, my paralegal, and Sam, my investigator, (formerly the second bedroom and nursery, respectively) were at various stages of deconstruction. Today, Stu had applied some ungodly smelling goo to the walls to remove the wallpaper, and he was now pulling up old carpeting as he waited for the goo to do its job. Why he needed a drill and a hammer to accomplish these tasks was a mystery.

The tool noises stopped. My shoulders relaxed in the silence, and for a short time, I was able to focus on the motion for summary judgment MJ had drafted earlier in the week. The motion related to a civil suit over trademark infringement where we represent the defendant, Pole Polishers, Inc., our largest client. Normally, I handle only criminal cases for Pole Polishers, which are plentiful given the character of its business.

According to its brochure, "*The professional staff at Pole Polishers provide personalized services for clients wishing to find a release from life's pressures.*" In other words, Pole Polishers offers sex-for-hire, and its employees are referred to as *Care Bares*. The firm is owned and operated by one of my best friends, Tuwanda Jones, who was herself a Care Bare until she took over management of the company about a year ago.

The trademark infringement suit had been brought by the principals of Post Polish, a local fencing firm. Post Polish claimed that Pole Polishers was a deceptively similar name, entitling Post Polish and its owners to injunctive relief and monetary damages. In my opinion, the plaintiff's position was weak—if Post Polish was losing clients to a firm engaged in prostitution, name confusion was the least of its problems. However, I still needed to convince a judge to take my side, and when it comes to judicial outcomes, all bets are off.

Judges are as biased and subjective as the rest of us. The problem is, when a judge expresses an opinion, it becomes law.

I barely made it through the first page of the draft motion when I heard the groan that wood makes before it breaks, followed shortly by the sound wood makes when it breaks.

Then I heard "shit," which is the sound Stu makes when something jolts him out of his usual state of near-unconsciousness.

"Shit" never meant that something good was happening in Stu's world.

"You okay?" I shouted rhetorically; if Stu was hurt, his vocabulary would be more extensive and descriptive. Stu never missed an opportunity to remind us of the risky nature of his work, and he exaggerated the effects of every sliver, banged thumb, or strained muscle resulting from his minimal efforts.

"I'm fine," he called back. "You got a hole in your

floor, though. You should have it fixed before someone falls in and gets hurt. Do you want me to give you an estimate for the repair cost?"

I sighed, put down my pen, and pushed my chair back. "Be out in a second," I shouted.

I knew what would likely happen next: I would see a freshly made hole that Stu would insist was a pre-existing condition he had just now discovered and narrowly missed injuring himself on, and I should be grateful he didn't sue me for everything I own, the extent of which I'm sure he greatly overestimated.

I trudged into Sam's office, the former nursery, and found Stu crouching on the floor next to a jagged hole with about a two-foot circumference.

"Looks like a fresh break to me," I said, pointing to the light-colored wood at the break line. "And I could have sworn I heard something that sounded like breaking wood." I might as well get the discussion rolling and over with.

"I didn't hear nothin', and I was right here. Plus the carpet was covering it, so it would take a long time to turn dark," Stu retorted.

"Wouldn't someone have fallen through the carpet by now?" Some perverse urge prompted me to pursue an argument I would not win. Regardless of what caused the hole, it had to be fixed before start of business on Monday. I didn't know how to fix it and Stu did.

"You'd think so. You're damned lucky no one did," Stu said with a straight face.

Right. Lucky. Not the word I would use. "Could you have it fixed by Monday?"

Stu rolled back on his heels and assumed the put-upon expression of the unreasonably burdened that he acquired whenever I asked him to complete anything by a specific date.

He made tsk-tsking noises and shook his head slowly, also a part of his standard response. "I'll have to charge you overtime, cuz it's the weekend," he said.

"No," I responded flatly.

"There could be more damage than this hole. It could be the whole floor is rotted out and needs to be replaced."

I bounced on the balls of my feet a few times to test the remaining floorboards. "It seems fine to me," I said, while at the same time silently praying, *Please, God, don't let that be so. I can't afford to replace the entire floor.*

I stared at the floor speculatively and then got on my knees to inspect the hole. "Do you have a flashlight?" I asked. I didn't know what I expected to find, but it was worth a try.

Stu handed me a small penlight, and I shined it around the area where the floor had given way. One of the broken boards had not yet fallen into the black space below and hung tenuously from a thin string of wood fiber. I reached down and pulled it out, doing my best to blot out visions of furry creatures and monsters lurking in the darkness and waiting for the opportunity to bite any human stupid enough to invade their space. (Such creatures and monsters, along with clowns, snakes, ticks, and red lipstick are among the fears leftover from my childhood).

I managed to remove the board without attack and injury, and I peered closely at its underside. I'm no expert, but I didn't see the telltale black dots of dry rot. What I did see, though, were deep gouges, as if someone or something had scraped and scored the wood with a hard object. Teeth marks maybe? They looked too long to be a rat's gnaw-marks. Great. I was back to the monster theory.

Stu grunted impatiently, took the piece of wood from me, and scrutinized it the same way I had.

"The bottom of this board is scraped. Maybe someone tried to remove the floor, but then changed his mind. Anyway, someone needs to get under there and find out the extent of the damage." Stu's tone when delivering this last pronouncement clearly indicated that that "someone" was not going to be him.

Well, it's certainly not going to be me, I thought with an involuntary shudder.

I heard the front door open. "Kate? You here? " shouted Beth, my secretary/administrator/cookie habit enabler. (Freshly baked cookies are my drug of choice and the ability to provide a steady flow of them is a non-negotiable part of Beth's job description).

"I'm in Sam's office with Stu," I called back, getting back to my feet and dusting my hands on my jeans.

Seconds later, Beth appeared in the doorway wearing

a flowered dress, white shoes, and a wide-brimmed white hat with enough flowers on it to qualify it as a Rose Bowl Parade float.

"I was driving by on my way back from Bible study and saw your car parked ..." Beth stopped in mid-sentence when she saw the hole in the floor. "Oh dear lord, Stu, what did you do this time?" (Her automatic assumption that Stu had caused the damage was rooted in precedent. Among other things, Stu had once painted the reception area black in the mistaken belief that since black is a somber, dignified color it was the perfect choice for a law office.) Stu started to object to Beth's implied accusation, but I cut him off. "It looks as if the floorboards were weak." I said, pointing to the piece of wood still in Stu's hand.

"We need someone to crawl underneath the house and check out the extent of the damage."

Beth jerked her chin at Stu. "That's *his* job. Stu, you get down there. Now!" Beth has several children and even more grandchildren, and when she uses her 'don't you dare talk back to me' tone of voice, usually no one does.

But Stu drew his lips together into a tight line and looked ready to dig in and hold his position. "No. I won't. There's not enough room for me to stand up," he said with finality.

Beth placed her hands on her ample hips. (Beth eats more cookies than I do, for quality-check and comparison purposes, she claims.) "What the hell are you talking about? That's a crawl space down there. You have to *crawl*.

Give me a damn flashlight. I'll shine it down there while you climb in and then I'll hand it to you so you can look around."

Stu tried to give her the penlight he'd taken back from me, and she slapped his hand away. "Not that piece of crap. A *real* flashlight."

Stu shrugged and said, "That's all I've got."

"Oh, hell," said Beth disgustedly. "Wait here. I'll be right back."

She stomped out, and we soon heard her rummaging around in her desk. She returned carrying a large, black, military-style flashlight *cum* bludgeon. I wasn't surprised. Beth had an arsenal of weapons in her desk: guns, knives, Tasers, Mace, you name it. So far, she'd never had to use any of them, which proved, to her way of thinking, that collectively, they served as an effective deterrent.

She flipped the flashlight's switch and ran its laser-like beam around the edges of the hole. "Look at that," she said, pointing to a rectangular groove in the floor surrounding the hole. "If Stu can pull out these nails, I bet this whole section will lift out. That should make it easier to repair."

Beth got high marks for good eyesight. The floor had been varnished and re-varnished so many times that the rectangle-shaped groove had all but disappeared. I could barely see it even after I got down on my hands and knees again to inspect.

Beth aimed the light into the hole. She was right. There was enough room for a person to crawl around on all fours. But none of us would be the one to do it. The skull, its sightless eye sockets eerily luminescent in the harsh light, was clearly that of a human. This was a matter for the police.

Chapter 2

Beth made the 9-1-1 call. Stu volunteered to wait outside for the police, no doubt motivated more by the need to escape the grisly tableau than the desire to help. I went into my office, sat down, laid my head on my desk, and closed my eyes. I fought back nausea and tried to block out the remnants of pink-rosebud fabric clinging to the small skeleton and the plastic baby-doll with time-faded features lying next to it. I forced myself to focus on what I knew about the house's history.

According to the real estate agent's report, the title was first conveyed by the then-territorial governor to John McDougall, who built the home sometime in the mid-twenties. Title passed from John McDougall into the McDougall family trust when John died in 1946, and the house was leased out to a succession of tenants until it was sold to me by the trust. I vaguely remembered that a couple of the longer leases had been recorded, but since short-term residential leases are rarely recorded in the county records, the remaining tenants couldn't be determined by simply examining the title report.

I cringed, remembering that I had once joked with my friend Joyce that, because of the attractively low price of the property and great downtown location, I was good to go so long as it wasn't a hazardous-waste dump site and there were no bodies buried anywhere.

I don't even remember requiring much of an inspection before closing because I figured that most of the wiring and plumbing would need to be redone anyway as part of the remodel.

Beth knocked on the door lightly and came in, not waiting for a response. Since even a light knock was unheard-of protocol in this office, I knew she was trying to give me a chance to pull myself together.

Usually, Beth's flawless, rich, honey-colored skin, inherited from her Kenyan dad, and her inquisitive bright blue eyes, inherited from her northern Italian mom, belied her real age. But now she looked every one of her sixty-plus years, and then some.

She had removed the flowered hat and her bun was unraveling; the escaped follicles of her graying hair stood at attention in corkscrew wisps.

"The police are here," she announced flatly.

"Who'd they send?" I asked without raising my head off the desk.

"The usual: Webber and his crew."

Webber was the detective in charge of two previous

murder cases in which I had been involved, and, in addition to the mutual distrust common between defense attorneys and members of the law-enforcement community, we had a personal dislike for each other. He was a rigid law-and-order kind of guy, and, to him, someone who hung around with hookers and employed a gay investigator was an anathema.

I was beginning to think he'd been permanently assigned to any case in which I was involved, in which case he should be grateful to me for providing him with job security.

"We meet again," said Webber from behind Beth.

Beth stepped aside, and Webber appeared in the doorway, looking balder and more pot-bellied than the last time I'd seen him, which wasn't that long ago. The waistband of his brown polyester pants was stretched to the breaking point. Despite the advertising claim of "no ironing required," his suit jacket looked creased and rumpled. He hadn't bothered to button it, but then, I doubt that was even possible. His tie was striped white and a color I had never seen before, and for good reason— no dye company would create that color on purpose. Webber must have found it at a sale of irregular (and unimaginable) clothing.

Beth looked at me questioningly. I shook my head slightly, and she left, closing the door behind her. She and I both knew that this was a mere formality since the walls were paper-thin, and she would hear every word Webber and I said.

I straightened up and did my best to look unruffled. I tried to act as though finding skeletons under one's floor wasn't a big deal. But I couldn't keep my voice from wavering when I spoke.

"Did you see what we found?" I asked.

He gave a short nod and his sardonic expression turned serious.

"May I?" he asked, gesturing toward one of the two chairs facing my desk.

I waved my hand in an "I don't care" motion.

Webber plopped into the chair and slid down, legs splayed in front of him. He looked weary.

"You're probably going to ask if we have any idea who she is," he said.

I noticed that he, like I, had no question about the skeleton's gender.

"I'll save you the trouble," he continued. "We don't have a clue. We searched your address on our system right after Beth put in the 9-1-1 call. There're no missing person reports, or any other police reports for that matter, listing this address. Yet."

I thought his last comment was unnecessary—but not at all unusual coming from him. I chose to ignore it.

"I can't add anything to what you already know," I said. "I'll ask Beth to make copies of the disclosures and other information I received in connection with the building's purchase. You can take it with you when you leave." I was hoping that would be sooner rather than later.

Webber ran his hands over his eyes. "This is coming at a bad time," he said. "I may have to hand this one off."

I couldn't believe it. Macho, invincible Detective Webber admitting he had too much on his plate? Admitting, in effect, to weakness? I pushed my chair back a few inches in case he was infectious.

A spark of the old Webber tough-guy cynicism flashed in his eyes but quickly faded. His eyes reddened and filled.

"It's my daughter," he said. "She ran away. She's only thirteen and we haven't heard from her in over twenty-four hours."

A petty part of me wanted to snap, *she ran away? What took her so long?* But, despite our past differences, I couldn't bring myself to say such a thing. There was genuine anguish in his eyes, and his pain was palpable. I guess even police officers as hardened as Webber have feelings.

"Have they posted an Amber Alert?" I asked softly.

The Amber Alert system, in effect in Arizona for about a decade, notified the public to be on the lookout for lost or kidnapped children within minutes of a child's reported disappearance. I hadn't heard any alerts today, but I hadn't watched TV or listened to the radio since I'd left for work this morning.

Webber nodded sadly. "Nothing. We called all her friends and classmates, too."

"Did she say anything before she left about where she was going?"

"The usual 'I gotta get out of here,' 'you don't let me have a life,' 'I hate you,'" kind of stuff. We get that all the time. My wife says it's because of puberty. Her latest blow-up was because we wouldn't let her hang out with her friends at the mall."

Webber had a wife? "Could she have gone to the mall anyway?" I asked.

Webber shook his head. "If she did, she never showed up. Her friends didn't see her there."

I stared at my hands, sharing, however minimally, in his desperation and frustration.

"Is there anything I can do to help?" I asked, more out of the desire to assist than the ability.

"Actually, there is," he said, swiping at his eyes and then staring at me intently. "You have connections out there I don't."

I did? I looked up at him inquiringly.

"Like your pervert son and that psycho lady."

Sadly, I knew immediately who he meant by my "pervert son." Larry Larkin was a homeless man I'd first helped out when he was charged by my then-boss, a nutsoid—my word—county attorney with Old Testament concepts of revenge, with a major felony for exhibitionism. Later, I helped out Larry again after he discovered the body of a murder victim. I first met Detective Webber in connection with the latter incident. When Webber placed Larry in my custody to make sure Larry attended his court hearings, Larry misunderstood the limited nature of my representation; since then, he has insisted that I am his adoptive mother and therefore responsible for his security and upbringing. Since Larry is in his forties, the upbringing part is a *fait accompli*. But every so often, Larry shows up and demands his allowance or quality time. I go along because I feel sorry for him. Plus, Larry once saved my life.

I was having a hard time placing whom Webber meant by the "psycho lady," though.

"Do you mean the *psychic* lady? Venus Butterman?" I asked. Venus was the grandmother of a former client and claimed to have psychic powers, including the ability to talk to the dead. I halfway believed she did, because she had once come up with information regarding the identity of a murderer that only the murder victim could have known.

"Psycho, psychic—same difference," shrugged Webber.

He had to be desperate to ask me to seek help from Larry and Venus, people who, in his law-and-order world, were irredeemable social outcasts.

I hesitated, but only for a moment. Webber and I may have opposing views on redemption—and just about everything else—but I don't care who you are, concern over a lost child is a universal emotion.

"Do you have a picture of your daughter you could leave with me?" I asked.

Webber pulled a piece of folded paper out of his pocket, placed it in front of me, and smoothed it open. It looked like a color copy of a standard school photo. There was nothing standard about the subject's appearance, though: long, thick, blonde hair hanging in soft waves framed her face; a small, straight nose perfectly tilted at the tip; surprisingly dark eyebrows; full lips; and penetrating green eyes. Her skin was tanned, with the kind of unblemished perfection that only exists before the inevitable onset of teen acne.

I gasped involuntarily and blurted, "She's beautiful." I looked back and forth from Webber to the photo and wondered about the possibility of generation-skipping genes.

"She's smart, too," said Webber, the pride showing in his voice. "And she's a good kid. The bad mouth and attitude are recent developments. Like I said before—my wife says it's puberty."

I remembered that age thirteen was about the time I developed an attitude. I hadn't lost much of it.

"Her name's Emily," he continued, his voice again dulled by despair.

"I'll show this to Larry and Venus—and to everyone else I can think of," I said. Then I looked back at the photo. "I can't believe anyone who saw her could forget this face."

After a short nod, Webber stood and visibly regrouped, straightening his posture and fixing his jaw in a determined scowl.

"I will let you know what we find out about your skeleton. In the meantime, it'll take us a couple of hours to finish up here. If you don't want to stick around, that's fine. We'll lock up when we leave."

Despite Webber's offer, I stayed. Leaving cops alone in a building with hundreds of criminal defense files was not something I was willing to do, no matter how much I wanted to go home to my little condo, get in bed, and hide my head under the pillow.

Chapter 3

For the record, the police investigation took more than "a couple of hours." By the time they left—six hours later—it was past eight o'clock and dark.

During the day, the early May weather had hinted at the searing summer heat around the corner. But at night the temperature was in the mid-seventies. A soft breeze ruffled the leaves of the eucalyptus tree in the front yard, carrying the tree's light scent with it. I stood on our small porch, closed my eyes, and let the warm air caress my face.

I had sent Stu away after speaking with Webber and told Beth to go home after she finished copying the purchase file for the house. She resisted at first but gave in after I assured her I had plenty of work to do and didn't mind in the least waiting for the police to finish. This last part was a lie, but there was no reason for both of us to suffer. Before she left, she asked me if I was going to "ask around about that little lost girl." I thought she was referring to our skeleton at first and then I realized she was talking about Emily. (As I said, the walls are paper thin). When I told her I planned to, she looked pleased.

"It's the Christian thing to do. Detective Webber may be difficult to get along with, and God knows he hasn't done our clients any favors, but that's not his daughter's fault. A child out alone in this town is hard to think about without your heart getting involved."

"Amen to that," I'd said, noticing that, although Beth had been the administrative assistant for a succession of county attorneys before coming to work for me, her loyalties now lay with our clients, most of whom had been charged with crimes by her former employers.

After Beth left, I called MJ and Sam and told them what was going on. I explained that Sam would need to move into MJ's office until his office floor was repaired. Sam seemed more horrified at the idea of sharing an office with MJ than he was at the news that he had been sharing his office with a skeleton for the last six months.

"She has a collection of biologically incorrect *lemurs* for God's sake," he wailed. (It's true: after several of her china lemurs were broken during a burglary, MJ glued them back together without regard to lemur—or any other—anatomy.) "Plus, she's a pig—she keeps *French fries* in her drawer" (also true). "And she constantly sings old Rolling Stones songs" (ditto). After listening to his irrefutable logic, I agreed he could work out of the kitchen, but only if things got really bad.

Bryan, my on-again, off-again significant other, called

twice—first to decide where we should go to dinner, and, after I told him what happened, once more to find out how I was holding up. He was at work too, trying to catch up with the mountain of paperwork that is part—his least favorite part—of his job as acting sheriff for Maricopa County. Bryan is tall, blond, and gorgeous, and he has the long suffering patience of Job. We have, more than once, been on opposite sides of a case, and while he admires my conviction, a lot of times he doesn't recognize, much less understand, the rational basis for it. Chemistry can overcome a great deal, but our differing points of view on the rights of the accused versus the desire to lock up troublemakers *tout de suite* were becoming a frequent source of conflict.

Standing outside enjoying the soft breeze helped to calm my nerves, but I was still wound up from the day's events. I no longer felt like hiding my head under my pillow, because I knew it wouldn't help; my mind would only replay everything that had happened over and over. On the other hand, I didn't feel much like hanging around other humans either. I knew that Bryan would be more than willing to come over and keep me company, but he has a tendency to lecture whenever things out of the ordinary happen to me (which is often), and I wasn't in the mood to listen and take notes. The company of Ralph, a large dog of indeterminate breed that I adopted from a dude ranch almost two years ago, was a good alternative. Unfortunately, Ralph was at a sleepover with Tuwanda's dog, Walter, a miniature poodle at whose paws Ralph worshipped.

I was mulling over my limited options when I opened my purse to get my keys and saw Emily's picture. I remembered putting it there after I'd spoken with Webber, intending to pass it around at church the next day and then take it to show Larry and Venus in the afternoon.

I slid into the driver's seat of my little Honda Civic and turned on the overhead light so I could inspect the photo more carefully. The same breathtakingly beautiful child-woman stared back at me, but this time, maybe through a trick of light or imagination, I noticed the stubborn set of her jaw and a glint of defiance in her eyes. I bet Emily was a handful; this was a child who would not take direction easily. I know the look. It is the same one I have on my face in every photo taken of me since early adolescence.

Suddenly, it seemed very important that I look for Emily sooner rather than later. I decided to pick up sandwiches at Jack in the Box and drop by to see Larry. After I softened him up with food, I would show him Emily's picture. Besides, as I said, I wasn't ready for full-on human contact and Larry was a good compromise.

Larry spends most nights on the roof of the Sacred Bleeding Heart Shelter on Washington Street. He prefers the roof to being indoors because he's subject to severe bouts of claustrophobia. The shelter only has one public phone, so contacting Larry is always a challenge. You never know who will answer, and, since most of the guests have psychological problems, you need to tailor your request to fit each one's particular form of insanity.

I punched the shelter's number into my mobile phone. Someone finally picked up after the eighth ring.

"God?" a woman's voice asked.

"Yes," I said. "And I need to talk to Larry Larkin. Is he around?"

I heard the receiver bang against the wall and then the sound of quickly receding footsteps. About ten minutes later, Larry's voice came on the line.

"God?" he asked uncertainly.

"It's Kate, Larry," I said.

"It's my mom," he said to someone in the background. His voice sounded muffled, so I guessed he was covering the mouthpiece with his hand. "Sometimes she likes to kid around. You can stop kneeling and grinding your teeth, Jilly."

I heard, but couldn't quite make out, a reply—presumably from Jilly.

"Yes, I'm sure, and maybe you think it's gnashing, but it sounds like grinding to me. Why don't you go somewhere and practice your gnashing for when God really calls," said Larry, sounding annoyed.

"What you want, Mom?" he said, coming back on the line.

I ground my teeth upon hearing this appellation—or was it gnashing? I didn't bother to correct him, though. It wouldn't have done any good.

"I was thinking of stopping by Jack in the Box for a sandwich. You want me to pick something up for you, too?"

A long silence followed, and I thought maybe he'd left. "Larry?" I asked.

"You know I prefer organic food, and I don't know what, if any, healthy options that particular establishment offers."

This from a man who considers Twinkies one of the major food groups, I thought. "I believe they have a tasty chicken wrap with veggies you might like," I said.

"Perhaps. Do they have anything for dessert?"

I knew where this was going. "I'll stop off at Circle K and pick up a package of Twinkies, too."

"I guess that would be okay."

I knew the offer of Twinkies would hook him.

"Oh, and don't bother stopping at the front desk when you come in. Come straight up to the penthouse. I'll make sure the doorman knows you're coming," he added magnanimously.

"See you in about a half hour," I said.

A little under a half hour later, I was climbing the stairs at the Sacred Bleeding Heart Shelter holding a grease-stained paper bag from Jack in the Box and a plastic bag from Circle K. I tried to ignore the nauseating combination of urine, Pine-Sol, and fried food smells. The generally accepted logic is, if you breathe through your mouth instead of your nose, you won't smell anything. But the idea of sucking in nasty particulates without the benefit of the nose's filters made me even more uncomfortable. Maybe I'd been hanging around Sam too long; Sam is incredibly germaphobic.

Once I'd ascended the final set of stairs and stepped out onto the rooftop, I took a deep, cleansing breath of fresh air before looking for Larry. I spotted him at the other end of the roof, sitting on one of two plastic chairs arranged on either side of a small plastic table. The area was softly lit by security lights. He put down the book he was reading when he heard my approach. I greeted him, sat in the empty chair, and started to unload the bags.

"What are you reading?" I asked conversationally.

Larry held the book up so I could see its title. "*Little Women,*" I read aloud. "What part have you reached?"

"Beth died," said Larry. A tear rolled down his cheek. "That sucks. I really identified with her character."

I nodded. I remember taking Beth's death pretty hard myself.

I pushed his chicken wrap toward him and popped open a can of Coke for him and a Diet Coke for me.

"You shouldn't drink that stuff, Mom," said Larry, chin-gesturing to my soda. "It's not good for you."

"It's one of the few vices I have. Don't rain on my parade," I said.

Larry looked up into the starlit sky. "It doesn't look like it's going to rain."

Sometimes Larry can be very literal-minded.

We munched on our sandwiches for a while and looked out over the city. I decided that living on a roof wasn't half bad, at least in this kind of weather.

When we were through with our sandwiches and

Larry was digging into the Twinkies, I pulled out Emily's flyer and placed it on the table between us.

"Have you seen this girl around?" I asked.

He squinted and scrutinized the photo, and, after licking a blob of Twinkie cream off his finger, reached over and repositioned the flyer several times, looking at it from different angles. Then he turned the flyer over. "Where's the back of her head?" he said.

I sighed before answering. "It's not a 3-D photo," I said. "You can't see the back of her head."

"That's stupid," he commented. "A lot of times I only see people from the back."

That's because most people walk away from you, I thought. *Snarky sarcasm is not helpful,* a wiser, kinder part of my brain lectured.

"Maybe you could try *imagining* what she would look like from behind," I suggested.

Larry closed his eyes and appeared to concentrate. "I think I saw a girl with hair like that this morning," he finally said, opening his eyes. "I only saw her from the back, but I'm pretty sure it was her."

"That's wonderful! Where did you see her?" I asked excitedly.

"Over on Nineteenth Avenue, by the Goodwill store. Except her hair was black and shorter when I saw her."

What the heck?

"Let me get this straight: you think you saw this girl, but you only saw her from the back, and her hair was shorter and black."

Larry nodded, his eyes somber.

I placed my hands over my face and shook my head wearily. Some fatalistic urge prompted me to pursue the matter. "Why, then, do you think it was her?"

"Because she had this," he answered, pointing to the photo. I followed the direction of his finger and noticed for the first time that Emily had what at first looked like a small cowlick. I looked more closely and saw that a small clump of hair stuck up from her head nearly vertically and was much shorter than the rest of her hair, as if someone had pulled out a patch, or maybe she had had an injury that required hair removal for stitches.

It wasn't much to go on. Still, it was something. I considered calling Webber and passing on the information, but decided it wasn't worth raising his hopes over. Maybe I would take a detour on my way home and check out the area around the Goodwill. This would be a big detour, as it would take me about five miles in the opposite direction from my condo.

"Thanks, Larry," I said, putting the photo back in my purse. I started to shove the detritus left over from our meal into one of the bags.

"I'll keep my eyes open and let you know if I see her again," said Larry, snatching an empty Twinkie wrapper out of my hands and smoothing it out carefully on the table. I'd forgotten that he collects them.

"She a friend of yours?" he asked.

"No. I've never met her. She's the daughter of a fr …

I mean an acquaintance," I corrected myself. "He's very worried about her."

Larry nodded. "He's right to worry. A lot of bad things happen to people. Look what happened to Beth."

I was confused at first, thinking perhaps he was referring to my secretary, Beth, and then I remembered he was reading *Little Women*.

"No need to escort me to the door," I said as I stood, even though Larry hadn't made a move to do so.

"Thanks for dinner, Mom," he said.

Chapter 4

I drove east to Nineteenth Avenue and then headed south, straining to see in the darkness beyond the dim halos of the street lights. I thought about how lonely and frightened Emily must be, and prayed that no harm would come to her. I thought, too, about how frightened the little girl under the floor of Sam's office had been if my worst-case-scenario-imaginings about the last moments of her life were true. I could do nothing for her now, but I might be able to do something for Emily.

I slowed as I passed the Goodwill Industries facility, a large, low building used primarily as a storage and distribution center with a small retail outlet in the front. The facility was closed at this hour, but security lights lit the front parking lot and loading platforms in the back. I took a turn around the parking lot and then drove down a narrow alley to the back of the building. I circled the potholed loading area, paying particular attention to the spaces underneath the loading docks. I could see makeshift beds in some of them but no occupants. Perhaps the evening was too nice to spend "indoors." I pulled up to one of the docks and put the car in park, leaving the motor running. I knew it was a long shot, but I still couldn't help feeling disappointed. (Although I affect worldliness as part of my professional persona, at heart I still believe in miracles.)

I was startled by a rap on the glass. A large black man wearing a security guard's uniform motioned for me to lower the window.

I lowered the window halfway and asked, "Is there a problem?"

The man chuckled and said, "I thought that was my line. Ma'am, if you're dropping something off, you need to come back during business hours when there's someone here to take it inside. If you leave anything outside now, it'll be gone by morning. Some homeless guy will take it."

I was struck by the irony of his remark; it's good to contribute clothes and other items to charity so they can be resold to raise funds for the homeless, but it's not good if you cut out the middleman.

"I didn't come to make a drop-off," I said. "I'm looking for someone." I pulled Emily's picture out of my purse and showed it to him. "Have you seen her around?"

He took the picture from me and looked at it. "No, ma'am. I think I would remember a face like that."

"She may have altered her appearance—dyed her hair black and cut it shorter," I said.

He squinted at the picture and I could tell he was trying to imagine her with dark hair.

He shrugged after a few seconds. "I don't know. Lemme ask around. He scanned the loading platforms and yelled, "Basil!"

I startled again. Either I was getting jumpy or people were unpredictably loud lately.

Taking a few steps toward the docks, he yelled, "Basil," again.

Still no answer. He stomped over to the last dock at the far end of the building, leaned over, and growled, "Basil, damn it, I know you're under there. A lady here needs to ask you a question."

The pile of blankets under the dock moved, and a thin man with a gray ZZ Top beard emerged clutching a large bottle half full of an amber-colored liquid. He wore a suit coat and mismatched suit pants, a T-shirt with a picture of Barack Obama and *I want change but cash would be better* printed on the front, and flip-flops.

"Duane, you are interrupting my musings," he intoned in a Shakespearean voice.

"More like I'm interruptin' your hallucinations," Duane the security guard shot back.

Basil seemed to notice me for the first time. "Who is she?" he asked.

"Like I said, there is a lady here who wants to ask you a question. *She* is the lady," Duane explained patiently.

"What, pray tell, is the basis for your determination she is a *lady*?" Basil questioned haughtily.

I shifted uncomfortably, waiting to hear how Duane responded.

"Cuz she didn't offer to sell me sex or drugs," said Duane.

The bar was set low. I relaxed.

Basil nodded and appeared satisfied with this answer. I thought things were progressing fairly well, but then Basil looked from Duane to me again and asked, "Who's that woman in the car?"

This was going to take a while. I turned off the motor and got out, taking the photo with me, and walked to where Basil and Duane were standing. I hoped that, if I stayed in Basil's line of vision, he might be able to maintain focus.

"Hello. I'm Kate Williams," I introduced myself. I did not extend my hand in greeting because, although it's shameful to admit, Basil's dirt-caked fingernails and filthy hands gave rise to fears of giardia, E. coli poisoning, and cooties.

Basil continued to stare at me suspiciously while Duane provided the remaining introductions. "I'm Duane Sadiki, and this is Basil Wentworth."

"Sadiki," I said thoughtfully. "Isn't than Kenyan?"

A broad smile split his face. "Yes, it is. My father is from Kenya."

I returned his smile. "My secretary's father was Kenyan."

"Really? What is her name?" asked Duane.

"Beth Portucci. But her maiden name is Abasi."

"No way! Beth is my godmother. Her parents were good friends of my parents. Beth goes to my church."

Basil cleared his throat. "This is lovely. I am touched. May I return to my video, now?"

"You're watching a video under there?" I asked in disbelief, peering into his blanket-strewn lair.

"No. In here," he answered, tapping his forehead.

I shot Duane a concerned look, and he shrugged.

"This won't take long," I said. "If you, um, could maybe hit the pause button, I'd like to ask you a question."

"You've already wasted too much of my time. I've missed the movie's apogee. I will need to rewind, and rewinding weakens the tape."

Sounds like the tape is already pretty weak, I thought sardonically. "I only want to know if you have seen this girl around," I said, holding up the photo of Emily. "She might have dyed her hair and cut it shorter, but maybe you recognize her face."

Basil took a gulp of the amber liquid in his bottle before scrutinizing the photo. Oddly, I didn't smell any alcohol.

"What are you drinking?" I asked.

"Apple juice," he answered distractedly. "I don't drink spirits, but I feel compelled to keep up appearances. People have certain expectations about street people, and I don't want to disappoint my audience."

I experienced an *Alice Through the Looking Glass* moment. Maybe Basil didn't drink spirits, but I could have used a shot of some about then.

"I believe I have seen this girl," he announced after a tension-building pause to take another swig of apple juice.

"When? Where?" I asked, not bothering to restrain my excitement.

"This morning. Here. She was going through some clothes somebody dropped off before hours. She was unaware that we in this community have a sign-up sheet for pillagers, who are called, in order, to take advantage of items dropped off before or after business hours. It was Abby Adler's turn, and Abby did not take this infringement upon her rights well; she went after the interloper tooth and nail. The girl was feisty, though, and managed to grab a bag of clothes before taking off. It was a plastic Safeway grocery bag. I noticed because I am a collector and remember thinking the artwork on the bag was mundane. I prefer the decorated holiday bags. I especially like …"

"Do you remember in which direction she ran?" I broke in.

"Toward the sun," he said, sounding annoyed that I'd interrupted his critique of plastic bag art.

"You said it was this morning. So that would be east," I said, half to myself.

"This time of year, it's usually to the north," he corrected.

I looked at him to see if he was kidding. He looked dead serious.

I dug into my pocket for a business card and asked

Duane if he had a pen. He handed me a plastic ballpoint with *Green Acres Funeral Home; We Dig Our Work*, printed on it.

I wrote my home and cell phone numbers on the back of the card and then added my condo address as an afterthought. I asked Basil to give it to the girl if he saw her again. I didn't ask him to call me because I was reasonably sure he didn't have a phone, or if he did, it was in the same place as his video player. I also handed one of the cards to Duane, this time asking that he call me if he saw her.

"Thanks very much. Both of you," I said, returning the pen to Duane. "Duane, I'll let Beth know I saw you."

"Do that," said Duane with genuine warmth. "I should probably call her. I haven't talked to her in a while. She goes to the early service at church, and me and my wife and kids usually don't make it until the eleven-thirty."

Basil carefully stowed my business card in the inside breast pocket of his frayed suit coat.

"Maybe you can do something for me," he said.

I fully expected a request for money. Instead, he asked, "Do you have any plastic bags?"

As a matter of fact, I have quite a cache of them in the trunk of my car. Whenever the grocery store gives them to me, I assuage my environmentalist-induced guilt by promising myself that I will re-use them. But then I always forget to take them out of the trunk when I go into the store again, and end up collecting more plastic bags.

I gestured for Basil to follow me to my car, where I

opened the trunk and waved at the pile of bags inside. "Be my guest. Take as many as you want."

Basil culled through the bags excitedly. His pleased exclamations grew louder and more frequent as he got closer to the bottom of the pile.

"My God," he said when he was finished. "You have some fine vintage bags in here."

I guess I hadn't realized how long I'd been tossing them in there, and I chastised myself for being such a rotten steward of the earth.

"Are you sure you don't mind if I take them?" he asked.

"Please," I said in all sincerity. I obviously wasn't going to do anything with them, and I could use the extra trunk space.

Chapter 5

Once I was in my car, driving in the direction of my condo, the feelings of desolation and sadness returned. I decided that being alone wasn't such a great idea, so I relented and called Bryan. He agreed to meet me at the condo, and we would watch what he referred to as "one of my chick flicks," his tone implying that, in doing so, he was making the ultimate male sacrifice.

As it turned out, despite initially complaining he was going to grow breasts as a result of watching the movie, he seemed to actually enjoy it. But instead of hanging around for some R-rated action of his own, Bryan left as soon as the movie was over, saying he had an early meeting. This was very un-Bryan-like conduct. This is a man who would take time out from a heart attack for a quickie. Maybe he was more overworked and exhausted than I'd thought.

So I ended up having the bed to myself—a rare occurrence. Usually, Ralph or Bryan slept with me, sometimes both. Being able to spread out to the bed's four corners was a luxury.

I fell asleep quickly and slept well, despite my earlier reservations, but something woke me up before I'd even come close to the recommended eight hours. It was still pitch-black and my digital clock-radio showed a time of four thirty. I had no idea what had awakened me. Then I heard someone moving around outside my bedroom.

"Bryan?" I called out, thinking maybe he changed his mind about staying over.

No answer. I grabbed my robe from the foot of the bed and quickly donned it. Before my feet hit the floor, the bedroom door opened and a hand reached in and felt around for the light switch. I retracted my legs and pulled the covers up to my chin, acting on the regressive logic that nothing can hurt you if you're under the covers.

"Don't shoot." The voice sounded young and nervous.

"I don't have a gun," I said reflexively and then gave myself a mental head slap. *Why did I admit I was unarmed? I should have said I had an M-16, a flame thrower, and a howitzer trained on the door.*

The hand located the switch and flipped the lights on. The door opened wider, and a small form slipped into the room. He/she/it wore a too-large black rain coat with the collar turned up and a stretchy black cap pulled down to eye level. The overall effect was that of a Burqa.

"Are you a burglar?" I asked. Under the circumstances, I thought it was a reasonable question.

"No. But I could be. It was real easy to get into your apartment. I have a talent for getting into locked places, and yours was a piece of cake" he/she/it answered.

"Who are you, then?" I thought this was an eminently reasonable follow-up question on my part.

He/she/it removed the black cap and became a she, which cut down on the number of pronouns I needed to use, but still didn't answer the question. Her face looked familiar, though. "Do you have a name?" I prodded.

"Depends," she answered. "Are you gonna tell my dad?"

Emily! Of course! I thought. *Ignore the hair color and style, and ignore the nose piercing—which looked new and unhealed—and this was the girl on the flyer. What had this kid done to herself in less than two days?*

I sat up, letting my protective shield [blanket] fall to my lap. "You are Emily, I take it. Did Basil tell you I was looking for you?" I asked.

"If you mean the old guy who sounds like Macbeth, yeah," she answered.

At least the kid knows who Macbeth is; a high five to the public school system. "Your father and mother are very worried about you," I said sternly, although I'm not sure how much of an authority figure I was, since I was wearing a robe covered with Tweety Birds.

"That's why I came over here. I want you to tell my *mother* not to worry; I'm doing okay."

It was clear her concern over her parents' feelings did not extend to her father.

"*Are* you doing okay?" I asked.

"I just *said* I was," she retorted, her tone reflecting some of the "attitude" her father had mentioned.

But I noticed that her eyes slid away from mine when she answered.

"Where are you staying?" I asked.

"I've got friends, I ..." She broke off and looked at me sharply. "I'm not falling for that. You'll tell my parents."

I didn't like this. She was too young and too pretty, and I don't care how clever she was, no one is ready for life on the street at thirteen. I couldn't let her go back out there. I made a snap decision and the words were out of my mouth before the dwindling number of wise cells in my brain could get their act together.

"If I promise not to tell your parents where you are, will you stay here?"

Emily looked at me with narrowed, distrustful eyes. But then I thought I saw a flash of hope. She took a business card out of her pocket—my business card—and read aloud.

"*Caitlin Williams, Esq., attorney at law.* I think I've heard my dad talk about you," she said, contemplatively.

That can't be good. I thought.

After a few beats of silence, she continued, speaking half to herself. "It had something to do with a case where an attorney was found floating in the canal. Dad said some insane lady-lawyer had gotten involved, claiming to represent a homeless guy who went bobbing for booty when he discovered the dead guy in the canal. I remember giggling at the word 'booty' and my mom explaining the way my father used it was as in 'pirates' booty,' not as in 'shake your booty.' Anyway, you're the insane lady he was talking about, aren't you? He called you 'Hate Williams' and lots of other things, too. My dad doesn't like you."

Her tone of voice turned respectful. My enemy status appeared to work in my favor.

"It's true," I said. "Your dad and I don't get along well. We're kind of on opposite sides. I work to achieve justice and he works to put people in jail. Unfortunately, those are often conflicting goals. But you can see how concerned he is if he asked *me* to help find you."

"Not really. It just shows what an asshole he is; asking somebody who probably doesn't give a damn to find me."

Somebody who doesn't give a damn so much she spent a large chunk of the day worrying about you and most of her evening trying to track you down, I thought.

I spent a lot of time in my first year of practice representing clients in juvenile court, and I had often dealt with the egocentric, irrational defensiveness of teens. Ongoing dealings with the egocentric, irrational defensiveness of attorneys further contributed to my pool of experience. Based upon this, I knew not to argue with Emily's logic. Arguing with teenagers and lawyers about logic is the verbal equivalent of trying to hold onto a soap-covered dog that is determined to jump out of the tub and roll in the most disgusting, smelly thing it can find, which is something I have lots of experience with, too. "So if I don't like your dad, why would I tell him you're staying here? Wouldn't I rather make him suffer not knowing where you are?" I pointed out.

"That kinda makes sense," she said reluctantly. Then her eyes narrowed again in suspicion. "Where would I sleep?"

"On the couch," I answered without hesitation. "There's a powder room with a shower off the living room you can use. You can come and go as you like. I would offer you a key, but you don't seem to need one."

"I bet you don't even have cable," she sneered. But I could tell she was weakening because she was still standing there.

"With premium channels. I need to tell you: I have a dog, Ralph. He's at a sleepover tonight, but he'll be back in the morning. So if you're allergic to dogs, we may have a problem."

Her eyes lit up. "A dog? I love dogs. My parents won't let me have one. Mom says they're dirty, and dad says all they do is shed and shit."

"Well, Ralph is a *big* dog, and he does shed and, um, poop. He gets his hair done every week, though, and he's fairly neat, and he only poops when I take him outside to his favorite pooping spots. Maybe you can help me out by taking him for walks once in a while."

"I would *love* to. I will take him for *all* his walks. Will he sleep with me?" Emily asked with child-like enthusiasm. It was the first time she sounded thirteen instead of thirty.

"I doubt you will be able to stop him. Ralph is big on body heat. Here, let me get you a blanket, sheets, and a pillow," I said, getting out of bed. "You're probably tired, and I want to grab what few hours of sleep I have left before I need to get up."

I showed her the couch and provided her the promised linens.

"This is a crappy couch," she commented.

I did not take offense. It *was* a crappy couch. Its red velveteen upholstery was worn out in places, and several tears in the cushions were held together with duct tape.

"It has sentimental value," I said. "That couch and I have been through a lot together."

"Gross!" she said, making a face.

"Oh, for God's sake. I mean it's been through a burglary—that's how the cushions got ripped—and has supported me throughout several periods of convalescence."

She looked at me questioningly.

"I hit my head a lot. Smoke inhalation seems to be a favorite, too," I said ruefully.

"Wild," she said.

"See you in the morning. *Later* in the morning, that is." I gave her a little wave and went back to my bedroom.

Reasonably assured that she would not leave, at least until morning, I shut the door behind me, grabbed my mobile phone out of my purse, and then went into my bathroom, where I also shut the door. Sitting on the toilet without bothering to put down the lid, I dialed Webber's number. He answered on the second ring, sounding tired and worried.

"It's Kate," I said in a half whisper. "I found Emily. She's okay."

"Thank God. Where is she?" His relief was palpable.

"She made me promise I wouldn't tell you. She's in a safe place, but she said she'd leave if I told you where she is."

"You *have* to tell me. Please. We have to bring her back. No place is safe out there. She needs to be home," Webber's tone alternated between wheedling supplications and loud threats.

"You need to give her time. Let me try to talk to her," I said, still speaking in a half whisper, although the way Webber yelled into the phone during his cyclic threats, I don't know why I bothered. Emily and everyone else on the floor could probably hear him. Maybe I lucked out and she was in the powder room with the water running. It occurred to me then: I could use some screening noises, too, so I turned on the shower.

"What the hell are you doing?" screamed Webber. "Are you taking a *shower*? Wait. You don't want me to hear something. She's there with you, isn't she?"

I never said Webber was dumb—just mean.

"Hell, no. You call that a safe place? You're a walking disaster area, and your condo is like a testing ground for burglars in training," he yelled.

I held the phone away from my ear to prevent [further] hearing damage. "Hey, that's not …" I started to say.

"Fuck. Your best friend is a hooker," he continued, now in a full-blown frenzy.

"Tuwanda is in management now. She no longer …"

"I'm coming over there right now," he screamed.

"No! She'll run away again. Please, please. Let me try to talk to her first. She seems to really hate you. I think …"

"Hate me? What are you talking about? She said that?" He still sounded furious, but at least he was listening now, kind of.

"Yes," I answered. While it's true Emily hadn't used that exact word, it was clear to me that was how she felt.

"Why?" He sounded sincerely bewildered.

I didn't know the specific reasons for Emily's feelings toward her dad. I had to restrain from suggesting a few reasons of my own, though. "I don't know," I said. "But she seems upset and extremely determined not to go home."

I heard a woman's voice in the background at Webber's end. Webber responded, addressing her as Missy. I didn't know if that was her real name or if Webber was being a jerk.

An intense discussion followed, during which Missy, after expressing tearful relief upon hearing that Emily was okay, took the position that Webber needed to give Emily space and they all needed to go to a family therapist because both he and Emily were out of control.

I was embarrassed to be privy to such an intimate conversation, but not embarrassed enough to hang up.

Although I had never met Missy and until yesterday hadn't even realized that Webber was married, much less had a kid, I was rooting for Missy's side. She sounded stressed to the limit and was desperately fighting to save her family. I thought Webber's stubborn resistance indicated a complete lack of understanding and anything close to sensitivity.

"You're overreacting," I heard him say to her. "You're letting her manipulate you with her crap. She needs a strong hand. You spoil her."

I couldn't quite make out Missy's response, but then Webber said, "Fine. Leave me. I don't give a shit. I don't give a shit where Emmy goes either. The both of you can go to hell."

The line went dead, and I figured that Webber had finally realized I was still on the line.

Whew! If this exchange was any indication of how the Webber household functioned, I didn't blame Emily one bit for jumping ship. I needed therapy after just listening to them.

I shut off the shower and tiptoed out to the living room to check on Emily. She was curled up under the blanket, snoring softly, not having bothered with the sheets. She looked so small and vulnerable, and a wave of panic hit me.

In the back of my mind, I'd assumed that Emily would go home once she had a good night's sleep and could see things more clearly. But what if she didn't? Good intentions aside, what did I know about taking care of a teenage girl? I am a barely competent dog owner. My friends and neighbors have had to step in and care for Ralph too many times to count when I was caught up at work, busy tracking down missing clients or murderers, being kidnapped, in the hospital—jeez, my life *was* a mess. Obviously, I was not mom material.

Then I had a brilliant idea. *Macy*! *That's it! I'll ask Macy to help out.*

Macy owns the condo across the hall from mine. She's a retired real estate agent from Brooklyn, New York. Although she is in her late seventies, she has more energy than I do, and she is an amazing cook. She also has the biggest heart of anyone I know. Having a daughter and a granddaughter of her own, she would know how the parenting thing worked.

I went back to my room and got in bed, glancing at the luminous numbers on the demonic clock radio sitting on my bedside table. (There is nothing uniquely evil about this particular clock. I dislike all clocks and resent the power they have over my life). I still had a couple of hours left before I had to get up. Having come up with the Macy plan, I quickly fell asleep.

Chapter 6

My clock radio was set on a classic rock station, and I was awakened by The Rolling Stones' "Gimme Shelter," which I considered apropos to Emily's circumstances. The smell of coffee and bacon drifted in from the kitchen, which was confusing. I didn't know if I even had bacon.

I looked around for my robe and then realized I hadn't bothered to take it off last night when I went back to bed. I got up and stumbled to the kitchen, noticing en route that Emily was not on the couch.

Tuwanda and Emily were sitting at the kitchen table. Tuwanda, who looks like a black Angelina Jolie, was wearing an elegant designer suit with a skirt short enough to show off her incredible legs but long enough to still qualify as business-like attire. Macy was at the stove, her gray hair inexplicably covered by a doo rag, and she was wearing a fluffy pink robe with matching Uggs slippers.

She looked like a hip yard gnome. Ralph was lying on Emily's feet, looking up at her adoringly. A string of saliva hung from his mouth.

"Did I miss the invitation?" I asked as I pulled up a chair and sat at the table.

"Hi, Kate," said Tuwanda through a mouthful of scrambled eggs. She paused to swallow before continuing. "I was droppin' Ralph off an' met Emily. She tol' me she was stayin' with you, an'—no offense—I know you never have any food aroun' here, so I knocked on Macy's door an' asked if I could borrow a few things."

"A few things? My weekly shopping list is shorter," interrupted Macy in her strong Brooklyn accent.

Tuwanda did not take offense. "I figured if I was gonna get provisions I might as well get enough for all of us."

"It was easier to bring over some food and cook somethin' up," said Macy.

"Macy said if she sent over anything that you couldn't microwave, you wouldn't know what to do," Emily added.

Macy placed a plate piled high with eggs, bacon, and toast in front of Emily. "Here's seconds, sweetie. You need to eat more. You're too skinny." Directing her attention to me, she continued, "Yeah, and I told her about the time you blew up a Stouffer's spinach soufflé because the direction on the box to make a slit in the cellophane cover was too complex for you."

Emily looked up from her eggs and giggled.

"I still say that container was defective," I muttered defensively.

I couldn't hold a grudge, though: Macy's cooking smelled wonderful, and I was starving. "Can I have some eggs and bacon, too?" I asked meekly.

"May I, sweetie," she corrected. "Normally, I let your bad grammar slide, but there's a young lady at the table, and I don't want you to set a bad example."

"When have I ever set a bad example?" I huffed.

Macy rolled her eyes and slammed a plate of bacon, eggs, and toast and a cup of coffee in front of me.

Macy is normally upbeat and supportive, but I think I knew what was going on. Tuwanda, whom I had called yesterday from my office, must have mentioned our discovery to Macy, and Emily's mere presence signaled something else was amiss. The end result: Macy was concerned about me, concerned about Emily, and concerned about Emily *with* me. She knew my weaknesses too well.

"I hate to deprive you all of my stimulatin' presence, but I gotta go home and get to bed," said Tuwanda as she pushed back from the table and motioned me to follow her out. "Thanks for dinner, Macy. It tasted real good."

Seeing Emily's confused expression, I explained. "Tuwanda works nights. So this is her dinnertime."

Emily nodded and said, "It was really nice meeting you, Tuwanda. I hope you come to visit again."

Clearly, Emily had no intention of leaving.

"It was nice meetin' you too, Emily. Addressing me

this time, she said, "Katie, walk me to the door. I got some bid'ness to talk to you about."

I followed Tuwanda into the hallway outside my condo, where she bent down to pick up my newspaper. I noticed Macy had already gotten hers.

"Did you tell Macy what we found at my office yesterday?" I asked, speaking in a half-whisper.

"Din't have to," Tuwanda answered, adopting the same half-whisper. "Why can't you get on the front page for somethin' pleasant?"

I winced. "Not again," I moaned.

An article about a fire at Venus's house had appeared on the front page of the Phoenix newspaper about a month ago with a bold-faced heading reading "Attorney Sleeping with Client Caught in Fire." Even worse, the article included a full-color photo of me running from the burning house in the altogether, holding Venus's dog, Precious. Unfortunately, Precious is a very small dog. For the record I was *not* sleeping with my client; I was staying at his grandmother's house with Tuwanda and MJ while we were hiding out from a murderer (which, come to think of it, doesn't sound much better than the paper's version of the facts).

The headline of today's lead story read "Bones of Girl Found under Attorney's Floor." The article started out, "Ms. Williams, Esq. apparently ran out of closet space and is storing skeletons under her floor—literally." The rest of the article contained few facts but was heavy on innuendo. Beneath the text were two pictures: one of my office building and one of me running from the fire at Venus's house. Language under the latter identified it as a stock photo.

I vowed to stop my subscription to the paper and then remembered that I hadn't renewed it last time around. Despite this, the papers kept coming. I needed to stop *delivery.* I'd already stopped payment. It says something about the quality of a product when you don't even want it for free.

"An' now you got some pretty young girl stayin' with you. Some reporter finds out about that, they gonna start rumors that you're like that man in California with a fetish for young girls—dead or alive," Tuwanda hissed.

"That's disgusting!" I said, forgetting to whisper.

"I'm just sayin'," said Tuwanda. "Them reporters at the paper don't like you for some damn reason. They don' like you at all. I wouldn't put it past them to come up with a nasty story like that."

It's true; the Phoenix press doesn't like me. I guess it's because I was less than forthcoming with them about some of the high-profile cases I've been involved in. Also, I may have referred to the reporters as scurrilous sensationalists in a couple TV interviews, and as "brainless rumor mongers" in a speech I gave at last year's Arizona Bar convention.

"Where did Emily come from?" demanded Tuwanda, interrupting my ruminations.

"She's Webber's daughter." I said. "She ran away from home."

Tuwanda's eyes grew big. "You got *Webber's* daughter in there? He ain't gonna like that at all. Tha's like one of Pat Robertson's kids hidin' out at Hefner's Bunny mansion."

She cut me off before I could protest the inappropriate analogy. "I hope to hell you tol' him where she is. You do *not* want to get involved in whatever shit is goin' on between Webber and his kid."

"I think I'm already involved," I said.

"What you gonna do with a thirteen-year-old girl with a slew of hormones?" she asked.

I had no idea, but a part of me thought I could help Emily. I sensed in her some of the childhood pain I still carried with me. I ran away too—when I was a year older than Emily. The loneliness and fear of being on my own were outweighed by the fear of returning home. The police found me a couple days later, one town over, and, although I resisted to the best of my fourteen-year-old ability, took me home. I hadn't been able to save my child-self, but maybe I could save Emily.

If a psychologist had read my mind, he or she would have identified a case of projection. But there weren't any mind-reading psychologists in the hallway, and, at the time, I missed the connection between my own experience and my strong feelings of protectiveness toward Emily.

I couldn't explain my reasoning to Tuwanda since I wasn't real clear on the issue myself, so instead I said, "Emily won't be here long enough for me to have a detrimental impact on her, or *any* impact for that matter. She'll be home with her parents in no time."

Even if I have to take Webber and Emily to a therapist at gunpoint, I thought.

"Good luck with that," Tuwanda said, sounding skeptical. "When this whole thing blows up in your face, don' say I din't warn you.

"I'm goin' home to bed, an' I'm gonna say a prayer for you, though with all the other things God's got on his mind I doubt it'll do much good."

Emily and Macy were rinsing dishes and putting them in the dishwasher when I got back to the kitchen.

"Hi, doll. I put the rest of your food in the microwave. Give it a thirty-second zap and it should be fine," said Macy.

I passed on the leftovers, but grabbed another cup of coffee.

"Macy says she's going to tell me how to make knishes," announced Emily.

"Don't you have to go to school?" I asked.

"It's Sunday," Macy pointed out.

My internal clock was really screwed up. I could have sworn it was Monday. "But you've got school tomorrow, right?" I asked, trying to show I wasn't a complete idiot.

Emily shrugged. That meant "yes" from what I remembered of teenage-ese.

"Where do you go to school?" I asked casually, trying to give the impression I was filling dead air and didn't really give a darn, when of course I did.

Emily made the sound I make when I have to clean hair and gooky stuff out of the tub drain. "Our Lady of Perpetual Grief," she said scornfully, taking a vicious swipe at a plate with the scrubber side of the sponge. The plate, an innocent bystander in the wrong place at the wrong time, squeaked in protest.

I looked at Macy questioningly. "I think she means Our Lady of Perpetual Succor," she said.

I thought that sounded worse. When I was Emily's age, my classmates (and I), would have had a field day with a word like succor.

I must have still looked unenlightened, because Macy added, "It's on Third Street between Camelback and Indian School Roads. It's a big, Spanish mission-looking building. Real pretty."

I remembered it now. Emily's school was only a few blocks from my office. I'd driven by it thousands of times, although until now, I hadn't known it was a school. Every time I see it, I can't help but admire its dark-orange tile roof, white stucco walls, and graceful arches surrounding a blemish-free grassy courtyard.

"It's none of my business, *bubeleh*, but you don't like school?" Macy asked Emily.

"They don't teach me anything I don't already know or can't pick up on my own," she scoffed, "and the sisters are totally out of touch."

"I remember thinkin' that," said Macy kindly. "I was in a public school, so we didn't have sisters, but some of the teachers were *meshuggeners*. I bet you got lotsa friends at school, though, and friends make it better."

"It's a *girls'* school," Emily said disgustedly. "All they

care about are clothes, hair, make-up, boys, and tearing each other down.

"I hate them," she added with feeling.

Now *that's* the part *I* remember about middle school. My school was co-ed, but this hadn't made things any different, or better.

"It can be rough, I know," I said sympathetically. "But school is important, and you have to get through it. I'll be happy to drop you off tomorrow on my way to work."

Emily shook her head ferociously and spun around to face me. She had the same expression Mel Gibson had in the big battle scene in *Braveheart,* minus the blue paint. I half-expected her to scream *freedom.*

"I *can't* go to school. I got suspended for a dress code violation."

She had shed her over-large overcoat some time during the night, and underneath, she was wearing jeans and a T-shirt with daisies printed on the front. It didn't look too bad to me.

Maybe daisies are a gang sign now, I thought, then giggled as an image of tough guys wearing daisy T-shirts in a Sharks *vs.* Jets-type stand-off popped into my mind.

"It's *not funny!*" She sounded so angry that Ralph, who had been hovering at her side looking for more affection and a few handouts, shot across the room in alarm and hid behind my legs.

"I wasn't laughing about you being suspended. I was laughing at how anyone could consider your clothes offensive." Not exactly the truth, but I didn't want to get into the daisy-gang thing.

"It wasn't about what I'm wearing now," she said with slow enunciation, as if she was explaining something to a child. She made kissy noises in the air and called Ralph's name, and he obligingly returned to her side, manically wagging his tail. "We have to wear uniforms to school. I got in trouble because I rolled up my waistband so my skirt came up over my knees."

"Wow," commented Macy. "Those nuns are tough. I see girls outside the public schools wearin' *really* short skirts. I got underpants that come down lower than them skirts."

A disturbing visual popped into my mind.

"And the tops they wear," Macy continued, probably attributing my grimace to a shared disdain for too-short skirts. "Even on cold days you can see their belly buttons an' décolletage."

Emily had dropped down on her knees while Macy was talking and was scratching Ralph's stomach. She seemed to have calmed down. "What's décolletage?" she asked.

I hurriedly explained what it meant before Macy pulled up her shirt and used her own substantial cleavage as a visual learning tool.

"How long is your suspension?" I asked.

"A week," Emily said bitterly. "Plus I can't go to the school dance next Saturday."

It occurred to me Emily might be exaggerating to get

out of going to school. A week-long suspension sounded excessive for a dress code violation as minor as a short skirt. I knew if I'd been suspended every time my skirt went above my knees, I'd still be in sixth grade.

"Maybe I can pick up your homework at school so you don't fall behind," I suggested, thinking I would also check her story while I was there.

"If you've got a computer, I can pull it off the 'net," she said. "The assignments are posted on the school's website."

I offered her the use of my laptop, but I still intended to check on her story about the suspension. If it was true, maybe she ran away because she was afraid to tell her parents. I felt a wave of compassion as I remembered how difficult it was to have every aspect of your life scrutinized by adults and how your parents' disappointment was the worst kind of punishment.

We established that the knish-making operation would take place in Macy's kitchen, due to the embarrassing lack of equipment in mine. Emily asked that Ralph be allowed to observe, and Macy consented, with the proviso that she would have to put a bib on him because "sometimes his drooling gets out of control, and the floor gets real slick."

She asked if I was going to come over and help with the knishes, adding, "With strict supervision, I don't see how you could screw things up too bad."

"No thanks, Macy," I said. "I have to go to my office and check on the … er, some work."

Macy looked at me knowingly.

Emily, who had found my laptop and powered it up, said, "You're going to try to find out what's going on with the dead girl they found under your floor, aren't you?"

I shot Macy a narrow-eyed look. "I didn't say anything," she said, raising her hands defensively, palms out.

"It's on here. Look," said Emily, turning the computer so we could see the screen. A box to the right of the Google logo bore the caption "Off-Beat News." Several short articles followed. The third one down was headlined, "Girl's Skeleton Found under Law Office Floor." The thumbnail photo underneath was my nude-running-from-burning-house photo. I was mentioned by name in the article. So was Webber.

Great. "What the heck does that picture have to do with what happened at my office?" I sputtered.

"It's not very flattering," commented Macy. "But look at the bright side: you got national exposure. It might help you get business."

"From whom? Aficionados of arsonist-porn?" I shrilled. I stifled further comment when I saw Emily's sober expression.

"You're going to be talking to my father, aren't you?" she asked, her tone flat, her shoulders visibly tensing.

No sense lying. She knew from the article that her dad was assigned to the case and we were bound to be speaking soon and often. "Yes. But I promise not to tell him where you are." I didn't add that I didn't have to because he already knew. "In fact, I won't talk about you at all."

"By the way, Emily," I said, quickly changing the subject. "Maybe you can help me with Ralph. I work long hours, and I know Ralph gets lonely. If you feed, walk, brush, and play with him every day, I'll give you room and board in exchange for your services."

Emily appeared to give the idea consideration. "How about room and board *plus* five dollars a day?" she countered.

This kid had a great future as an attorney.

"Done deal," I said.

Macy nodded approvingly and said, "Now that you're employed, maybe later today or tomorrow we can go out and get you a work wardrobe."

I silently congratulated Macy for raising the issue and agreed to swing by the condo around three so we could do some shopping at Fashion Square, a gargantuan mall at the corner of Scottsdale Road and Camelback.

I provided Emily with the essentials, (a toothbrush, toothpaste, shampoo, conditioner, and a clean pair of underwear, upon which was embroidered "Keep your sunny side up" (hey—Victoria's Secret had a sale, they were my size, end of story), and then I retired to my bedroom to change, slightly jealous that Ralph didn't hug my heels as usual but chose to stay at Emily's side.

Chapter 7

I didn't take long to get ready. Weekend work clothes for me are jeans, a well-worn pair of Tory Burch loafers, and any shirt that doesn't need laundering, a fact that I establish with the underarm sniff test.

A half hour later I turned onto Third Street and had entered the final approach to my office when I noticed that the front door was sealed with bright yellow police tape. Webber hadn't mentioned anything about sealing the building. The investigation team must have come back last night after I left.

Webber did this to annoy me, I grumbled, remembering the time his department kept me out of my condo for hours while they conducted an investigation of a burglary they never had any intention of solving.

I pulled into my parking space and stared disgustedly at the tape. The disgust was not so much directed at the tape as it was at me: I couldn't believe I was stupid enough to leave the case files for the next day's court hearings here. I should have anticipated that something like this would happen.

The little voice in my brain that has gotten me into more trouble than I care to admit said, *It's just a piece of tape. It's not like you're going to disrupt a crime scene. You won't go near Sam's office and the hole in the floor* (which the police had enlarged by some three feet)*, and any evidence that might have been in the other rooms is long gone.*

The law-abiding cells in my brain awoke, stretched, yawned, and then cautioned without conviction, *But it's against the law to go into a sealed building unless you have police permission.*

The trouble-making voice countered, *Wimp. It's* your *damn office.*

I got out of my car, climbed the two steps to the small front porch, and, in an attempt to reach a compromise between the warring factions in my head, examined the tape to find a way to bypass it without disrupting the seal.

"Looking for something?" asked a voice behind me.

I whirled around to find Webber standing in the driveway. He must have been parked somewhere waiting for me because I didn't hear his car pull up.

"You scared the hell out of me," I blurted. "What are you doing here?"

"Odd as it may sound, but when I'm assigned a case, I sometimes actually conduct an investigation."

"I thought you were going to transfer this case to

someone else because you have too many other things going on."

"I decided to stay on this one and move some others around. I like being around you that much."

So you can keep track of me and pump me for information about Emily, I thought.

I smiled sweetly. "My hero!" Then I added, not so sweetly, "I need to get into my office."

"How's Emily?" he asked.

I got the message: I bring him up-to-date on Emily, and he lets me in my office.

It's his daughter. He has a right to know what's going on, screamed the sane pile of neurons.

Sanity and empathy prevailed.

"She's doing fine," I said. I told him about our morning with Macy, Emily's new job caring for Ralph, and our shopping plans. I did not mention that Tuwanda had joined us for breakfast and kept quiet about Emily's school suspension.

"What about her school uniform? My wife said she didn't take anything with her. What will she wear to school? How will she even get to school?"

"We have it all under control," I answered, evading a direct response to his questions. I wasn't exactly lying. Things were under control, kind of. Emily was safe, and as far as I was concerned, that meant everything was hunky-dory.

Webber narrowed his eyes and glared at me, as if trying to figure out if I was telling the truth. I put on my court face, which consists of a neutral expression accomplished by internally repeating the phrase, "I will not react no matter how much I want to scream/swear/hurl negative comments about ancestry at the judge/opposing counsel/my client."

"If she's not home in three days, I'm calling Child Protective Services," he said.

I returned his glare.

"May I go into my office now?" I asked, figuring the glaring was nonproductive.

Webber looked like he wanted to strangle me, but then he shrugged and said, "Be my guest."

I started to tear off the police tape and then hesitated. "Could you write up a permission slip and sign it?"

I wouldn't put it past Webber to threaten to conveniently forget that he consented to my entry whenever he wanted more information.

"I don't have paper or pencil," he answered.

I pointedly directed my gaze to his breast pocket where the ends of several pens were sticking out. One of them had leaked and his shirt was stained with black ink. I shifted my glare to his side pocket where the top of a small spiral notebook was visible.

"Oh for God's sake," he muttered. "Nobody trusts the system anymore."

"What system is that?" I snapped back.

Webber pulled out the notebook, opened it to a clean page, and took out a pen. I thrust out my hand. "Give it to me," I said. "I'll write the authorization and then you read and sign." I wasn't going to give him the chance to mess with the verbiage either.

As soon as he signed the authorization I'd written, I checked his signature (I wouldn't put it past him to sign the name of a fictional character), ripped out the page, pocketed it, and handed back the notebook.

He watched as I removed the police tape but made no move to follow me into the building. I slammed the door behind me and looked through the window to make sure he left.

Chapter 8

I stared at the motion I was reading—or supposed to be reading. I was having a hard time concentrating on trademark infringement. My mind kept wandering to the hole in the floor of the room across the hall. Stu wouldn't be able to get around to fixing it until Tuesday, and even though the police techs had cleared the area of evidence the night before, the mere fact of the hole and what had been found in it bothered me immensely. Even with two walls and a hallway in between, I felt, or maybe imagined I felt, the damp cold from the ground underneath the house touch my shoulder. Then it moved through me and traveled down my arm until I felt it on my hand. Air drafts are not supposed to act this way.

I placed my hand on my forehead to check whether I had a fever, thinking maybe I was experiencing pre-flu chills. It felt fine to me, but then according to Tuwanda, who had taken a couple of nursing courses at the community college, feeling your own forehead is not the best way to tell if you have a fever.

"If you got a fever, your hand's jus' as hot as your forehead, so you don't feel no difference," she'd informed me.

"Don't be sick!" I ordered myself out loud. "I can't afford to get sick." Literally, if I don't work, the bills don't get paid.

The cold air patted my shoulder. *Great. I'm not getting sick. I'm going insane,* I thought morosely. Either way, the firm's bottom line would be negatively impacted.

I looked at my watch. It was only eleven thirty and the partial breakfast I had eaten earlier was not going to carry me through the afternoon. I figured I could pick up something later at the mall, but I needed a snack to tide me over until then. I opened my desk drawer and found my emergency supply of Snickers bars, which I had hidden from MJ, the office food thief, under a stack of printer paper. I would have checked the kitchen for cookies first, but I knew that the batch Beth had made on Wednesday had not survived much beyond Thursday morning. Sam had acquired a cookie addiction almost as bad as mine, and it went without saying that MJ ate a lot of them too, although her addiction was to food in general and was not cookie specific.

I bit into the Snickers, relishing its not-quite-empty calories. (I rationalize that the peanuts are a source of protein and the caramel and chocolate fulfill my daily calcium needs—I have a creative, albeit self-serving, system of rationalization.) My eyes drifted over to the real estate file Beth had copied for Webber the day before. She had set it on the edge of my desk, probably thinking I would want to look at it again before she re-filed it.

I picked it up and flipped it open. This time, I took my time reviewing its contents. It was too bad that sellers were no longer required under Arizona Law to disclose if a murder or suicide had occurred on a property. But then, how many sellers would answer truthfully anyway? No one was going to say, "Oh yes; I murdered my mother-in-law here a couple of years ago and buried her in the back yard," or "not yet, but I get *really* depressed on weekends."

I pulled out a fresh legal pad and took notes between nibbles of my Snickers, barely noticing the candy was colder each time I picked it up. I wrote down the names of the two owners and those of the lessees reflected in three recorded leases. Though, as I mentioned before, residential leases of less than a year are usually not recorded, so this was not a complete history. I also wrote down the names of the signatories to all easement grants—water, sewer, telephone, and sidewalk. I knew that the police investigators would pick up on the chain-of-title issues, but they might not realize that many times the lessee, as well as the owner, is asked by utilities to sign off on grants of easement to cover all the bases. Utility company payment records were also a great resource because lessees are often responsible for making utility payments.

When I was through, I had about thirty or so names listed and a starting place for my investigation.

Yes, *my* investigation. I knew damn well I should leave it to the police, but I also knew the police department, like every governmental agency, was underfunded and overworked and would assign a low priority to a death that was obviously not recent. I, on the other hand, was highly motivated: not only do I own the property where the skeleton was found, a fact that triggered my curiosity as well as an irrational sense of responsibility, but the avenging angel side of me had been aroused, and when that happens, there's no letting go.

Once, in the midst of a heated conversation about my interference with a federal investigation of Mexican cartel activities, Bryan had suggested that my need to protect the underdog and solve the world's problems had a deep-seated psychological basis and I would do well to subject myself to extensive analysis with regard to it. I believe my response was something along the lines of, "Oh, yeah? *You're* the one who needs help." In my defense, I had just been through a house fire, a kidnapping, and two car crashes at the time, so I wasn't on top of my game. I, however, do not consider an obsession for truth to be a mental abnormality but rather an indication of strong character.

Finding the truth in this case was going to take long hours of research. The house had been built in the early part of the twentieth century. Even with the efficiencies provided by the Internet, a review of records covering the last eighty-plus years was daunting. I figured that I could safely ignore the last decade in light of the skeletonized condition of the body, but that still left a lot of years to cover.

Since I needed to work my investigation around my regular schedule, some serious prioritizing was necessary. I sat back in my chair and closed my eyes to give the matter some thought, but my brain brought up the picture of the piteous little skeleton under the floor. I pushed the image away, but, as I did, the tip of an idea emerged. I rewound and did a freeze-frame, focusing on the faded features of the baby doll lying next to her: it had a small round hole in the middle of its kiss-puckered lips.

I had a doll like that when I was little. You filled a little plastic baby bottle with water and inserted the tip in the doll's "mouth." You then fed your pretend baby by letting the water drip out of the bottle into the doll's tummy. After the feeding, you could squeeze the doll, and the water would squirt out of a hole in the doll's butt, an anatomic abnormality that caused me problems in my grade-school science class. This gave you the opportunity to moan dramatically, chastise the doll for wetting its pants, and then change its little cotton diapers like a real mommy. The ability to urinate was the doll's sole selling feature. I had inherited mine from an older cousin who, unfortunately, had experimented with liquids other than water, so the doll's pee had a distinctly bad odor. I felt this added to the authenticity of the experience, though, so I didn't mind.

Try as I might, I couldn't remember the doll's brand name.

I wondered if Google had ever considered developing a search engine that could be implanted in a human brain—one where all you needed to do was think of a word and your brain would automatically and efficiently conduct a search of your memory bank. I could use something like that.

A cold blast of air on my face interrupted my mental meanderings. I searched my office for possible sources of the cold air, without success, and forced myself to refocus on the little girl under my floor.

I decided to call her Betsy. The name popped into my mind, which is odd because it's not a name I particularly like, and I never knew anyone named Betsy or even heard the name that often except … *that's it! It was a Betsy Wetsy doll.*

I searched the name on my desktop computer and found information about the doll in *Wikipedia,* a site that has information about absolutely everything. Though much of the information is questionable, the site was still a good starting point. According to *Wikipedia,* the doll was issued by the Ideal Toy Company in 1934, and had enjoyed the height of its popularity until the 1950s. This information shaved another two decades off the relevant search period.

I was entering the name of the previous owner of my building on the Google search page when my phone rang. It was Bryan, who had come up for air from a pile of paperwork to ask me if I wanted to go to lunch, saying he had something important to discuss.

"I don't have much time," I said. "I need to pick up Macy and Emily at three and I was hoping to get some work done before that."

"We'll make it quick. By the way, who's Emily?" he asked.

"I'll explain over lunch. How about we meet at El Barrio for enchiladas?"

"Sounds good. See you there in fifteen," he said enthusiastically. Bryan is similar to Ralph that way. Mention his favorite food, and his mental processes are replaced by a maniacal focus on that item.

Now I was sorry I had eaten the Snickers because knew I would succumb to the siren call of Maria Garcia's enchiladas. Beth, who had known Maria since childhood, first introduced me to Maria and her cuisine a few months after El Barrio first opened, and I'd been a devotee ever since. Maria had started the restaurant a year ago in a seedy neighborhood near the downtown area. She did not advertise, but word got around that the northern Mexican cuisine at El Barrio was the best in town—in a town that has more Mexican restaurants than pizza parlors, that is high praise. These days, on most weekdays, the office workers in downtown Phoenix relocated to El Barrio around noon. I usually avoid it for that very reason. To quote Yogi Berra, "Nobody goes there anymore. It's too crowded." But at this hour on a Sunday, we shouldn't have a problem getting a seat.

I grabbed my purse, stood, and closed the search screen upon which I'd entered the phrase "McDougall

Phoenix," hoping to narrow the search to local families. As I did, the air around me became frigid again. I was overwhelmed with feelings of sadness and something worse: fear. Fear is normally not part of my emotional repertoire unless someone is pointing a deadly weapon at me with the intention of using it. Experiencing fear while standing in my empty office made no sense.

I leaned against my desk and shook my head to clear it. I felt the cold air pat my shoulder again, after which the room's temperature returned to normal, and the blanket of fear and sadness lifted. I shook my head again and then jotted down a reminder on my calendar to ask Beth to get a heating and cooling company over to check the air conditioning system and vents. One of the reasons I moved to Phoenix was for the warm weather, darn it. These arctic blasts had to stop.

When I got to El Barrio Bryan had already arrived and was ensconced in a back booth—a choice location since Maria waited the tables in that section. Maria always made sure your meal got that extra Maria touch, which usually meant the portions were doubled, not that this Snickers-muncher needed an extra-large portion.

Bryan waved at me and lifted his margarita glass with an inquiring look. After a brief internal debate, I nodded, and he summoned the waitress, who was, indeed, Maria. He was already putting in an order for another margarita when I slide into the seat opposite him.

"Hi, Maria," I said.

"Hi, Kate," said Maria smiling broadly. "It's good to

see you. You're still too thin. I'll make sure you get extra of everything."

Maria thinks everyone is too thin. She is less than five feet tall and must tip the scales at over two hundred pounds, so, comparatively, most of the population of Phoenix *is* too thin. Seeing her reminds me of one of my of my father's sagacious pieces of advice: "You wanna' look thin? Hang around with fat people." No one ever accused Dad of being overly politically correct.

Maria recommended the chicken and cheese enchiladas, so of course that's what we ordered. She was back in milliseconds with a pitcher of margaritas and another glass. Bryan poured me a drink, then topped off his own.

"Are you sure you can do this?" I asked Bryan, gesturing at his drink.

"I'm heading to my apartment for a marathon nap after we're finished," he answered wearily. "Except for our movie date last night, I've been on the job nonstop for over seventy-two hours. I need a break. Lack of sleep does not make for wise decision making."

"I know. I hadn't slept in twenty-four hours the day I decided to adopt Ralph," I said wryly. I had found Ralph, a stray, at a dude ranch I visited a while back. The kitchen staff irregularly fed him scraps of food, and he was skinny and dull coated when we first met. He was now pleasingly plump—the vet wants me to put him on a diet—and his coat looks better than my hair, thanks to weekly grooming sessions at Doggy Divas. I joke about him, but my friends know I adore him, and so does he.

I explained to Bryan about Emily and, after expressing his surprise (along with a light spray of taco chips), when I told him who she was, he proceeded to state the obvious. "You are screwed. You know you're in a no-win situation, right? If Emily disappears again, her dad will hate you, and if she prefers staying at your condo over going home, her dad will hate you."

I was fully aware of this conundrum, so I didn't find Bryan's comments helpful or enlightening. "What was I supposed to do?" I snapped back. "Throw Emily back out on the street? Or maybe you think I should have tackled her, tied her up, thrown her in the trunk of my car, and taken her home

"Emily and her parents have to work things out. In the meantime, she needs to be in a safe place, not out on the street." I paused to chug the rest of my margarita. But I was on a roll. "Dammit, Bryan. They found the skeleton of a young girl under the floor of my office building. God only knows what horrible thing happened to her. I can't do anything to bring Betsy back, but I can do something to help Emily."

"Betsy?" asked Bryan.

I made an exasperated noise in my throat. "That's what I call the little girl under my floor. The doll lying next to her was a Betsy Wetsy doll. I had one when I was little."

I thought I glimpsed of flash of annoyance in his eyes, but then his expression slide into an unreadable mask. Maria arrived at that moment and placed two steaming plates of enchiladas in front of us.

Despite the post-Snickers promise I'd made to myself to eat a light lunch, I dug in and kept going. I blame my lack of will power on the margarita.

The conversation we worked in between bites consisted of polite inquiries and equally polite responses about friends, family, and pets—mine and Tuwanda's. Bryan had no pets of his own but had assumed some parental duties with respect to Ralph because, as he said, "Ralph needs a male role model."

When we finished, we both ordered coffee, but even after a few shots of caffeine, Bryan looked sleepy and ready for a long nap.

"Why don't I drop you off at your apartment?" I asked. I wasn't concerned about him being pulled over for a DUI—he hadn't drunk enough for that—but there was a real possibility he would fall asleep at the wheel. The guy was exhausted.

"Kate, I need to talk to you …" Bryan started to say, but Maria appeared at our table again, carrying our checks.

"Sheriff, you look tired," she remarked.

"I said the same thing," I said. "We were discussing whether he needs a ride home."

Bryan started to protest, but Maria interrupted. "I will take the sheriff home. My shift is about over, and Bryan and I live in the same building."

"I didn't know that," I said in surprise. I've visited Bryan's condo many times—sometimes staying overnight, although we both preferred sleepovers at my place—and

I thought I had met, or at least seen, all of the of the residents in his building.

"I live in the penthouse and have my own elevator, so I don't run into anyone too often." I could hear the pride in her voice.

"Wow," I said, genuinely impressed. "I've seen the top level from the street. You've got a patio that runs around the building. The view must be amazing from up there."

"You and the sheriff need to come up for drinks and see for yourselves. Would you have time to drop by Wednesday around six?"

"I can make it," I answered. "Bryan, how about you?"

"Absent an emergency at work," which we all knew was not only possible, but probable, "I'll be there."

"Good," said Maria. "I will make mini-tacos and quesadillas for a snack, and my special margaritas, of course. If the sheriff can't make it, Kate, you and I will have a party of our own.

"Give me a second to get my sweater, Sheriff, and then I will take you home." But Maria made no move to leave. I got the feeling she had more she wanted to say, and I was right.

"When you come over, maybe I can ask you about something," she said to me with forced nonchalance.

I was expecting a request for legal advice. Friends, acquaintances, and even strangers pumping me for free services is part of the gig, and I don't mind general requests for information. But I really resent it when people ask me what they should do in specific circumstances. I'm supposed to get paid for those kinds of answers.

Maria wasn't interested in free legal advice, however.

"I read about the skeleton under your floor," she said. "It is a sad thing. I lived near your neighborhood when I was little. I want to tell you what I remember. Maybe it will help."

Bryan's law enforcer's point of view kicked in. "You should call the police if you remember anything."

Maria shook her head sadly. "The police have enough to do. Because the little girl died a long time ago, it will not be an important to them. But I have read the news stories about Miss Kate. She will want to know, and she won't give up until she finds out."

This was one of the nicest things I'd ever heard. I had been afraid the media's coverage of my cases gave people the impression that I was a borderline psychotic. (I mean, when the newspaper's stock photo is me running naked from a fire holding a Chihuahua, people are bound to get the wrong impression.)

Bryan scowled, but didn't say anything. Even he had to admit the truth of what Maria said. Had the case fallen within the jurisdiction of the sheriff's office, you can bet it would go to the bottom of the list.

As Maria trotted off to retrieve her sweater, I glanced at my watch and slid out of the booth. "I'd better get going," I said. "I want to get some work done before I pick up Emily and Macy."

"I'll call you later, Kate. Will you be available?"

"Sure," I said lightly, wondering about his serious tone.

I went back to my office, and, despite the margarita—or maybe because of it—I managed to get about an hour of work done before leaving to pick up Macy and Emily.

They already were standing in front of my condo building, even though I was a few minutes early. Macy got into the front passenger side, and Emily jumped into the backseat.

"We left Ralph at Macy's," Emily announced. "He fell asleep, and we didn't have the heart to wake him."

"How did the knish cooking lesson go?" I asked.

A lively narrative followed, with a few interruptions and corrections by Macy, during which I learned Emily is a natural at knish preparation.

I suggested, time permitting, we stop in at the mall pet store and look at the puppies. Normally, looking at adorable doggies in glass cages makes me kind of sad, and I want to rescue them all and take them home with me. But I knew Emily would be thrilled, especially because the store will take the puppies out of their cages if you ask, and you can get some on-site cuddle time.

Emily loved the idea—so much, in fact, that she was willing to blow off the clothes shopping and head directly to the pet store. She changed her mind, however, when Macy offered to lend her some of her clothes if she didn't want to buy new ones. I love Macy, but pastel-colored, rhinestone-studded, sequined jogging suits, sweaters, and spandex pants (Macy loves anything that sparkles) do not appeal to teenagers.

I found a parking space on the second floor of the mall's four-storied parking garage, and we set out, planning to go to Nordstrom's junior's department first and then to Forever Twenty-One at the other end of the mall, stopping at all points in between.

An hour and a half later, we were still at Nordstrom's.

How can it take so long to decide on a [T-shirt, pair of jeans, hoodie], I thought for the umpteenth time.

She finally decided on a T-shirt but almost backed out at the cash register when she had second thoughts about the color (light blue). The transaction was completed only after the sales clerk told Emily that Fergie of the Black-Eyed Peas said light blue was her favorite color.

Two hours and four stores later, Emily had found a pair of jeans, a couple more T-shirts, and a hoodie, and I had found a Starbucks. We had left Macy at the fountain in front of the movie theater two stores ago, promising to come back for her when we were through. She said something about needing to soak her feet, or maybe it was her head. I forget which.

I was all for picking up something at the food court and heading home, but Emily insisted that we visit the pet store first. We stopped off at the fountain to pick up Macy, who seemed to have perked up. I noticed that her shoes squished when she walked.

I volunteered to get some takeout at the food court and meet the other two at the pet store. Emily voted for pizza and Macy wanted Chinese food. I wanted hamburgers, and since I was paying, my vote was the only one that mattered.

I waited in a long line of similarly minded people, and when it was my turn at the counter, I ordered six hamburgers (we each needed two, right?), three jumbo fries, and three chocolate malts. My caloric intake for the day was already astronomical, but I wanted comfort food, so I ignored the nagging little-miss-perfect-voice in my head.

Lugging a grocery-sized bag of fast food, I walked to the pet store and spotted Macy and Emily in the back admiring an adorable little French bulldog playing at their feet. Several other dogs had been let out so the patrons could pet them and, hopefully, bond on the spot so there would be a few purchases as a result of the pet-fest.

"Hi, guys," I called out as I headed toward them. I recognized my grave error too late.

The Jack Russell's nose started to twitch and then he twisted himself out of the arms of the little girl holding him. A golden retriever sniffed at the air, crouched, and leaped over the side of her wire-sided playpen with the grace of an Olympian athlete. A poodle and a rottweiler followed suit. The French bulldog and a dachshund were no slouches either, and both of them headed toward me with alacrity. The dogs in the glass-fronted cages could not get out, but they participated in the brouhaha with a lusty chorus of barks and howls.

The pack of loose dogs headed for me—or, more precisely, for the bag of hamburgers I was carrying. I am a trained professional with years of courtroom experience requiring trigger-fast decision making and strategizing. I tossed that background out the window and panicked. I ran like hell, holding the bag of food over my head. The dogs went after me, dodging the reaching hands of sales clerks and store patrons, and yipping joyfully.

I ran to the down escalator, reasoning, it seems defectively, that dogs, especially young dogs, would be afraid of moving metal stairs. The buggers didn't even hesitate. Only the dachshund fell back a stride or two when he realized the weird moving floor turned into steps that were too steep for his short legs to handle. When the steps flattened out at the bottom, though, he took off after the rest of the pack.

I was in pure panic mode now. I remembered something about water being a deterrent because the dogs would lose the scent. Or was that bees? Of course, it never occurred to me to toss the bag of food at my loyal following, an action that would have put an immediate end to the chase. For some reason, protecting those hamburgers was important to me. Looking back on the event later, I saw it as a sort of metaphor for my life: I will sacrifice everything to protect things, or people—and whether they care, or even are capable of caring, is irrelevant.

The closest body of water was the fountain Macy had rested beside earlier. I spotted it six or seven stores away, at the midpoint of the mall, and sprinted toward it.

It was near closing time, so relatively few people were still wandering around the mall. I saw several of them take pictures with their cell phones.

I made it to the fountain and leaped into the pool

of water surrounding the two-story high waterfall in the middle. Unfortunately, the heel of my loafer caught the edge of one of the surrounding benches, so I went in head first and landed in a position far different from what I had intended. Both the food bag and my purse went flying, and when I surfaced, the dogs were in the fountain snapping up the hamburgers and fries. The little dachshund wasn't able to make it over the knee-high wall surrounding the pool. Instead, he was chewing on the handle of my purse, which, miraculously, had landed outside the pool.

A small crowd gathered around the fountain, and I was surrounded by a ring of cell phones aimed in my direction. I was miffed that no one bothered to ask how I was or offer a hand to help me up.

As I struggled to my feet, I saw Emily push through the crowd toward me. As it turned out, though, it wasn't me she was concerned about. She stepped into the water and fished out the little French bulldog, who had his jaws locked around a quarter-pounder. "Poor doggie," she murmured as she wrapped her new hoodie around him.

Macy arrived panting up a few seconds later. "I ain't been trained for this, doll," she gasped between gulps of air.

Who is? I thought. *This isn't exactly a recognized sport.*

At least Macy was kind enough to offer me a hand and help me out of the fountain. I emptied the water out of my shoes, and, as I was wringing out my shirttails, a security guard strutted up. Dressed in a spiffy beige uniform, his pelvis thrust forward, the thumb of his right hand stuck in his belt, his left hand resting on his flashlight (mall cops aren't allowed to carry guns)—everything about him screamed, "I am a self important asshole who should, in a fair world, be treated as a god."

"Ma'am, no people allowed in the fountain," he intoned. "I'm afraid I'm going to have to ask you to leave."

"Are dogs allowed in the fountain?" I snapped, gesturing toward the golden retriever and the poodle, who, even though the food was gone, were still leaping playfully around in the water.

This seemed to stump him. Apparently the mall rules he had, no doubt, committed to memory did not address this issue. Most people, by extrapolation, would reason that, since dogs are not allowed in the mall, they are barred from the fountain as well, but mall cop-guy fell into that category of people with a literal understanding of the laws. A lot of law enforcement folks, ultra-conservative politicians, and school principals fall into this category.

Mall cop guy regrouped and re-focused on the one thing he knew for sure: people are not allowed in the fountain. Period. "If you do not cooperate, I have the authority to arrest you for trespass, and believe me, ma'am, I will exercise that authority."

Oh, I believed him. Arresting dangerous ol' me would be the highlight of his day; he'd be a hit at the neighborhood bar after work tonight. To avoid ruffling his feathers, I refrained from pointing out that if he did arrest me, he would have to call in a *real* cop to make it official.

"As soon as I snatch my purse from the jaws of that over-sized bratwurst," I said, pointing to the dachshund, "I'm out of here, sir."

"See that you are, ma'am."

Sheesh. This guy made Barney Fife look like a Navy SEAL.

I retrieved my purse, but the dachshund remained attached, his teeth still locked on the handle. As I was shaking the purse to make him let go, Macy rushed over, cradled the little dog in her arms, and gently pried his jaws open, murmuring, "What a sweet, sweet, little doggy. I'm not gonna let the mean lady hurt you."

The mean lady had about had enough. "I am going to my car," I snarled. "If you and Emily aren't there in fifteen minutes, I will leave without you, and you can take the damn bus back."

I heard Macy ask, "What's *she* so upset about?" as I squished away.

I waited more than twenty minutes and was still moist by the time they got to the car. Macy had stopped off to get more hamburgers, and, although I appreciated the gesture, I never wanted to see another beef patty again in my life.

"Yer buns dried off yet?" she called out merrily as she got into the car.

"No, as a matter of fact they are still soggy," I said, squirming uncomfortably.

"Wow!" commented Emily enthusiastically. "That was so great. My parents are never that much fun."

Oh God, I hope Webber doesn't hear about this.

Little did I know—this would be one of the better experiences of the week.

Chapter 9

We went back to the condo and I ended up skipping dinner and going to bed early. Ralph got my share of the burgers, which Emily said was only fair since Ralph had missed out on all the fun and food at the mall.

The next morning, Macy came over and made breakfast again. Since the newspaper-boy hadn't been by yet, I had to forgo my routine of coffee and catching up on the local news. (Yes, I admit it: I don't like the paper's editorial policies but I still read it). I didn't feel too deprived. The Monday paper in Phoenix is usually thin and weak on substance, as if all the staff's energies were poured into the huge Sunday edition, so that on Monday, even if an alien ship landing on the building's roof, the reaction would be along the lines of "*feh*."

Emily woke up and rolled out of her couch-bed as I was leaving. The forlorn expression on her face when I told her I needed to go to work tugged at my heartstrings. Despite her display of indifference the day before, I knew she would miss being with her friends at school and felt flattered she considered me an acceptable substitute.

"How about I stop off at your school on my way in and have a sit-down with the principal to see if I can get her to drop this suspension-thing?"

Emily's reaction was loud and immediate. "No! I don't want you talking to that bitch." Her tone reflected a mixture of horror and distain.

"Don't curse," I reprimanded reflexively.

Emily glared back at me defiantly and looked like she might launch into the teenage equivalent of a grand mal seizure. But then the fire went out of her eyes, her little shoulders slumped, and, in a much quieter voice added, "Besides. It wouldn't do any good. Sister Mary Grace never changes her mind when it comes to punishment and sentencing."

Talk about rough justice. At least in the adult legal system, you have the right to appeal.

I changed the subject and asked her what her plans were for the day. She explained that last night she and Macy had come up with an idea for a dog walking business and were going to make fliers and pass them out to the building's residents. At the time, I thought that was a superb idea.

On the way to work, I changed my mind about not pleading Emily's case with her school's principal, impulsively taking a hard right onto Seventh and then turning left into the parking lot of Our Lady of Perpetual Succor. At eight forty-five, the log jam of parents dropping off students was beginning to break up, and the driveway was clearing out. I noticed that the school's buildings housed an elementary school in addition to the middle and high schools, which explains why children in a wide range of ages emerged from the vehicles pulling up to the curb. The chaos at the disembarkation point was somewhat organized: adults—probably teachers or other school staff members—escorted the smaller children from their cars and then through the entrance to the elementary school wing.

I waited for a huge Suburban driven by a harried-looking petite blonde to pull out and then parked my car in the space she had vacated. After turning off the engine, I remained seated for a while and stared through the window at the school's entrance, trying to reign in the feelings of panicky dread I have experienced since kindergarten whenever I'm in the vicinity of teachers and school administrators. (I was not a bad kid; I always seemed to be in the wrong place at the wrong time, though. I mean, like who knew the fire alarm would go off if you hung a poster on it. In retrospect, I probably shouldn't have used a nail.)

I got out of the car and strode with forced confidence through a door to the right of the main entrance over which hung a metal plaque with the word "Administration" engraved on it.

The anteroom into which I walked was typical of the

school genre—two uncomfortable-looking faux-leather couches faced each other, and a scuffed wooden coffee table covered with copies of *Catholic Digest* and school newsletters stood between them. A woman wearing a pink suit and high-necked blouse *circa* 1960 stood behind a counter at the back of the room. (I think I saw Doris Day wear the same outfit in *Please Don't Eat the Daisies*. Before you start doing the math, I should tell you that I watched the movie on the Turner Classic Movies channel—not at its premier). Her blonde hair was pulled back tightly into a French roll (another Doris Day touch), and a pair of tortoise-shell glasses attached to a pink beaded eyeglass holder were perched on the tip of her nose. Once I made it past the retro-garb, though, I realized she was probably only in her early thirties. Her unlined face and neck gave her away.

She was addressing a student, a gangly red-head with bad skin, who had apparently asked for a late pass.

"Miss McCarthy," she said severely. "This is the second time you have been tardy this year. Classes start at nine in the morning, not nine-oh-five. If you are tardy one more time, you will face the possibility of suspension."

The way she said "suspension" made it sound like a medieval torture. This *was* a tough group.

The girl took the slip the woman handed her like it was the Holy Grail, and, practically curtseying, murmured, "Thank you, Miss Dresky."

After the sinful Miss McCarthy left, Miss Dresky turned to me.

"May I help you?" she asked pertly, affording me the politeness reserved by school administrators for adults.

"Yes," I squeaked. *Pull yourself together, Williams,* I lectured. *You're a lawyer for God's sake. What are you afraid of? That they'll keep you after school? Make you stay in for recess?*

I tried again, this time managing a more authoritative tone. "Yes. I would like to speak to Sister Mary Grace concerning Emily Webber, one of your eighth-grade students."

Miss Dresky, whom I had already nicknamed Drecky in a surge of sophomoric inspiration, tilted her head slightly to the side. "We do not give out information on a student except to their parent or guardian. I know both Mr. and Mrs. Webber. What might your capacity be?"

"I'm Emily's attorney," I shot back. "Mr. and Mrs. Webber are aware that I am representing their daughter." Well, kind of. I mean, they knew Emily was staying with me. I figured that was close enough for purposes of this conversation.

I placed one of my business cards on the counter in front of Drecky. She picked it up, scrutinized it, and said, "Please wait here." Then she disappeared through a door behind the counter, holding my card in front of her in a two-fingered grip as if it were hazardous waste.

I sat on one of the couches, picked up an issue of *Catholic Digest,* and settled in to read an article about the sliding moral values of today's youth. It was very similar to articles published about sliding moral values when I was in high school. I mused that there must have been an intervening generation during which values soared, otherwise we'd be in subterranean territory by now. I was well into the article when Drecky returned, followed by a short, stout woman with iron-gray hair and a kindly expression. She was wearing a Hillary Clinton-esque navy-blue pantsuit and low black heels. I tried to hide my strappy Manolo Blahniks under the coffee table and tugged my skirt down over my knees.

Once again, the rebel contingency spoke up. *What is your problem? You are a well accomplished adult. Stop acting like schoolgirl, and a wimpy one at that.*

I rose to my feet and extended my hand to the newcomer. I was a good foot taller than she.

She beat me to the punch on introductions. "I am Sister Mary Grace." She sounded like Betty White.

"Kate Williams," I responded in a businesslike voice. I was not fooled by her grandmotherly demeanor. All school principals are tough as nails, and many are meaner than snakes, too. Sometimes they have to be, but I still nursed a childhood grudge against them.

"I understand you have come to talk about our Emily," she said.

I nodded briskly and looked pointedly at Drecky. "What I need to discuss is better discussed in private," I said.

Sister looked thoughtfully at me with a little Mona Lisa smile. I stared back at her, stone faced. *Oh man,* said the goody-two-shoes brain cells. *You are in T-R-O-U-B-L-E.*

An unreadable look flashed across her face. "Please, why don't we go into my office?" she suggested, the little smile back in place.

"Thank you. That would work fine," I said graciously.

Neither the principal nor Drecky made a move to leave, however. Both remained in place and stared at me, the former benignly; the latter malignantly.

I cleared my throat. Still nothing.

"After you," I said, sweeping my arm in the direction of the door through which the principal had entered.

"Dear, why don't you go into my office and make yourself comfortable," said Sister Mary Grace/Betty White. "I need to talk to Miss Dresky about some school matters, but it won't take me long. Go through that door. My office is at the end of the hall."

I looked at my watch, not because I was late for anything but because I wanted to give the impression that my time was limited and valuable. "Very well, then," I said with a short nod.

Where the hell did that come from? I thought. *I never say "very well." English butlers say "very well."*

I hurriedly pushed through the little swinging half-door in the counter and went through the door leading to the office area before I blurted out something along the lines of, "Will there be anything else, ma'am?"

The principal's office was as I expected: large, wood paneled, and lined with bookcases. Centered in the middle of the room was a carved wood desk, behind which was a comfortable-looking leather wing-back chair. Two uncomfortable-looking straight-backed chairs faced the desk. I was tempted to sit in the leather wing-back chair, but the goody-two shoes brain cells talked me out of it.

I sat in one of the straight-backed chairs and scanned the titles of the books in the bookcases. My father always told me you could tell a lot about a person by the books they read. Based upon what I saw, Sister was a Roman Catholic school administrator. Big surprise.

I noticed with interest that one shelf was packed with yearbooks dating back to 1941. The school is close to my office, and I wondered if Betsy had attended here at any time. Without a name, though, it would be impossible to find out.

I heard the door open and straightened my back and crossed my legs neatly at the ankle. Talk about conditioning.

"Now then," said Sister Mary Grace, sitting in the big chair behind the desk and placing the file she had been carrying in front of her. "Tell me why you are here."

"It is my understanding that Emily Webber was suspended for a week due to a dress code violation …" I began.

"Is that what she told you?" interrupted Sister Mary Grace.

"Yes, ma'am," I answered, using a form of address I usually reserve for judges, (female judges, of course although there is one male judge I could think of who would probably prefer this salutation, at least in private).

"Emily has indeed been cited several times for wearing an inappropriately short skirt, but this was not the basis for her suspension. Emily stole another girl's backpack. The theft was reported last Friday morning, and another student spotted it later in Emily's locker."

"Are you sure?" I asked.

"We do not make or take such charges lightly," Sister Mary Grace said sternly. "And in light of the especially heinous nature of the crime, I believe a one-week suspension was light punishment."

"Heinous?" I repeated.

"At the time of the theft, Emily's skirt was hiked up over her knees."

Dear God; she sounds as if there is a special ring of hell reserved for thieves with the hubris to wear short skirts. I had to fight back a giggle.

"I think I need to talk to Emily again," I said, fighting for composure. "I want to hear her side of this. Also, I will need a copy of all reports in Emily's student file relating to this matter."

"Of course. But I believe you will find that our decision to suspend Emily is soundly based." Sister punched the button of an outdated intercom and asked Miss Dresky to bring her a copy of Emily's suspension file. Then she turned her attention back to me and looked at me thoughtfully as she fingered the file in front of her. She seemed as if she wanted to say something but wasn't quite sure if she should.

She apparently decided to take the plunge. "I recognized your name immediately when Miss Dresky told me you were here. You've been in the newspapers a few times lately."

Oh heck. She saw my running-naked photo. So much for my attempt to make a professional impression.

I looked at her brightly and tried to regroup. "Why yes," I said, as if I she had just paid me a compliment. Then, assuming a suitably somber expression, I added, "The circumstances were unfortunate. There was the fire, and then of course, most recently, the discovery of a skeleton at my office."

"Yes," said Sister Mary Grace. "And this morning's article about the incident at the mall."

I felt the blood drain out of my face. "I don't believe I've seen that one yet," I said in a strained voice.

"Oh, well, let me show you. I have a copy of the paper right here." Sister pulled a newspaper out of a carry-all hanging from her chair-arm, placed it on her desk, and pushed it toward me. I picked it up gingerly and looked at the front page.

The picture showed me standing in the fountain at the mall with a wet hamburger wrapper stuck to my hair and my sopping clothes clinging to my body like spandex. The dogs in the fountain with me looked charming—like the cute little puppies you see on calendars.

The headline read "Attorney Goes to the Dogs."

I tried to derive comfort from the thought that at least this photo wasn't as bad as the running-naked photo.

"The article is continued on page four," said Sister Mary Grace.

I turned to page four, and there was the running-naked photo.

I covered my face with my hand and groaned.

I heard Sister shuffling papers.

I felt a terrible sense of foreboding. *Oh God; there's more.*

Sister cleared her throat. I let my hand drop back into my lap and stared at her, glassy-eyed.

She pulled a newspaper clipping out of the file in front of her and handed it to me. I flinched as my hand came in contact with it, and thought, *here we go again.* But I had already seen this article—it was the one about the skeleton at my office.

"I think I may have some information that might help you identify the remains found at your office," she said. "I can't guarantee it is relevant, but on the off chance it is, I would like to tell you about it."

This was the last thing I expected her to say. I breathed a sigh of relief and hoped she wasn't going to smack me with a ruler and make me stand in the corner after all.

"I would appreciate anything you can tell me," I said humbly.

Sister opened the file in front of her again and took out a photograph. She handed me the picture after glancing at it briefly. I could have sworn I saw a flash of grief in her eyes.

The photo was black and white and showed a girl of about eleven or twelve, with long, light-colored hair hanging around her shoulders in ringlets. She was smiling slightly, but the smile did not match the sadness in her large, dark eyes. I studied the picture more closely, and thought I recognized something else in her expression—nothing as strong as fear, but perhaps wariness.

Although her ringlets were reminiscent of a pre-World War II Shirley Temple, the picture looked more like the type of school photo taken in the fifties.

"This is a picture of Lily Ignacio," said the Sister. "She attended this school for a short period of time in the early fifties when I was here."

I looked up at Sister's face in surprise. If she had been the principal of the school in the fifties, she had to be at least in her late eighties by now. She looked terrific for her age.

Seeing my expression, she said, "I was a student here. Lily and I were in the same class."

Oops.

"Lily attended Our Lady of Perpetual Succor for about six months. I remember her, because her mother would drop her off in the morning and wait for her outside until school was over in the afternoon. All of us—the other students and I—thought that was strange.

"Moreover, Lily's mother didn't let her talk to anyone before or after school, and I remember her watching Lily through the fence during recess. I'm sorry to say we all avoided Lily because of her mother's possessive behavior. Plus, she was a quiet child by nature and seemed somehow, I don't know, distrustful, so making friends would have been difficult for her under any circumstances. Still, there was something about her. She was lovely, of course, you can tell by looking at her photo, but she seemed older than the rest of us, more experienced.

"The fact that we avoided her didn't mean we weren't curious about her. We tried to follow her home one day but chickened out when her mother spotted us. At the time, they were heading in the direction of your office."

She paused and then said softly, "The newspaper article said the skeleton looked like that of a young girl. That's terrible."

I thought so too. "You said her last name was Ignacio. She doesn't look Hispanic, although it's hard to tell in a black-and-white photo," I said, returning the photo to her. "Was she from Mexico?"

Sister Mary Grace blushed deep red. "That is unlikely," she said stiffly. "Children of ... a certain type did not go to Our Lady of Perpetual Succor in those days."

"You mean children of color?" I asked bluntly.

Sister nodded. "Those days are well past, though," she hurried to say. "It's possible she was Spanish, though. She had blonde hair, but her eyes were brown. Her mother had dark hair and eyes, but after all my years as a teacher and then as a principal, I've seen many students that looked nothing like either parent. Genes are funny things. And then again, it's possible she was adopted."

"Did you ever see her father?" I asked.

"Never. If she had one, he never came to school."

At that moment, Miss Dresky came in with what I assumed was my copy of Emily's file. She handed it to

Sister, and Sister glanced through it briefly before handing it to me. Then she surprised me by handing me the file out of which she'd taken Lily's picture as well.

"I'm giving you a copy of Lily's file, too," she said. "There's not much in there, but it does contain a copy of her school registration form, which reflects her full name, birth date, and emergency phone numbers. It's at least something."

I thanked Sister and stood to leave. I extended no like expression of gratitude to Miss Dresky, who had planted herself beside Sister's chair with crossed arms and a sour expression.

"I know it's a long shot, but if it turns out that little girl you found is Lily, will you let me know?" Sister asked.

Her eyes reflected concern and sadness. I would have to remember to tell Emily that at heart, Sister Mary Grace was a caring person, even if her definition of "heinous," could use work.

"Of course I will," I said kindly.

"Please feel free to give me a call at any time," she said. "If I am not immediately available—I am required to attend a fair number of meetings in my line of business—leave a message with Miss Dresky, and I will get back to you as soon as possible." She then jotted a couple phone numbers on a writing pad, ripped off the page, and handed it to me. "Here are my home and cell phone numbers in the event you cannot reach me here at the school."

Miss Dresky made a low, strangled noise in her throat—half gasp, half groan.

She then accompanied me as far as the half door in the counter, probably not so much as a courtesy but as a way to make sure I left.

As I pushed the door open, she said, "Mrs. Williams, I urge you not abuse Sister's generous offer of accessibility. It was an offer sincerely meant, but Sister's time is in great demand. I would appreciate it if you could address your future concerns to me, and I will pass them on to Sister if and when appropriate."

I turned to face her and stared directly into her eyes. "Miss Drec ... I mean Dresky: First of all, it is *Ms.* Williams, not Mrs. Second, unlike the young lady who, when I arrived, was throwing herself on your mercy to obtain a grant of a late pass, I am not cowed by you or anyone else in this school. I will conduct myself according to my own needs and according to the demands of my profession." I then let the door swing closed behind me (okay, I may have given it a little help), and it smacked into her with a gratifying thwack, which prompted an even more gratifying, "Ooph," followed by an expletive that undoubtedly qualified her conduct as heinous.

A freckle-faced, pudgy girl had entered the room during my speechifying. She stared at me, open-mouthed, her expression reflecting a mixture of fear and reverence; she quickly backed away as I passed her on my way out. I think she was expecting lightening to hit me and wanted to get out of range.

Part of me was thinking the same thing, and I glanced up nervously as I speed-walked to my car.

I tossed the two files in the backseat, making a mental note to fax a copy of Lily's file to Webber (after I read it, of course). I would let Emily look over her own file when I got home tonight. I didn't want her to think I was going behind her back to dig up information about her, although that was exactly what I'd done. I figured it would make things better if I 'fessed up about talking to Sister Mary Grace, then gave her the file and told her she didn't have to share anything in it with me unless she wanted to. My underlying strategy was to use negative psychology to prompt Emily to tell me her side of what happened to bring about her suspension.

Sam's, Beth's, and MJ's vehicles were already parked in the small circular drive-way in front of my office building when I arrived. Since all the good parking was gone, I had to leave my car on the street. Since the only spot available was under an ancient African Sumac, I could expect to find a load of bird poop on my roof at the end of the day.

The members of my staff were sitting in the reception area drinking coffee when I came in. When empty of clients, the reception area is our version of the water cooler.

I was startled to see that MJ looked as if she had been crying. So far as I knew, MJ never cried. Angry outbursts were her coping strategy of preference.

Sam and Beth, who were sitting with their backs to the door, turned around when they heard me come in. I could tell they, too, were fighting strong emotions.

"What's going on?" I asked in alarm.

First MJ, and then Sam and Beth exploded into loud guffaws, and I realized that MJ's tears were not tears of sadness but rather tears of laughter.

"You're on YouTube," MJ chortled. "Your video is the top pick of the day."

This can't be good.

I marched into my office, threw my briefcase and purse on the credenza, and sat with some force at my desk. I waited impatiently for my computer to power on and then went directly to the YouTube website.

Sam, Beth, and MJ had followed me into my office and were lined up behind my desk.

The video, captioned *Sic'em*, showed my desperate dash down the mall and into the fountain, followed by a joyous pack of puppies. Some shopper had likely recorded the incident on a cell phone.

I experienced a rush of hatred toward modern technology.

"At least they didn't identify me by name," I said. "Since I held the fast food bag over my face most of the time, a lot of people won't know it's me."

"Scroll down to the comments section," said Beth helpfully.

I did, and the first comment by someone calling him or herself, "News Junkie," not only identified me by name but included a copy of the newspaper's stock photo.

Several more comments followed, but I quit reading them after the first few because they made me feel worse. One was a tirade against attorneys in general and recommended that the pursuing puppies be awarded a lifetime supply of dog food for their wisdom and valor.

"Did you see the newspaper article?" I asked dismally.

"Which one?" asked Sam.

Resting my elbows on my desk, I put my face in my hands and considered changing my name and moving to a different state.

"Kate, it's not that bad," said Beth, massaging my shoulder lightly. "Remember that old saying: any publicity is good publicity."

"Tell that to Tiger Woods," I muttered through my hands.

"I'll go bake some cookies," said Beth.

Beth is a wise woman: when the chips are down and words fail, fresh cookies will bring me back from the precipice quicker than Prozac.

Feeling a little better about my recent notoriety, I lifted my head. "Heavy on the chocolate chips please. Thanks, Beth."

The show being over, MJ and Sam left for their offices—or rather MJ's office, since the hole had not yet been repaired. As Beth was heading for the kitchen, I remembered the problem with the air conditioning and called out, "Beth, before I forget, could you get a hold of the air conditioning and heating service? I noticed something wrong this weekend. The air is freezing cold at times. Hopefully they can fix whatever is causing it."

Beth looked at me strangely. "I haven't felt anything like that. Is it happening now?" she asked.

"No … wait. Yes it is. I feel a cold current right here," I said, wiggling the fingers of left hand, which was resting on my desk.

Beth retraced her steps, and waved her hand in the air over me. "I don't feel anything," she said, shrugging her shoulders. Then she placed her hand over mine. "But my lord, your hand *is* cold. Maybe it's not the room's circulation that's off. Maybe it's yours."

I added possible illness to my list of concerns, but a specific diagnosis would have to wait. I hate doctors, and I hate waiting even more, and every time I go to a doctor's office I have to wait a half-hour or more until my name is called, after which I spend another half-hour or so sitting on a hard examination table dressed in a paper napkin.

Seeing my dismal expression, Beth quickly added, "I'd better get out to the kitchen and make those cookies. I'll be sure to call the refrigeration guys and set up a service check, too."

"*Lots* of chocolate chip, I reminded her.

"Of course."

At least there was that.

I started on the stack of motions I needed to review and letters I needed to sign and worked without interruption the rest of the morning. Each time I experienced the frigid air phenomenon, I massaged the affected body part and then pushed the matter out of my mind. At noon, I checked in with Macy to see how things were going with

Emily. When she answered the phone I could barely hear her because of all the barking in the background.

"Sounds like the dog-walking business is good," I shouted.

Macy yelled, "Keep it down," presumably at the dogs, but she didn't cover the mouthpiece so I couldn't be sure. "Yeah. It's goin' great," she said wearily, I think addressing me this time. "Emily's a real help. What time you coming home?"

"I don't know—around six maybe?" I answered. Based on the way she sounded, I thought maybe her child-care duties were taking too much out of her.

Her response undid this theory. "Take your time," she said. "We're doing great."

"Want me to bring dinner home?" I asked.

"Yeah. And maybe some more dog food."

This was odd. I had picked up a fifty pound bag of Doggy Delight—Ralph's favorite—two days ago. I needed to talk to Macy and Emily about overfeeding him. Now was not the time for lecturing, though; not when Macy sounded so close to exhaustion.

"Will do," I said. "Tacos okay?"

"Get that out of his mouth," she screamed.

I wasn't sure if this was a yes or a no.

"Tacos are fine," she clarified, then hung up.

MJ stuck her head in my office. "Did I hear you mention tacos?"

The woman has a sensitive, highly discriminatory auditory system capable of picking up any mention of food, food-like substance, or food-sound, regardless of intervening barriers such as walls, buildings, or even thousands of miles of space. If an astronaut circling the globe so much as opened a bag of dehydrated peas, MJ would no doubt hear it and get a hankering for snack food.

I knew MJ was angling for a free lunch, but I went along with it because I was hungry and could use the company. I could not play favorites, though, so I invited Sam and Beth to come too.

Sam suggested we go to El Barrio, and even though I had been there the day before, it sounded good to me.

"It's gonna be crowded, you know," said MJ as we walked to my car. "It always takes forever to get a seat around this time of day."

"I've got connections," sniffed Sam.

I looked at him questioningly. I knew of Beth's longstanding friendship with Maria, but Beth wasn't the type to impose. I had no idea Sam knew her too.

"El Barrio does the catering for our weekly talent shows," he said.

Sam and several hundred of his closest friends got together every week at As You Like It, an offshoot of Pole Polishers that caters to gays and transvestites (Sam was both). Everyone was invited to come in costume, and, for a small fee, could purchase five minutes worth of stage time to perform any song, skit, poetry reading—whatever— they chose. Winners were decided by applause. I had never been to one of these soirees, but MJ tells me that, although they can get pretty rowdy, the entertainment is primo.

As we neared the restaurant, I spotted the back-up lights of a car parked not far from our destination. I stopped at a polite distance behind it, and we waited for the car to pull out. The vehicle was being piloted by a woman with black hair arranged in a bun. (At least we assumed it was a woman because of the hair; we couldn't see her face.) After several long minutes, during which a string of passing drivers blasted their car horns at us for blocking the lane and then angrily accelerated around us, the car still had not moved.

"What the hell," huffed MJ. "What's taking her so long?"

"Maybe you should back up and give her more room," contributed Beth.

"She's got plenty of room. This is stupid," countered MJ.

Before we could stop her, MJ was out of my car and on a fast approach to the driver's side of the parked vehicle. MJ can be aggressive when she has low blood-sugar, or, more correctly, more aggressive, since even on a full stomach she has never suffered fools gladly.

At this point I should also mention MJ is into "extreme fashion," as she refers to it, although if Sam is within hearing range, he will invariably counter with, "extremely bad taste, you mean." However, maybe because they are intimidated by the legal process in which they are ensnared, our clients seem not to mind and indeed are comforted by MJ's bizarre attire. I think perhaps it offsets the scary formality of the legal system.

Since today was Monday, and Monday is a traditional day of mourning for MJ, she was wearing black fishnet stockings and had stuffed her massive derriere into a too-small, shiny latex, black miniskirt, Doc Martens, and a low-cut, black T-shirt with *Ask Me about My Explosive Diarrhea* printed in white, accessorized with a bicycle chain necklace; an armful of clanking bangle bracelets completed her ensemble. MJ's hair and nail colors were always thematically consistent with her garb, so today they were, of course, jet black. When combined with her various piercings and tattoos, the overall effect inspires reactions ranging from concern to fear among those who do not know her. The sight of an angry MJ thus attired heading toward them would make most people lay rubber and get the heck out of there. But the parked Toyota Prius didn't move.

MJ banged on the closed window and yelled, "Are you leaving anytime soon? Or are you thinking of making this your permanent address?"

The woman did not respond. MJ pounded on the window again and lowered her head to make eye contact with the driver. Suddenly her hand dropped to her side, and she stepped back.

"There's a problem here," she said in a subdued voice.

Chapter 10

Sam got out and joined MJ, and together they looked inside the car. He paled, took out his cell phone, and hit three numbers. We all listened while he reported the discovery of a body and gave a description of our location. I pulled my car over as far as I could, blocking the parked Prius, and turned off the engine. Beth and I both got out and went to stand next to MJ and Sam.

"It is, or was, Maria," Sam said tersely.

I glanced quickly into the window to confirm Sam's identification. The woman stared straight ahead, her mouth slightly open as if in surprise. There was no question; it was Maria. Her employee name tag was still intact although most of her chest was not. MJ probably had not spotted the gaping hole at first because Maria was wearing a red cardigan sweater, and because visibility was partially obscured by the tinted windows. I suddenly felt faint and swayed forward. Beth, who looked like she could use some help herself, caught my elbow and held on.

"Are you sure she's …?" I asked in a near whisper.

"Yes," said Sam without equivocation. "She's dead."

The sound of sirens became louder, and a police car followed by an ambulance and a dark- colored sedan pulled in behind my Honda. The uniformed officers waved back the crowd that had begun collecting on the sidewalk, and a man wearing a god-awful brown polyester suit got out of the unmarked car and walked toward us. It was Webber.

"For crying out loud. Are you the only detective on the force?" I blurted.

"Lately, it feels like it," he said as he wiped his forehead with a crunchy-looking handkerchief that looked like it was primarily for nose blowing, not wiping.

Sam shuddered. "Serve and defend, my ass," he whispered out of the corner of his mouth. "More like serve and offend."

"Maybe if you'd quit finding bodies, we wouldn't be so damn busy," said Webber, once he was an arm's length away. He'd lowered his voice so the members of the public who stood on the sidewalk ogling wouldn't overhear and perhaps think less of our boys in blue, or, in the case of our local force, the boys in beige.

He unenthusiastically put his hand out to shake mine, and Sam, a well-documented germaphobe, probably fearing he was next, muffled a shriek. He needn't have worried. Webber dislikes Sam intensely and didn't bother extending his hand to Sam, probably because he was afraid of getting gay cooties, or worried that Sam would get the wrong idea and think it was foreplay.

Webber bent at the waist and looked inside the car, shading the window with his hand to cut down on the reflection. I couldn't see his face, but I heard his quick intake of breath. For a detective as seasoned as Webber, this was an expression of high emotion.

He straightened and turned back toward our little group. "Did any of you touch anything?" he asked brusquely. The shock and sadness in his eyes belied his professional manner. Webber, like most of the people who worked downtown, had probably known Maria.

MJ raised her hand dispiritedly and volunteered, "I knocked on the window before I realized she was dead."

"That's it?" he asked. We all nodded somberly in response.

"I need all of you to wait over there," he said, pointing to a spot on the sidewalk. "I'll get your statements when we're though here. You know the drill."

Sadly, we did.

Addressing the gawkers on the sidewalk, he asked in a loud voice, pointing to my Honda, "Whose car is this?"

"Mine," I said.

Webber looked at me and then back at the car.

I think I heard him say, "I should have known," under his breath.

"We were waiting for the driver to leave so we could take her spot. When we realized what had happened, I pulled my car in back of hers so it wasn't blocking traffic," I explained.

"Well now you're blocking us and interfering with an official investigation. Move it, and then return immediately."

Prick, I thought.

Sam touched my arm. "Are you okay to drive?" he asked.

"I'll be fine," I said, and in fact my annoyance at Webber's assholeness had revived me.

In defiance of his order that I find a parking place and return immediately, I went to a Jack in the Box and picked up chicken wraps and Diet Cokes for me, Beth, and Sam, and two hamburgers, fries, and a milkshake for MJ. Since the lunch crowd was thinning when I returned, I had no difficulty finding a spot a block north of where the Prius was parked. The police had already set up the crime scene tape and chased most of the onlookers away by the time I strolled up carrying the Jack in the Box bag. The tech team had arrived and was photographing, swabbing, printing, and whatever else tech teams do. (One of the team members was under Maria's car doing something that required a lot of grunting and cursing.)

A man I recognized as one of the cooks from El Barrio was talking to a police officer. Tears streaked his face, and his shoulders shook. Webber or one of his men had probably summoned him from the restaurant.

Webber and a member of the coroner's office were standing by the open driver's side door of the Prius, looking on while a photographer clicked away like he was at a fashion shoot taking photos of a famous model.

I walked up to Sam, Beth, and MJ and held up the bag. I'd lost my appetite as soon as I saw the Prius. Sam and Beth thanked me politely, but they, too, didn't seem in the mood for food. MJ did not disappoint, however, and snatched the bag out of my hands. Digging through its contents, she said, "What, no onion rings?"

"How can you eat at a time like this," hissed Sam.

"I compartmentalize," she answered through a mouthful of fries.

"The root word being 'mental,'" countered Sam.

The temperature was getting uncomfortably hot, and Sam, MJ, and Beth were crowded under a measly looking eucalyptus tree, which was the sole live piece of vegetation in the area. We have very few trees in Phoenix, so shade is at a premium. I have seen people come to blows over which of them has the superior claim to the only shaded spot in a parking lot. The developers and city planners apparently thought that trees wasted valuable land. Obviously none of these people had walked down a Phoenix street in late spring, summer, or early fall when the temperatures rarely dip below a hundred degrees and the heat, first absorbed and then released by the pavement, ups the ante another twenty degrees.

I moved a few yards away and sat on the curb, taking advantage of a patch of shade provided by a monster SUV parked two cars down from the Prius. Beth joined me and rested her head on her knees with her face toward me. Tears rolled sideways down her cheek.

"How did you and Maria first meet?" I asked gently.

"We met at a group home when we were both ten years old."

"Group home?"

"Foster care. The state placed me in foster care when my parents were arrested because of their non-citizen status." Beth was born in Phoenix, but her mother emigrated from Italy and her father was Kenyan. "Maria went into the system when her mom got sent to prison. She never knew who her father was."

"Beth, I had no idea. How long were you in the foster care system?"

"Both Maria and I were in for three years. I went home and she got adopted. We were lucky, I guess. Lots of kids stayed in foster care until they aged out." Beth buried her head in her knees and her shoulders shook.

I've handled a few juvenile court matters. A couple of the kids I represented (*pro bono*, of course) lived in foster care. I knew a little about the system, but not much. I knew, for instance, that in foster care-ese "aging out" means the child has reached the age of eighteen without being adopted and is no longer the state's responsibility. I also knew that under Arizona's current system, when a "foster," as they're referred to by the caseworkers, turns eighteen, he or she may opt to stay in the system for another year. Most kids, even those with no job prospects or plans for living arrangements, don't re-up for another year. It's pretty much Parenting 101 that love and consistency are the pillars of child-raising. A lot of fosters get neither, and at eighteen would rather be on their own than continue to deal with the red tape love of CPS (Child Protective Services).

The Arizona system was revised in the nineties to be more child-centered but was still plagued by underfunding, a high rate of caseworker turnover, and gaps in caseworker accountability and supervision. I could only imagine how bad it was in the fifties when the citizenry considered foster children second-class citizens—shameful outcastes tainted by bad blood or pitiable urchins who should be grateful for every benefit they received. I remembered my mother's disparaging remarks about a girl in my third-grade class who was placed temporarily in a neighbor's home after her father deserted her mother and her mother became ill. My mother said she did not come from a good family, the implication being that the child therefore suffered from some permanent defect in character that rendered her unfit company for those of us with better bloodlines. Even then, at an age when most children accept their parents' words as gospel, I thought there was something unfair about her analysis. After all, people don't choose to be born, much less whom to be born to.

Beth started to speak again. "We were in the home with ten other kids, five to a room. They don't allow that now; they limit the number of young children that can be placed in a single home. But even regular families were bigger then, so it didn't seem strange to us.

"Maria and I hit it off right away. We were the same age and were both going through a tomboy stage. We'd been inspired by the movie *The Adventures Tom Sawyer* at school—the one with Tommy Kelly and Jackie Moran."

I shrugged and lightly shook my head; I'm not *that* old.

Beth smiled at the memory of her childhood adventures with Maria, but the smile quickly faded, and her tears increased in volume.

I put my arm around her and held her as she cried.

Two scuffed black shoes appeared in my line of vision, and I looked up to see Webber glaring down at us.

"No talking to each other until after you've been interviewed," he ordered.

"Is crying allowed?" I asked, dripping sarcasm.

Webber grunted and started to walk away.

"Hasn't anyone ever told you not to wear black shoes with a brown suit?" Sam pointed out loudly from behind me.

Webber hesitated, but did not turn around. "Thank you, Perez Hilton. Sometimes this job distracts me from the really important issues in life, like color coordination."

Beth roused from her misery long enough to deliver her verdict. "Asshole," she hissed in my ear.

MJ came over and we butt-hopped down the curb to give her some shade.

"This sucks," she said.

I nodded in agreement. "Any idea what's going on?" I asked, noting that MJ and Sam's shade-spot was closer to the action than mine.

"I heard the cop talking to Gilberto, one of the cooks at El Barrio. Gilberto said Maria opened the café at ten this morning so the cooks could prep, but left soon afterward. He said she said something about meeting a guy who knew the social worker assigned to her as a kid. She didn't say why, and Gilberto figured it was probably kind of a roots thing; you know, where people try to figure out where they came from and what it was like. Apparently Maria was adopted when she was thirteen."

Beth lifted her head and said, "That's right. Her mother died in prison."

"No talking," yelled Webber.

"Fucking asshole," growled MJ.

Webber finally got around to interviewing us. He talked to Sam first, maintaining such a far distance that I was surprised they could hear each other. Then, he talked with MJ, Beth, and finally, me. He was probably bummed that we didn't have much to say. None of us had seen anyone around Maria's car, and we didn't know of any enemies Maria might have had. We found the body. Period.

At the end of my interview, Webber got in my face (or, rather, more in my face), and, with barely controlled anger—a state I didn't find particularly disturbing since he's always upset about something—if he'd been pleasant, now *that* would have made me nervous—said that Miss Dresky had left a message on his voice mail telling him that I had stopped in to see the principal that morning and the Sister was concerned as to why he chose to send legal counsel rather than talking to the her directly.

I doubted that Sister Mary Grace had said any such thing. Drecky was the only one who seemed bothered by my visit.

"I was simply dropping by the office to let them know Emily would be staying with me for a while and to give them my name, address and phone number in the event of emergencies," I said innocently. "I couldn't lie and say I was a relative, so I told them I was Emily's attorney."

If there was any truth to that Pinocchio-thing, Barbra Streisand was going to seem pug-nosed compared to me.

"Her attorney? And that's *not* a lie?" he spat back.

I shrugged and tried to look apologetic even though a vocal minority of my brain cells was in favor of screaming, *I am doing you a favor by caring about and for your child, dammit. Be grateful and lay off.*

"If the school contacts you about Emily for any reason, you tell me ASAP," he continued, struggling to keep his voice low so the others couldn't hear. "And I want you to call Sister Mary Grace and tell her you are *not* Emily's attorney. Tell her you're a family friend or something."

I raised an eyebrow. "So it's not that I lied, it's that I told the *wrong* lie?"

We were eyeball to eyeball now. "Nothing had better happen to my little girl while she's staying with you," he growled from the back of his throat without moving his mouth. Edgar Bergen would have been impressed.

Thank God he hasn't read the paper yet, or this could get really ugly, I thought.

"And stay out of fountains," he added and then pivoted on his heel and stomped away.

I walked dispiritedly over to my little band of employees, who were huddled together under the eucalyptus tree looking hot and tired. Even Sam, impeccably dressed as always in a Hugo Boss suit and dress shirt, Hermes tie, and Gucci loafers, looked wilted, his face covered by a light sheen of sweat.

MJ looked different somehow. I gave the matter some thought, and then asked, "When did you take off your stockings?"

MJ grunted, and opened her hand to show me a balled up pair of fishnets. "I took them off while you were talking to Webber. It's too damned hot for pantyhose."

"But how …" I started to ask.

Sam shuddered. "She took off her shoes, hiked up her skirt, and rolled down her hose and stepped out of them. She did not bother to use a vehicle, plant material, or other object for screening. We have witnesses." He pointed toward three police officers standing about ten yards away. One of them was looking in our direction, red-faced, his pen frozen in mid-air above an open notebook. The other two looked ashen. Apparently the sight of MJ partially disrobing in public had a more stunning affect on their psyches than a gunshot victim.

"What's the big deal?" MJ said defensively. "We're all adults here."

"Some of us more than others," I sighed. "MJ, at least pull your skirt back down."

She started to protest about the heat again, but something in my face must have warned her that I wasn't in the mood for contradiction, so she clamped her mouth shut and tugged her skirt down those last critical six inches.

"Did Webber say we're free to go?" asked Sam.

"Not in so many words, but since we've all given our statements and he hasn't asked us to stay put, I vote we leave," I said wearily.

The others nodded in agreement, and Beth, who was no longer crying but whose red, puffy eyes threatened more tears, said, "The ayes have it."

"I'm parked one block up," I said, motioning for the others to follow me. I figured if Webber wanted us to stick around, when he saw we were leaving he would yell at us to come back, or at least fire a warning shot.

MJ caught up to me. "What were you and Webber talking about back there?" she asked.

"Um, finding Maria's body in a parked car," I said, giving her a, "duh," look.

"I mean after that. He looked like he was ready to strangle you. Don't get me wrong, he always looks at you like he hates you, but today it was worse."

I stubbed my toe against an uneven chunk of sidewalk and stopped to massage the injured leather of my expensive pump, as if rubbing it would make the scratch disappear.

"God, no. Not the Manolo Blahniks," Sam cried, bending over to look at the damage.

Sam gets emotional about expensive shoes. I think he may even give them names.

"Which one was it? Lulu or Tina?" he asked.

See?

"Are you okay?" asked Beth worriedly.

At least Beth cared more about me than she did about Lulu and Tina.

"I'm fine. Damned sidewalk. Why doesn't the city repair the things once in a while?" I growled.

I straightened and headed for the car again.

"You didn't answer my question," said MJ hurrying after me.

"What question?" Sam chimed in.

"I can't remember," I said curtly.

"I asked you why Webber was so in your face," MJ repeated patiently.

"Yeah. What *was* that all about?" asked Beth who seemed, momentarily at least, distracted from her grief.

I sighed. "I'll explain everything once we're in the car."

Once we were in the car with the air conditioner going, I told them about the situation with Emily from start to finish, leaving out no details.

After I finished, there was a couple of beats of silence before anyone said anything.

"To summarize," said MJ, "You have Webber's daughter staying at your condo with a seventy-eight-year-old babysitter..."

"I asked Tuwanda to stop by and check on them once in a while," I interrupted defensively.

"… and a hooker looking in on her from time to time; the kid was suspended from school for either a dress-code violation or theft—you're not sure which; her father is in the dark about both Tuwanda and the school suspension; the principal thinks you're Emily's attorney; and, if so much as one hair on the kid's head is damaged—which has already happened since she you say she cut and dyed her hair and pierced her nose as soon as she got out of the house—your ass is grass. Does that about cover it?"

I nodded miserably.

"Don't forget the part about how Webber is going to stick to you like white on rice until his daughter comes home, which means he's going to get in our way, too," added Sam.

I nodded again.

"He'll use the police investigations of our skeleton and Maria's death as an excuse to harass us," said MJ glumly.

At the mention of Maria's name Beth started to cry again. Sam, who was sitting in the back seat next to her, put his arm around her.

"Sister Mary Grace, the principal at Emily's school, gave me the file of a student she thinks might be our skeleton," I said hurriedly, trying to distract Beth.

It's a bad day when you have to use a skeleton to take someone's mind off a shotgun victim.

"Are you going to give it to Webber?" MJ asked curiously.

"Of course," I said. I could feel everyone look at me. "After I've had a chance to look at it."

"Good girl," said Sam. "I mean, we all know ID-ing our house guest is a low priority for the police. They'll be spending most of their time on … more recent matters."

Fortunately, Sam caught himself before he mentioned Maria's name. Beth wasn't fooled, however, and the sobbing got louder.

"Yeah, and besides, she's *our* skeleton," said MJ, raising her voice to be heard over Beth.

We had arrived at the office, and I pulled over and parked along the street. Before we got out of the car, I explained my plan to do a records search to find out who had lived in the house during the fifties and sixties. MJ and Sam both volunteered to help, although MJ added the proviso that she not be docked in pay due to working on a non-billable case.

Sam told her she was crass and uncaring and smacked the back of her head, but I assured them that time spent on what I considered an in-house matter could be billed to the firm—the firm being me—and would not affect anyone's paycheck.

Maybe I was redirecting my sadness over Maria's death to something I had more control over, I don't know. But suddenly, I wanted more than anything to find out who the child under the floor was and how she got there.

Chapter 11

As soon as I got back to my office, I called Bryan to let him know what happened. He already knew about it, of course, since the sheriff's office and the police department work closely together on matters subject to dual jurisdiction. I repeated what I had told Webber and reassured him that, as distinguished from previous incidents, my sole involvement was as co-discoverer of the victim.

Bryan did not seem convinced, though, and warned me in no uncertain terms to stay out of the investigation from here on in. I had stuck my head into Bryan's side of the business on several previous occasions, and each time it happened he got more irate. I got the feeling from the way he said it that this last warning was a test. Maybe even he, patient man that he was, had a breaking point. And I was beginning to wonder if I was getting too close to it.

"It's important to me that you keep a low profile," he emphasized.

"I get it, I get it. I'll try not to interfere in this one."

"Not just this case; not any of my cases, ever."

"What? Why? What's going on?"

He paused before answering. "That's what I wanted to talk to you about. I've decided to run for sheriff in the November election."

"Why, Bryan, that's great. I think you'll win hands-down. You've been a great interim sheriff, and ..."

"Maricopa County is very conservative, Kate, and I'll be running on a law-and-order platform. My campaign committee is advising me that I need to work on my image."

It started to dawn on me what he was trying to say.

"And I'm a liability," I said flatly.

"You don't *have* to be Kate. If you would just ..."

"What? Quit my job as a defense attorney? Join the prosecutor's office again?" I had tried that once before. It resulted in the arrest of both my boss and Bryan, and had nearly led to my death.

I took slow breaths and tried to listen to my understanding, reasonable side. (All right, maybe it wasn't quite a whole side; more like a small section.) I told myself I had enough on my plate with the skeleton mystery and being a first-time mother and all—I do *not* consider Larry to be an older child, despite his claims to the contrary—and I half-heartedly agreed to stay out of Maria's case.

Of course, as soon as I hung up, I had second thoughts. It was strange that after Maria said she might have information regarding our skeleton girl, she had arranged a meeting with the social worker assigned to her when she was in foster care. It's possible that Maria was seeking information from the social worker about her past for her own benefit, but it wasn't too much of a stretch—at least for my fertile imagination—to think she could have been trying to get information to confirm her suspicions as to the identity of our skeleton before she talked to me on Wednesday.

Was it possible that our skeleton girl was in foster care? Since Beth was in foster care during the same period as Maria, Beth might have the same information as Maria.

Of course, if the histories of Maria, Beth, and our skeleton, and possibly even Sister Mary Grace, seemed inextricably intertwined, I needed to stick my nose into the investigation of Maria's death to some extent. And there was no need for Bryan to know unless it was absolutely necessary.

I would put off talking to Beth until she was in a better state and could discuss Maria without bursting into tears. In the meantime, I had another avenue of information to pursue.

Chapter 12

Of course, if I was honest with myself, I would admit that I wanted to find out who was responsible for Maria's death, too. I had seen enough when I looked through her car window to know there was no weapon in sight. Even assuming you could shoot yourself with a shotgun, which is tough to do unless you have extremely long arms, you would not live long enough to hide the weapon. I was 99.9 percent sure that Maria had been murdered. Maria was a good, kind woman, and, although I had not known her for as long as Beth had, her death hit me hard.

I told my staff they could leave early if they wanted, but nobody took me up on the offer. I think all of us felt better being among other people, and I, for one, thought that work would serve as a distraction from the grim business of Maria's death. I spent some time trying to prepare for oral argument on a motion to suppress evidence scheduled for ten o'clock the next day, but my powers of concentration were weak. When I reviewed the case file, every word I read triggered some memory of the day's events or a new idea on a line of inquiry I could pursue in my skeleton and murder investigations.

One of those lines of inquiry was a tad outside the box (okay, a lot outside the box), and would likely not result in any useable evidence. But, maybe, it could give us direction. I had gotten to know Venus Butterman when I represented her grandson, Arnie, in a murder case. Venus claimed—and Tuwanda believed and I kind of believed—that she communicated with the dead. The problem was, she did not summon spirits through séances or other targeted methods, but she bumped into them randomly or was contacted by them on an *ad hoc* basis. That being the case, it wasn't a sure thing she could find people (or rather ex-people) who knew anything of value about a particular matter. From past experience, though, I knew that she had pretty good luck getting in touch with a particular subject at a location the spirit would likely choose to hang around or visit because of some special meaning associated with that place.

Venus had been at my office before and hadn't remarked on the presence of any spirits, but then maybe she hadn't been paying attention. I remember Venus saying something about how she had to open up certain extra-sensory channels and concentrate before she could communicate with spirits. "Otherwise, I couldn't never get no sleep for all the whinin' and yammerin'," she explained.

I picked up the phone and punched in Venus's number which I knew off the top of my head because I had loaned Venus one of my own cell phones when she retained us to represent her grandson. Her grandson's case was long over, but I was still footing the bill for the phone since Venus also considers herself an employee of my firm—according to her, she is one of my "'vestigators"—and the phone was therefore necessary for the performance of her duties.

Venus answered on the second ring. "Butterman 'Vestigations; we see dead people," she said.

"You've set up your own business." I replied, surprised.

"Yep. I was meanin' to call you about it. You need to make my checks out to Butterman 'Vestigations now. On the advice of my tax lawyer, I set up a limited liability comp'ny."

"You have your own tax lawyer?" I asked. *I* don't even have my own tax lawyer.

"You bet. Daisy Reman, a friend of mine from church, has a son who's a tax lawyer. She sent him over an' now he does my taxes in exchange for me tellin' him what his wife is sayin' about him."

"His wife?" I asked weakly.

"Yep. She passed away 'bout two years ago. I'm guessin' it wasn't a good marriage, 'cuz she bad-mouths him all the time."

Prompted once more by a fatalistic impulse, I pursued the matter. "Then why does he want to hear what she has to say? I wouldn't want to know if someone was saying unkind things about me in the afterlife."

"I guess he gets to missin' her from time to time, and bein' reminded about how nasty she is makes him feel better about her passin'."

In an odd way, this made sense to me.

"You callin' 'bout somethin' in particular? 'Cuz I got the clock runnin'," Venus informed me in a businesslike voice.

"Have you raised your rates?" I asked.

"We charge a hunnert dollars an hour," she promptly answered. After a few beats, she added, "But I'm given you a special rate 'cuz you're my boss."

My office has a firmly established policy, put in place, and fully supported, by my staff, that I am not, at any time, allowed to deal with the firm's business matters. The consensus is that my talents lie in legal work, and any matter involving money or mathematical calculations should be handled by Beth. When it comes to asking for, or agreeing to pay, people money, I'm a complete pushover.

"I think you need to discuss this with Beth," I said hurriedly. "I'll give you another call after you and Beth have gotten things settled."

"Tell you what," said Venus before I could cut the connection. "I won't charge for a consultation. But as soon as I start communicatin' with the designated spirit, the clock starts runnin'."

That sounded fair.

"Okay," I said hesitantly.

"So what you callin' 'bout?" asked Venus.

I briefly outlined the skeleton situation and asked if she could drop in tomorrow and, if there were any spirits hanging around, ask them some questions.

"Let me check my calendar," she said. I could hear the rustle of paper in the background. "I got an appointment tomorrow at the Super Saver at ten. The manager thinks spirits are meetin' there at night an' eatin' cherry Popsicles. I tol' him spirits can't eat nothin', them not bein' able to digest and all, but he says they tryin' because ev'ry mornin' he finds melted Popsicles on the floor. I can drop by your office after. It'd be aroun' eleven. That okay?"

"I have to be in court at ten, but I should be back by then," I said, "so eleven will work fine."

"You c'n pay me my retainer when I get there," she said.

"What retainer?" I'm bad at business but my memory is good, and I didn't remember discussing a retainer.

"A hunnert dollars up front. I prefer cash, but I'll accept a check provided I c'n call your bank an' verify the availability of funds."

I repeated my mantra. "Talk to Beth," I said.

"Okay. I'll give her a buzz and let her know what we agreed to."

"I haven't agreed to anything," I countered, raising my voice. But Venus had already hung up.

I went out to Beth's desk to tell her to expect some hard negotiating from Venus tomorrow. She was resting her head on her desk next to a stack of balled-up Kleenex.

"Beth," I said softly. "I think you should go home.

Do you want me to call your husband and ask him to pick you up?"

She shook her head without raising it. I noticed the blotter on her desk was soaked with tears. "He's out of town on business. I talked to him on the phone, and he said he'd come back early, but he won't get here until tomorrow or maybe even the next day."

"Do you want to come home with me?" I asked. The offer was sincerely meant but unfortunately not well thought-out, since I only have one bedroom and the couch was already taken.

"I'd like that," she answered in a muffled voice.

Maybe Beth or Emily could stay in Macy's spare bedroom.

I stuck my head into MJ's office to let her and Sam know that Beth and I were leaving. The scene reminded me of pictures of the Berlin Wall. All that was missing was the barbed wire and the circling helicopters.

Sam had managed to move his furniture into MJ's office and their respective desks now faced each other, separated by a foot of no-man's land and a wall of books, files, and oddly-shaped china lemurs. MJ's side was decorated in what is best described as a post-apocalyptic style. Her desk and the surrounding floor were covered by a jumble of papers, snack-food wrappers, and Coke cans. Sam's half was neat and uncluttered, and I could smell the distinct odor of Lysol. They had not yet noticed I was there, and when MJ coughed, Sam, without looking up from the file on which he was working, removed a

Lysol can from his drawer and liberally spritzed in MJ's direction. MJ, likewise without looking up from the paper in front of her, hurled a potato chip at Sam's head. It got hung up on one of the lemurs and, judging by the number of chips lying on and around the other lemurs, she was having trouble clearing the wall.

"Beth and I are leaving. I'm taking her home with me," I announced after lightly tapping on the open door.

"Where's Dale?" asked MJ. Dale is Beth's husband.

"Out of town on business. He won't be back until tomorrow or the day after," I explained.

"Don't you already have a house guest?" Sam pointed out.

I nodded yes. "I don't think Beth should be alone, though. She's having a hard time dealing with Maria's death."

"You need us to do anything?" asked Sam.

"I need some background information on how Child Protective Services, or whatever its predecessor was called, operated in the fifties and sixties and where, and even if, records from that period are kept. If you have time yet today to look into it, I'd appreciate it."

Sam saluted and said, "Will do."

We stopped off at the grocery store on the way home and I bought a bag of dog food and a couple more essentials, including two bottles of chardonnay. Then we swung by the Teepee, a Mexican restaurant not far from my condo building, and got enough carry-out food to feed Macy and my growing household.

Beth helped me carry up everything from the garage to my condo, for which I was grateful; even with the two of us, our arms were full. I was carrying Ralph's dog food bag with one of the take-out bags balanced on top. Beth had the rest of the take-out and the groceries. Neither one of us had a free hand so I had to hit the elevator button with my hip, which is not an exact science. I ended up hitting all of them so we stopped at every floor before reaching mine.

I heard the barking as soon as the elevator door slid open. Either Ralph was watching his DVD of the Westminster Dog Show (a Christmas gift from me—he's fascinated by the toy breed class), or Mrs. Goldfarb, at the end of the hall, was hosting another party for her Shi Tzu. Since I didn't hear Ralph's bark among the chorus of yapping—his way of cheering for his favorite breed I guess—I figured the latter scenario was more likely. Ralph had been black-balled by Mrs. Goldfarb due to an unfortunate incident involving a min pin Ralph mistook for a chew toy. I still say it wasn't Ralph's fault. Who dresses a dog in a plush purple jogging suit? In Ralph's defense, he dropped the little dog as soon as it yapped and seemed more startled and upset than the min pin.

I tapped my foot on the door, but the barking had gotten louder, and I don't think anyone inside could hear me. I tried another piece of anatomy, and slammed my knee loudly against the door.

The door opened part way, and a hand reached out, grabbed my sleeve, and dragged me inside. Once I was inside, Macy slammed the door shut behind me.

"Beth's out there!" I protested.

Ralph hurtled toward me and tried to wedge himself between me and the door.

"What's the matter with …" was all I managed to get out before a pack of dogs flew around the corner. The combined smells of the bag of dog food and the Mexican food further incited them, and they tried, with varying degrees of success, to jump up and grab whatever food they could get.

"What the hell …" I screamed.

"Sorry, Beth!" yelled Macy through the door, trying to be heard above the canine cacophony. "I'll let you in. Just a sec."

"That's okay," responded Beth, her voice muffled by the door. "I'll stay out here for a while. You take all the time you need."

Emily appeared with another five or six dogs dancing around her feet. Their perpetual motion made an exact count difficult.

One of the dogs managed to rip off a corner of the dog food bag, and "meaty little pellets of lamb and rice," according to the description on the bag, spilled in a steady stream onto the floor until all I was holding was an empty sack. Macy grabbed the take-out bag before it fell onto the floor as well.

The dogs instantly quieted as they went for the dog food.

"I hate to pry, but *what is going on?*" I enunciated through gritted teeth, focusing on Macy, the only other adult in the room.

She looked harried and exhausted, and, despite the fact that my pantyhose were shredded and my skirt was covered with sticky drool, I felt a stab of pity for her.

Emily answered for Macy. "It's my fault. Don't blame her," she said. I detected defensiveness with undercurrents of challenge.

I didn't say anything but looked at her expectantly.

"Most of your neighbors walk their dogs before they go to work and then again later when they come home at night, so they don't need a dog walker. What they really wanted, though, was day care, because the dogs get lonely while they're at work. So we set up a doggy day care camp."

"In my apartment," I said in disbelief.

"We tried to take them to a park, but there was too many of them, and Macy couldn't get them all in her car—a Mini-Cooper. So we brought them up here. We tried to set up activities for them, but it turns out dogs are mainly interested in sleeping, eating, and smelling each other's butts, not dress-up, kick-ball, and paw painting."

I was afraid to ask, but I had to. "Paw painting?"

"Like finger painting but with paws," contributed Macy helpfully. "Some of the dogs were pretty good at it, but most of them just tried to eat the paint."

At least this explained why some of the dogs had splashes of yellow, green, and/or red paint on their coats.

I woodenly walked into my living room and gazed numbly around at what had once been a habitable space. The song "Teenage Wasteland" played in a continuous loop in my head.

I sat wearily on my paint splotched, dog-hair covered couch. I figured that my skirt was already ruined, so a little paint and hair wouldn't matter. Before I could settle in, the couch cushion squirmed and yapped. I jumped back to my feet and nervously checked my rear end and then the couch.

A tiny Yorkie shot me an offended look and then leaped off the couch.

"That's Bob from 204," explained Emily.

Ralph had followed me to the couch and now leaned against my legs, looking up at me as if to say, "None of this was my fault. You've got to believe me."

In the meantime, Macy had let Beth in, although the latter continued to express a preference for staying in the hall until matters were sorted out. But Beth immediately proved to be a valuable asset. She has five grown children and sixteen grandchildren, so crowd control is one of her specialties.

Beth directed Macy and Emily to return the dogs to their homes and then, "Come back and clean up this god-awful mess." I retreated to my bedroom to clean up and change clothes. Thankfully, my bedroom door had been shut during the doggy day care experiment, so the room was relatively unscathed. I say "relatively" because one of our house guests—I'm guessing one of the larger breeds—had managed to get in and relieve himself next to my bed.

When I re-emerged about a half-hour later, all but two of the dogs, not counting Ralph, were gone. Macy explained that the parents of the remaining dogs would not be able to pick them up until later.

We all pitched in to clean what we could—the already much-abused couch had taken the brunt of the dogs' enthusiasm—then sat at the table to eat the take-out Mexican food.

I wanted to ask Emily why she had lied about the reason for her school suspension, but I didn't want to embarrass her in front of Beth, who was a relative stranger to her. Instead, we discussed alternate business opportunities for Emily, and, after a heated debate during which Macy and Emily defended the idea of a dog grooming business, everyone agreed that Emily would limit her entrepreneurial talents to walking Ralph and maybe one or two other dogs, and she would allocate time for cooking lessons from Macy, homework, and another lesson of her choice—either dance, there was a dance studio down the street, or guitar. Macy had a friend in the building who taught guitar, and Macy was willing to lend Emily her Fender Stratocaster. I had no idea that Macy had a Fender, but this new information explained the Led Zeppelin riffs that woke me up in the wee hours from time to time.

Macy offered, and Beth accepted, the use of Macy's guest room for the night. As soon as they left, I grabbed the opportunity to speak to Emily about her suspension. I did not approach the subject obliquely, but told Emily straight-out that I'd talked to Sister Mary Grace and heard a different version of the facts. I had left the files Sister May Grace gave me in my car, but I'd skimmed

Emily's earlier and found nothing of note in addition to what Sister told me except for the name of the girl whose backpack Emily had stolen: Chelsea Robinson.

Emily said nothing after I finished.

"Well?" I asked.

My verbal nudge didn't work. Emily set her jaw and clamped her lips tightly together.

"Emily, I'm tired, my house smells like a kennel, and I'll be picking dog hair out of my mouth for a week. I'm not the enemy here. Tell me what happened."

"Why should I? You aren't going to believe anything *I* say," she sulked.

"Try telling me the truth," I snapped. "I'm a real sucker for the truth."

"You won't believe me. Adults always take the side of other adults."

I had a flash of inspiration. "I'm not your parent or teacher. I'm your attorney."

She looked at me interestedly. "My ... attorney?"

"Anything you say to me is privileged, which means I can't tell anyone else," I said in my business voice.

"You can't just decide you're my attorney," she said. "I have to hire you or a court has to appoint you."

"Did you learn that from your dad?"

"No. *Law & Order*," she said smugly. But then she appeared to think the situation over.

"I'm not sure I'm old enough to hire you (she wasn't), but if I do and it means you can't tell anybody what I tell you, that would be cool. How much do you charge?"

We worked out the business details, the upshot being that Emily would pay me an hourly rate of one dollar, which I would deduct from her salary. I was glad Beth wasn't there. This was the sort of deal-making she, MJ, and Sam were trying to prevent.

"Now, back to the subject: tell me why you were suspended."

"Chelsea is a bitch," she announced with great emotion.

"Don't swear," I said before I could catch myself. Attorneys don't criticize their clients' vocabularies; parents do. I had to remember which hat I was wearing. "Tell me why you believe Chelsea is the b-word."

"Chelsea sent everyone a text that said I was a lesbian and I hit on her."

Wow. Chelsea *was* a bitch.

"So you took her backpack to get back at her?" I, personally, would have slapped the fair Chelsea.

"I took her backpack because I thought her cell phone was in there. I was going to send a text from it telling everyone that what she said about me was a lie and she only said it because she's a lesbian and has a crush on me," Emily explained. "But her cell wasn't in her backpack, and she ratted me out to Miss Dresky before I had a chance to return it."

"Why didn't you tell Sister Mary Grace about Chelsea's text?" Even as I asked, I knew it was a dumb question. It's a cardinal rule of kid-dom that you don't report what amounted to name calling, no matter how slanderous, to adults.

Emily didn't bother to answer, as well she shouldn't.

"That sucks," I added lamely.

"Is that your legal conclusion?" she asked, a smile playing around her lips.

I nodded yes.

Her expression turned glum again. "It gets worse. Chelsea is really pretty and is the most popular girl in my class—probably in the whole school."

I thought back to life in middle school and ventured a guess. "You mean guys like her and pay her lots of attention, so all the other girls want to hang out with her to get attention by association?" At that age, it's always about boys.

Emily nodded miserably. "All my so-called friends won't cross her because they're afraid she'll cut them out of her crowd."

"Do you know why she picked on you?" I asked, although I think I knew the answer. Emily was a beautiful girl. Chelsea probably viewed her as competition for the all-important male attention.

Emily put her arms around Ralph and hid her face in his neck. Pets are good that way. They're a great source of non-judgmental body heat. I reached out and clumsily patted Emily on the head.

"They think I'm weird," she said in a muffled voice. "I like to read. Sometimes I enjoy reading more than hanging out. I want to be a famous writer someday.

"Plus, my dad is pretty strict about my social life, so it's not like he'd let me hang out much with my friends anyway. I mean, I'm not like a hermit or anything. I do have friends, and I sneak out all the time, but it's usually to wander around town and see, well, see life. You know, watch people, especially kids, and see how and where other people live. My dad would kill me if he found out. He has this vision of me as this perfect girl—good grades, popular, into sports.

"What are your friends like?" I asked.

"They're cool. Most of them are neighborhood kids that go to the public school. We talk about important stuff like what we want to do and about our feelings, and we listen to music. I like groups like the Rolling Stones. I think Justin Bieber sucks, though—yet another thing that separates me from my peers at school."

"Is that why you cut and dyed your hair?" I asked softly. "To look different because you feel different?"

"Kind of. After I ran away from home, I went to a hair place, thinking that if I changed my hair, somehow I would change too."

I couldn't accuse Emily of defective reasoning. Most women feel this way.

"The stylist who worked on my hair said black was really big with the fashionistas, and shorter hair would make me feel totally different—give me more confidence and stuff. Before I had a chance to think about it, he'd already started."

The scene Emily described sounded painfully familiar. "Was his name Christopher by chance?" I asked.

"Wow, you know who he is. He told me he was really famous, so as least that part of what he said was true," she said.

I couldn't believe it. A hair stylist by the name of Christopher had dyed my hair bright red a couple of months ago, insisting it was auburn and giving me that line about fashionistas. I dyed my hair brown to get rid of the red, and then gradually lightened it to its original near-blonde, but the red color still bled through between touch-ups. Christopher should have been disbarred, or whatever the equivalent was for beauticians. He was a threat to hair follicles everywhere.

"Do you like your new hair style?" I asked.

Emily shook her head glumly. "I guess it'll grow out, though," she said.

Emily went on to explain that she had spent every cent she had made from babysitting over the last year on her hair. This was child abuse, plain and simple. I resolved to pay Christopher a visit and, at minimum, get Emily's money back.

"What about the nose piercing?" I asked.

"I tried to do that myself. It hurts too much, though, so I'm letting it grow back."

I shuddered. No way did I want to know the details of that little experiment.

"Kate," said Emily in a small voice.

"Um," I answered, tearing myself away from a vivid revenge fantasy involving Christopher, an electric shaver, and permanent ink magic markers.

"Please don't tell Sister Mary Grace about Chelsea. It'll make it worse."

I nodded. I knew how cruel middle school girls—and

boys—can be. With Facebook, texting, and Twitter, the gossip spread by word of mouth when I was that age could now be shared at the speed of light with a large audience and, should the sender wish, be shared anonymously. No more, "Don't tell anyone I told you this," a shtick that never worked anyhow—the source was always revealed. Now, by using an untraceable user name, gossipers could avoid accountability. But tattling to adults was then, as now, a recipe for the dreaded persecution-by-snubbing. Exclusion from social groups, no matter how much of a loner you were, was *the* worst punishment for a middle-schooler.

I gave Emily a hug. "Have you given any thought to how you and your parents can reconcile?" I asked. Notice I said, "How," not, "if."

"I don't care if I ever talk to them or see them again," said Emily defiantly. "If my dad knew any of this he'd kill me. He always sides with the school and anyone else who says I'm wrong. I like it here. Things are fine the way they are."

What had happened between Emily and her parents to cause her to prefer an uncomfortable, dog-hair covered couch, take-out food, and chaos to a stable home with parents who loved her? *Give her time,* the patient, loving side of my brain urged. *I need my life back,* screamed the selfish, immature side.

I'd let the two sides fight it out in my subconscious.

Chapter 13

I said good night to Emily, and fifteen minutes later, I was in bed and deep into the REM stage of sleep. I dreamed a green-furred Ralph was chasing Christopher, while Sister Mary Grace, dressed in traditional nun's garb, stood outside a closet in which Emily and I were locked, hurling condemnations at us while Miss Dresky took notes.

When the alarm went off at seven, my sleep-addled brain seemed to think it was important that I get a copy of Miss Dresky's notes. I was searching for paper and pen to write a reminder to file a motion to compel discovery before I was fully awake.

Needless to say, I did not feel well rested.

Once again, the smell of coffee wafted from the kitchen, and I found Emily, Tuwanda, Beth, and Macy in the kitchen. Tuwanda was becoming a regular at my breakfast table.

"Hey, Tuwanda," I greeted her as I poured myself a cup of coffee.

"Hey, yourself," she said through a mouthful of pancakes. "You look like shit."

I pushed the hair out of my eyes and squinted at her through sleep swollen eyelids. "No swearing around the child," I said sternly.

"You look like crap. That better?"

We turned to Macy for a ruling.

"Crap's borderline," she said. "You two ought to learn more Yiddish. Yiddish has got some great words, and since it's a foreign language, it doesn't qualify as swearing."

"Macy's teaching me Yiddish," said Emily seriously. "Today we're learning adjectives."

Great. *Here's your daughter, Webber. Oh, by the way; she cut her hair and dyed it black, thinks dog hair is a condiment, and speaks Yiddish.* The kid had been at my house for only two days. I didn't want to think about what could happen in a week.

Tuwanda looked meaningfully at her watch. "Shouldn't you get movin'? You goin' to work today, right?

"Yes," I said tersely. "I don't need to be in court until ten o'clock, though."

"I know. I'm goin' with you," she said.

Then I remembered that the motion I was arguing related to one of the Care Bare cases. Tuwanda seldom showed up for such procedural matters, though. I raised an eyebrow and looked at her inquiringly.

"I figgered we could get lunch afterward," she said,

keeping her tone casual. Too casual. She was up to something.

"I have a meeting at eleven," I said, studying her carefully. "We can go to lunch after that."

"Sounds good to me," she said, suddenly becoming very interested in the bacon on her plate.

Whatever it was, it wasn't something she wanted to talk about in front of Emily or Macy, or maybe both.

Tuwanda polished off her bacon and wiped her mouth daintily. "I'm gonna go home and catch some z's," she said.

Beth, who until now had remained quiet but seemed to be, if not enjoying, then at least distracted, by the banter going on around her, got up from the table with Tuwanda. "Tuwanda offered to drop me at my apartment on her way home so I can change clothes before work."

"Beth, maybe you should take the day off," I said softly, placing my hand on her arm.

Beth shook her head decisively. "No. It's better that I work," she said. "I need to stay busy."

I nodded understandingly. Work was how I coped with personal problems, too.

"I'll meet you at court before the hearin'. If for some reason I can't make it, I'll be at your office at eleven," said Tuwanda, as she and Beth headed out.

"Why not come by later for lun …" I broke off before I finished. I had figured out what she was up to. Tuwanda is fascinated by the spiritual world—obsessed even, you might say. (Or is it possessed?) She's known Venus longer than I have and has often consulted with her on otherworldly matters. "Did you happen to speak with Venus yesterday?" I asked.

"I did. So I'll be seein' you later then?" asked Tuwanda.

Clearly she didn't want to pursue the subject of Venus's visit in front of Emily. I didn't either, so I let it drop.

After Tuwanda and Beth left, I ate a quick breakfast and then got ready for work. Later, as I got into my car to drive to work, I caught sight of Sister Mary Grace's files in the backseat and remembered that I had yet to review Lily's files. I would need to find time today to get to it. I would ask Beth to make copies for Sam and MJ as well.

Beth had not arrived yet when I got to the office, which is not surprising since I had a head start. Sam's Toyota and MJ's motorcycle were parked outside, though.

The motorcycle had been a birthday gift from MJ's boyfriend, Mitchie. It was a pink, late-model Harley Davidson Fat Boy with purple and orange flames and the words *raging hormones* painted on the sides. I was concerned about MJ's safety at first, but drivers give her bike lots of leeway. Some go so far as to pull over to the side of the road and wait until she rides out of sight.

I poked my head into Sam and MJ's shared quarters to say good morning. Sam had removed the lemurs and was supplementing the barrier between their desks with yet more books and files. MJ's aim and arm seemed to have gotten better; Sam's side of the office was littered with potato chips.

"MJ, stop throwing potato chips at Sam," I chastised. After sniffing the air, I added, "And Sam, stop spraying Lysol.

Jeez. I thought I'd left the parenting duties at home.

"Hi, Kate," greeted Sam, sneaking in a final spritz before he put the can away. MJ hurled a Cheese Curl at him, then immediately turned to me and said, "You said no potato chips. You didn't say anything about Cheese Curls."

I wondered if I should use the kitchen as a time-out area.

"Sam, did you have a chance to look into the issues I talked to you about yesterday?" I asked, trying to establish a semblance of a business atmosphere.

"I've got some background information on CPS," he said, handing me a manila file folder. "I'm planning on calling them once their office is open to find out if records from the fifties and sixties are even available."

Government offices are supposed to open at eight and it was already eight-thirty. But if you were serious about talking to someone, you had to wait until after nine.

"Oh, and Bryan called you. I left the message on your desk," he added.

"Brown-noser," hissed MJ.

"Doing your job is not brown-nosing," countered Sam.

I left before getting caught in the middle of the crossfire. I was wearing a white blouse, and I didn't want to show up in court covered in orange Cheese Curl powder.

I called Bryan as soon as I got to my office.

"Hi, stranger," he said as soon as he picked up the phone. This was not his office's standard greeting, so he must have seen my name on caller ID before he picked up.

"The phone goes both ways, you know. You could have called before today," I said, annoyed and still feeling hurt that apparently my liability to his political career outweighed our relationship.

"I didn't want to distract you from your parenting duties," he said. He tried to sound teasing, but I picked up on the sharp edge in his voice. "Maria's death has hit everyone around here hard. The deputies and police officers working out of the downtown offices all knew her either through El Barrio or through her volunteer work with the DARE program at Central High School."

"It's tragic that all she was and did ended the way it did," I said somberly. "I can't believe no one heard the gunshot. There are usually lots of people in that area around noon."

"That's because she wasn't killed where you found her. I don't know how much you could see through the window, but there was too little blood for her to have been shot inside the car, and the techs didn't find any blood in the area where the car was parked. The crime investigation guys think that, because of the pattern of blood smears on the seat, she was probably shot first and then loaded into the passenger seat. Her killer then drove her to where you found her and pushed or dragged her to the driver's side. Her foot was either placed or fell on the brake, so the brake lights were on.

"We don't know why she was placed behind the wheel or why the car was left running. Maybe it was to delay discovery—a person sitting in a car with the windows closed on a hot day would draw attention, but a running car, presumably with the air conditioner on, would pass notice. Plenty of people wait in their cars for one reason or another, but no one does so without the AC on this time of year."

"Prints?" I asked.

"MJ's on the window, Maria's all over inside and out. The tech guys found only one unidentified partial."

"No one saw anything?" I pressed.

"It looks like she was sitting there for over an hour. I don't know how much gas was in the car to begin with, but the tank was almost empty and the engine was close to overheating by the time the police got there. That means she could have been left there as early as eleven yesterday morning—before traffic in the area really picks up."

This fit with what Gilberto, the cook MJ had heard the police questioning, said about Maria leaving the restaurant as early as ten.

"So where does that put the investigation?" I asked. I had no right to know, but I wanted to capitalize on Bryan's chattiness, a condition that is rare and usually only occurs when he's exhausted or nervous.

"Up against a wall," he said with vehemence. "We need to find someone who saw something, and I guarantee we're not going to stop until we find whoever did this to her."

"We?" I asked. "I thought this was a police investigation. Is your office involved too?"

"Yes. As a courtesy and by choice. Plus, until we know where Maria was shot, we don't know who has jurisdiction," he said.

In other words, the law enforcement guys were taking this one personally.

"Do you have time for lunch tomorrow?" he asked. "I'm assuming dinner tonight is out of the question unless we go to MacDonald's for a happy meal."

"Emily's thirteen, for gosh sake. She's already eating adult food," I said.

"Not if she's staying at your house," he chuckled. "Unless you're feeding her chardonnay and crackers— that's usually all you have around."

I was going to counter with, "Hey; I'm a good mother," but decided that would be too weird.

Instead I said, "Lunch sounds fine provided you're not planning on any more lectures."

He probably realizes he told me too much and needs to reinforce his non-interference message. Tough cookies.

"Truce," he laughed, but he sounded uncomfortable.

We agreed to meet at Wally's the next day for lunch and signed off.

I skimmed the information on CPS Sam had given me and saw that the agency was not formed until after the enactment of the Child Abuse Protection and

Treatment Act in the mid-seventies. Before that time, adoptions and foster care placements were handled, somewhat haphazardly it seems, if at all, by a division of the Arizona Department of Health Services. To confuse matters more, prior to the sixties, many adoptions and placements were handled by privately funded orphanages, so, although birth and death certificates were maintained by the Arizona Department of Health Service, there was no central repository of records regarding what happened in between.

Maybe the police would find the name of Maria's social worker through a search of her personal records, because the public records weren't going to be much help. In the meantime, I would focus on the lead Sister Mary Grace gave me on our skeleton investigation, and if, for some reason, it led to information about Maria's death, then, well, so be it.

Chapter 14

I looked at my watch and noticed that it was time for me to leave for court. Nine times out of ten, hearings are delayed due to the court's busy calendar, but if I was late it would be my luck—this time, the court would be on schedule. One does not tempt fate in this profession.

When I walked into Judge Schwartz's courtroom at five minutes to ten, I was surprised to see Tuwanda sitting in the gallery. I had to control my shock when Schwartz, who is notorious for being late, not only showed up on time, but called our motion first. Because I am an experienced attorney, I knew this meant that nothing else would go right today.

The motion was a run-of-the mill request to suppress evidence of a prior criminal record, but Schwartz seemed to be unusually lively and attentive. I barely recognized him as the same man who had dozed and then fallen off the bench during a DUI trial. Of course, at the time, he adamantly denied that this had been the case, and he accused counsel of lack of respect for the judiciary when she suggested that he wipe the drool off his cheek. At some point, I noticed that the judge kept glancing at Tuwanda, and guessed his performance was intended to impress the knockout in the back.

The prosecutor and I finished our arguments, and the judge took the matter under advisement. I swear I saw him wink at Tuwanda before he left the bench.

Once we were outside the courtroom and beyond the hearing of the prosecutor, I hissed, "What was that all about?"

"You wuz there. What the hell. It was an evidentiary hearin' on a motion. You had me fooled. I coulda' swore you wuz payin' attention."

"Very funny. That's not what I mean and you know it. What's with you and Schwartz?" I continued as we walked toward Tuwanda's parked car *cum* parade float. Tuwanda drives a 1984 pink El Dorado with spinners, dual exhausts, red leather seats, and lots of bright shiny chrome. It is the least subtle car I've ever seen. I would say it's the least subtle *vehicle* I've ever seen, but MJ's Harley wins by a hair in that category.

Tuwanda looked across the street where two picnic tables sat on a square concrete area surrounded by a low brick wall and empty planters, which is Phoenix's idea of a park. "I don' understand why a city in the middle of the damn desert can't put shade structures up here and there. Ain't no one gonna sit on a concrete pad with the hot sun beatin' down 'cept for folks that got no other place to go," she muttered.

And in fact, the only people in the park were two homeless men with their worldly possessions piled high in grocery carts. One of them looked familiar. "Hi, Basil," I called out. I gave him a friendly wave when he looked up to see who was calling his name.

"Hey, bag lady," he said cheerfully. "Did you find the girl you were looking for?"

I nodded, "Actually, she found me," I answered.

He grunted in approval and went back to what he'd been doing before I interrupted him, which, to anyone without knowledge of Basil's internal audio visual system, would appear to be staring at a bench.

"Friend of Larry?" asked Tuwanda.

"No. I met him the other night when I was looking for Emily.

Tuwanda tsk-tsked, and said, "Kate, I don't mean to be critical, but don' you think it's weird that most of your friends is hookers and homeless people? You a well educated white woman with money. Shouldn't you be hangin' out with members of the Junior League or somethin'?"

I shuddered. "The 'junior' part is a misnomer. My mother is a member of the Junior League," I said, making a wry face. "She has no time or sympathy for people she deems less than perfect, and if the other members of that organization are of the same ilk, I want nothing to do with them."

I felt a twinge in my hand and realized I held the straps of my purse in a death grip.

Tuwanda looked me intently. "I guess you feel like you're one of those imperfect people, an' maybe you feel comfortable aroun' people who ain't in no position to judge," she said softly.

I knew what she said had a grain—or more like a silo full of grain—of truth, because I felt like crying.

Quickly looking away, I said, "I don't know how we ended up on this subject, but I know I started by asking what was going on between you and Schwartz, and you have avoided answering me, to the point of engaging in the unauthorized practice of psychiatry in the middle of a damned sidewalk."

If Tuwanda was hurt by my verbal push-back, she didn't let on. "I jes' know how touchy you attorneys get about your damn ethics an' conflicts of interest."

I groaned. "Please don't tell me Schwartz is one of your clients."

"Oh, oh," said Tuwanda. "Looky there."

We'd reached her car and she was pointing at the expired meter.

"I better get movin' before I get a ticket. They real strict around here."

Before I could follow up on the Schwartz issue, Tuwanda was in her car and on her way.

Vowing to follow up on the Schwartz issue when I got back to my office, I trotted off in the direction of my car, which I'd parked on the other side of the courthouse.

When I got there, the evidence of a meter maid attack was tucked under my windshield wiper. I put it in my glove compartment with the others.

Tuwanda's car was already parked outside by the time I got back to my office. Since Venus doesn't drive, I had no way of knowing if she was there yet.

That question was answered when I got to the front door, just as Venus pulled up in a taxi and stepped out.

"You owe him seven dollars," she said, chin jerking toward the driver. "I like to tip 20 percent, so that makes for a total of eight-forty."

"Is payment for your transportation costs part of our deal?" I asked.

"They is unless you wanna pick me up an' drop me off at my place," said Venus, as she pushed her way past me.

I paid the cab driver, who told me to thank Venus for the tip, and then I followed her inside.

Tuwanda was sitting in lotus position on the floor of our reception room. Her eyes were closed, and she was mouthing something ohm-like.

Beth looked up from her desk and shushed me. "Tuwanda's trying to clear her mind," she whispered loudly.

"Unless she usin' the met'physical equivalent of a snow plow, we gonna be here a long time," quipped Venus, who was busy pouring herself a cup of coffee.

Tuwanda opened her eyes and glared at her. "For someone who can hear dead people, you ain't at all sensitive to the livin'," she said.

Beth, who was puffy-eyed but seemed a lot better than yesterday, looked at me disapprovingly. "I was not aware that you had a meeting with Ms. Butterman," she said, tapping her desk calendar with her pen.

I did a mental head slap. *I violated the cardinal rule that all appointments must be calendared by Beth.*

"Fortunately, because you were appearing in front of Judge Schwartz this morning, I assumed the hearing would go into overtime, so I didn't schedule anything else before noon," she said primly.

We were safe. We had skidded to a stop at the edge of the black hole of chaos that Beth was convinced would result if her organizational rules were not followed.

"I'm sorry I forgot to tell you, Beth," I said humbly. "I guess with all the insanity at my house last night, it slipped my mind."

Neither Tuwanda nor Venus bothered to inquire as to the nature of the insanity to which I alluded. Insane occurrences at my house were par for the course.

"I've asked Venus to try to contact the spirit of our skeleton," I explained.

Beth, who is one of the most grounded people I know, does not believe in Venus's, or anyone else's, ability to talk to the dead. She rolled her eyes and muttered, "I need a vacation."

"Let's go into my office, shall we?" I said, shepherding Venus and Tuwanda ahead of me, the latter having unfolded herself and risen to her feet during my exchange with Beth.

Tuwanda sat in a comfy client chair, and I gestured for Venus to take the matching chair next to it. But she shook her head and said, "I ain't gonna sit in someone's lap. You better find me another chair."

"You see a spirit?" asked Tuwanda excitedly, leaning forward and swiping her hand back and forth through the air above the chair.

Venus, arms akimbo, angrily asked, "What in the name of Jesus are you doin', Tuwanda?" Then, turning to the empty chair, she said, "Sorry, honey. Sometimes hardbodies is real assholes."

"Hardbodies," is the term Venus uses for the living.

I hurried to MJ and Sam's office. They looked up in surprise at my abrupt entry. "MJ, I need to borrow one of your chairs," I said as I began to tug an ugly, green-striped armchair toward the door.

"Allow me," said Sam. He pulled a box of plastic gloves out of his desk drawer, donned a pair, and picked up the chair effortlessly. "To your office?" he asked, holding it out in front of him so no part of it part of it came in contact with his suit.

"Yes, please. Thank you." I said.

I trotted after Sam, and MJ, who was wearing neon yellow leggings and a T-shirt with *Sunshine's nice but moonshine's better* written on it, heaved herself out of her chair and followed.

Sam placed the chair where I indicated and then looked around questioningly.

"You're expecting someone else?" he asked.

"No," said Tuwanda excitedly. "Venus says there's already somebody sittin' in that other chair—a spirit."

"So what's the matter with sitting on it?" scoffed MJ "It's not like you're gonna squish 'em."

"It's common courtesy," said Venus primly. "How would you like it if someone planted their butt in the middle of your essence?"

We were all quiet as we let Venus's reasoning sink in. Since the underlying assumption, or fact, if you will, was that there was such a thing as a spirit remaining after the physical body died, the skeptics among us, (MJ and Sam, and me, kind of), had a hard time accepting Venus's logic. But none of us carried the debate further because you can't argue a fact into existence—either it is or it isn't—and if someone accepts as true something that can't be proved, arguing about it is a waste of time.

"Can we stay and watch what happens?" asked MJ, breaking the silence.

"No," said Venus. "The presence of non-believers interferes with my abilities."

I wondered if Venus spotted my skepticism and meant to include me as one of those who should be excluded. But when she majestically extended her arm in front of her and pointed to Sam, then MJ, and then pointed at the door and said, "Out," it seemed okay for me to stay. Venus probably figured that since I had asked her to come over and was paying the bill, I was enough of a believer that the static of my aura wouldn't interfere with her abilities.

Sam and MJ left, with MJ closing the door behind her

harder than necessary. I wasn't fooled. I knew darn well they would listen to us from the hallway. The walls of my office are paper thin.

Venus sat in the green chair Sam had brought in and smoothed her skirt over her knees. Her gray-white hair covered her head like a halo. When I first met Venus, she tamed her hair with massive amounts of gel and pulled it tightly back into a bun at the nape of her neck. Of late, though, she had let it frizz and float in joyous freedom as homage to her black heritage. She had also taken to wearing brightly colored dashikis, but today she was wearing her business clothes, consisting of a navy-blue skirt and jacket made of a material whose elastic properties were tested to the limit by her plump body. Her blouse gapped open between the buttons, and the buttons themselves were barely holding it together.

Venus took a spiral notebook and a pen out of her capacious black purse, and settled back in her chair. She wasn't finished with the adjustment process, though. She bent over at the waist and hauled her knee-high, beige support hose up a notch or two. The skin of her calves bulged over the tops, and I wondered if they cut off her circulation.

I scooted my chair around my desk and placed it next to Tuwanda's then sat down and waited in anticipation as Venus readjusted her skirt over her knees.

"Now," she said, uncapping the pen and flipping the notebook open. "Tell me your name and address."

It sounded like a job interview. I had expected candles and maybe some incense and an incantation or two.

Venus appeared to be listening, but she did not write anything down on her pad. Her expression reflected growing concern. "I can't help you if that's how you feel. This lady here you're talkin' about don't got the gift of understandin' spirits, so's the only way you can commun'cate with her is through me."

Venus listened again, frowning. "You don't gotta trust me. All I do is tell people what you say. I'm like a translator—you know, them people who translate somethin' like Spanish into English so's people who don't understand Spanish know what the heck is goin' on. If you don't think I'm sayin' it right, you explain to me what I'm sayin' wrong, and I try it again. It ain't my job to do anythin' other than listen an' translate. I ain't gonna use what you tell me any other way."

Tuwanda and I were like spectators at a tennis match, looking at Venus when she spoke and then at the empty chair when she listened. Of course, to make the analogy perfect, it would have to be a tennis match with only one player.

"She a whore," Venus said after another short period of silence.

Tuwanda leaned over and whispered in my ear, "She talkin' about me."

I wondered why she thought clarification was necessary.

"No, she here 'cuz she fascinated by what dead folks say," said Venus. "I guess maybe it's better'n what she hears from live people. In her line of business, I 'spect hardbodies make noises, aroun' her, but don't use words a lot and when they do, they just sayin' the same stuff over and over."

Unable to restrain herself in the face of Venus's condescending reasoning, Tuwanda blurted out, "Who you talkin' to? Who you tellin' them things to? I'm sittin' right here. You got any questions about Tuwanda, ask me straight out." Tuwanda directed this last statement to the empty chair.

The chair's demeanor did not change. If it was a person, I imagined it would be filing its nails in bored disinterest.

Venus made a disgusted noise in the back of her throat. "She gone," she said. "I hope you's happy. An' because your nasty ol' friend scared her off don't mean you don't owe me my fee."

"Who you callin' nasty?" snarled Tuwanda, half rising out of her chair. "You jus' tol' someone I was a lonely hooker who don't hear nothin' but gasps and groans all day. You sum'rized my complex character by emphasizin' a tiny little fraction of my life experience."

Tuwanda is taking a course titled "Psychology and Self Awareness" at a local community college, and it has affected her outlook and vocabulary. Believe me—this was way better than the time she took a course on self assertion. Tuwanda taking a course on self assertion is like a cat taking lessons on aloofness or Ralph taking lessons on drooling.

"Were you able to learn anything from the spirit?" I

asked before Tuwanda could whip herself into a frenzy of speechifying.

"Not much." Venus shrugged nonchalantly, unruffled by Tuwanda's attack stance. "She only wants to talk to Kate. She don't trust no one else."

"Me?" I squeaked in surprise. "But why? Did you explain I can't communicate with spirits?"

"You heard what I tol' her," said Venus. "She says you felt her presence and that all you needed to do was focus more and quit blamin' the air conditioner."

I made the connection right away—the arctic blasts of air I had felt in my office on Sunday.

"Did Beth tell you about the air conditioner acting up this weekend?" I asked suspiciously.

"What, you think I got nothin' better to do than call your secretary jus' to ask about your air conditionin'?" Venus huffed. "Like I got some kinda' obsession about climate control?"

"What 'xactly was it you felt?" asked Tuwanda interestedly, sitting back in her chair and appearing to have lost interest in speechifying.

I closed my eyes in concentration and tried to remember the sensation I'd experienced. "My shoulder felt cold and then the cold air moved to my hand and my candy bar. I remember thinking the candy bar tasted like it had been in the refrigerator."

"Tha's what some spirits feel like when they present. They got no substance, but when they tryin' real hard to communicate with someone, they can affect the temperature," Venus said, nodding knowingly. "Some of 'em c'n even move things aroun', but they had to have had a lot of experience in focusin' an' lots of energy just before they died so their residual got some oomph left. People who were real sick and weak before they died have a hard time makin' a hardbody notice 'em, unless it's a hardbody like me who's sensitive to more subtle stuff."

"But why me?" I asked again.

"The spirit didn't give me much in the way of information, but I picked up right away that it's the spirit of a young girl. It's possible she's a spiritually undeveloped adult female, but that's pretty rare. No matter how much you try to protect yourself, life takes a toll, so with older folks there's a weariness of spirit you don't see in young ones. It wasn't too hard to figger out, too, that she got some real trust issues, which usually means somethin' bad, or a lot of things bad, happened, and the people who shoulda' protected her didn't, or maybe even did the bad things themselves."

"Like maybe she was a victim of child abuse," I said.

"Maybe. Interestin' that you would fall on that bein' the reason. I don't know 'xactly what this child went through. I do know though that pain knows pain," Venus concluded ambiguously.

"What do you mean by 'pain knows pain'?" I asked.

"I mean that folks who go through somethin' bad will trust other folks who know their kinda sufferin' more'n they do other people, no matter how well intentioned them other people is." Venus, after having made this pronouncement, looked at me speculatively.

"Well, Katie here has been through a shitload of stuff," commented Tuwanda. "But it's mainly been clients an' other people she workin' for tryin' to kill her."

"Maybe that's it," I acknowledged, although I slightly resented Tuwanda's characterization of my past troubles. She made it sound like I was a bad attorney and a worse employee, but I let it pass. "Maybe someone hurt her and didn't want anyone else to know about it."

"Is that why *you* so distrustful?" asked Tuwanda.

"I am not distrustful of all people," I said heatedly. "I tend to be wary of people who kidnap me at gunpoint or come after me with knives, however." The words were already out of my mouth before I remembered that Venus's grandson had been among the latter group.

A spasm of pain flashed through her eyes, and she looked away for an instant. Then she quickly resumed eye contact and pretended she didn't pick up the connection.

"I've done about as much as I can," she said, standing. "If you wanna' get more detail from this spirit, you better practice your communication skills."

"How do I do that?" I asked, still skeptical but intrigued.

She sighed and fixed me with an intense stare. "You gotta concentrate on listenin' and lookin' for cues, an' pay attention to stuff your mind norm'ly filters out. It ain't gonna be easy, 'cuz with you bein' a lawyer, you got a pretty dense filter."

"I'm dense?" I'd been called a lot of things, but never that. People usually think I'm pretty quick.

"I don't mean dense as in slow," Venus explained patiently, "I mean dense as in you look at the world a certain way, an' if somethin' don't fit into with how you see things, you automatically delete it before it even gets to the thinkin' part of your brain."

I wondered if Venus was taking the same community college course as Tuwanda.

"So if she opens her mind and pays attention, she will hear what the little girl's sayin'?" asked Tuwanda.

"It ain't like all of a sudden you hear this voice talkin' to you," said Venus. "It's more like you feel things: sometimes it's emotions, like all maybe one day you wake up hating turnips, an' before that you haven't given much thought to turnips. Tha's a spirit talkin to you. Katie, I think you oughta' start with focusin' on painful memories. That's where this little girl's feelin's gonna pop up, an' you'll figger things out."

Great. I wasted an hour of my time only to find out that I need to get in touch with my feelings. No thanks. I prefer to rely on hard evidence.

I had to face the fact that the only way I could identify our skeleton was through the dry, laborious process of searching records that might not exist and interviewing the few people still alive who could remember something that happened more than fifty years ago.

I thanked Venus for her efforts, and she reminded me about her fee. I told her she needed to discuss it with Beth. She patted my shoulder sympathetically as she passed by me on her way out to see the holder of the operation's financial power.

Tuwanda waited until the door closed behind Venus before speaking, "She right, you know. Even if you wasn't tryin' to find out who that little girl was, you should learn to pay attention to what your own self is tellin' you. You gotta be more self aware."

"I *am* self aware," I said testily, as I pushed my chair back behind my desk, "and I don't think sitting around staring at my navel is going to help one bit with this investigation. This whole thing is ridiculous. I don't know why I asked Venus to come over. I would be better off going on the *Jerry Springer Show*."

Tuwanda stayed seated and looked at me solicitously. "Maybe we c'n talk about it at lunch," she said. "Low blood sugar don't create a good environment for consideration of new ideas."

"I will not go to lunch with you unless you promise to avoid the topics of self-awareness, self-discovery, self-analysis, self-examination, self-improvement, self-help, do-it-yourself, or anything else even tangentially related to any of that bunk," I said, perhaps more shrilly than the circumstances required. After a couple beats I continued more calmly. "Now, where should we go to eat?"

"I guess anywhere that ain't *self*-serve," quipped Tuwanda.

I gave her a weak smile. "How about El Barrio?" I suggested. I of course had an ulterior motive. I wanted to talk to some of the staff members, and to Gilberto the cook in particular, to find out if anyone knew more about Maria's plans the day she died.

"I don't think it's open," said Tuwanda. "Maria's funeral is today at one o'clock, so I'm guessin' the restaurant will be closed outta' respect."

"It's today?" I gasped. "I had no idea it would be so soon. The police usually hold the body for a while for testing."

"I guess the cause of death ain't a question mark here, so's there's no need. Anyway, they prob'ly took a bunch of blood and tissue samples before they released her body, so's there's no need to hold things up," commented Tuwanda, sadness creeping into her voice.

"Where is the funeral being held?" I said as I grabbed my purse.

"Saint Teresa's Chapel of the Bloody Robes," provided Tuwanda.

I had to hand it to the Catholics for creativity. My people, the Presbyterians, tended to use unimaginative names like First Presbyterian Church, Second Presbyterian Church, and so on.

"Then that's where we're going," I said.

"For lunch?" Tuwanda asked. "You gonna' crash a funeral for snacks?"

I stopped to glare at her after having only applied lipstick to my lower lip. "Of course not, I …wait; is it a private funeral?" I asked. A private funeral did not seem consistent with the way I thought Maria would want to be remembered, but many people don't leave instructions, so it's up to their family decide.

"I believe so. At least that's what Beth tol' me before

you got here from court. Maria's brother—stepbrother I guess—is in charge of the arrangements."

"Is Beth going?" I asked, surprised that Beth had not made a point of telling me as soon as I walked in the door.

Tuwanda shook her head. "Nope. She called the stepbrother this morning—his name is Mario Batista— an' he tol' her it was for immediate family only."

"Are there a lot of relatives?" I asked. I hadn't even been aware of the stepbrother, but then I didn't know Maria well enough to know all her relatives or even how many there were.

"Beth said Maria didn't have many family connections, and those she had weren't all that strong, so it seemed strange, and kinda' mean, that Maria's close friends aren't invited. Beth acted like she didn't care, but I think she does, and she's real hurt about it."

"Maybe they're planning a memorial for later where anyone who wants to can come," I suggested.

"I dunno. Beth didn't say anythin' 'bout that," said Tuwanda.

I went out to Beth's desk to ask. She looked as if she had been crying again, and I almost backed out of raising the issue, afraid it would trigger more misery. "Tuwanda told me about the closed funeral," I said softly. "Is there a memorial service planned for later? If so, I would like to go."

I wanted to provide support for Beth, but, selfishly, I also wanted to see who showed up and even talk to some of the attendees—exercising the utmost in discretion, of course.

She shook her head no, and the tears started again. I came around behind her and hugged her.

Tuwanda, who had followed me out of my office, went to our kitchen and returned shortly with a glass of water. "You cryin' so many tears you gonna run out of water, Beth," she said, placing the glass gently in front of her.

"We're going to Maria's funeral," I announced decisively and with absolutely no rational forethought. Beth needed closure, and I needed information.

"We gonna just march in?" asked Tuwanda. "Beth's okay in that navy skirt, but ain't no way I'm gonna blend into a crowd of mourners in this purple dress. Besides, don't they got bouncers checking names at the door?"

"What if they do? What's the worst that can happen?" I said, now thoroughly fired up and ready to go.

"That we get tossed down the steps, which ain't at all good for a person," said Tuwanda doubtfully. "Saint Teresa's got a real impressive entry: lots of cement steps an' statues— an' some of them statues got pointy parts: arrows, swords, and thorns and such like. Saint Teresa's don't pull any punches when it comes to depictin' sufferin'."

Beth, usually the most moderate of the three of us, stood abruptly and grabbed her purse. "Let's go," she said with grim determination.

It was already twelve forty-five, so I drove as fast as traffic would allow, with Tuwanda shouting directions from the passenger seat. Somewhere in between swearing at traffic and Tuwanda's yelled instructions, we came up with a plan whereby I would cause a diversion while Beth and Tuwanda sneaked into the church. Of course, I had no time to get to the details, such as how I would create such a diversion, but I figured it would come to me when we got there. I pride myself on my ability to think creatively under pressure.

I dropped off Beth and Tuwanda at the side of the church—an impressive gothic structure, kind of like a mini-Notre Dame without the flying buttresses, and quickly found a parking place. The area was surprisingly devoid of parked cars, which, unless the family members came by bus or taxi, meant it was a small gathering, so melting unnoticed into the crowd was not a viable strategy. Beth and Tuwanda would need to hang out in the shadows at the back of the sanctuary when—and if—they got inside.

A hearse was parked out front, and two men stood on either side of the church's large, carved wooden doors. One door was propped open slightly to allow latecomers to enter quietly. The men really did look like bouncers. To the right of the entry and in the middle of the steps stood a statute of Saint Sebastian, who looked amazingly calm despite all the arrows piercing his body. To the left of the entry and further down on the steps was another statue, a young woman. I assumed she was Salome, holding a platter upon which the head of John the Baptist lay. John, like Sebastian, seemed blasé about his predicament.

I took a deep breath and climbed the six steps to the

front door, keeping my head down and my shoulders rounded in sadness. When I got to the top of the steps, the two men moved simultaneously to block the entrance. Both wore suits that stretched tightly over muscular chests and arms. They would be right at home at a wrestle-mania event; unless the church was now hiring thugs to literally twist the arms of potential converts, this was not these men's normal milieu.

"I'm sorry, ma'am," said the man on the right, a Hulk Hogan lookalike. "This is a private service."

"I need to pray," I said. Actually, I was already praying, but they didn't need to know that.

The man on the left, who did not appear to have a neck, said, "You'll have to find some other place to pray, lady." He sounded like Barry White. I suspected steroid use.

"I have an appointment with God," I insisted, silently apologizing to the almighty for fibbing.

"You'll have to tell him to meet you somewhere else," said no-neck. "Try texting him," he added, snickering.

I disagreed with his choice of pronouns, but I didn't think this was the time or place for a debate about religion.

I dropped to my knees, sacrificing my pantyhose to a good cause, and cried out, "Blasphemers. You defile this holy place."

"Jesus, lady, keep it down," said Hulk looking around nervously, which was the last thing I wanted him to do.

I'd have to try a different tactic. I began babbling

incoherently. You'd think that would be easy, but it's not. Try as I could, I kept delivering recognizable words, in order, using appropriate grammar. I discarded my attempt at nonsensical muttering and focused instead on non-sequiturs, lowering my voice so they would come closer to hear me. "Malts are good but fattening. Alpo causes diarrhea. You should recycle. Rashes are never good. Ferrets make lousy pets."

The men seemed fascinated by my stream of consciousness and leaned down to listen. If they were waiting for plot development, they were going to be disappointed.

"Why do ferrets make bad pets?" asked the Hulk interestedly.

"Ducks don't like water—they pretend they do," I said with conviction.

Out of the corner of my eye I saw Tuwanda and Beth tiptoe up the steps on the far side of Sebastian and John and then slip into the church. Once I was sure they were safely inside, I abruptly stood, brushed off my knees, and glanced at my watch.

"Wow," I remarked. "I'd better get going or I'll be late for my mani-pedi."

I descended the steps sedately and walked around the corner. Once I was out of sight, I ran a block down, crossed the street, and then doubled back. Except for the few cars parked by the church, the neighborhood showed no signs of habitation. I hid next to the porch of a house not far from the church, using a shrub as a screen, which was a poor choice from the point of view of comfort since it was prickly as heck. I had a clear view of the front of the church through its leaves—or more correctly, thorns—so I put up with the scratches.

After fifteen minutes or so, my knees and ankles were getting sore and planning a coup. So I abandoned my crouching position and sat on the slightly damp ground, thereby shifting the pressure to my tailbone, which, unless I land on it hard, does not take such things personally.

Fifteen more minutes passed before the doors of the church opened, and a few people filed out. I counted five of them, excluding no-neck and the Hulk—two women and three men. All were dressed in black except for the last man to emerge who was wearing a brown suit and a jarring red, white, and blue tie: Webber.

The man can't even dress decently for a funeral.

I snapped a couple of pictures with my cell phone's camera, after which I pocketed the phone and scrutinized each of their faces in turn. Except for Webber, I didn't recognize any of them. The two women and one of the men looked Hispanic. The remaining man was a well-dressed, elderly Anglo who, despite his cane, had the regal bearing of someone used to power.

The stocky Hispanic man with the pock-marked face acted as if he was in charge. I fingered him as the stepbrother, Mario Batista, Tuwanda had mentioned. He took position facing the hearse, and the others obediently lined up next to him. A coffin perched on a gurney rolled out of a street-level side door, pushed by another dark-suited man whose face bore the practiced solemnity of a professional. The attendees didn't seem afflicted by any obvious infirmities, and I wondered why a few of them had not volunteered to carry the coffin as was more traditional. Heck; the Hulk probably could have tucked it under his arm and carried it solo. Even though he was a likely a hired hand, it would be more personal than schlepping Maria around on a dented stainless-steel gurney with a defective wheel that spun without direction or purpose.

The gurney stopped short at the edge of the curb when one of its wheels became wedged in a rut. While the others looked on impassively, the pusher first rocked the gurney back and forth and then finally rolled it back a few feet, made a running start, and cleared the curb. After positioning the gurney in back of the hearse, he opened the hearse's tailgate and shoved the coffin into the back. He tried unsuccessfully to shut the tailgate, regrouped, and gave the coffin another shove. This time, the tailgate slammed shut with finality.

The members of the group on the sidewalk made no move for their cars but wordlessly watched the hearse pull away and then appeared to await their next instruction. Maria's stepbrother looked at his watch, said something first to Webber and then to the others, and left, heading around to the back of the church where there was a parking lot. Webber bowed slightly to the remaining attendees and climbed back up the church's steps to where the Hulk and no-neck still stood. He spoke to them briefly, and the Hulk responded, first holding his hands in a prayerful pose and then pointing to where I had knelt on the steps. Webber covered his eyes with his hand and shook his head. I was pretty sure the Hulk had ratted on me.

When the Hulk finished pantomiming what looked like a beaver (maybe it was his version of a ferret), Webber glanced toward the large wooden doors, then appeared to ask another question. No-neck answered with a brief nod.

Webber disappeared into the church with the two guards following. He had probably guessed what happened and was looking for my accomplices. I hoped like heck that Tuwanda and Beth already managed to get out.

I frantically scanned the vicinity for any sign of them.

The group on the sidewalk had disbanded. The two women left together in an ancient Buick Regal. The old man with the cane got into a black Mercedes Benz sedan with heavily tinted windows. The car had materialized swiftly and smoothly from a side street. Since I had not seen the elderly man make a call, I assumed the driver had been waiting and watching for him.

I abandoned my search of the church grounds and scrutinized the windows of the building with the sinking realization that Tuwanda and Beth had not yet made it out. I saw a flash of purple behind a second-story window. The window opened, and a purple-sleeved arm emerged, waving frantically. I shaded my eyes and squinted at it. Tuwanda now had her head out the window and was looking in my direction. She'd spotted me from her higher vantage point and seemed to be mouthing something, but I'll be darned if I could tell what. I raised my shoulders in an exaggerated shrug.

"Pull the damn car up to the side of the damn building," she screamed.

If her cover wasn't blown before, it sure as heck was now; a subtle escape was no longer possible. Being the patron saint of lost causes, however, I obediently sprinted the distance to my car, threw myself behind the wheel, and simultaneously turned the key and hit the accelerator. I traveled the hundred or so feet between me and my destination going fifty (at least, it felt let fifty, but it was probably more like twenty since my Honda hadn't had a tune-up in a long time and took about a half-hour to go from zero to fifty), and screeched to a halt at the side of the church, Bonny and Clyde–style. I looked apprehensively at the second-floor window and wondered how they were going make the two-story drop. Seconds later, I had my answer. The tip of a rope, hastily made of lavishly colored material, appeared in my line of vision and dangled a few feet from the ground. Then I remembered Tuwanda had some experience with second-story escapes—she and MJ had once tied sheets together to enable us to escape from the upper bedroom of a house that had the bad manners to catch fire.

Tuwanda shinnied down the makeshift rope, and Beth followed at a much slower rate. As soon as Beth's feet hit the ground, Tuwanda shoved her into the backseat of my car and hurled herself in after.

"Go!" she ordered." Her voice sounded muffled because her face was smashed up against Beth's shoulder.

I took off, glancing nervously at my rearview mirror, expecting Webber to come out of the church any minute and give chase.

"What happened?" I asked breathlessly.

"We saw Webber comin' in as we was goin' out, so we ran up the steps and hid in a room at the top of the steps. It said, "Private," an' somethin' else I didn't understand, but it wasn't locked or nothin'. It was a nice-sized room with fancy robes and hats hangin' in glass cabinets an' on the wall. There was a bathroom off the room, which I thought was real convenient in case we had to hide out there for a while. Beth here had more immediate plans for it, though. The bathroom door was partly open an' she pushed it all the way open. Damned if there wasn't a man in there with nothin' but his boxers on."

"It was the priest," said Beth in a hoarse whisper. "We're going to hell."

"I already got a room assignment in hell, so it don't matter to me, but Beth, I'm real sorry if your chances at a heavenly life everlastin' is ruined," said Tuwanda sympathetically.

"What did he do when he saw you?" I asked, trying to forestall further thoughts and commentary on the hereafter.

"He screamed," said Beth miserably.

"Yeah, an' what he screamed wasn't too priestly," contributed Tuwanda.

"What did you do then?" I prompted before they took off on another theological discussion.

"Beth here's a quick thinker. She slammed the door shut and shoved one of them little rubber door stops under it," said Tuwanda proudly.

"I imprisoned a priest in a bathroom," Beth rephrased.

"That's when I looked out the window to see how much a drop it was to the sidewalk an' saw you hidin' in the bushes. I tol' Beth to start tying them robes together cuz' it was too far down to jump, an' then I got your attention an' told you to drive up to the side of the buildin'."

"You *yelled* out of the window. How come Webber didn't hear the priest or you yelling? He should have been trying to beat down the door by then."

Tuwanda shrugged. "I dunno. Them old building's got thick walls. Plus some guy started playin' an organ real loud so you pro'bly couldn't hear too much out in the hall."

"I made a rope out of priest vestments," said Beth dully.

I didn't hear any sirens, and the road behind us was clear of flashing lights, so I figured we made good on our escape.

"I'm going to go to buy us lunch," I said. "I think we'll all calm down once we've had something to eat. "Then maybe we can discuss what happened at the funeral."

Since I didn't hear any dissent from the backseat, I turned right on Central Avenue and headed for Durant's, a restaurant that has been around as long as anyone can remember and caters largely to a professional crowd. The interior is dark red, the booths are large and comfortable, the fare is basic Americana, and the bar is well-stocked. People in the know park in back and come through the kitchen to the main dining room.

Fifteen minutes later, we were sitting in a cozy, relatively isolated booth in the back of the restaurant. Tuwanda had ordered a bottle of wine when we were coming through the kitchen, so we were already sipping chardonnay as we scanned our menus. We would never be seated this fast during the mid-day rush, but at close to two o'clock, the restaurant, although still busy, was not as crowded as it no doubt had been an hour before.

Beth still looked glassy eyed, but I think the wine was helping. At least she'd stopped crossing herself and murmuring prayers of supplication for forgiveness. Still, I waited until we had ordered, our food had come, and the wine bottle was empty before I asked about the funeral.

"Dry as a bone," answered Tuwanda.

"How do you mean?" I asked.

"No one there except for Beth shed so much as one tear. The stepbrother—an' I'm guessing that's who he was 'cuz he thanked everyone for coming—kept lookin' at his watch. We mostly saw the back of everyone else's heads, but when the old guy with the cane got up to leave, I swear he looked like he was tryin' not to smile. The two women looked sad, but it was kind of an 'I lost my favorite pair of sunglasses' sad as opposed to 'someone I loved has died' sad. You know—no head shakin', cryin', holdin' each other or moanin'. Webber sat behind the four of them an' cleaned out his ears; puttin' our tax dollars to work. "

"Beth, did you recognize any of those people? Aside from Webber, that is," I asked softly.

"I recognized Mario, Maria's stepbrother. I haven't seen him in a long time, but, except for the gray hairs and a few more wrinkles, he looks the same as he did the last time I saw him, maybe thirty years ago at Maria's parents'—her adoptive parents'—house. She didn't talk about him, and I got the feeling they weren't close, or maybe even had a falling-out. Maria was the kind of person who liked to talk about people and what they were doing, especially her friends, but only if she had something good to say. The two women are Mario's twin daughters. Maria showed me their newspaper photos when they graduated from high school."

"What about the elderly man?" I prodded.

"He looked familiar, but I can't place him," she said, shaking her head rapidly, as if she was trying to wake up the dormant brain cell that held the information. It must have gone into hibernation, though, or maybe it was watching television.

"I know what you mean," said Tuwanda thoughtfully. "He looked kinda' familiar to me, too."

I tried to think of where Tuwanda's and Beth's lives could overlap in such a way that they both would recognize someone, other than a famous public figure who everybody with reasonably good eyesight would recognize. (Since I'd seen the guy myself, I knew he wasn't the latter).

I knew Tuwanda went to El Barrio every so often and knew Maria on a superficial basis. "Maybe you saw him at El Barrio," I suggested.

"Uh, uh. I don' think so," said Tuwanda. "Plus, he don' look like the kinda' man who goes to restaurants with no valet parkin.'"

Beth nodded in agreement as she distractedly chewed on a piece of roast beef. "I don't think it has anything to do with Maria—I mean, me thinking he's familiar. It's something else."

"I'll talk to Webber," I said. "He probably knows who the guy is."

"You gonna talk to Webber?" asked Tuwanda in amazement. "You mean, *intentionally* talk to Webber? An' he jus' gonna tell you whatever you wanna know, jus' like that?"

I smiled smugly. "I think I have a little leverage."

"You mean 'cuz you got his chil' stayin' with you? That's a nasty trick, even for a lawyer."

I shot Tuwanda a narrow-eyed look. "I'm not going to use Emily to blackmail him for information. I have an obligation to talk to him about the status of his daughter; other things may come up in the conversation."

"So you've gone from avoiding Webber to cozying up to him?" asked Beth, her disapproval clearly evident in her tone.

"I am not cozying up," I shot back, shuddering at an

unwanted image. "I've decided to manage the situation in a positive way instead of avoiding Webber, which seems to make him angrier and want to meddle even more.

"You think *Webber* is meddlin'? Kate, I think you oughta' take this self-awareness thing more to heart. You got some serious issues. You decide you can take care of his kid better 'an him, an' on top a' that, we stickin' our noses into his investigations, not that I mind that last part."

I opened my mouth to lash back, but then realized there was some truth—okay, a lot of truth—to what she said, so instead I said, "You're right. I've got to talk to Emily tonight. I haven't done much to get her to reconcile with her parents."

I suddenly felt unreasonably cranky. "Does anyone want dessert?" I said, throwing my napkin on the table.

"I'd like a night cap," said Beth.

I looked at my watch. "It's three in the afternoon," I pointed out. "You'll fall asleep at your desk."

"I didn't get much sleep last night. Could I have the rest of the day off?"

I chided myself for being insensitive. Beth had been through so much, and not just mentally; shinnying down a rope isn't easy at any age, so I could only imagine what it had been like for a sixty-three-year-old woman whose idea of exercise was to walk from her car to her front door.

"Of course, Beth," I said. "After you finish your drink, we'll drop you off at your house."

Beth and Tuwanda each ordered three fingers of Glenmorangie Scotch. I had a Diet Coke because I was the designated driver. After they finished, I paid the tab, and we headed out to the car.

I noticed that both Beth and Tuwanda were a little unsteady. "You guys doing okay?" I asked.

"Yes," said Beth, slurring a bit so it sounded more like "yesh."

Tuwanda did not bother to answer but got into the back seat and lay down.

After Beth got into the passenger seat, I buckled her in, during which process she grabbed my forearm and said, "I think God has forgiven me for defiling …" She seemed to have a problem coming up with the appropriate term for what she'd defiled and settled for, "all that shit."

"I'm sure she did," I said comfortingly, disengaging her hand from my arm.

Beth's husband was still en route to Phoenix and wouldn't be home until later that evening, but I managed to track down her godson, Duane (the security guard I'd met in the Goodwill Industries parking lot the night I was looking for Emily), through his employer, and he graciously offered to meet us at Beth's house. I thanked him profusely. Not only did I not want to leave Beth alone, but I was going to need help getting her into her house. She was pretty far gone.

Duane was kind enough not to ask any questions when his godmother greeted him with, "Hey, Duane. Long time no see. How they hangin'?" and then burst into tears and mumbled something about funerals and, "priests' private parts."

At that point, Tuwanda, who had fallen asleep before I left Durant's parking lot, woke up and yelled, "Keep it the hell down, or I'll call the manager." Seconds later, she was softly snoring again. I didn't want to disturb her again because Tuwanda does not take sleep interruption well at all, so when I reached my office, rationalizing that she should sleep some of the alcohol off before driving home anyway, I parked under a shade tree, opened all the car windows, and left her to continue her nap in the backseat.

My plan was to find out if I had any appointments scheduled (I had resisted getting a BlackBerry and still relied on Beth's calendar and my appointment book for such matters) and check on MJ and Sam. If my afternoon calendar was clear, I would maybe take the files for tomorrow's cases home with me and call it a day. I could defer waking Tuwanda until I was ready to leave, and if she still seemed woozy, I could drop her off at her apartment on my way home.

I got as far as Beth's desk when I heard a loud crash. It sounded like it came from MJ's office, so I hurried back and opened the door without knocking, afraid someone had been hurt. A china lemur flew by my head and shattered against the wall in back of me. Just as quickly as I'd opened the door, I slammed it shut.

"What is going on in there?" I yelled.

"I'm under attack," Sam shrieked. "She's crazy."

There was no question in my mind who "she" was.

"MJ," I intoned. "Stop it."

"He started it," she accused loudly.

"I'm coming in and there'd better not be any more flying lemurs, or any more flying anything for that matter," I said sternly.

I waited through a few beats of silence, and then went in.

MJ's office was in shambles. Open files spilled paper onto the floor, lemur fragments and potato chips littered every surface, and pens and books lay everywhere. MJ was holding an apple core, her arm locked in firing position. The smell of Lysol was heavy in the air. Sam was crouching on the floor behind his chair looking for a reload.

"What happened?" I demanded.

MJ lowered her arm but continued to glare at Sam. "He kept touching me—poking me with his finger!"

"I wasn't even near you. How the hell could I be touching you?" Then, appealing to me, but not taking his eyes off MJ's throwing hand, he said, "I was sitting on my side of the office working quietly on our skeleton girl case, and out of the blue she yelled at me to stop. When I asked her what I was supposed to stop, she threw a file at me."

"Yeah, and then he poked me *again*!" spat MJ.

"How, pray tell, could I possibly poke you from over here?" countered Sam.

I saw Sam's point. He would need six-foot arms to reach MJ from his chair.

"I don't know, but you *did*," said MJ, winding up for the pitch.

"Stop it, both of you! I don't care who did what. Clean

up this mess, and, Sam, come to my office when you're through and give me an update on the research project I gave you this morning."

I stomped to my office and slammed door behind me before either of them could further defend their respective positions.

The first thing I did was call Stu, whom I had seen neither hide nor tail of since Saturday. The call went into his voice mail, and I left a bristling message asking him to please repair the floor in Sam's office ASAP.

I had to take a few deep breaths to settle down before I could focus on work. I checked my schedule and saw that Beth had only written in one appointment for that afternoon and, thankfully, it wasn't until five. The appointment was with Roy McDougall, whom Beth, in her neat handwriting, described as, "a possible new client."

It's a damn good thing Mr. McDougall didn't show up early," I thought. *Flying china lemurs would make a heck of an impression—both literally and figuratively.* I absently rubbed a spot on my head that had been hit by a piece of lemur that had ricocheted off the wall—collateral damage of the war between MJ and Sam.

I wondered if Roy was a relation of the McDougall family who used to own this building, but I dismissed the idea as too much of a coincidence. McDougall wasn't exactly a common name, but it was not unique either. There had to be a fair number of them in a city the size of Phoenix.

I scanned the next day's schedule and made a list of the files I would need. Normally, Beth would stack the files on the corner of my desk after lunch so I could bring myself up to speed on whatever I needed to do the next day, but Beth was, of course, to put it politely, indisposed.

Just as I finished the list, I heard a light tap on the door and Sam entered.

"Finished so soon?" I asked.

"I think she's possessed," he said unresponsively.

I sighed and rubbed my temples. "I've had kind of a tough day, Sam. Let it go. I ..."

A thought occurred to me. *Possessed. No. It couldn't possibly be ...*

"Sam, is the air conditioning working okay in MJ's office?" I asked, motioning for him to sit down.

He looked surprised at this abrupt transition to maintenance issues. He took a few seconds to think about it, and then said, "Odd you should ask. I know you said you felt blasts of cold air in your office last weekend, but the air conditioning guy Beth called showed up earlier and everything checked out. Then when MJ was getting touchy, or, 'touched,' if you believe her version, I felt these weird currents of frigid air. Actually, currents isn't the right word. They weren't like breezes or blasts of air. More like sudden changes in temperature."

"What were you doing when the whole, er, situation with MJ started?" I asked.

"I was going through a list of people employed by

the Arizona Department of Health Services between 1950 and 1970. I wangled the information out of one of my friends who works in DHS's personnel department. Unfortunately, the records haven't been put into computer files yet, and many of them were handwritten by people either in a hurry or with lousy penmanship or both. I was trying to narrow the field to employees who worked in the children's social services area, including social workers. I had just mentioned an especially odd name to MJ when hostilities broke out."

"An odd name?"

"Adolph Heiler. I mean, most of the people around then had either fought in World War II or had family members who did. It was still pretty fresh in everyone's memory. If I had a name like Adolph Heiler, I would change it or live a quiet life in a remote area."

"In the fifties and sixties, Phoenix *was* a remote area," I reminded him.

"Still, the huge bump in population growth during that time was largely due to returning soldiers who were based in Phoenix at one point or another during the war—not exactly people who would appreciate a name like that," said Sam, not willing to concede the point.

"That and the invention of the air conditioner," I said, referring to Phoenix's post-World War II growth. "So what you're saying is anyone with the name Adolph had to have some serious personal issues?"

"Either that or he had tremendously thick skin," said Sam.

"Are there any Heilers listed in the phone book?" I asked.

"I haven't looked yet, but I'll search current listings for all the names soon as I complete my list of likely candidates," he said, fishing a piece of a potato chip out of his hair and flicking it into my wastebasket.

My cell phone rang. Normally I would ignore it during a meeting, but I saw Macy's name on the screen.

"I'm sorry, I need to take this," I said to Sam as I hit the "accept call" button.

Sam looked at me questioningly and mouthed *should I leave?* I shook my head and motioned for him to stay seated.

"Macy? Is everything okay?" I said into the phone.

"No, it isn't," answered Macy. "Before you get upset, Emily isn't hurt—at least not physically. But you gotta' come home and talk to your kid. She's got a problem."

"She's not my kid," I corrected, "and what's wrong?"

"This morning, we was talking, and I told her what a good job she was doing with the dogs. Then I mentioned how, when I was her age, all I wanted to do was hang out with my friends. I didn't want a job, and I sure as heck didn't want to hang out with adults. That got me to thinking. Even though I told her it was okay, Emily doesn't phone her friends or have any of 'em over, and hasn't asked for permission to go meet 'em somewhere.

"A little while ago, I went across the hall to my place to get something, and when I came back, Emily was doing something on your laptop. But she slammed the lid down as soon as she saw me. I asked her to take Ralph out for a walk earlier than usual because I thought he looked nervous. Of course the reason he looked nervous was because I stepped on his paw, and I apologize for that, but I needed a diversion.

"Anyway, after Emily left with Ralph, I checked to see what she was doing on the laptop. Her Facebook page was still open, and I read some of the comments people were posting. My daughter tells me parents gotta keep tabs on what their kids are doing on the Internet, so I figured it wasn't invasion of privacy so much as a safety check."

More like nosiness, I thought, remembering the time my mother read my diary.

"I copied out the page for you to see it. The comments are real mean, and most of them are by girls her age, if you believe the pictures on their pages. Sometimes weirdos use pictures of someone else to fool you into thinking that they aren't weirdos, so you can never be sure.

"Some of the comments about Emily are outright threats. You being a lawyer and all, I think Emily will trust you telling her it's libel or slander or whatever you call it, and she shouldn't stand for it. I'm a powerless old lady. She'll figure I'm out of touch and can't relate, and even if I'm not, which I'm not, what the heck can *I* do to help? At least you can sue them."

The problem is, you can't make a living out of suing mean girls, I thought.

"Shoot!" Macy's voice dropped to a whisper. "She's back. Katie, she looks so sad. You gotta talk to her."

I felt a tug at my heart and big wallop of guilt. Emily was going through a difficult time, and I wasn't providing her much emotional support. I wasn't even trying especially hard to encourage her and her parents into counseling.

"I'll be home in fifteen minutes, traffic willing," I said and ended the call.

"Sam, I need you to stand in for me at my five o'clock appointment. Beth's note says it's a prospective client. Apologize for me not being there, listen to what he needs help on, explain our specialty areas and billing practices ..."

Sam held up his hand palm out. "I know the drill," he said. The, looking down at his feet, added, "I guess I'd better lose the Jimmy Choos."

They were an elegant, strappy, gold pair. "I wish you and I wore the same size," I said, for probably the millionth time.

"I wish everyone was as open-minded as you," he said, standing. "Then not only I, but my shoes as well, could come out of the closet."

I grabbed my purse and hurriedly pulled the files for tomorrow's cases out of Beth's filing cabinet. As I exited through the front door, I heard MJ loudly accuse, "You were touching me again," and Sam, equally loudly, responded, "I was in Kate's office for God's sake. How the hell could I touch you?"

When I got to my car, I was momentarily startled to see a body in the backseat, then remembered I'd left

Tuwanda there. I wasn't looking forward to waking her up at what, in Tuwanda-time, was the middle of the night.

"Tuwanda," I whispered softly.

She didn't wake up, of course. Stronger measures were required.

I deposited the files and my purse in the passenger-side front seat and then opened the back door and prodded Tuwanda gently on the shoulder. I increased the pressure of my fingers when she did not respond until it was close to stabbing level.

"Whuh?" she said finally, lifting her head.

"Tuwanda, we're at my office. Do you feel like you can drive home, or should I drop you off?"

She raised her arm and looked at her watch. "What the hell. How long we been here?"

"About an hour. You've been in the car in the car sleeping."

She abruptly sat upright and fixed me with a flame-shooting glare. "You left me in the car?"

"I left the windows open," I said defensively.

"Next time why don' you tie me up in the backyard? You coulda' left me a damned bowl of water at least."

"I wanted to let you sleep," I countered. Now I was getting annoyed. *Hey,* I thought. *I was trying to be nice.* "Now, do you want to take your car, or should I drop you off?"

Tuwanda dropped back against the seat. "I think you better take me home with you. I can't go into work. I'm too tired. Marge can handle things for one night."

Marge was Tuwanda's über-efficient assistant. She could run a country; being in charge of Pole Polishers for one night would be a piece of cake. I was worried, though; in all the time I've known Tuwanda, she has never taken a day off.

"Are you okay?" I asked, concerned.

Tuwanda sighed and placed a hand over her eyes. "I dunno. This class I'm takin' is gettin' to me. I been wonderin' why I am who I am and why I do what I do. I need to think. I jus' need to get away an' think."

To my condo? "Tuwanda, you know you're welcome to stay with me, but I'm not sure how much thinking time you're going to get. Emily's living with me, remember. And what are you going to do with Walter?"

Walter was a good, well-trained dog, but even he couldn't hold it in for more than twenty-four hours.

"We better stop by my place and pick him up. An' you don' need to worry 'bout Emily bein' there. I don' wanna be alone, an' one more person in the room ain't gonna matter to me."

I wondered where I was going to put three people and two dogs in my small, one-bedroom condo, and I hoped Macy's spare bedroom was available again. At the rate I was going, I should probably start paying her rent.

By the time we got to her apartment, Tuwanda had started to doze off again, so I asked her for the key and told her to wait in the car while I went inside to get Walter.

"Don' forget to crack open the windows for me," she mumbled.

I found Walter sitting inside the door of her apartment. He looked especially sharp in the blue-and-white sailor suit Tuwanda had dressed him in that morning. I loved the little hat. I had once tried to put a little doggy business suit on Ralph, but he ate it. I haven't tried to dress him up since.

Walter was overjoyed to see Tuwanda and leaped into her lap as soon as the car door was open. Tuwanda cradled him in her arms and baby-talked to him nonstop during the trip to my condo. I like to think Ralph and I have a more mature relationship.

On the way up in the elevator, I explained what I knew of the situation with Emily, and told her I was going to need some alone time with Emily to talk it over.

"No problem," said Tuwanda. "Walter an' I'll go sleep in your bedroom an' leave you two alone.

"That's a real tough situation for Emily. Kids can be mean, especially girls. I'm thinkin' part of the problem is that Emily's real pretty. Lots of girls gave me a bad time in junior high 'cuz of my remarkable good looks, but I jus' beat 'em up when they did."

"I'm not going to recommend that approach to Emily," I said.

"Hell no. Ain't no such thing as a good knock-down these days. You slap a kid an' he'll pull a gun on you."

The scene inside my condo was not good. Emily was sitting on the couch with her knees drawn up to her chin and her head bowed. She didn't bother to look up when Tuwanda, Walter, and I came in. Ralph, however, who had been lying on the floor in front of Emily, jumped up and hurled himself excitedly at Tuwanda's legs. Tuwanda placed Walter on the floor, and the two dogs launched into a frenzied spate of butt sniffing, which I guess is their way of catching up. I could hear Macy in the kitchen rattling pans and knew we were in for a special treat for dinner—cooking is Macy's way of coping. Last fall, she had a fight with her daughter and ended up having a party for the whole building to get rid of all the food she made—which included an eight-tiered wedding cake. (It was a really bad fight.)

Tuwanda jerked her head toward my bedroom and mouthed, *good luck.* The dogs finished their greeting ritual and followed her. I got the feeling *I* was going to be the one sleeping in Macy's spare room.

After the bedroom door closed, I placed my files and purse on the coffee table, sat next to Emily, and stroked her back.

"Emily, what's wrong?" I asked softly.

She shook her head and then buried her face into the back of the couch.

"Macy told me about the Facebook comments," I said.

"She had no right to look at those," retorted Emily in a muffled voice.

"As your attorney, I'm telling you those people had no right to write what they did," I said in my business voice. "Further, I am advising you that, if you can identify who these people are, you can sue them for libel and slander."

Emily rolled her head sideways to look at me, and I saw a flash of hope in her eyes. The bleak stare returned quickly, though.

"Maybe what they're saying is true. And anyway, what good what it do? They'd hate me more." She turned away, but not in time to hide the tear rolling down her cheek.

"I'm sure that's not so," I said weakly.

I heard the kitchen door open, and Macy appeared in my line of vision. She looked almost as miserable as Emily did. She stopped next to the couch and mutely handed me several sheets of paper. I recognized the Facebook logo on the top page.

"Emily, do you mind if I look at these?" I asked, holding them up for Emily to see.

She rolled her head sideways again, glanced at them, shrugged, and hid her face in the cushion again. "It doesn't matter. Macy'll tell you what it says anyway." I heard a soft sob.

Actually, I thought the sob was a good sign. Seriously depressed folks don't cry. They have what psychiatrists refer to as a "mask of depression"—flat eyes and no expression. As soon as folks stop caring and hoping, the possibility of self-injury, the ultimate expression of which is suicide, becomes real.

My agitation grew as I read the pages until it evolved into full-blown rage.

"This is not only libelous. This amounts to criminal harassment," I said through gritted teeth. "Do your parents know about this?"

"No. If I told them, Dad would blame me, and Mom would tell me to tough it out, or at least she'd say, 'this too shall pass,' which basically means the same thing."

"Emily, I think you should talk to your parents," I said in a soft, pleading voice. "They're your family, and they love you very much."

She raised her head to look at me. "You're my family, too," she said, her voice wavering. The tears were coming fast now. "And Tuwanda, and Macy, and Ralph, and ... who's this?"

Walter, with the amazing empathy of pets, had recognized a person in distress. He'd jumped up next to Emily and offered his head for petting. Ralph, equally empathetic, lay on the floor in front of her, rolled over, and thumped his tail expectantly, as if to say, "I know you're sad, but if you scratch my stomach, all your problems will disappear."

"That's Walter, Tuwanda's dog," I said in response to Emily's query.

"I love his outfit! He looks like a little sailor," said Emily, gathering the small dog into her arms and lowering one of her feet to the floor to stroke Ralph's tummy with her toes.

I thought it was sweet she didn't forget about Ralph during the excitement of meeting a new dog.

Emily scratched Walter behind the ears, then gently removed his little hat and stroked his head.

Animals have a way of providing comfort to otherwise inconsolable people.

I didn't want to interrupt the moment, so I held my tongue a few beats before I spoke again. "We all love you, Emily. But if you added all our love together, it wouldn't amount to a fraction of how much your parents love you. The love of a mother and father for their child is the deepest, strongest, most unshakable form of love there is."

I felt my eyes swell up with emotion but then the distrustful, paranoid skeptic in my head crossed its arms and held forth. *That sounds like something you lifted from the last fifteen minutes of a Disney movie. You know damn well some parents abuse their kids, either emotionally or physically and sometimes both. Don't tell Emily her parents will be there for her because maybe they won't, and then she'll never trust you again, either.*

A more rational voice entered into the discussion. *You have no idea whether Webber and his wife are bad parents. That's for Emily and her parents and professional counselors and psychologists to figure out. You have no business inserting yourself into their lives.*

But both these voices were drowned out by my overwhelming compulsion to rescue people—as well as animals, for that matter. In Chicago, I once spent a frantic couple of hours trying to return a young bird to the nest out of which it had fallen. The bird came out okay, but the fire department had to come out and get me down from the tree I'd climbed and could not un-climb.

Not only do I have to rescue those whom I perceive as helpless—I also to have to put everything right that was wrong in the first place.

"Emily, dear," I continued softly, "we will support you no matter what and make sure you are safe. To help us do that, I would like to show the Facebook comments to Sister Mary Grace. I think she should know and the school should take action to control this kind of bullying."

Emily's body stiffened. "Please, please, please don't tell Sister. It'll make it worse," she hoarsely whispered. "Everyone will *really* hate me then. I'd have to go to a different school."

"What if this happens to someone else, though?" I said. "People like this won't stop hurting other people because one of their targets goes away. Bullying is how they exercise power and control over people; it's how they manage their universe. Also, I know this may sound like a contradiction, but the bullies need help, too. What they're doing comes from a sad, fearful, insecure place inside."

"How do you mean?"

I had her interest now. "I mean people who believe they are nothing unless they are popular, pretty, or have nice stuff—things that have nothing to do with a person's heart, soul, or character—are desperate to keep those things because without them, they have no substance."

Emily appeared to mull over this theory.

I heard Macy stir beside me, and I looked over my shoulder at her. She had tears in her eyes, and when she caught my glance, she gave me a thumbs-up.

I was glad for the positive reinforcement because I had not planned this speech and didn't know where the words were coming from. It's not that I didn't believe in what I was saying. On the contrary, I was surprised at the depth of the feelings that prompted me to say it.

"What do we do now, then?" asked Emily, hopefulness creeping back into her voice.

"We talk to Sister Mary Grace *and* your parents. Give the folks who care most about you a chance to help you."

"Sister cares?"

I detected scoffing in Emily's tone. I had tried to shelter Emily from the details of our skeleton matter, but I decided to tell her about my conversation with Sister Mary Grace, which I felt was evidence of her great caring. I explained to Emily how Sister had been so saddened by the discovery and told her about Sister's guilt over how she and her classmates treated a little girl in her class—a little girl she thought might be our skeleton.

Emily uncurled from her fetal position in a sudden motion that startled Ralph as both her feet landed on his stomach. Toe tummy-tickling was one thing. Full-on feet-to-tummy contact was an entirely different matter.

"Do you think she was murdered?" asked Emily excitedly, forgetting all about Facebook and mean girls, at least for the moment.

I shrugged. "We don't know. We've been focusing on trying to figure out who she is. It's up to the coroner's office to determine how she died—if they can." I was so thrilled that Emily was distracted from her problems that I was more than willing to pass on any information I had regarding our skeleton. Not that there was much to tell. It didn't seem like we'd come very far in our investigation.

I left out the parts about Venus and Maria, largely because I was embarrassed to mention the former and thought the connection between the skeleton and the latter might be too nuanced for Emily to comprehend. I told her about my suspicion that skeleton-girl had been part of the foster care system and the results of Sam's research thus far.

Emily furrowed her brow after I finished bringing her up to date on the investigation. "You really haven't found out much," she said critically.

She was definitely Webber's daughter.

"Is my dad trying to find out about her, too?" she asked.

I nodded my head and had to bite my tongue to keep from saying, "But he's not trying too hard."

She pursed her lips and looked thoughtful. "Dad is always busy and tired and angry at me. Maybe, if I can help you find out who the little girl is, he can relax. Maybe he even won't think I'm such a loser."

"You are not a loser," I said automatically. I knew, though, that anything I said had only a fraction of the power of a parent's opinion.

I didn't want to burst her balloon by telling her the last thing her father wanted was for people to butt into his job. But then I rationalized that maybe the investigation would give them something to talk about—or scream about—but at least communicate with each other. In my defense, I was exhausted when I came up with this theory.

"Maybe you could start by checking census forms from the fifties and sixties to find out who lived in my office building during that time," I suggested.

Emily raised an eyebrow, and I explained what censuses were and how you can find census information on the Internet. She caught on immediately and wanted to start her research right away, but I convinced her to wait until the next morning. In the meantime, we would eat dinner and then I would help her with her homework. (Emily said she was having trouble with geometry. I knew that geometry fell into the general category of math, but that was extent of my knowledge. I was hoping it would come back to me.)

An hour later, Emily, Macy, and I were sitting at the table in the small dining room off my living room. I didn't wake up Tuwanda because I value my life.

I was right about the meal. Macy's culinary coping strategy had resulted in matzo ball soup, two roasts (one beef and one pork), double-baked potatoes, corn soufflé (made from scratch and not out of a Stouffer's box), corn bread (also made from scratch), and knishes (ditto), and for dessert, a chocolate cake with two inches of frosting and *Emily Rocks* written in white icing on top. The selfish part of me hoped Macy's life became more of an emotional roller-coaster. My better instincts told the selfish part to go sit in the corner.

Macy entertained Emily with stories about growing up in Brooklyn. I'd heard the stories before, though, so my thoughts wandered to other matters while she talked.

While we ate and they talked, I mulled over the two cases. I was still disturbed by Maria's brief, impersonal funeral. It was as if her stepbrother wanted to push her under the carpet (or soil) and forget about her. According to Tuwanda and Beth, her eulogy had not included any recognition of her business and personal successes or the big hole her death left in the hearts of her friends and, for that matter, in the fabric of our community.

I wanted to know more about the stepbrother and his daughters—and the older man as well. I knew, of course, that Webber would also be looking into their backgrounds; their behavior was too weird to go unnoticed by even an emotional brick like him. But then, the danger of interfering with Bryan and Webber's investigation was becoming less and less important as my crusader instincts continued to beat back the opposing forces.

I was curious as heck to find out what the police had found thus far on Maria's case and that of skeleton-girl, and I was thinking of ways to get the information out of Webber without arousing his suspicion when Emily tapped on my shoulder.

Macy had disappeared into the kitchen to retrieve dessert plates, so we were alone. "I think I can find out what the police know about the little girl," whispered Emily.

The child is a mind-reader. I'd have to censor my thoughts as well as my language. "How?" I asked, stifling my alarm at such a prospect.

"I'll call my dad to let him know I'm okay and then I'll ask him."

It was, in a sense, ironic that a dead little girl, whom no one cared enough about to bury in a marked grave, might bring about the reconciliation of a present day girl with her parents, or at least the start of reconciliation.

"And he'll tell you? Just like that?"

"I'm giving you the gist of what I'm going to ask. How I ask it is way more complex," she said seriously.

When Macy returned, Emily clamped her mouth shut and gave me a "not now" shake of her head.

Together we polished off half the cake. As we were winding down and eating the last few bites of our respective slices, Tuwanda staggered in, caught sight of the cake, and glared at us accusingly. She then sat down and proceeded to consume the remaining half using my fork, which I had immediately surrendered to her when she growled, "Gimme that."

She finished the cake in record time and then went into the kitchen to see what she could find in the way of leftovers.

I grabbed the empty cake plates and took them into the kitchen. Tuwanda stood over the sink eating the last of the pork roast. The empty beef roast pan sat on the counter.

"Tuwanda, why don't you take that out to the table and sit down?" I suggested.

I ain't got time," she mumbled. "I got a schedule to keep."

"I thought you weren't going in to work."

"I wadn't," she said, spraying me with bits of roast. "My cell phone is what woke me. Marge's sick and ain't goin' in. If Marge ain't there, then I gotta be there. With us both out, my bid'ness is like a wheel without a hub. Marge and I are hubs. We can't operate hub-less.

I sighed. So much for a relaxing evening at home. "I'll get my keys," I said resignedly.

When we left, Macy and Emily were at the table staring intently at the screen of my laptop. I got a nod and a couple of distracted waves when I told them where I was going.

I dropped Tuwanda off at my office and politely waited until she was in her car, with her motor running before pulling out to leave. Then I noticed the light was on in MJ/Sam's office, so I stopped, backed, and parked again, thinking someone had probably forgotten to turn off the lights, and MJ was the more likely culprit since Sam was meticulous about saving energy. The front door was unlocked, though, so either one of them was not only careless but extremely careless, or he or she was working late—the latter being an uncommon occurrence indeed.

"MJ? Sam?" I called out, thinking maybe I should add, "Burglar?" to my list of inquiries.

"Kate?" answered Sam's voice. "What are you doing here?"

I flipped the switch for the lights in the reception area and headed for his temporary office. "I could ask the same of you," I said.

He wasn't in MJ's office though; he was across the hall in his own office. "Stu repaired the floor!" I said in surprise. This was fast work for Stu.

"Not exactly," he said, pointing down.

Someone had placed a large price of plywood over the hole. Sam had moved his desk and chair back in, shoving then up against the far wall, clear of the plywood.

"I picked the wood up this afternoon," Sam said by way of explanation. "I wasn't getting any work done in MJ's office. Even when she wasn't throwing food at me, the smell of French fries was overwhelming and distracting. And then she brought in a bag of pork rinds and …" Sam shuddered, unable to complete the sentence.

"Anyway, that's why I'm here; I'm trying to catch up on work."

"Any more air conditioning problems after I left this afternoon?" I asked.

"No. McDougall arrived less than ten minutes after you left, and since then I haven't felt any eccentric temperature changes."

I was seized by a sudden wariness, which made no sense at all. I attributed it to being overtired and a bit freaked out by the plywood, or rather what it covered.

"How did it go with McDougall?" I asked quickly, hoping Sam hadn't noticed my odd behavior.

If he had, he didn't let on. "It went okay," he said. "He's got a dispute with a neighbor over an easement on one of his properties. By the way, I didn't know he was the scion of *the* McDougall family."

"*The* McDougall family?" I asked, trying to ignore the fact that my wariness had grown into outright fear. "Are they related to the McDougall who owned this house?"

"He didn't mention anything about it, but it's possible. The McDougalls are an old Arizona ranching family. At least that's what they did until the sixties. Then they became developers and made a bundle from sub-dividing some of their ranches into residential lots and selling them to the newcomers. They still own a lot of land in this area. All those cotton fields west of town? Those are theirs.

"Even if the McDougalls held title to this house, with all the property they own, they might not have realized it. People like that hire managers and lawyers to take care of their assets."

I was not one of those people, but I'd met enough of them to know this was true.

"Roy, the guy who came in today, is the oldest member of the last generation of McDougalls," continued Sam. "He never got married and keeps a low profile. If you check the society pages of the newspaper, you'll see lots of pictures of the younger McDougalls—his brother's and sister's kids, though."

Sam paused and gave me strange look. "Kate, are you all right?"

No, I wasn't all right. I was terror stricken and unable to move from where I stood. I looked around wildly to see if maybe I'd caught sight of something out of the corner of my eye that could have triggered this.

"Maybe you'd better sit down, Kate. Sit here," he said standing and gesturing to his chair. When I didn't move, he rolled the chair over to me and nudged it against the back of my knees. I sat down stiffly and clutched its arms, my knuckles whitening. "Should I call a doctor?" asked Sam worriedly, bending over and placing his hand on my arm.

Then he straightened abruptly. "What the hell is that?" he asked.

I felt it too. The air was suddenly cold. Not, "oh gee, I need a sweater," cold, but down-jacket cold.

A thought occurred to me out of the blue—which was the color I was probably turning. I reached stiffly into my purse and took out my cell phone. After several tries, I hit the right icon and brought up one of the pictures I'd taken outside the church after Maria's funeral. I showed it to Sam, who was now leaning against his desk looking thoroughly nonplussed.

"Why do you have a picture of McDougall on your phone? I thought you didn't know him." he asked through teeth gritted against the cold.

The air warmed, and my feelings of terror vanished.

Without waiting for me to answer, Sam added, "I think we should call it a night and get the hell out of here. I'm calling that air conditioning guy back tomorrow. This is ridiculous. I will not work in a meat locker."

Although he blamed the air conditioning system, I could tell he was as freaked out. So was I.

We studied each other's ashen faces for a couple beats. The Sam grabbed my hands and pulled me out of the chair.

"Now!" he said. "We're leaving now. We'll talk about this in the morning."

I nodded mutely, and we fled the scene, leaving on all the lights and locking the doors behind us. Sam waited for me to get in my car. "Do you want me to follow you to make sure you get home safe?" he asked solicitously.

"No," I responded shakily. "Do you want me to follow you home to make sure *you're* safe?"

His teeth gleamed in the streetlight as he flashed me a big smile. I couldn't tell if it was forced or not, but I'd take it either way.

Chapter 15

When I got home, I found a note telling me Macy had taken Emily out for ice cream to reward her for finishing her homework.

I envy the ability of the young to eat anything and still fit into their jeans.

During the drive home, I hadn't let myself think about what had happened at the office, and I continued to block out the incident as I got ready for bed. *Thinking about it isn't going to do any good,* I told myself. *It's one of those things in life that doesn't make sense. Let it go, Williams.*

I crawled into bed, staying to the right because Walter and Ralph were hogging the left side. Amazingly, I fell asleep quickly, but it wasn't a deep sleep. All night, I floated between the land of dreams and the abyss of nightmares. I won't go into detail, but the latter involved irate lemurs, potato chips, talking floorboards, coffins, and cranky priests.

The next morning, the alarm woke me at six o'clock. The fact that I had intentionally set the alarm for that hour did not get the clock off the hook, though. I bashed it with my fist as if it had come up with the idea all by itself.

Still tired and not at all refreshed, I staggered out to the kitchen fully expecting to be the first one up, which meant, as if it weren't crappy enough on its own, that I would have to make my own coffee. I was wrong. The coffee was on, and Macy sat at the small kitchen table with a grim look on her face.

Based upon my years of experience of living with me, I poured myself a cup of coffee and took a gulp before risking a conversation.

"Is everything okay?" I asked, post-gulp.

"You'd better sit down," said Macy in an ominous tone.

I suddenly remembered that I hadn't seen Emily on the couch when I walked by. My legs gave out, and I fell into the chair more than sat. "Is it Emily? Is she all right?" I managed to get out.

"Emily's fine. She's asleep in my spare room. I figured she needed a break from the couch, and, since none of your friends was using it, she might as well have a night in a real bed."

I got the hint; I was using Macy's apartment as a hotel for my overflow guests. I really needed a bigger place.

I waited for Macy to light into me about taking advantage of her good will one too many times, but, to my surprise, she reached over and gently placed her hand over mine.

"We drove by DeRoys last night and saw Bryan in the parking lot," she said.

Rats. Bryan. He'd left a couple of phone messages for me yesterday, and I never got back to him. I completely sucked as a significant other.

"That's nice," I said, uncertainly, not sure where this was going.

"He was with someone," she said. Her expression was one of great sympathy. This was not good.

"Oh?"

"A tall yo ... I mean a tall brunette," she said softly.

I knew the word Macy was going to use before she stopped herself: young.

I felt as if I had been kicked in the stomach. I knew that Bryan and I were two very different people, but we had something good together, or I thought we did. We were both ambitious people with high principles who lived for our jobs. Never mind that our principles and jobs made us polar opposites.

As I stared at my coffee cup, trying to let what Macy had said sink in, Tuwanda walked in. I looked up, almost grateful for the distraction. Almost.

"How did you get in?" I asked peremptorily.

She held up a key. "I took Macy's key and had a copy made so's you wouldn't have to bother lettin' me in," she said.

"What makes you think I'm not bothered by you letting yourself in?" I countered.

Tuwanda gave me a hard look. "So what the hell you so touchy about today?" she asked.

Macy shook her head slightly and mouthed, "Not now."

Tuwanda looked from one to the other of us. "What's goin' on here?"

Macy mouthed, "Bryan."

"Oh for God's sake, Macy," I said. "I'm sitting right here. I can see what you're doing."

Tuwanda immediately sat down and crossed her arms on the table. "What about Bryan?" she asked.

"I saw him last night with a young ... I mean with a brunette," said Macy.

"So what? He was pro'bly meetin' with a colleague, or a witness, or somethin'."

I looked at Tuwanda gratefully. Maybe Macy had misread things.

"Colleagues don't play tonsil hockey," Macy said stubbornly.

Tuwanda smiled evilly. "Depends on what kinda' business you're in."

At this point, they must have realized that I had my head down on the table.

"Hell, Kate," said Tuwanda softly. "You know you too good for him. He's a persecutor ..."

"Prosecutor," I automatically corrected.

"Same thing," Tuwanda shot back. "Anyways, you an avengin' angel for the weak an' downtrodden. There ain't no middle ground between his philosophy an' yours."

"He's running for sheriff in the November election. His handlers think I'm a liability. I guess he does, too,"

I said morosely. "Avenging angels apparently make lousy girlfriends. He wants a nice, safe ... neutron."

"A what?" asked Tuwanda.

"It's that little thing inside an atom that is neither negatively nor positively charged. It just ... is."

Tuwanda tsk-tsked. "This is what happens when depressed people watch the *Discovery* channel."

"I like Bryan," said Macy. "I think, overall, he's a fine man. But in this situation, I'm taking the position that he's an asshole."

Tuwanda placed her hand over Macy's and mine in a show of solidarity that I found sweet.

After a few quiet moments of group pity for me, Macy said, "You should lift your head off the top of your coffee cup before you get a dent in your forehead."

I reluctantly raised my head. "Too late," said Tuwanda. "Rub it real good when you wash your face an' it'll pro'bly go away."

I stood and shuffled over to place my coffee cup in the sink.

"You don't want any breakfast?" asked Macy. "Not even more coffee?"

I shook my head. "I have three hearings this morning and two this afternoon, and I haven't looked at any of the files yet. I've got to get moving."

Before the kitchen door swung shut behind me, I heard Tuwanda say *sotto voce* to Macy, "Emotionally distraught with low blood sugar—that ain't a good combination at all. I hope she gonna' be okay."

I was tempted to defend my mental stability, but I couldn't work up the energy.

I dressed according to my mood: a black suit with black pumps and a black silk blouse. All I was missing was the black hat and veil. I stood and scowled at myself in the mirror, then went into the bathroom and added a few more layers of makeup.

People have often compared me to Christie Brinkley. But today I looked more like Morticia.

When I left, Macy and Tuwanda were gone. As I walked by Macy's condo, I could hear them inside laughing and talking with Emily. I found this annoying and thought, somewhat irrationally, that if they were truly good friends, they should be empathetic—and therefore as depressed as I.

Since I had picked up the case files for the morning hearings the day before, I had no reason to stop at the office. I drove downtown and parked in an exorbitantly priced parking place and then went into the courtroom where my first case would be heard. I slid into a bench in back to review my files.

Fortunately, none of the scheduled motion hearings involved complex matters. Despite my lousy frame of mind and low-key presentation, the judges hearing my cases that morning, while all taking their respective matters under advisement, indicated that their eventual rulings would be favorable to my clients.

At noon, I raced to my office. Beth handed me a sandwich that I ate hurriedly at my desk while I reviewed the files for my afternoon hearings. Although Bryan and I had made lunch plans the day before (apparently in happier times), since he had not called to confirm, I figured our mid-day date was off.

Beth looked worse than I felt, but she was back on the job and as efficient as ever.

Sam tried to catch me on my way out, and I told him he would have to wait until I got back from court to talk.

The afternoon hearings, both of which were in front of my nemesis, Judge Wiener, did not go as well as those in the morning. He was his usual grumpy, irrational self and accused the prosecutor and me of presenting the wrong case when it was he who was working off yesterday's calendar. He would, of course, not back down even in the face of fact, so I diplomatically asked that the hearing on our matter be accelerated, and he grudgingly acquiesced. (My theory, one that I would never share with the judge, was that his attitude was the result of a tortured childhood, and it would have been better for him and the rest of us if his parents had changed their last name before the young Wiener reached school age.)

I had planned to head back to my office once my hearings were over, but en route, I made a sharp turn into the parking lot of the *Phoenix Republic,* the primary local rag. The impetus for my spontaneous visit was two-fold: first, I wanted to buttonhole one of the editors and let him or her know in no uncertain terms that if the paper continued to use the woman-running-from-fire picture as a stock photo, I would sue them for every cent they had; and, second, I wanted to search the paper's archives for the twenty-year period from 1950 through 1970 for any mention of Lily Ignacio, (the little girl whose name Sister Mary Grace had given me), addresses at or near my building, Roy McDougall, Maria, or the Arizona Department of Health Services. A search this broad would be time consuming, and I wasn't likely to finish today. Plus, if the paper hadn't gotten around to scanning its archives from the fifties and sixties into a computer database, the search time would be significantly increased, and either I or Sam would need to come back another day to finish.

According to the receptionist, none of the editors on staff were available for a face-to-face meeting. However, she took no time to figure this out, and I got the feeling that my name was on the newspaper's "do not give this woman any information and pray she leaves right away" list. Conceding round one to the paper, I left a written message for the editor in chief to call me as soon as possible regarding a potential lawsuit. The receptionist placed it on top of a stack of other messages lying on her desk. I wondered how many of those were threats, too.

Upon my request, the receptionist pointed to a door at the end of the hall with a sign on it that read *Archives.* I could feel her eyes on my back as I walked down the hall. Inside the room, I was met by yet another receptionist: the poker-faced, humorless counterpart of the woman at the front desk. Receptionist number two led me to another room in the back where several microfiche machines were lined up on a high wooden table. Wooden stools sat in front of each machine—not the most comfortable arrangement. It was probably planned that way to discourage long-term visitors. A copy machine and a printer were located at the room's far end.

A microfiche search is not as inconvenient or messy as a manual search of newspaper hard copies, but it is about as time consuming.

Receptionist number two asked me if I had ever operated a microfiche before, and I assured her that I had.

I certainly had. As recently as fifteen years ago, storage of legal documents on microfiche was the height of technology and the method of choice in many county recorders' offices for storage of thousands of recorded real estate documents. While larger counties have converted almost all their files to searchable computer databases, some smaller counties have retained their microfiche systems due to the cost of converting their records.

The receptionist informed me prissily that if I intended to print out copies, the cost was fifty cents per copy, and she would need to hold a credit card to assure payment.

I figured I had discovered the paper's profit center. Fifty cents was a steep price for one lousy copy.

I didn't have a lot of leverage under the circumstances, so I handed her my American Express card.

"Visa or MasterCard only, please," she said, handing it back.

I rummaged around in my purse and produced a MasterCard. I rarely used it—I generally prefer the "pay as you go" method over the temptation of interest-only payments.

She disappeared into yet another room and returned a minute or so later with a stack of microfiche reels, which she placed next to the nearest machine.

Before she left the room she said, "Enjoy," which we both knew was an insincere suggestion and an impossible goal.

She's probably going back to her desk to do some Internet shopping with my credit card, I thought cynically.

I was surprised that she trusted me to be alone in the room. Most of the time, the folks in charge of these machines watch you like a hawk to make sure you don't try to slip one of the reels into your pocket. Then I glanced up and around and saw the lenses of several security cameras. So much for trust. I waved jauntily at the camera trained on my station and popped the first reel into the machine.

Although Phoenix had only two major daily newspapers during the period I was interested in, I chose to focus only on the *Republic* based upon the assumption that, since both it and its sister paper, the *Gazette,* (published in the afternoon), had the same publisher, their news coverage would be similar.

The McDougall name was mentioned frequently during this period but mostly in connection with civic and business matters that had nothing to do with the subjects I was interested in. I did learn, however, that the McDougall family had generously contributed to several charities, including a local orphanage operating under the name Southwest Children's Home.

It was already four o'clock; it had taken me slightly under two hours to skim through 1951 and 1952. At this rate, it was going to take at least a couple more days to finish. Maybe Sam, MJ, and I could divvy up the remaining research, and we could cover more ground in less time.

At the thought of Sam, I remembered I'd promised him that we would talk when I got back from court. He was probably wondering what had delayed me and was angry as heck that I hadn't called.

I sighed, hating to stop before I found anything of real value. I decided I'd better finish my review January of 1953, which I'd already started, then head out.

An item appearing in the January 28 issue caught my interest. According to the article, the good citizens of Phoenix were at the brink of riot when a large donor visiting a foster home run by the Southwest Children's Home discovered that "a white child was being housed in the same building as coloreds." A case worker for the Children's Home interviewed by the reporter explained that the error had occurred because of the Hispanic-sounding last name of the white girl. Regardless, members of the public on both sides of the racial barrier were highly offended, and the girl was immediately moved to another, presumably all-white, home. A follow-up article, on January 31, indicated that another major donor to the home, a member of the McDougall family, was looking into the problem and would make sure it would never happen again.

I remembered that Sam had seen the name Adolph Heiler on the list of Department of Health employees from the fifties, and I wrote the name of the case worker, A.D. Heiler, on a legal pad. I had no idea if Mr. Heiler had any connection to our skeleton, but if he was still alive, he might remember Maria's case worker. Phoenix was, after all, a relatively small town in the early fifties.

Chapter 16

I didn't make copies of the articles I found because I refused to give the *Republic* my pound of flesh for the privilege.

It was five thirty by the time I wrested my credit card from receptionist number two and drove back to the office.

Beth looked up from a pile of files when I entered.

"Judge Wiener hold you after school again?" she asked.

Judge Wiener was notorious for running late on his calendar.

"Not this time. He was unreasonable as usual, but he was unreasonable in a timely manner," I said, smiling ruefully. "I stopped off at the *Republic* to take a look at the archives."

"You still trying to figure out who our skeleton is?"

I nodded and thought, *among other things.*

I wasn't sure if Beth was up to talking about Maria's

murder yet, but I thought I'd give it a try. Because of her longtime relationship with Maria and the similarity of their early childhood circumstances, Beth might know more than she thought.

"By the way," I said. "Do you remember a case worker named Heiler from when you were in foster care?"

I figured this was an oblique enough question to start with.

Beth grunted dismissively. "He wasn't *a* case worker; he was *the* caseworker. The state didn't invest a lot in child services in those days. They had started to phase out orphanages and farm kids out to foster homes at that time. Kids like me and Maria weren't a priority. Not a lot of planning went into where we ended up. "

I remembered reading, in Sam's notes, about the transition from orphanages to foster homes in the fifties. "I guess the theory is that the children get more individual attention in foster homes," I commented.

"Maybe, but it also meant less state supervision," said Beth. "It's harder to keep tabs on a bunch of foster homes than it is to supervise one orphanage. There were lots of abuses in the system. Probably still are."

"You mean, like children being placed in homes with unfit parents?" I asked.

"I mean like kids being placed in homes with people who never intended to be parents in the first place— people who wanted household help or … other services. Some of those children were no more than slaves to their adoptive or foster families."

The thought sickened me, although I knew that this sort of thing was still going on today.

"Were you treated that way, Beth?" I asked softly.

"No. I was lucky. My parents were still alive and were going to come back for me once they got everything at immigration sorted out. But Maria ... after her mom died in prison—I'm thinking more and more that may be what happened to her. We kind of lost touch for a while, but I know she wasn't close to her adoptive family, and the times I was at her house, they treated her like a servant. But she never complained, so I thought maybe it was okay.

"Later, after she'd grown up and left her adoptive family, she changed her name from Batista back to her birth name.

"It's sad, because even after she became a successful businesswoman, there was a part of Maria that seemed beaten down and scared, and she never talked about her years with the Batista family. I think that's why she worked so hard—she had a lot of bad memories to forget."

I felt a prick of anger that Maria had been treated so poorly both in life and in death by the Batista clan.

"I think she got the last laugh, though," continued Beth. "Before she died, she wrote up a will leaving everything to the Foster Care Association. That's the group that buys clothes and school supplies for foster kids and gives them money for things like summer camp. If not for that will, everything would go to her stepbrother."

"How did you find out about the will?" I asked curiously.

"Gilberto, the cook over at Barrio's told me. He said the police found it in her safe at the restaurant."

"You talked to Gilberto?"

"Yes. I called him today. I'm organizing a memorial for Maria at my church for next Saturday, and I'm inviting everyone I can think of."

"Good for you!" I said enthusiastically. "Please let me know what I can do to help."

"You're helping me enough by paying my salary while I arrange a memorial service instead of working," she said sheepishly.

I patted her shoulder. "MJ, Sam, and I will pitch in with the filing and docketing. You do what you need to do."

I started to walk to my office, then thought of something else. "Did Bryan call today?" I asked with forced nonchalance.

Beth looked at me sympathetically and shook her head.

Oh heck, I thought. *She knows. Tuwanda probably called her. Or maybe she picked up the sound waves when Macy told me this morning.* I wouldn't put it past her. Beth, like MJ, has radar hearing.

I realized, of course, that if Beth knew about the Bryan situation, so did MJ and Sam. There is no such thing as a secret in this office.

Even though, technically, it was my turn to call since I hadn't returned Bryan's two previous calls, I wasn't about to make the first move. If he wanted to break up with me, he'd have to man up and do it face to face. I wasn't going to make it easy on him by confronting him over the phone. I wanted him to be within striking distance when he told me.

I dropped my briefcase off in my office and went to see Sam, feeling guilty that I had blown off our earlier meeting to do research in the newspaper archives.

The plywood in Sam's office was still there, and his desk was still pushed up against the wall, but he'd managed to fit another chair into the remaining useable space.

I made my apologies for being so late for our meeting and asked if he had gotten hold of the air conditioning guy.

"He insists there's nothing wrong with the system and suggested that I go see a doctor because chills are a sign of illness. He mentioned liver disease as a possibility. I think he was projecting. He looked like a drinker."

I sat in the extra chair and looked across the desk at Sam. After weighing what I was about to ask, I took the plunge. "Sam, is it possible we're surrounded by spirits of the dead?"

"You mean, do I believe in ghosts?"

I thought his tone was unnecessarily mocking.

"Yes," I said firmly. "That's another way of putting it."

"I think Venus and Tuwanda are getting to you," he said, running has hand over his face.

"How do you explain how Venus knew who murdered Mitchell Alvarez?" I asked, referring to a previous case where Venus had discovered information she couldn't possibly have gotten from anyone else but the victim.

"She's incredibly intuitive, I'll hand her that. But I

don't think she's a ghost whisperer," said Sam. "And as for what happened last night, I think it was late, we were both tired, and, regardless of what Adam and Eve's Plumbing, Heating, and Air Conditioning Service says, we have a duct problem."

"Adam and Eve?" I asked, temporarily distracted.

"Yeah. Their ad says, 'Providing good service since the beginning of time; ask us about our snake.'"

"Maybe we should get a second opinion on the air conditioning issue," I commented. "But you have to admit, you were freaked out last night, too."

"I was freaked out because *you* were freaked out," said Sam. "You should have seen the look on your face. You looked like you'd seen a ghost." Then, catching himself, he said, "Let me rephrase that."

I continued to push the topic of weirdness. "Don't you think it was a huge coincidence that Roy McDougall was at Maria's funeral and then showed up here for a meeting the same afternoon?"

"Maybe McDougall saw your name in the paper in the article about Maria and thought, 'hey, maybe I should hire her to handle my easement issue.'"

"Do you think it was the naked woman running from fire photo that hooked him?" I asked sardonically.

"So what do *you* think—that the guy buried the kid under our floor, then years later kills Maria on a whim, immediately after which, to tie up loose ends, he sues his neighbor over an easement dispute? What's the connection? What's his motive?"

"I don't know yet," I said, sighing in exasperation. "I can't explain it. I have this feeling."

"What feeling? I think you and MJ need to go to a psychiatrist. You're both imagining things."

I thought his comments were tremendously unfair, not to mention unkind. In any event, it was clear that this discussion was going nowhere. "Let's get off the subject of the supernatural," I said.

"*You* brought it up in the first place."

"I know, I know. So let's talk about the status of the investigations you're working on," I said, silently wondering why Sam was so testy about the subject of ghosts. Maybe he was more disturbed than he let on about what had happened last night, and maybe at a sub-conscious level he, too, thought there was something other-worldly about the whole thing. But, then again, it was also perfectly possible that he thought I was a nut.

Sam brought me up to speed on several matters he was working on, most of them involving cases scheduled for trial in the near future. I made a few suggestions, and Sam conscientiously took notes.

When we got to Roy McDougall's case, Sam ran through a list of issues and research ideas.

"By the way—did you know that McDougall's family *did* own this house?" he asked, then quickly added, "And don't get started again. The guy is a paying client. Leave it alone."

But I wasn't about to leave it alone. I told Sam about the connection I'd discovered in the newspaper archives between the McDougall family and the orphanage and foster homes operating in the fifties.

"The McDougall family has been involved in charities for years. A wing of the Scottsdale Civic center is named after them, they've got a hospital in Glendale named after them, the African Veldt exhibit at the zoo was donated by them, they …"

"I get the point," I interrupted him testily. Then I told him the name of the social worker I had found in the article about the misplaced Caucasian girl.

"So this is what we have so far: we think we can fix the age of the skeleton by reference to the Betsy Wetsy doll, and Maria said she had information about our skeleton, but was shot before she could tell me." I held up my hand as Sam started to protest, and I said, "I'm not saying there's a connection. I'm only telling you what we know.

"Next, Sister Mary Grace gave us the name of a young girl to check out, and … wait a minute." I remembered I'd given the Ignacio file to MJ. "MJ," I called out. Are you still here?"

"Who wants to know?" MJ called back.

"*I* do. Could you come into Sam's office? We're discussing skeleton girl."

There was a pause and then I heard a series of scraping and bumping noises, and MJ came in, pushing her chair in front of her. She parked it just inside the door and sat down. "I'm not getting anywhere near that man," she glowered.

Sam looked up at the ceiling and moaned, "Gawd.

Give some serious thought to the psychiatrist, Kate. Maybe you and MJ can get a group rate."

I ignored his comment and asked MJ if she'd had a chance to look at the Lily Ignacio file.

"Yeah," she said, fixing Sam with a hate-glare. "It looks like she lived in a foster home."

MJ, who is into seasonal coloring, had dyed her hair pastel purple the night before and was wearing a matching lavender miniskirt and a purple Def Jam T-shirt. She looked like an overweight Popsicle.

"So Lily was in *foster care*," I said, shooting Sam a triumphant look. "Did the file say who her biological parents were?"

"Deceased," said MJ.

"What about the name of her foster family and their address?"

Nothing. The phone number listed was for someone named A.D. Heiler. I looked up the address an old directory, and, at the time, it was the location of the Southwest Children's Home."

I felt a twinge of excitement and threw Sam another significant glance. "'A' as in Adolph? I bet that's the same DHS employee you saw listed in the personnel records. Beth said Heiler was the name of the social worker assigned to the foster home where Maria was placed *and* A.D. Heiler was the name of the social worker mentioned in the newspaper article I told you about."

Things were clicking into place—not a lot of things, but enough to reassure me that I was headed in the right direction. Whoever this Heiler guy was, if he was still alive, I needed to find him.

"Was there any other information of interest in the file, MJ?" I asked.

"Some handwritten reports from different teachers. Lily got high marks for being quiet, studious, and polite. But one report—by a teacher named Sister Mary Margaret—raised concerns about Lily's failure to make friends or fit in. She described Lily as 'remote and seemingly without affect.' She also mentions—in a nice way—that the foster mother was a bit overprotective."

This corresponded with what Sister Mary Grace had said about the little girl and her mother.

"The reports end after a few months," continued MJ, "and the last thing in the file is a signed slip withdrawing Lily from the school. The reason given was relocation of the child to a different home."

I turned this information over in my mind. "Beth mentioned a girl in her foster home—the same one Maria was in. Based on what Beth and Sister Mary Grace said, I think she might be the same girl who attended Our Mother of Perpetual Succor. Beth and Maria wouldn't have gone to the school, because the school was whites only at the time."

Then I told MJ about the article I'd read about the uproar over the discovery of a white child staying in the same home with people of color. "Do you think it's possible it's the same child?"

"Could be. But even if she is, that doesn't get us anywhere," said Sam.

What a wet blanket.

"It does too," I said, not bothering to hide my irritation. "Lily Ignacio was a white child with a Spanish name. The article I read said that was the reason the Department of Health Services gave for the confusion. I'm going to broaden my search of the newspaper archives to include any follow-up articles that tie the child to our address or mention McDougall or Heiler again."

I was really heating up now.

"*You* may think it's a friggin' *coincidence* that McDougall goes to Maria's funeral and then shows up here the next afternoon. And you may blame the frigid air and the skin-touching sensations on MJ's imagination, my paranoia, and the damned air conditioning, but I *don't*. Either you can cooperate with this investigation or you can get the hell off of it."

Sam and MJ looked at me in shock. I had never exhibited this level of anger in front of them before. (Well, maybe once—but that wasn't my fault. I had accidently taken some LSD, thinking it was aspirin. I don't remember much of what happened, but Beth, MJ, and Sam reported afterward that I was fairly out of control.)

"Where did *that* come from?" Sam asked in a stricken voice.

To tell the truth, I didn't know where it came from.

"Did you take any more aspirin?" asked Sam, making quotation marks in the air around the work "aspirin."

"No!" I said, shrugging helplessly. "It's like what happened last night, only then I felt terrified instead of angry. I don't seem to have control over my emotions anymore."

A meaningful look passed between Sam and MJ.

"Maybe you should, er, get your hormone levels checked out," suggested Sam in a kind voice.

"I am *not* menopausal!" I yelled. First Bryan took up with a younger woman, and now my staff was more or less implying I was old. No wonder I was angry.

"I will schedule a couple of hours to help you search the archives tomorrow," said MJ in a soft, "Let's placate the crazy lady," voice.

"I will too," volunteered Sam, adopting the same tone.

I glared exasperatedly at them in turn. They stared back at me implacably. After a few beats, I relented and went in a different direction. "Great," I said clapping my hands together enthusiastically. "We've got eighteen years to cover—1953 through 1970—so that gives us six years each. Since I've already started on 1953, I'll take 1953 through 1958. MJ, you take 1959 through 1964, and Sam, you take the rest. I'll give you a list of the information I'm looking for tomorrow morning.

"Now, unless anyone has anything more to say, I think this meeting is over."

Sam and MJ shook their heads to indicate they sure as heck didn't have anything more to add to the conversation.

As I walked out the door, I heard MJ say, "I was *not* imagining the touching thing, you asshole."

When I glanced at my watch and saw the time, I

picked up the pace and quickly grabbed my briefcase and the files Beth had left on the corner of my desk with a copy of tomorrow's schedule. It was six thirty, and I hadn't checked in with Macy all day. For the thousandth time that week, I chided myself for being a bad child caretaker and a worse friend.

I needn't have worried. When I got home I found every surface of my living room covered with fabrics, patterns, scissors, and fashion magazines. A basket full of tape measures, pins, thread, and needles was perched on the coffee table. Macy and Emily were sitting on the floor looking at one of the magazines. Walter and Ralph were on the couch, eying the scene with interest.

"Hey, doll," said Macy, looking up. "We're designing fashions."

"Now I don't have to be restricted by current fashion," bubbled Emily. "I can express who I am through the clothes I wear."

"Cool," I said weakly. I inspected the fabric more carefully and saw, with a sinking feeling, that black was the dominant color. If white makeup and black lipstick were part of the plan, she was going Goth.

"What happened to the guitar lessons?" I asked, hoping to raise the possibility of a safer alternative.

"Too loud," said Macy. "By the way, you got a notice from the homeowners' association about that. It was stuck to your door. It mentioned the guitar and something about dogs barking, too. I personally think they're infringing on your First Amendment rights."

Or those of the dogs, I thought, wondering what penance the HOA would exact for the noise control violations.

"By the way, I checked census records for 1940, 1950, 1960, and 1970 for Phoenix," said Emily proudly. "Your office address only shows up in the 1950 census. A woman, Marci or Marcia Ratomski—it was hard to read the handwriting—lived there alone."

"Excellent job, Emily," I said enthusiastically. "That was a lot of work."

"Macy helped," she said humbly.

"Macy didn't help much, doll," said Macy. "My eyesight is crap, and those census records are written by people unfamiliar with the English alphabet."

I put my briefcase and files on the dining table and sat on the couch, using a right-to-left butt-shove to make space between Walter and Ralph.

We sat in companionable silence for a while, and I watched as Macy and Emily flipped through magazines.

"I talked to my dad today," said Emily casually, putting an end to our quiet time.

"Emily, that's wonderful!" I said. Regardless of how their conversation went, the fact that they were speaking was good news.

I wanted to know what Emily and her dad talked about, but I didn't want to pry. But a general inquiry could hardly be considered prying, right? "Did it go okay?" I asked.

"Yeah. I told him about being suspended from school," she said.

"I'm proud of you Emily. That was a tough thing to do," I said encouragingly, reaching out and gently pushing her hair out of her eyes.

Ralph leaned into me and nudged my shoulder with his nose as if to say, "Why are you petting *her* when I'm sitting *right here.*"

"He was really upset," said Emily without meeting my eyes. "I asked him about your office skeleton too."

That must have been an interesting segue, I thought. I didn't press her for details though. I was leaving it to Emily to decide how much say.

"First, he wondered how I knew about it, and I told him I saw it on the Internet, which is true." She looked at me for affirmation.

I nodded and kept my expression neutral.

"He said the lab guys confirmed it was the skeleton of a young female, between nine and twelve years old and figured the bones were fifty to sixty years old." Her voice had become official-sounding, and I knew she was mimicking her dad.

This meant our archival search-time would be cut in half. I would have to remember to tell MJ and Sam.

Emily's eyes slid away from me. "He said they didn't find any signs of injury, but all they have are bones. It doesn't mean she wasn't hurt in some way that wouldn't show up in the bones." Emily gulped before continuing, and I could tell she was struggling to hold back tears. "He said that's what happens when girls run away from home; they get hurt and some get killed."

That brought me up short. I didn't want to interfere in Webber's relationship with his daughter (at least not any more than I already had), but scaring Emily like that was wrong.

Macy did not share my reservations about interfering. She looked up from her magazine and said, "What kind of a thing is that to say? You're staying here, and nothing bad is gonna happen to you here."

"How does he even know she was a runaway?" I blurted out in violation of my non-interference rule.

Emily shook her head miserably. "I don't know exactly. He said they'd found out from someone named McDougall that the house was leased by three different families between 1950 and 1960, and none of them had children. So I guess he thinks she had to be a runaway."

If that was the case, he'd stretched logic pretty far.

"Did he mention the names of any of the families who rented the house?" I couldn't help myself. It wasn't the best form to milk Emily for details about the skeleton case when she was in such a fragile emotional state, but I had to know.

The question seemed to have a positive effect on Emily, though, because she lifted her head, brushed away a tear, and said, "No, but I bet we could track down this McDougall guy and ask him."

We? Apparently Emily considered herself a part of my investigation team. Heck, if it distracted her from her personal problems, I was all for it. I would draw the line at unsupervised field work, however. Beth and Tuwanda sneaking into churches and climbing out of windows was bad enough. I didn't need another burgeoning V.I. Warshawski working for me.

"Emily, would you like to go to my office with me tomorrow?" I asked. "We can meet with MJ and Sam, and you can tell them about what you learned. Then we can get a game plan for where we take the investigation next."

"Yes!" Emily said, her eyes clearing. But then she looked at Macy, "I mean, if that's okay with you, Macy. We can maybe do the sewing the next day."

That answered another question. Emily's conversation with her dad didn't result in plans for a homecoming, at least not one in the near future.

"No problem, sweetie," said Macy, reaching over to pat Emily's hand. "In fact, as much as I love bein' with you, I could probably use some time to catch up on housework."

And sleep, I thought sympathetically. Macy wasn't used to keeping up with a teenager. Neither, for that matter, was I.

"Are you guys interested in going out for pizza?" I asked.

"Yes!" answered Emily. "Can we take the magazines with us and go over which outfits express my inner light so I can embrace my differences?"

She'd either been talking to Tuwanda or watching too much Oprah. Either way, I was surrounded by people engaged in self-realization. I was too reality-bound to put stock in such things, but if it helped Emily and Tuwanda, more power to them.

A voice shouted out in contradiction from the deep recesses of my brain. *You don't want to remember anything that happened to you, but you're helpless to forget.*

I told the voice to shut up and shoved the memories responsible for the outburst back into the walled-off section of my brain from which they'd escaped.

Chapter 17

After dining on pizza with extra sauce and extra cheese (nice and stringy when you pull it apart), and Diet Sprite for Emily, scotch for Macy, and chardonnay for me, we spent a peaceful evening looking at fashion magazines, with each of us circling our favorite outfits in a different color. The outcome was foreseeable for the most part: I tended toward St. John suits and J. Crew blouses and skirts, and Emily liked anything worn by Kristen Stewart, who, Emily patiently informed me, plays Bella, the female lead in *The Twilight* movies. Macy was the wild card. She went for what I would call the "underwear used as outerwear" line of fashion: skin-tight dresses the size of a hand towel showing lots of leg and lots of cleavage—or "chest-wrinkles," to use Emily's jargon. I don't know how Emily handled it, but the image of Macy in those dresses disturbed me. Think Danny DeVito wearing a wig.

The next morning, we left Macy in charge of Walter

and Ralph. Tuwanda had dropped off some more of Walter's clothes, and today he was wearing a green jogging suit. Emily and I went to my office. In honor of the occasion, Emily was wearing a denim skirt and one of my silk blouses that was so large on her she could have done without the skirt and worn it as a dress. Her professional image was somewhat marred by her Sketcher tennis shoes, but in my office, with MJ in Doc Martens most of the time and Sam in women's heels, she would fit right in. At least it wasn't Friday. MJ's idea of casual Friday was more like, "show up dressed as your favorite Tim Burton character" day. I didn't think Emily was ready for that.

Beth was thrilled to see Emily again and immediately launched into grandmother mode, asking Emily what kind of cookies she would like and whether she preferred lemonade or milk. MJ emerged from her office, probably because she heard cookies mentioned, followed shortly by Sam, who was probably wondering what MJ was up to. MJ wore a tight hot pink T-shirt with *Goddess* printed on the front, a yellow, polka-dot miniskirt, a bicycle chain necklace, and ankle-high steel-toed boots. As a nod to the warmer weather, she was bare legged. She'd dyed her hair again, and today it was black with pink highlights that coordinated nicely with her shirt—as did the nose ring, from which dangled a pink enamel flower charm. Sam was wearing a navy Brooks Brothers suit and red, strappy high-heeled sandals. I noticed he'd painted his toenails to match the shoes.

MJ pulled up short upon catching sight of Emily. "New legal associate?" she asked. "You know if you paid better you could probably find an adult willing to work here."

As opposed to you? I thought.

Sam stepped in front of MJ and extended his hand. "Hi," he said. "I'm Sam." Head-cocking toward MJ, he added. "This is MJ, the village idiot. Beth, why don't you give MJ your keys to play with so she doesn't bother us?"

This of course earned Sam a slap upside the head from MJ.

"Ignore him. He has PMS," said MJ.

I hadn't warned Emily about my unusual staff. She wouldn't have believed me anyway. Her expression had gone from one of mild shock to one indicating a desperate effort to stifle giggles.

"Hi. I'm Emily," she said, shaking first Sam's hand and then MJ's.

"Hey, you're Webber's kid, right?" said MJ.

Emily nodded, and I prepared to intervene, expecting a snide remark from MJ about Emily's heritage. To my surprise and gratitude, though, she said, "Cool," and left it at that.

"Emily, would you mind waiting out here while MJ, Sam, and I discuss the status of our current cases?" I asked. "I'll leave the skeleton case until last, and come and get you before we start."

"Sure. I brought a stack of typing paper and pencils to make fashion drawings," said Emily, motioning at her backpack. "That'll keep me busy and off the streets and out of sex n' drugs n' stuff."

Her delivery was straight-faced, but her tone was teasing.

MJ guffawed. "You're okay, kid," she said. "By the way, if you need pointers on fashion, I'll be glad to offer instruction and guidance over lunch." Looking at me, she said, "I assume Kate will be taking us out for Mexican food around noon."

I hadn't planned on treating my staff to lunch and wasn't at all sure exposing Emily to MJ's fashion advice was a good idea—actually, I thought it was a very bad idea—but I didn't want to ruin Emily's image of me as a kind, tolerant human being by strangling MJ in front of her. (Not that this was the image she had of me, but it was certainly the image I wanted her to have.) So I smiled ambiguously and shepherded Sam and MJ toward my office.

As soon as the door to my office closed behind us, Sam said, "Oh for God's sake, MJ, don't scare the child like that."

"What did I do to scare her?" snapped MJ.

"You exist," Sam shot back.

MJ responded by raising her middle finger. I ignored their behavior and gestured for them to sit.

"So why are we having another status meeting?" MJ asked after she plopped down in a comfy armchair. "We went over everything last night. And what's the deal with calling Emily in to discuss the skeleton case?"

I told them what Webber had said to his daughter about the status of the police investigation and touched lightly on Emily's difficulties with her classmates and why she needed a distraction.

"Girls that age can be such bitches," MJ commented with feeling. It sounded as though she had experience with the matter.

"So can boys," added Sam, nodding energetically in agreement with MJ's assessment—probably for the same reason.

"I'll get Emily, and we can go over what we've found out so far. Since our search period has been cut in half, you guys can split the work between the two of you."

I trotted out to get Emily and returned with her a minute later. She had what I suspected were cookie crumbs on her chin. I was jealous because Beth had cut off my supply pending a weigh-in.

Sam politely gave Emily his chair and sat on a small couch against the back wall.

I summarized where we were in the investigation, including the information Emily had gotten from her father. When I was finished, Sam raised his hand.

"Yes, Sam?" I felt like a classroom teacher.

"I found out something else this morning. Remember that friend of mine at the Department of Health Services? He looked up Adolph Heiler's personnel file, and it turns out the guy is still alive. His retirement payments are being sent to The Pearly Gates Home for the Elderly on Glendale Road and Thirty-Fifth Avenue. I Googled it and you'll never guess the name of the biggest contributor to the Home: The McDougall Family Trust!" he proclaimed, looking smug.

"That's wonderful!" I said enthusiastically.

"What: that Adolph is still alive or McDougall is a very giving man?" grumped MJ.

I knew she was mad because Sam—and not she—had discovered these nuggets of information.

"Emily, do you want to come with me and see if we can talk to Mr. Heiler?" I figured this was a safe plan. *What could happen to us in an old folks' home?*

Emily, who had been sitting quietly staring at her hands ever since she finished her part of the presentation, looked up. Her empty-eyed stare was unsettling. It was if she were looking through, not at, me. "He's a bad man," she said, her voice hollow.

Sam, MJ, and I looked at each other worriedly.

"We don't know that, Emily," I said softly. "For now I would like to find out if Mr. Heiler remembers if a child, who was likely part of the foster care system lived, here or near here between 1950 and 1960. He may not remember anything."

"Or can't," said Sam. "The Pearly Gates is an assisted care facility, and they've got a floor for residents with dementia or Alzheimer's. The place is not cheap, by the way. Even with state funding and charitable contributions, it costs ten thousand a month, minimum, to stay there."

I looked at Emily, who still seemed to be out of it. "Are you okay, sweetie?"

The Emily I knew reappeared in the eyes of the young girl staring at me. "*That* was weird," she said in her Emily-voice. "Hey, can I see where you found the skeleton before we go visit Mr. Heiler?"

I nodded, relieved to hear what was a normal request for a curious thirteen-year-old.

I asked Sam to act as tour guide. Before he and Emily left my office, I instructed MJ and Sam to do their best to review the remaining archives by noon.

"What time we will meet at Paco's for lunch?" said MJ.

"Noon. My treat," I said, caving in, even though I knew I shouldn't encourage MJ in this regard. The woman has never picked up the tab in all the time I've known her.

As I went in search of Beth, MJ, Sam, and Emily left to take a gander at the plywood sheet covering the hole in Sam's office floor. Although MJ had seen it before, the encounter was a brief because Sam wouldn't let MJ into his office until she submitted to a search for weapons. He even made her leave a package of potato chips outside.

I found Beth in the kitchen stirring a bowl of cookie dough. I looked at her hopefully.

"Uh, uh. No. These are for Emily. You're on a diet," she said.

"I am *not* on a diet."

"Are you trying to tell me your clothes aren't getting tight on you?" she asked, head-jerking toward my skirt.

I adjusted my jacket to cover the button I hadn't quite been able to get closed that morning. "No," I lied.

"You have an addiction, and I'm not going be an enabler anymore," she asserted firmly. "You're like a little child when it comes to cookies."

I came close to throwing a tantrum, but I restrained myself because it wouldn't have done much to build a case in my favor. Instead, I changed the subject to the skeleton girl in my office, and asked if she remembered if a little girl named Lily had ever lived in the foster home with her and Maria. She stopped stirring and pursed her lips. "Lily? Let me think."

I selfishly wondered why she couldn't stir and think at the same time. I was salivating in anticipation of fresh-baked cookies.

"I remember a girl—Leah or Linda—yes, it could be Lily. I remember her because she was white. She wasn't at the home long, though. One day a group of people came in to tour the foster home—and see us, I guess. I remember feeling real uncomfortable. They all but pinched our arms to see what we were made of. Afterward they stood out on the front yard talking loudly. They seemed agitated about something. The next day, the sheriff, Mr. Heiler, and a well-dressed guy came and took her away. We thought she'd done something wrong, but our foster mom explained she was just going ... my dear lord in heaven!"

I checked nervously to make sure nothing bad had befallen the cookie dough—like maybe an insect flew in or something—to bring about this remark. (Cookies are still my number-one priority, despite being presently classified as forbidden fruit). Once I was reassured the dough was unmolested, I asked Beth what was wrong.

"The man at the funeral was the same man we saw with the sheriff that day," Beth said excitedly. "He was a lot younger then, of course, but it was him. I remember because Maria and I thought he was the best-looking man we'd ever seen. He still has the same air of … entitlement—or confidence, maybe. Of course, that's not how I would have described him then. Then I thought he was handsome and rich."

Not only was it probable that the white girl was Lily Ignacio, but the man who came with the sheriff to liberate her from the "coloreds' house" was McDougall. I silently exulted that I had been right or at least on the right track.

"Do you know where the girl went?" I asked.

"No. I don't. Like I started to say, our foster mother told us she went to a new foster home. She didn't say where. For a long time, we thought maybe she'd moved in with the rich, handsome man, but we saw him once or twice after that, and she wasn't with him."

"Why did he come around again?" My eyes bored into Beth's face. I was in full cross-examination mode. I couldn't believe one of the chief witnesses was under my nose—both a friend and an employee no less—all this time. Of course, I could be excused: Beth had been in no condition for interrogation the last couple of days. I had been treading lightly.

But Beth didn't have an answer to my question.

I told Beth where Emily and I were going and why, and asked if she would like to come along.

She furiously shook her head. "I have no fond memories of Mr. Heiler. When he showed up at our foster home, it meant one of us kids was going away, and it wasn't to go back to their parents. If you went back to your family, your family picked you up, not Mr. Heiler."

"Do you remember anything about him that might help when we question him?" I asked.

"Only that they said he was a social worker, but he wasn't social and I didn't see him do much work either. He ordered people around and lectured us kids about how we would never amount to anything and we'd be lucky to get jobs as maids and janitors."

From what I'd heard so far, Mr. Heiler was not shaping up to be one of my favorite people.

I gave Beth a quick hug and told her about our plan for everyone to meet at Paco's for lunch at noon. During the hugging process I accidentally dipped my sleeve into the cookie batter, and I was happily sucking at it when I found Emily, who was still in Sam's office with Sam and MJ. The plywood was slid back, and they knelt next to the hole, staring into the blackness—out of which a damp chill arose.

"Come on, Emily," I said with forced chirpiness. "We need to get going."

I was furious with Sam and MJ for uncovering the hole. It was macabre and disturbing, especially for a thirteen-year-old. I didn't chastise MJ and Sam in front of Emily, though, since I was still clinging to my "Kate the Perfect" image.

Emily pushed herself back onto her feet and stood. Her serious expression reflected sadness and pain.

"She's here," she said without inflection.

"Who's here?" I asked unsteadily.

"The little girl. She's here."

I squinted at MJ and Sam and gave them a, "this is your fault" look.

Sam got off his knees and stood. I noticed that he was wobbling a bit. I had never seen Sam wobble—even when he was wearing six-inch heels. "The board was pushed back when we came in," he said. "We didn't do it."

Now it was my turn to be the cynic. "Stan was probably here and removed the plywood so he could repair the hole," I said dismissively.

"He's not here," said MJ in a wavering voice. "I called him on my cell to make sure. He's at a contractors' convention in Tucson. I could hear people talking, glasses clinking, and country western music in the background."

That certainly sounded like the kind of contractors' convention Stan would attend.

"Then maybe Beth …" I started to say.

"No. No one was in my office this morning except me," interrupted Sam.

We all looked at one another, each of us thoroughly spooked.

Chapter 18

"Well," I said after a few beats of silence. "I'm sure there's some logical explanation. *(I wasn't sure at all.)* In the meantime, we've got work to do."

My Disney-esque "everything is fine" approach didn't fool them. Nobody moved. I clapped my hands twice and said, "Chop-chop, let's get moving."

Chop-chop? My grade school PE teacher, who was universally detested, would say that to encourage us to pick up the pace. I always thought the phrase sounded mildly racist. I had never used it until now.

As Emily followed me out of Sam's office she commented, "You sound like my PE instructor."

Maybe being told to say "chop-chop" is part of the standard curriculum for PE teachers.

Emily and I were getting into my little Honda when Tuwanda drove up in her Caddy. I swear, her car is big enough to be turned into condos.

Its convertible top was down, and B.B. King's *The Thrill is Gone* was blasting from the CD player.

Tuwanda turned off the music with a flick of her hand.

"Where you two goin'?" she asked loudly.

I reversed action and trotted over to her.

"Shouldn't you be in bed?" I asked.

"Yes, I should. But all the interruptions over the last few days have screwed up my internal clock, an' I can't get to sleep."

The tone she used implied that somehow I had been responsible for the interruptions.

"Take a sleeping pill," I said, unable to keep the irritation out of my voice.

Tuwanda glanced in Emily's direction. "Why the hell you encouragin' me to take drugs in front of a young chile'?" she asked *sotto voce*.

Giving Emily a little wave, she called out, "Hi, Emily. Stay off drugs, sweetie."

"Okay," Emily called back.

I sighed and shook my head.

"So, you was jus' about to tell me where you goin'," said Tuwanda.

I was more in the mood to tell *her* where to go but opted for conflict avoidance and gave her an abbreviated version of our plan.

"I'll ride in the backseat," said Tuwanda, getting out of her car.

"No, Tuwanda. I don't want you going with us. It's

going to be difficult enough for the two of us to get in to see Mr. Heiler," I said firmly.

"I didn't say I was goin' with you to visit anyone," she said as she headed toward my car. "I jus' said I was gonna ride in the backseat. I got to get me some sleep, an' I sleep good there. You know how parents get a cranky baby to fall asleep by drivin' 'em around? It works the same way with me. It's the vibratin' or somethin'. Knocks me right out."

Emily looked at me questioningly as Tuwanda climbed into the backseat.

"She's going to sleep in the back," I said.

Emily was getting used to the weirdness that is my life; she nodded without comment.

After Tuwanda was settled, I moved my seat into its original, upright position, and slipped in behind the driver's wheel.

"Seatbelts on," I ordered.

Emily dutifully buckled up, but I got resistance from the backseat.

"Belts don't fit when you're hor'zontal," said Tuwanda. Then she giggled. "Hey, tha's like a pun or somethin.' Get it? 'Whore-zontal.'"

I glared at her in the rearview mirror, and then, remembering who was in the car with us, she hurriedly added, "Yeah, like hore as in horehound—them nasty little candies."

I rolled my eyes. *What a lousy save.*

A few beats later, I heard her mutter to no one in particular, "Besides, I don' do that stuff no more."

"Buckle up," I repeated.

"Uh-uh," she said. "We just gonna have to take the chance you know how to drive."

"It's the other Phoenix drivers you need to worry about, not me," I snapped. I gave Emily a "do you see what I have to deal with?" look and started the car.

It took us a while to get to the address Sam had given me. The elder-care facility was at the end of a cul-de-sac, accessed via a rabbit warren of streets that stopped and then started again a block up or block down from the cross street. This happens quite a bit in Phoenix. Whoever planned Phoenix's roads must have been a Tetris addict.

I parked across the street from the Pearly Gates under a tall eucalyptus tree. Emily and I paused to stare at the building before getting out of the car. Tuwanda would be staring too but for the fact that she was sound asleep. (Her legs were twitching the way Ralph's do when he's asleep. I always assumed that Ralph was dreaming about chasing squirrels or rabbits when he did this. I didn't have a clue what Tuwanda was dreaming of.)

The Home was a u-shaped, three-storied, pink stucco affair. The front door and the windows on the first two floors were covered by bars painted in sky-blue, yellow, and green. The attempted message was probably, "hey, we're bars, but we're *happy* bars." I don't care what mood they were in—the place still looked like a jail. This overall affect was not softened by the gold-lettered sign over the door, held up on either side by carved stone angels with sappy expressions, that said *Welcome to the Pearly Gates*. The only parking lot in sight was a small area with room for only four or five vehicles. I guessed the residents weren't allowed to keep cars, which meant, even if one of them managed to slip out, the only means of escape was hoofing it.

"I hope I never end up in a place like this," said Emily, half to herself.

"Ditto," I said. I touched her softly on the shoulder. "Are you ready to go in?"

"As long as we can get out again."

We left the windows open for Tuwanda and went to the front door. An intercom was set into the wall, and I pushed the call button. I scanned the entryway, but I didn't see any video equipment.

There was no response, so I pushed the button again, this time holding it down for a while.

The intercom crackled and then a tinny voice said, "Dammit. Is that you again, Carl?" Then, sounding fainter, the voice said, "Mike! I think Carl's got out again. Go look out the window."

For a high-cost operation, the AV technology was pretty lame.

"I'm not Carl," I said loudly into the intercom. "I've come with my, er, daughter, to visit Mr. Heiler."

I shrugged apologetically at Emily. I didn't know what else to say.

"You sure?" said the voice.

"Reasonably," I responded dryly.

"You see an' old guy out there wearin' a red T-shirt and Depends?"

"No," I said, looking around to make sure. I secretly hoped that Carl had gotten away, although with a description like that, he wouldn't be hard to track down.

"Be down in a second," the voice said wearily.

A minute or so later, the front door opened and a large woman dressed in black slacks and a stained white smock decorated with yellow happy faces emerged. She stopped behind the gate and glared at me. I squinted through the bars to read her name tag (a large plastic happy face, of course). *Bunny* was written in large block letters between the happy face's black dot eyes and its inane grin. A bunny is not the creature that came to mind. A bulldog, maybe, or an orangutan, but certainly not a bunny.

I introduced Emily and myself but didn't extend my hand in greeting. I didn't think my arm would fit through the bars.

"You relatives of Adolph?" she asked suspiciously, without bothering to return the introduction. She probably thought the name tag provided all the information I needed.

I had been hesitant to use Heiler's first name in place of his initial in case either I'd guessed wrong or he'd had the common sense to change it. Bunny's question confirmed that I hadn't, and he hadn't either.

I nodded. "Daughter and granddaughter." I quickly did the math and added, "My mother was much younger than he."

"Adolph never mentioned having any kids, and you're not listed in our records. I checked before I came down," she said, sounding proud of her efficiency.

"I am illegitimate," I said.

She did not look convinced. But, after appearing to consider my bona fides again, she surprised me by saying, "I guess it's okay for you to visit him. God knows he doesn't have many visitors, and it's not like you're gonna sell him some worthless crap or pull some other con. He doesn't have any money, and he can't sign anything because, even on a good day, he can't remember his name. Don't expect to share memories either; he goes in and out of focus, and even if he does remember something, you can't understand it because it doesn't make any sense."

My heart sank. I was afraid of this. Since we were already here, though, it was worth a try.

I glanced at Emily to see how she was handling the situation. She looked nervous and scared.

Bunny must have picked up on Emily's emotions as well, because she said, "Don't worry. Adolph's not dangerous. He's got problems with gas, and his farts are evil-smelling—they'll burn the hairs on the inside of your nose. Other than that, he's harmless."

She took a key out of a deep pocket on the front of her smock and scratched her head with it before inserting it into the lock on the metal-barred gate.

Maybe the oil in her hair works like a lubricant, I thought, looking distastefully at her greasy, unwashed, yellow-blonde tresses that were styled in a shag, *à la* Carol Brady.

As soon as we stepped inside, the gate clanged shut behind us, and I knew how convicts must feel their first day at a penitentiary. Inside the Home, the combined odors of urine and Pine-Sol were overwhelming. If Heiler's homegrown gas overpowered this ubiquitous fragrance, it was indeed a force to be reckoned with.

The foyer was small, and no attempt was made to soften the institutional effect of cracked, beige linoleum floors and off-white walls. The only picture on the wall was a large framed print of Escher's *Dream*. I wasn't sure the theme (a huge insect hovering threateningly over a sleeping man) was a good choice in a facility for people suffering from dementia.

We followed Bunny's large derriere up a narrow set of stairs to the second floor, where we stopped and waited for Bunny to unlock yet another set of barred gates. Although I'm no expert, I thought the set-up had to be in a violation of government safety codes: what if the Home caught on fire or there was an explosion? The residents would have to wait for Bunny or some other employee with a key to unlock the doors before they could escape.

A few orderlies were sitting and drinking coffee on a sagging green couch in the large room behind the gate. Several elderly people sat in wheelchairs arranged in a semi-circle in front of an older-model TV turned to ESPN. Most were slumped over in one direction or another, kept from falling to the floor by tied restraints. None of them seemed interested in what was on the TV. One ancient woman mumbled a steady stream of obscenities and picked fretfully at the fringe of a stained blanket draped over her lap. Her chenille robe was on its last threads, and her bony elbows protruded pitifully from areas of the fabric that had worn through. Next to her was an equally ancient man contemplating his lap with unblinking eyes. *I heart Justin Timberlake* was printed on his stained pajama top.

Another man was rhythmically sticking his forefinger in his ear and then smelling it. His mis-buttoned pajama top gaped open over his skinny, concave chest.

The only person in the group who seemed slightly with it was a woman wearing a ruffled pink tutu over her shabby gray jammies. Her gray-white hair was pulled into a tight bun at the top of her head. She looked at us haughtily, pointed a bony finger at Emily, and imperiously ordered her to "get off the stage" because she was "not on until the final act."

"Okay," said Emily timidly.

Bunny ignored this exchange and motioned for us to follow her down a poorly lit corridor that was lined on either side with closed doors, each of which had a small, barred window situated at eye level. So far, the overall effect of the facility was thoroughly depressing, and I saw nothing that justified the high cost of living there. I hoped that at least the private rooms were nice.

Bunny stopped at the last door at the end of the hall and peered through its window. Then she grunted, and this time, instead of unlocking the door with a key, she inserted a plastic card into a metal slot. A little green light blinked, and she opened the door. The smell hit us with full on gagging force. The urine/Lysol odor was French perfume by comparison.

A shriveled, elderly man with unwashed, long white hair was propped up in a wheelchair next to the room's only window. He was wearing Batman pajamas and his face was partly covered by a small, black plastic mask secured to his head by an elastic string. His chin was resting on his chest, and he appeared to be sleeping. I guesstimated the size of the room to be six by eight feet—prison-cell size. The off-white color scheme of the outside corridor had been carried into the room. The only difference was that the off-white walls in the room were covered with what looked like finger painting. My first thought was how great it was that the Home allowed its residents to express themselves so creatively, but a closer inspection of the wall art, which included an unintended sniff of the "paint", revealed that the artist's art supplies were likely food, medicine, and something more, uh, intimate.

Bunny immediately went to the old man, bent down, and sniffed his crotch.

"Do we need a change?" she asked him in the chipper, singsong voice of health care workers everywhere.

I hated the "we" thing. Did she want us all to check?

The muscles in Adolph's stringy neck tightened. Like a crane lifting more tons of cargo then it could handle, he slowly lifted his head, and, having achieved maximum altitude, opened his eyes partway and peered hatefully at Bunny. "Go to hell," he said in a hoarse voice that sounded like it hadn't been used in a long time.

He might have dementia, but his response sounded rational to me. I would have said the same thing.

Bunny straightened and instructed us in a brisk, businesslike manner to keep the door open until we left the room, limit our visit to no more than a half hour, and hit the red button next to the bed if we needed assistance. When were through, we were to find one of the orderlies to escort us out of the building. She concluded with, "Enjoy your visit, ladies," and left, her swaying hips barely clearing the door frame.

There were no chairs other than the wheelchair, so we stood awkwardly in the center of the room while I searched my mind for an opening remark. Before I could come up with something, Heiler barked, "Sit on the bed!"

We obediently side-shuffled to the bed and sat down in unison.

"Mr. Heiler," I began.

He held a bony finger attached to a heavily veined hand to his lips. "Keep your damn voice down," he whispered. He pointed furtively with the middle finger on his other hand toward an intercom on the wall. Since there didn't seem to be anything wrong with his other fingers, I figured his choice of the middle digit had significance other than merely providing directional information.

"Mr. Heiler," I began again, this time whispering, "I'm Kate Williams and this is my associate Emily Webber." He hadn't questioned our right to be there, so I didn't see any reason to reassign our ancestry again. "We were hoping you could answer some questions."

"And *I* was hoping you'd open your shirt. Get to the

point," he whispered, staring at my chest and leaning closer.

Maybe I should offer him a copy of the naked-woman-running-from-the-fire photo in exchange for information. He'd probably love it.

"Did you work for the Department of Health Services?" I whispered.

"I'm Batman," he answered.

"I see that. But I'm talking about before you became Batman."

"I have a Bat Mobile."

I smiled pleasantly and whispered, "I have a Honda. Did you ever work with, er ... orphans?"

I wasn't sure if the term "foster care" was in common use in the fifties.

He abruptly sat back, clenched his hands, and was quiet. I thought maybe he hadn't heard me.

"Mr. Heiler, I asked if you had ever worked with children who'd lost their parents." I spoke slowly.

"I saved 'em," he said. "They were damaged goods. Every one of 'em. Hell, even their relatives didn't want 'em."

"How did you save them?" I asked gently.

I heard footsteps in the hall, and Heiler looked at the doorway nervously. He seemed to relax when the footsteps faded away.

Directing his gaze back to us, he seemed to notice Emily for the first time. "Are you one of 'em?" he asked sharply.

Emily looked at me for guidance, and I gave her an encouraging nod.

"How do you mean?" she asked.

"You one of them mongrel kids with empty souls?"

"I'm not sure ..." she started to say.

But Heiler wasn't interested in her response and talked over her. "The soulless devils were headed for a life of crime, drugs, alcohol, and prostitution. I saw how them girls looked at men, sizin' 'em up for profit potential. I found 'em places to live where they could learn an honest trade and do good, honest work." Spittle flew from his mouth as his agitation grew. He was no longer whispering. His voice was loud and crackled with bitterness.

I heard feet pounding down the corridor toward Heiler's room.

"Mr. Heiler, did you know a little girl by the name of Lily Ignacio?" I asked hurriedly.

He tensed and grabbed the arms of his wheelchair, looking at me in wide-eyed surprise. Then, like a marionette whose strings have been cut, he slumped into his chair and covered his eyes with his hands.

I took that as a big, emphatic "yes."

I couldn't pursue the matter further, though, because at that moment a mountain of a man hurtled through the door, skidded to stop in front of Heiler, and looked around wildly.

When his eyes lit on Emily and me, he registered surprise and roughly asked, "What are you doing here?"

I recognized him right away. He was the Hulk—one

of the goons I had seen standing outside the church at Maria's funeral.

He didn't seem to remember who I was, though; not yet, anyway.

I started to feed him the line about me being Heiler's illegitimate daughter, but he was distracted by Heiler, who had begun to sob.

"I guess we'd better go," I said, grabbing Emily by the arm and pulling her toward the door.

We made it out to the hallway when I heard him say, "Hey! I know you. You're the one who hates ferrets."

I thought the comment was unfair since I'd only said they didn't make good pets, and that's a separate issue from whether or not I liked them in general.

"Run," I whispered to Emily as I pushed her ahead of me toward the stairway.

"We can't get out," she whispered back frantically. "The gate's locked."

We dashed across the TV room, which, thankfully, except for a couple zombie-residents, was empty, ignored the locked gate, and ran into the corridor leading to the wing opposite the one where Heiler resided.

I pulled ahead of Emily and started trying doors. I found one that was unlocked and pushed it open, pulling Emily in after me. I closed the door behind us but there was no way to lock it from the inside.

Chapter 19

"Why aren't you in your costumes yet?" asked the same imperious voice that had ordered us off the stage earlier.

We wheeled around and saw the lady in the tutu staring at us contemptuously from her wheelchair.

I listened for the sound of footsteps in the hallway and, thankfully, didn't hear any. The Hulk was probably still searching for us in the rooms on Mr. Heiler's corridor, but he was bound to widen the search area at some point when he didn't find us in any of them.

"We need a way to get out of the building," I said.

She cocked her head and gave us an appraising look. "Stage fright," she concluded. "Is this your first performance?"

"Yes," I said. I didn't think an attempt at an explanation would do any good. "How do we get out of the building?"

She shrugged. "Same way Carl Hanson does, I guess."

This was probably the same Carl that Bunny had mistaken us for when we first arrived—the guy in the red T-shirt and diapers.

"I think you should try changing into your costumes first, though," she continued. "Dressing in performance gear helps with the stage fright."

"We already gave our costumes to our, um, understudies," I said. "How does Mr. Hanson get out?"

"I have extra costumes here. Give it a try; put them on. You'll feel better."

I doubted it.

"If we put on the costumes and we still want to leave, will you tell us how?" asked Emily.

I shot her a 'What are you *saying?*' look.

"Yes," responded the tutu-lady. "But I think you'll change your mind about ducking out once you see how fabulous you look." She motioned toward a small closet. "The frog and puffin outfits are in the black bag hanging to the far right."

Frog and puffin? A factoid long lying dormant in one of my lesser-used brain cells popped up.

"Swan Lake?" I asked.

She gave me a severe look. "Of course. I can see why you're nervous. You seem horribly unprepared. Come to think of it, I haven't seen you at rehearsals."

"We may have missed a couple of practices," I said, then hurriedly added, "but you are the best … um … Odette I have ever seen. We greatly admire your work."

She beamed at us.

Both that the old lady danced the lead and that the lead's name was Odette were lucky guesses. I silently offered a prayer of thanks to Mrs. Schwartz, my fifth-grade teacher, who had forced us to watch a videotape of an abbreviated version of Swan Lake, starring her daughter in the part of Odette. (Her daughter was two years older than me and had been an insufferable snob. She got knocked up in high school by the kid who danced the part of Kaj in *The Snow Queen*. Apparently toes had not been the only body parts pointing at the ballet school).

"Remember, though—it takes hard work in addition to tremendous talent to be a *premiere danseuse*."

"Yes, ma'am," I said humbly.

"Please, dear," she said kindly. "Call me Madam Kanastokosolis."

I decided to go with Madam K.

"Now get dressed!" she ordered us with good-humor and shooed us toward the closet.

The closet, as it turned out, was larger than it looked from the outside. Its walls extended about four feet on either side of the access door. The clothing inside was packed in so tightly I doubted hangers were necessary; the items didn't need to be hung so much as wedged. A top shelf was piled high with masks and hats, and toe and tap shoes were stacked three deep on the floor.

I spotted two identical black clothing bags on the far right and wrestled them out. After placing the bags side by side on the bed, I unzipped one of them to reveal a long, red evening gown. That didn't seem like something a puffin or a frog would wear, so I unzipped the other bag, which was a lot heavier.

Variously colored net, tulle, and satin fabrics burst through the opening like stuffing out of a cushion. If fabric could talk, this bunch would, have sighed with relief and said, "thank God." I removed a bouncy tutu with alternating layers of white and black, a black leotard and tights, and a black vest with white lapels. Next, I found a long green catsuit-type affair that was covered with overlapping half-moon shaped pieces of fabric probably meant to look like scales. As a result of being packed haphazardly and then crushed, the scales stuck out crazily in all directions.

Biology was not my best subject (I got sick and had to be sent to the nurse's office the day we dissected frogs), but to my recollection, frogs did not have scales—maybe the costume designer had frogs confused with snakes or dragons.

The last items I removed from the bag were a tall, yellow feathered headdress and a green satin hood. The latter was adorned with a big, red, grinning, felt mouth; two eyeholes topped with felt Groucho Marx-style eyebrows; and a red, bulbous rubber nose. Rudolph the red-nosed frog? A frog with a drinking problem? I had no idea which character traits the designer intended to convey.

"You may each borrow a pair of my toe shoes as well," said Madam K, gesturing to the stack at the bottom of the closet.

"Um, what size are they?" I asked, looking at them doubtfully.

"Size six." As a visual aid, Madam K pulled up a pajama leg and wiggled a dainty foot.

"That'll fit perfect," said Emily, who appeared to be enjoying the whole "let's play dress–up" thing.

"I wear a size eight and a half," I said apologetically.

"You will find a way to get them on," Madam K declared with conviction. "Remember—one must suffer for one's art."

Maybe I could get by with hanging them on my toes.

I handed Emily the puffin outfit because I thought it was the less ridiculous of the two and I am a kind and caring person. There was no way the costumes would fit over our clothes, so I stripped down to my underwear and stepped into the one-piece catsuit. Emily turned her back to us, slid off her clothes, and donned her costume without showing anything in between. Only adolescent girls subjected to the indignities of gym class locker rooms are capable of this maneuver.

I awkwardly zipped up the back of my catsuit and searched for a mirror. Unfortunately—or fortunately, as it turned out—the only thing I could find was a small face mirror on top of the dresser. The only thing its limited reflective surface told me was that green isn't my best color.

Emily finished buttoning up the puffin vest and turned around for me to take a look. She looked adorable, and I told her so. She did not return the compliment.

I tossed her a pair of black toe shoes and snagged a white pair for me. I actually tried to shove my foot into one, but, after a jolt of empathy for the Chinese women forced by tradition to wrap their feet, I hung it on the end of my foot as originally planned. I did likewise with the other shoe and pulled the legs of my catsuit down to cover the deception.

I handed the feathered headdress to Emily and pulled the frog hood over my head. My aim was off and I had to reposition it so I could see through the eyeholes. Even with this adjustment, the world was green-tinged.

Emily stifled a giggle.

The good part was that we'd accomplished our clothing changes in record time. Fear of apprehension inspires that sort of thing.

"Now, don't you feel better?" asked Madam K.

Of course I did not, but didn't want to hurt her feelings.

"Yes," I exclaimed. "What a change it makes. (I winced over my unintended pun.) But we will still need to know how to get out of the building, so, when our performance is over, we can leave immediately. We, er, have another engagement tonight at a different venue."

"Ahh, the pressure of tight performance schedules. How well I know the feeling," she said reminiscently. "I wish the public was more sensitive. *Artistes* cannot be turned off and on like a light switch."

Time was running out. I didn't hear any searching sounds from the hallway yet, but the Hulk was bound to make it down here soon.

"We really need to know how to get out of the building," I repeated.

"It's quite simple. There are stairs behind the door at the end of the hall. Go to the third floor, take a left and follow the signs to the emergency exit, and then climb down the fire ladder."

I felt a wave of admiration for Carl Hanson, followed by a wave of disgust for the Home's administrators. *How are elderly people supposed to climb down a ladder in an emergency? Shouldn't there at least be a set of fire stairs? I thought that elder-care facilities were supposed to be inspected by the state annually. How could they miss such glaring safety violations? For that matter, why hadn't family and guests brought the matters to anyone's attention?*

I was so bothered by the unsafe conditions that, despite our need to rapidly depart, I asked, "Madam Kapa … Kopi … Madam K., do you have many visitors here?" I deserved credit for at least getting the first consonant right.

All signs of haughtiness disappeared from her face, and her expression collapsed into one of sadness. "No," she said softly. "I see Mr. McDougall once in a while, but he never stops in to talk."

You need to leave ASAP, ordered the survivalist part of me. *You may never have a chance to talk to this woman again,* said the truth-seeking-at-all-costs part. The latter won out.

"How do you know Mr. McDougall?" I asked. Emily moved closer to me and dug her nails into my arm. I did not know whether the message was, "OMG, we need to get out of here," or "OMG, keep going; this woman might know something."

"I was Mr. McDougall's secretary for over twenty years. I gave up my dancing career for him," she said bitterly.

I picked up on the fact that she said she left her career "for him," and not, "to work for him." It was an interesting distinction.

"When did you start working for him?" I asked excitedly. Emily increased the pressure of her nail digging, conveying that the "we need to get out of here" message was the one she'd intended.

"He convinced me to take the job after his secretary, Marni, disappeared in 1953. I had been Marni's assistant. I think Marni ran away to New York to dance. That's what I would have done. She thought Mr. McDougall was going to marry her, but he had other ... preferences."

"What was Marni's last name?"

Emily had abandoned all subtlety and was now full-out dragging me toward the door.

Madam K's haughty gaze returned, her posture straightened, and she slid back into her fantasy world of ballerinas. "Her legs were too short; she could never have performed the part of Odette. Mr. McDougall was right; she was only good for typing and babysitting those children he took in out of the kindness of his heart."

"What children?"

I heard the sound of opening and closing doors. The Hulk had made it to this side of the building.

"We need to go, now," I said to Madam K.

"Yes, your audience awaits," she said with a sweep of her arm.

Chapter 20

I heard a door open and, praying that this meant the Hulk was in the room-inspection-portion of the search-cycle, I opened the door and peered out. The hallway was empty, so I'd guessed right about the timing. I made a dash for the door at the end of the hall, towing Emily behind me. My ballet slippers flapped against the soles of my feet like flip-flops. Ours was not a subtle escape.

Once we were in the stairwell, we waited for the heavy metal door to whisper shut behind us before we, or rather I, clomped up the steps. (Emily was much lighter on her feet.) In an increasingly rare moment of rational thought, I removed my toe shoes, but not until after I had tripped, hopped, and finally crawled to the top of the steps.

"I look like Bjork and you look like, well, I don't know, but you look weird," whispered Emily. "There's no way they won't notice us."

"We just left the room of a woman wearing a pink

tutu. Before that, we were talking to a man dressed as batman. Don't worry; we'll blend in."

Still, I looked up and down the corridor and listened for voices before we left the stairwell. I spotted an exit sign with an arrow pointing to the left. I also saw something that put a serious dent in my theory that we could pass unnoticed among the equally strangely dressed population. The third floor was used for administrative offices, and, even worse, the fronts of all the offices were glass.

"Rats," I whispered.

"We're screwed," Emily said matter-of-factly.

"No. We'll use a cover story. If we get stopped, let me do the talking." I would tell anyone who stopped us that we were with a group of dancers who had come to perform for the residents—and I prayed they wouldn't ask us to actually dance.

The Hulk had already recognized me, so I didn't dare take off my frog hood. I don't think he got a good look at Emily, though; I'd pushed her ahead of me when we ran out of Heiler's room.

I opened the door and stepped into the hallway, motioning Emily to follow. Amazingly, each office we passed was empty and, moreover, appeared to have been hurriedly abandoned. Computer screens were still lit, and pencils and pens lay haphazardly on desktops next to open notebooks and legal pads.

It was a curious situation, but I wasn't going to look a gift horse in the mouth.

We came to a double window, over which was hung

an exit sign with an arrow pointing down. The fire ladder outside was attached to the wall under, but to the right of, the window.

It took a fair amount of tugging, and *sotto voce* cursing, to raise the window enough for us to squeeze through.

Once the window was open, we could hear voices coming from the street side of the building. One of them was louder than the others.

"What the hell you mean by sayin' a white lady an' a kid din't go in here earlier. Tha's a lie."

Tuwanda. The ruckus she was making out front probably explained why the staff members weren't in their offices. I know from experience that it takes more than one person—more than three or four, actually—to subdue an irritated Tuwanda.

Bless her little soul, though. She must have woken up and decided to go find us. The diversion she provided was a godsend.

"You lyin' to me 'cuz I'm a black woman. I don't see no black faces starin' out at me. You prejudice, that's what you are. *Prejudiced.*"

I couldn't make out the response, but it sounded placating.

I boosted myself up, pivoted on my stomach, and lowered my legs over the sill, feeling around with my foot for the top rung. I was irked that they hadn't put the ladder right under the window, this being the more logical approach. But then, the idea that elderly folks, who were likely disoriented even under non-emergency conditions, could climb down a three-story ladder was already absurd. The fact that it was improperly aligned seemed like intentional disregard for their welfare.

After my right foot made contact with the top rung, I slid my fingers sideways along the sill until I could place my full weight on the top rung of the ladder. Then, leaning into the wall, I slid my hands sideways over the stucco until I was directly over the ladder. At that point, still leaning into the wall, I moved my left foot down to the next rung and grabbed for the top rung. It was not an easy process. My admiration for Carl was growing.

I descended a few steps and then instructed Emily to swing her legs over the sill. I guided her feet to the top rung, then stepped up a rung and grabbed the sides of the ladder so my arms and body surrounded her like a cage, to keep her from falling. She made it to the ladder with far more agility than I had.

We climbed down, rung by rung, with me arching my body out so I could keep Emily in front of me.

The ladder ended about ten feet above the ground. I surveyed the area and spotted a pile of mulch with a suspiciously human-shaped indentation on top. This had to be Carl's landing pad.

"I'm going to aim for that mound," I told Emily. "Once I'm on the ground, I'll stand under you and you climb down and grab the lowest rung, then swing your legs down so I can grab them and lower you the rest of the way.

"Kate, are you sure …" Emily started to ask, but I had pushed off and was already airborne.

I tried to relax because I remembered reading somewhere that the risk of injury is greater if you are tense. My body was not receptive to this logic, however, and I landed like a board.

I learned two things: mulch is not as soft as it looks, and mulch is a generic term covering everything from cedar chips and leaves to evil smelling organic material of indeterminate origin—the latter being the stuff I landed in.

The wind was knocked out of me, and I experienced the now-familiar symptoms of a minor concussion. It could have been worse—my frog hood provided some padding.

After what was probably only few seconds but seemed like a lifetime, I regained my equilibrium as well as my ability to inhale and exhale. I guess practice makes perfect—and lord knows I've had enough practice with head injuries.

I rolled off the pile, stood, and staggered to the side of the building where I stretched my arms over my head as far as I could.

"Your turn, Emily," I said.

I was still dizzy, but I mustered every bit of mental and physical energy I had left for the task at hand.

I couldn't see Emily's face, but she had to be frightened, and I chastised myself for getting her into this mess. If she got hurt, it would be my fault. I should have let the Hulk find us. What was the worst that could have happened?

I would find out that something much worse would have happened, but that moment of realization was yet to come.

Emily swung her legs down, and I could just reach her ankles. I grabbed them and instructed her to "walk" down the wall with her hands. I kept my grip around her ankles until her feet were safely planted on terra firma, and then I gave her a big hug.

"I'm sorry," I whispered in her ear.

"Why?" she said, pushing back and looking into my face in surprise. "This was great."

I was pretty sure her parents wouldn't think so.

I could still hear Tuwanda making a fuss out front, but now, in addition, I heard the muffled sound of applause. I looked up and saw that a group of residents had gathered at the barred windows on the second floor and were applauding our escape act.

Madam K. would be so proud.

Emily took a bow while I scanned the high wooden fence surrounding the yard. In the back corner, next to a garbage can, I spotted a gate that looked like it led to a back alley.

I started for the gate, but Emily showed no sign of leaving her admiring fans. "Let's go," I hissed, wishing I had one of those hooks used to get people off the stage when they take too many bows.

After I gave her arm a few hard tugs, she got the message and followed me out the gate.

We hustled down the alley to a side street, where I told her to wait for me. Fortunately, I had left my car keys in the ignition in case Tuwanda woke up and wanted to turn on the air conditioning, since the weather can be toasty this time of year. Provided I could get her attention, I could signal her to drive around the corner and pick us up.

"You should take off the hood," suggested Emily. "Otherwise she won't know who you are."

Good call. I'd gotten so used to being a frog I'd forgotten about the hood.

I pulled it off and immediately felt much cooler, as the sweat in my hair and rolling down my face started to evaporate.

I hurried to the corner, turned right, and cut across the front yards of the houses on the cul-de-sac. I stayed down, running from one clump of vegetation to the next, until I reached a stand of blooming ocotillos in front of the house next door to the Pearly Gates. My bare feet had borne the brunt of numerous cactus assaults. I would need to spend some time with tweezers when this thing was over.

Tuwanda was standing on the front steps of the Home with her back toward me, staring down Bunny and a small crowd of orderlies, aides, and administrative types. The Hulk wasn't among them. He was probably still engaged in a room-to-room search of the first and second floors.

Bunny and her gang remained behind the barred gate.

Tuwanda said, "You people's crazy."

"You've got projection issues," said a middle-aged man in a bow tie and horn-rimmed glasses.

Tuwanda grunted in disgust. "I'm gonna call the damn police." She pivoted a hundred and eighty degrees on her heel and headed toward my car.

"Don't do that ma'am," said a distressed voice that

sounded like it might be Bunny's. The contingent from the Home had crowded forward, and it was hard to pick out individuals.

"We'll go look for your friends right now. Wait here," the voice continued, now with a pleading element overlaying the distress.

Yeah, I thought. *The last thing you want is for the police to see what's going on in this place.*

Tuwanda had reached her limit, though, and continued to march toward my car, mumbling loudly.

"Damn people think they can bullshit a little black woman. I'm gonna get the police and then I'm gonna get Reverend Sharpton to come down here to raise holy hell."

I motioned to her frantically as she drew even with the ocotillos. She must have caught the movement out of the corner of her eye—she looked in my direction and immediately spotted me, her eyes widening in surprise. I pressed my finger to my lips and then pantomimed holding a steering wheel and pointed in the direction of where I'd left Emily.

I had to hand it to Tuwanda. If I saw a woman dressed in a bright green, scaly catsuit waving at me, I would visibly react. Then, I'd probably say something like, "Oh dear God," and run in the opposite direction at the speed of light. But Tuwanda only nodded slightly and continued walking to the car without missing a beat.

I wondered if I should be impressed with her aplomb or offended because seeing me in a frog suit was not cause for surprise.

Chapter 21

I didn't wait to make sure Tuwanda was following instructions but sneaked, Wile E. Coyote style, back to the corner and trotted up the street to where Emily was still standing.

A tense few minutes later, my little car rounded the corner and pulled over in front of us. As soon as we jumped in, I began thanking Tuwanda profusely for unknowingly providing a diversion and then rescuing us.

She interrupted my stream of gratitude. "Why you dressed in a goddamned green ... whatever that is, an' why's Emily dressed like a Vegas showgirl?"

"It's a ballerina outfit," corrected Emily from the backseat.

"I've seen ballerinas an' I've seen showgirls. You look like a showgirl," Tuwanda responded obstinately.

I turned around to look at Emily. Tuwanda had a

point. The tutu was cute, but the feathered headdress pushed it over the top.

I started to explain to Tuwanda what had happened in the Home, but she cut me off again. "I'm gonna pull over an' let you drive, an' I'll trade places with Emily. I gotta finish my rest, which got interrupted 'cuz of the insanity surroundin' your lifestyle. Plus, I don' want anyone to see me drivin' this piece-of-crap car. I got an image to protect."

"Emily and I couldn't possibly have disturbed you. We were inside the Home. Who or what *did* wake you up?" I asked defensively. My thankful mood was disappearing; I wasn't about to take the blame for interrupting her sleep.

"I was in the middle of a great dream. I wasn't me in it, but I looked like me, an' I was bein' a doctor to lil' kids. Tha's a respectful position. Problem was, the lil' kids were all blue an' green, an' all I had to treat 'em with was a garden hose."

"A garden hose?" Emily asked interestedly.

Tuwanda pulled over, and we switched seats and responsibilities and left the garden hose question dangling until we were resettled.

"Yeah. One of them green ones. But it wasn't hooked up to nothin'."

"And this was a *good* dream?" I asked.

"Compared to most, yeah. Anyway, so I'm in the middle of this great dream, an' somethin' wakes me up. So I boost myself up on my elbow to take a look an' assign appropriate blame. I see this big black car, an' a guy who looks like he's takin' steroids is walkin' around the back to the passenger side. I figured it musta' been his slammin' the driver's side door shut that woke me.

"He opens the passenger door an' this ol' fart gets out, cane first. I reco'nized him right away—he was the same white-haired guy from Maria's funeral, the one who looks like he would probably make people call him 'massah' if he could.

"So the ol' guy heads for the Home an' gets half-way up the sidewalk when another man, who looks like he works out at the same gym as the driver and pro'bly takes the same drugs, comes runnin' out the front door. This one looks like one of the dudes standin' outside the church at the funeral, except he's dressed in blue scrubs instead of a bid'ness suit.

"So ape-man says somethin' to the old guy, but he's speakin' real low so I can't hear 'im. Then, the old guy turns around, he and his driver get back in the car, and they drive away. Ape man looks real unhappy, an' he looks aroun' before he goes back in the house. I ain't afraid of no one, but I ducked down so he wouldn't see me an' come over an' ask me why I was there. When I'm tired I don't feel much like socializin'.

"I din't like the way things looked, though, an' after waitin' a while for you to come out, I decided to look for you. Besides, I couldn't get back to damn sleep. Must be the vibratin' that works, and, as a rule, parked cars don't vibrate.

"I pushed the intercom button, an' a big ol' fake blonde come to the door. Her name tag says her name is Bunny. What the hell kin' of name is Bunny for a grown woman? If they was goin' for a nickname, "big-assed bitch" woulda' bin more descriptive.

"So *Bunny*," said Tuwanda, emphasizing the name with heavy sarcasm, "says neither you nor anyone matchin' your descriptions has bin there. I know that was a lie, 'cuz the reason I'm sleepin' in a damned cul-de-sac is that you wanted to visit some guy in that place.

"I tell her so, and she gets real nasty and insists I'm mistaken—which, in my book, is the same thing as sayin', 'you lyin', bitch.'"

I bit my lip to keep from cautioning Tuwanda about use of foul language in front of Emily. When Tuwanda's rolling out a stream of consciousness, it's best to not interrupt. When she's tired *and* on a roll, it's best to not be in the same hemisphere, but that wasn't an option.

Tuwanda paused to stuff Ralph's traveling blanket under her head to make a pillow before she continued. "So, I start to dispute the issue, employin' sound logic—and pretty soon, a whole bunch of people joined in on the fat blonde's side. They was all a bunch a' chickens, though, 'cuz they stayed behind that locked gate so's I couldn't max'mize my persuasive powers.

"I wasn't gettin' nowhere with them idiots, so I gave up and said I was gonna' call the police. Katie, you *know* how much I hate them police, but I was that aggravated. But I din't need to 'cuz that's when I spotted you, an' I want you to know how much stress it put on my organs not to laugh my ass off. You look like a damn salamander.

"By the way, not to be mean or nothin', but on top of lookin' amphibious, you stink."

"I fell into a pile of mulch," I said, sniffing my sleeve. I didn't think I smelled *that* bad.

"She was aiming for it," Emily piped in unhelpfully.

I started on the story of what had happened to Emily and me inside the Home, but after a few seconds, I could hear Tuwanda's soft snoring.

"We're supposed to meet everyone at Paco's for lunch," Emily reminded me.

"We can't go like this," I said horrified. But I'd left my cell phone in my jacket pocket, which I'd left in Madam K's room—so we had no way of calling to let them know we would be late—or a no-show. Plus, it was getting hot, and Paco's is in an urban area with very few trees. Tuwanda would fry even if I left the windows open.

I glanced at Emily. Without the headdress, she looked cute—like a kid coming from ballet class. If she didn't object, I could drop her off at Paco's, and she could get everyone caught up on what had happened while I got Tuwanda up to my condo and I changed clothes.

Neither Emily nor I had any cash on us, so maybe, for the first time in her life, MJ would have to foot at least part of the bill. I found the thought gratifying.

I told Emily what I was thinking.

"Sure," she said. "You'll come back won't you, after you drop off Tuwanda and change?"

"I'll try. The changing shouldn't take long. It's the dropping off that might take a while."

I pulled up in front of Paco's, but I didn't let Emily out until I made sure Beth's car was already in the lot and Emily had removed the offending headdress. The tutu collapsed as she passed through the too-narrow door, but it bloomed again once she was outside. I waited until she was inside the restaurant and then a minute or so longer, just to make sure she wasn't tossed out. Paco's has a loose dress code, but even that has limits.

As I drove to my condo, I mentally reviewed our conversations with Heiler and Madam K. We hadn't learned many hard facts from Heiler, if indeed *any* fact delivered by Batman could be trusted, but Madam K. had provided some interesting leads—with the caveat that our witness wore a tutu and thought she was a ballet dancer, a *prima donna* no less. Heiler had more or less confirmed that he had been placing children with families to serve as indentured servants. His comments about the seductiveness of the children had overtones of pedophilia, but I didn't know how that figured into the picture, if at all. His extreme response to Lily Ignacio's name was the most interesting, but I hadn't been able to pursue the matter because that's when the Hulk had showed up.

Madam K. had proved to be an unexpected source of information. She'd said McDougall employed a secretary named Marni who had disappeared the same year Lily was pulled out of Our Lady of Perpetual Succor. Also, she had mentioned that this secretary had romantic feelings about McDougall, but McDougall had, "other preferences." Given an innocent interpretation, this could be taken to mean he simply liked another woman. The way Madam K. had said it, though, led me to believe that she meant something more sinister; there had been an element of distaste in the way she pronounced the word, "preferences." The zinger, though, was that McDougall had taken in children. Is it possible that one of those children was Lily, and McDougall and Lily had lived at my address? This was, of course, piling guesswork upon un-proven assumptions, but it was an intriguing possibility—and, so far, my guesswork had been pretty darned good.

Of course, I could go directly to the source and ask McDougall about his activities, but I had a feeling he wouldn't tell me the truth. I needed more facts to get the answers I needed. (Law school 101: Don't ask a question on cross-examination unless you already know the answer.)

I pulled into the underground garage beneath my building and found a space close to the elevator. I got out of my car and, since it had apparently worked to wake Tuwanda before, loudly slammed the door.

"What the *hell*?" yelled Tuwanda. "Keep it down. There's people tryin' to sleep in here."

I glanced around the garage in case sleeping in cars was, in fact, as popular as Tuwanda made it sound; sadly, with the economy as bad as it was, she could be right.

Seeing no other irritated faces staring sleepily out of car windows, I opened Tuwanda's door and announced that she needed to change sleeping quarters.

"Why?" she asked stubbornly.

"Because I cannot keep driving around all day and it's too hot to park you outside. You can stay in my condo."

I thought I was being reasonable. Kind, even.

"You have no compassion for people sufferin' from insomnia," she grumbled ungratefully as she pushed up into a sitting position and slid out of the car.

She really did look exhausted. "I'll tell you what. I'll make you some warm milk," I said, sympathetically patting her arm.

"Does that work?" she asked.

"I don't know," I said, supporting her elbow as we walked to the elevator. It was with some surprise that I realized I'd never had a glass of warm milk in my life.

"What'd your mom do to get you to sleep at night? I always thought white women sang their kids lullabies an' stroked their hair an' shit."

"I am not singing you a lullaby, and the farthest I will go with the hair stroking thing is a quick pat on the top of your head. I have to change and drive back to Paco's to get Emily."

The elevator came, and we stepped inside. Tuwanda looked around blearily. "Yeah. I was wonderin' what you did with Webber's kid. Is she gettin' us food?"

"No. You need to sleep, not eat," I said firmly.

"I don't see as how they's mutually exclusive." She leaned against the back wall of the elevator and closed her eyes. I was afraid she was going to fall asleep again, but she roused when we got to my floor.

The dogs must have heard or smelled us coming, because they started barking wildly before we got to my front door. As soon as we stepped inside, Walter hurled himself at Tuwanda. Ralph was more circumspect. He sniffed my green suit suspiciously and then experimentally licked one of the cloth scales. Realizing it wasn't edible, he launched into his happy-to-see-you dance, leaping around and on me.

Tuwanda headed straight for my bedroom with Walter in her arms. Ralph and I followed, and I had to restrain him from joining the other two in bed.

I grabbed clothes and a pair of tennis shoes out of the closet and my cosmetics bag off the bathroom counter, and held everything in one arm so I had a free hand to grab Ralph's collar and haul him out of the bedroom with me. So as not to disturb Tuwanda, I would use the powder room off the entry to clean up, change, and redo my makeup, most of which had rubbed or sweated off when I was wearing the frog hood.

"Don't forget my glass of milk and head pat," I heard her mumble as I closed the door behind me.

I was concerned about Tuwanda's insomnia. To my knowledge, she'd never experienced this problem before. Even more worrisome was her sudden neediness. I didn't mind that she'd come to me for help; Tuwanda had helped me out in the past, and I was glad for a chance to return the favor. But relying on others was not Tuwanda-like. She took her independence seriously and resisted—vocally and sometimes physically—any real or perceived limitations.

Something was wrong, and she wasn't giving me any clues as to what it might be. I resolved to sit her down and demand that she confide in me. I would have to wait until after she had a good night's—or day's—sleep, though. I wasn't about to press Tuwanda on personal issues when she was tired and testy.

I took Ralph into the kitchen and gave him a treat to assuage his hurt feelings about being excluded from Tuwanda and Walter's nap time. Courtesy of Macy, I found a full carton of milk in the refrigerator with an expiration date that was actually in the future.

I filled a glass with milk and put it in the micro. I guessed one minute would do the trick, so I set the timer and punched the start button. So far, so good.

After thirty seconds, the milk boiled over the sides of the glass. I decided to let it cool off rather than start over again. In the meantime, I could at least wash my face, which felt stiff. A crust had probably started to form over it.

I pushed open the swing-hinged door of the kitchen, and froze.

Chapter 22

The Hulk was standing in the middle of my living room, still dressed in blue scrubs. He'd been standing with his back to me when I came in, but he spun around as soon as he heard the door swish open. He pointed the business end of a nine-millimeter at my head and gestured with his free hand for me to come all the way into the room. Ralph, the guard dog, wagged his tail and headed toward Hulk for a welcoming crotch sniff. The Hulk moved the gun from me to Ralph.

"No, Ralph," I said frantically. I was scared to death that the Hulk was going to shoot him. "Sit. Lie!" I ordered. Ralph ignored me. The only human words he understands are "walk" and "food" and any word that sounds like it might refer to something edible. (The breadth of his vocabulary is astounding when it comes to food items.)

"Food," I said. Ralph immediately trotted back and looked at me expectantly. The gun moved off Ralph and back to me. I hoped that Ralph appreciated what I'd done for him, but, judging by the look on his face that said, "So where's this food you were talking about," I don't think he did.

I wasn't in the hot seat long, though, because Walter began barking hysterically, and the Hulk pointed his gun at my bedroom door.

"What's that?" he asked nervously.

"My other dog," I said. "I put him in the bedroom because he and Ralph make a mess if I leave them together."

I didn't want to let on that Walter was not alone.

"Who's Ralph?" he asked loudly.

I pointed to Ralph, who, right on cue, started to bark back at Walter.

Walter's sharp bark had to have awakened Tuwanda, and if it hadn't, Ralph's would. I would need to shout to be heard over the cacophony, which was good—I figured that a loud exchange would warn Tuwanda about what was going on and, hopefully, keep her from storming out and blowing her cover. The more noise, the better, as far as I was concerned.

"We're going for a ride," said the Hulk, raising his voice to be heard over the barking.

"Who we?" I yelled. "Me, you, Ralph, and Walter?"

"Who's Walter?"

"He's the dog in the other room."

Hulk appeared to give the matter some thought. "Just you," he said.

"I need to feed them before we go, then," I yelled. "Otherwise they're going to rip the place apart while I'm gone."

He smiled nastily. "You ain't comin' back," he said.

The situation having now been clarified, my brain settled on frozen terror as the appropriate emotional response.

"I can't die in a green frog suit," I squeaked. While, objectively, this should be a minor concern in light of the more serious consequences, I was under a lot of pressure, and my mind seized on it as a major deal.

"Frog suit? What're you talking about?" he asked suspiciously.

At first, I was confused by his question, until I realized that he thought I meant the dive suits that Navy SEALs wear for underwater assignments. "Not frog*man* suit as in a scuba diving suit, but frog suit as in dressed like an actual frog," I explained.

"You do look pretty stupid," he commented— unnecessarily, I thought. "What are those things sticking out supposed to be?"

"Scales," I provided.

"Frogs don't have scales. Those are dragon scales. Or maybe an iguana."

I thought so, too, so I couldn't argue with his logic.

"It's a ballet costume," I said shrugging, "and it's supposed to be worn by the frog in Swan Lake."

"You should have tried out for the Odette part, or even the puffin part. Being a puffin beats being a frog."

My would-be killer was ballet literate, a fact totally at

odds with his appearance. I would have guessed him to be more of a wrestling or a NASCAR fan.

My face must have reflected my surprise, because he said, "My mom taught dance," by way of explanation.

"How about shoes? I need shoes. People don't drive cars without shoes. No one's going to believe it was an accident if I'm barefoot," I babbled, taking advantage of a lull in the barking.

This seemed to make sense to him. "Where are they?" he asked.

I pointed to the powder room. Without taking his eyes or his gun off me, he sidestepped over, reached in to the powder room, grabbed my tennis shoes off the counter, and tossed them to me. I sat on the floor and put them on, wincing as the shoes rubbed against the cactus needles protruding from the bottoms of my feet.

Ralph and Walter got their second wind and started barking again.

Slipping into his growly bad-guy voice, the Hulk said … well, I don't know what he said. I couldn't make the words out over the din.

"What?" I shouted.

He motioned with his gun for me to go to the door.

I couldn't continue to stall without putting the dogs and Tuwanda in danger, so I did as he said.

"Open the door!" he ordered, pushing the gun's nose into the small of my back.

My mind was racing. I had to get away before we got into a car. At the top of my list of possibilities was that someone in the building would see us and call the police. I didn't see how I could physically overcome the Hulk, so next on the list was the possibility that the Hulk had made poor lifestyle choices and would drop dead of a heart attack in the hallway.

What happened was kind of a combination of both. As I opened the door, I first heard the sound of metal hitting bone and then the sound a Hulk makes when it hits the floor.

The gun was knocked out of his hand by the fall, and it skidded across the hall. I retrieved it and, with shaking hands, pointed it toward the Hulk's inert body. Tuwanda was standing over him with a two-handed grip on my bedside lamp—a solid brass monstrosity that used to sit on my desk in my Chicago office.

"I'm gonna go back to my apartment," she announced. "They doin' construction on the floor above me, but hammerin' and drillin' ain't nothin' compared to the shit that goes on here."

"We need to call the police before he wakes up."

"I already called 'em on my cell when I was listenin' in the bedroom. This guy made his intentions real clear and they wasn't good. I didn't trust Phoenix's finest to get here in time, though, so I smacked him with the lamp."

"I'm glad you did," I said sincerely.

The elevator doors slid open and a bunch of police officers spilled out like circus clowns out of a miniature car. They were dressed in full riot gear and held their guns forward in firing position.

"What did you tell them?" I hissed to Tuwanda.

"That there was a gang of terrorists plannin' on bombin' the police station. Cops don't get motivated unless they own asses is threatened."

"Put the gun down, ma'am," ordered the lead officer, "and both of you put your hands out where we can see 'em."

"Can I put the lamp down?" whined Tuwanda. "Seems unfair I gotta keep holdin' this thing."

The officer ordered one of his men to take the lamp and be careful not to smudge any prints. He motioned for us to stand back and then moved cautiously over to the Hulk. Without lowering his gun, he nudged the Hulk with his boot toe.

"Is he dead?" he asked.

"Damned if I know. I ain't no doctor." said Tuwanda. "Since I was tryin' to stop him from kidnappin' my lawyer, I wasn't too careful about how hard I hit him. You know, when you under pressure you can't gauge that kinda thing."

The officer looked from Tuwanda to me. "You the lawyer?" he asked.

I nodded.

"Why're you dressed like that?" he asked.

One of the men behind him guffawed. "Maybe they finally passed a law that makes lawyers dress the part—you know, like snakes."

"I am not a snake," I said defensively. "I am a frog."

"I was gonna' say dragon," offered another officer.

The door to the fire stairs opened, and Webber

emerged, red-faced and huffing. I figured he and his pot belly couldn't jam into the elevator with the others and so he had to take the stairs.

"The dispatcher said there was a 9-1-1 call from your address," he said between gasps for air. "Emily, where is Emily?"

"She's fine. She's having lunch at Paco's with my staff," I said, hurrying to reassure him.

Webber ran a shaking hand over his face. "Thank God." Then he seemed to notice the Hulk for the first time. "Who's that?" he asked.

"I don't know his name," I said. "But he was one of the guys guarding the door at Maria's funeral."

Webber crouched down to get a better look at the guy's face. "Candy Roberts," he announced. "He's one of McDougall's bodyguards."

"Roy McDougall?" I asked in surprise.

"The one and only," said Webber. "McDougall was at Maria's funeral."

"I know," I said.

"Did you say this guy's name is *Candy* or *Andy*?" butted in Tuwanda.

"Candy, as in the sweet stuff that rots your teeth," provided Webber. Now that he knew his daughter was okay, he was being unusually responsive.

"No wonder he so mean. Damn. Candy. He musta' got beat up a lot at school," she said sympathetically. "I knew a guy named Christy once, but it kinda fit, if you get my meanin'.'"

The captain of the riot squad, probably realizing he was losing control of the situation, moved between me and Webber. "I'm going to need you and your friend to come down to the station to give your statements."

"What about him?" I asked, head-jerking to Candy.

"We've already called in the EMTs to take care of your victim."

"*Victim*?" repeated Tuwanda incredulously. "Oh no, you din't say that. He was holdin' a gun on Kate here. He ain't no victim. *We* was the victims."

"Ma'am, when we got here your friend was holding a gun on ... er ... Candy. Not the other way around."

"I *tol'* you what happened," snapped Tuwanda.

"And now I need to get it in writing," said the officer reasonably.

The elevator doors slid open again, and three EMTs emerged. One of them was pushing a gurney. We all moved out of the way so they could get to Candy.

"Hey," said the EMT pushing the gurney. "I know you."

I looked around to see who he was talking to.

"You, the one in the green outfit. You were in a fire once, right?"

"Well, I've been in a couple of fires," I started to explain.

"This was the one where you were naked," he clarified.

Ah, yes.

They rolled Candy onto his back, and one of the EMTs checked Candy's vital signs while another inserted an IV needle in his arm and slapped an oxygen mask over his face. I took this as a sign that Candy was still alive. Candy verified his un-dead status by slitting his eyes open and hoarsely whispering, "Bitch," into his mask.

I wasn't sure whether he was referring to Tuwanda or me.

The EMT who had recognized me removed a long, cloth-covered board from the gurney and positioned it next to Candy. Then he and his colleague lifted Candy a few inches off the ground while the remaining EMT slid the board under him. They quickly strapped him on and then hefted him onto the gurney, where they used more straps to secure the board and Candy to the gurney.

While this last part was going on, the elevator doors slid open yet again, and Emily lightly stepped out, still wearing her tutu. The hallway looked like that scene from *Night at the Opera* where the Marx Brothers and a bunch of passengers, waiters, crew members, and wall painters pack into a tiny stateroom.

Upon spotting me, Emily waved a white bag over her head and said, "I brought you some tacos." After a moment of hesitation, she added, "Why are there so many people here?"

Emily hadn't caught sight of her dad yet, but he promptly took care of that. "Emily, come here!" he ordered.

Emily stiffened at the sound of his voice and looked afraid.

The guy really needs a lighter touch, I thought. *He's talking to her the same way he talks to suspects.*

Webber started to push his way toward his daughter. She shot me a panicked look and hit the elevator's down button. The doors opened immediately, and Emily rushed inside.

The doors closed before Webber could reach her, but that didn't stop him from wedging his fingers in the space between the two doors and attempting to force them open. When the doors stubbornly refused to yield, he started kicking them. I don't know why he thought kicking would do any good. It probably made the doors angrier and more determined to thwart him.

Breathing heavily, he spun around and pointed an accusing finger at me. "This is your fault," he yelled.

After a few beats of uncomfortable silence, one of the EMTs commented, "Sheesh, this is like an episode of *As the World Turns.*"

Candy groaned. This seemed to refocus everyone, except Webber, on his situation.

"We need to get this guy to the hospital," said an EMT, as he pushed the gurney toward the elevator. His colleagues followed him, and the overworked elevator doors opened to let them in.

As soon as the EMTs left with their burden, the police captain reiterated his request that we accompany him to the station. Of course, I knew it was more of a demand than a request and if we didn't cooperate, he would arrest us as material witnesses and haul us in anyway. I was more than happy to comply, though, because I didn't want to be alone with Webber.

"At least I don't gotta call my lawyer," grumbled Tuwanda.

Webber trailed behind us, and I could hear him on his cell phone reporting a "runaway" and giving the name and a description of his daughter. I couldn't hear the police dispatcher's side of the conversation, but, after pausing to listen, Webber said, "That's none of your business."

The dispatcher had probably remarked on the fact that Webber and the runaway had the same last name.

On the way down in the elevator, one of the riot squad members said, "Someone stinks."

Everyone looked at me.

"I fell into a pile of mulch," I said.

There were murmurs of, "So that's what that is," "Thank God; I thought my uniform needed washing," and, "Jeez, Dixon; I thought maybe you'd had burritos for lunch again."

"Speakin' of burritos," said Tuwanda. "Did Emily leave the bag of tacos?"

"I think she took it with her," I said. For Webber's benefit, I added, "It's a good thing, too, because I hate to think of her out there with no food."

"She wouldn't have run if you hadn't poisoned her mind against me," snarled Webber.

"I did *not* poison her mind against you. Right, Tuwanda?"

"Tha's right," said Tuwanda." Emily's goin' through a rough time, detective. Maybe you should try listenin' an' understandin' instead of yellin'."

"Don't you try to tell me how to raise my daughter," warned Webber.

"Tuwanda's got a point," said one of the cops dressed in riot gear.

"It's none of her business," said another, siding with Webber.

This triggered a lively debate about child-raising practices.

"This elevator is awfully slow," the captain finally said, talking over his men.

"Did anyone hit the button for the ground floor?" I asked.

We all looked at the unlit panel.

"It don't look like it," said Tuwanda as she punched the ground floor button. "Guess that was an administrative oversight, right cap'n?"

The captain grunted and swiped the sweat off his face. The overcrowded elevator had gotten toasty.

Chapter 23

When the doors opened on the ground floor, we burst out of it. Outside felt relatively cool, even though the temperature had passed the ninety-degree mark.

Webber headed to his unmarked, yet still unmistakable, cop car. *Who drives black Crown Victorias—other than cops?* Tuwanda and I followed Captain Hamlin, who had introduced himself during our interminable elevator ride, and got into the back of the riot squad van with him and his men. The driver, a police officer in regular uniform, had waited outside in the van while the heavily armored and padded squad members stormed my building. The men removed all of their heavy gear after they sat down— except for the breathing masks hanging around their necks, which some of them placed them over their faces.

"Come on," I said. "I can't smell that bad."

"Yes, you can," said Tuwanda. Her voice was muffled

because she'd covered her nose and mouth with her hand.

I felt like a leper.

When we got to the station, we were taken to a small waiting room, given cans of Coke, and called in separately to give our statements to Captain Hamlin. Tuwanda was in the room with Hamlin for far less time than I—she probably omitted all the background information. However, I did not; I told Hamlin far more than he likely wanted or expected. I even told him that Maria had told Bryan and me that she had information about the skeleton found under the floor of my office and that she had planned to visit with her old social worker the day she was murdered; I also mentioned the Hulk and McDougall's attendance at the funeral, our interviews with Heiler and Madam K., McDougall's aborted visit to the Home, and I told him that the Hulk (I couldn't bring myself to call him Candy) had showed up at my condo with a gun and a request that I accompany him on a car ride from which I would never come back. I gave permission to Hamlin to tape the interview and told him that, once it was transcribed, I would be more than happy to sign it.

When I finished talking, he turned off the recorder, leaned back into his chair, and folded his hands on the desk in front of him. Objectively speaking—if one can ever be objective about such things—Hamlin was damned good looking: curly brown hair, green eyes, a straight nose, and full lips. Right now, though, his good looks were marred by a frown and scowl lines.

"What is this thing between you and Detective Webber about his daughter?" he asked.

"It's kind of personal," I responded, not wanting to air Webber's dirty laundry in front of one of his fellow police officers.

"It is not personal if it interferes with the performance of Detective Webber's duties. It appears that you have quite a bit of information on two cases that are currently assigned to Detective Webber. Whatever is going on between you two, whether consciously or subconsciously, affects the efficacy of the investigations, and in particular, your cooperation as a material witness."

I started to protest, but he held up his hand to silence me.

"I'm not saying that you are intentionally withholding material facts from an investigating officer. I am saying that the tension between you two is preventing open and honest communication."

The man had a point. Webber's overriding concern about his daughter caused him to teeter between bullying and cajoling to get information about her, and his first priority was clearly his child—not his cases.

I sighed and explained the situation involving me, Webber, and Emily from beginning to end. The captain did not interrupt, but the lines between his eyebrows deepened as I spoke.

When I finished, he excused himself and left the room, leaving me alone with my thoughts.

Even if Webber should be removed from the skeleton

case and Maria's murder case, Hamlin probably thinks that Webber is perfectly justified in being concerned about his daughter, who has been staying with a nutcase who took her to a retirement home where, after they gained access through false pretenses, the girl dressed like a puffin and escaped through a third-story window. I can't provide a stable environment for myself, much less for a thirteen-year-old girl.

After a few more minutes, during which I continued to beat myself up about being a lousy parent-figure, Hamlin returned and asked me to wait outside with Tuwanda until my statement was ready.

"Will the cases be transferred?" I asked.

"Your skeleton case will be transferred to another detective in our department. It's likely that we will cede jurisdiction over the Garcia murder case to the sheriff's office, since the matter is subject to dual jurisdiction anyway. Great. My relationship with the acting sheriff was even more strained than my relationship with Webber. I didn't want to go into it with Hamlin, though. I'd told him enough about my dysfunctional personal life.

I called Sam on a police department phone and asked him to pick up Tuwanda and me at the station in about half an hour. Then I settled in to wait for my statement to be typed. While I was in Hamlin's office, Tuwanda had stretched out on the waiting room couch and was now sound asleep. For a woman so picky about where she slept, it seemed to me she could sleep anywhere.

Sam arrived at the same time my statement was ready for my signature. I corrected a few typos, signed, and delivered it to the desk sergeant, whose name tag identified him as Sgt. Williams. No relationship to me—as far as I knew.

"Sergeant, I'm wondering if you could do me a favor," I said, leaning toward him flirtatiously. Let me tell you right now, flirtation does not work when you're in a frog costume and smell worse than a swamp. The sergeant recoiled and pinched his nostrils shut.

"You need a bath and a personal shopper, lady," he responded nasally.

Dropping the flirtatious attitude, I asked him if he could inform the lady in the reception area that her ride was here. I didn't tell him the lady in the reception room did not like being woken up, which was why I preferred he do it.

He obliged, and, as Sam and I waited at his desk, we listened for the explosion of expletives from Tuwanda. We were not disappointed.

"What the *hell*. I'm in here tryin' to get some sleep an' you come in an' bother me with your shit. Tha's mean. Tha's police brutality. It's 'cuz I'm black, ain't it? If I was a white woman you'd be bringin' in a blanket an' tuckin' me in."

The sergeant bolted out of the reception area and dove behind his desk. "What is her problem?" he asked, sounding shell-shocked.

"She hasn't gotten a lot of sleep lately, so she really hates it whenever she's finally able to grab some z's and someone wakes her," I explained belatedly.

"You set me up," he hissed.

I shot the sergeant a sweet smile that wouldn't be an effective salve even without the frog suit.

Tuwanda came out of the waiting room looking stormy.

"Why don't we go to El Barrio so you two can grab some lunch?" suggested Sam, cutting off Tuwanda before she could chastise the sergeant again.

I looked at Sam gratefully. Even though I didn't have much of an appetite and would have preferred joining the search for Emily, food was always an effective distraction where Tuwanda was concerned.

"Tha's a good idea, Sam," said Tuwanda, appearing to forget about Sergeant Williams and heading for the front exit. "Where you parked?"

"In the handicapped zone." Sam's car had handicap license plates, even though he is in no way handicapped that I'm aware of. I asked him about it once, and he said something about the existence of a handicap being a subjective determination. MJ says he got them because he's an asshole.

"Is El Barrio open?" I asked Sam as we trotted behind Tuwanda.

He nodded. "Under new management."

"Whose? How could Maria's estate be settled so soon?" The answer came to me then, and I answered my own question. "Her stepbrother is running the restaurant, isn't he?"

We reached Sam's car, and, as he opened the passenger

side door for me, he said, "I found out more about Maria's stepbrother. Something's off in the whole setup."

"You mean more off than Maria being treated as a servant by her adoptive family?" I asked angrily.

"I'll explain it over lunch, which, by the way, I have already eaten, so I will be present in my official capacity only."

After we were all in the car, with Tuwanda lying down on the backseat, I borrowed Sam's cell phone and called Macy. When she didn't answer, I left her a voice mail message explaining that Emily had run off again and asking her to be on the lookout for her in case she showed up at my or Macy's condo.

"I can't believe it will take the police long to find a teenager wandering around in a tutu," commented Sam.

"She might hide out until dark and then go to Goodwill's drop-off center and get some different clothes. That's what she did last time."

"Did you tell Webber that?"

"No, I guess I forgot to mention it in all the confusion—you know: the kidnapping, the rescue by Tuwanda and the lamp, and the arrival of the police riot squad and EMTs."

Sam grimaced. "I haven't heard the details of your adventure. It sounds wild, but, sadly, not atypical."

I punched him the shoulder, and the car swerved.

"Dammit!" Tuwanda commented loudly from the backseat. "Don't you know not to smack the driver? You gonna get us killed."

I ignored her. This particular driver deserved to be smacked.

"So, if the police haven't found Emily by nightfall, do you want me to stake out Goodwill Industries?" asked Sam, not sounding the least bit apologetic.

"I think we should both go," I said. "It's a rough area."

"How 'bout the three of us go?" asked Tuwanda.

Surprised, I turned to look at her. "Don't you have to go to work tonight?" I asked.

"Uh-uh. Marge is back, and she's gonna handle things for a coupla' days so's I c'n do some reflectin'."

"What do you need to reflect on?" asked Sam, sounding genuinely concerned.

"Life's purpose. My life's purpose in partic'lar. I gotta figure out what I'm meant to do."

I was taken aback by her response. All the time I've known Tuwanda, she's been proud of her business acumen and management skills, and moreover, completely unapologetic about the nature of her profession. I knew she was tired and needed a break, but I'd had no idea she was deeply questioning her lifestyle choices.

I didn't have a chance to delve into the developing crisis, though, because Sam had pulled into a parking space across from El Barrio and was politely waiting for us to get out before he turned off the engine—and the air conditioning.

It was already two o'clock, so there were only a few other diners when we walked in. The hostess was a young woman I recognized as one of the Batista daughters we'd seen at Maria's funeral. If she knew who I was, she didn't let on. In fact, she seemed incredibly bored and a little put out that we'd interrupted her in the middle of a vacant stare. On the bright side, she didn't seem especially put off by my frog suit and *eau de* garbage. Her antipathy was directed toward all of us equally.

I wondered if Mario and his clan could make a go of the restaurant in the absence Maria's welcoming presence.

Although there were plenty of other empty tables, she led us to the one closest to the restrooms. I didn't want to make a big deal out of it because I figured it was best we not bring unnecessary attention to ourselves. Even if the hostess, whose brain waves appear to have flat-lined, did not object to my frog suit, the other customers and wait staff might. Sam the germaphobe would have none of it, however. "Could we please have a table outside the flight pattern of particles containing fecal matter?" he asked.

The hostess looked at him uncomprehendingly.

"He don't want to eat next to where people poop," clarified Tuwanda.

"Sit any where you want, then," she said peevishly.

Her expertise and authority regarding seating selection having been questioned, she slammed copies of the menu down on top of a wood-paneled half-wall and stomped back to her hostess station.

I grabbed the menus, and Tuwanda and I followed Sam as he inspected tables further removed from the rest room area. He finally found one that satisfied his stringent standards. We sat, and I distributed the menus.

"Looks like the same food, anyway," commented Tuwanda.

I didn't notice any difference between the items listed and Maria's offerings either, which I considered a big plus.

I didn't recognize the waiter that came by our table. "I haven't seen you before. Did you just start working here?" I asked pleasantly.

"Yes," he said. "I guess when the previous owner died, a lot of the staff here left or was let go."

It sounded like the new boss might be a jerk

I ordered a pitcher of iced tea for us to share and one cheese enchilada. Tuwanda got the five-enchilada platter with rice, beans, sour cream, and guacamole. Sam and Tuwanda munched on taco chips dipped in hot sauce while we waited. I was too nervous about Emily to have much of an appetite.

Sam filled us in on what he and MJ had found during their search of the newspaper archives, which they had returned to after receiving the new information Emily had provided over lunch. The name Marni had appeared several times. However, most of the Marnis were too old or too young to refer to a woman of working age. The only Marni who fit the timeline and description was a thirty-two year old woman reported by her family as missing in May of 1953.

According to her employer, Miss Marni Radowsky

had left her job as a secretary to pursue a more lucrative career in New York. The family was concerned, however, because she failed to contact them before she left. At first, authorities pursued the possibility that a foster child previously placed with Radowsky had disappeared as well. However, Mr. Heiler of the Arizona Department of Health Services had reported that the child had been adopted by an out-of-state couple the week before, and he had produced records of the adoption. The names of the adoptive parents were hidden, ostensibly to protect the family's privacy.

Sam and MJ didn't find any follow-up articles, and Sam opined that, since no news is good news, perhaps the woman had gotten hold of her family and all was well.

Our conversation was interrupted when the food arrived, but we quickly got back to the subject as soon as the waiter was out of earshot.

"It's too much of a coincidence. Marni Radowsky must be the secretary employed by McDougall whom Madam K. said disappeared in 1953. The name is right, and the year is right. Plus, Madam K. said something about McDougall's former secretary babysitting kids he took care of out of the 'kindness of his heart.' She could have the facts wrong; maybe Marni was foster-parenting one or more children at McDougall's or Heiler's request."

"Even if that's true, how do you jump from that to finding a girl's skeleton under the floor of my office? We still don't know for sure if anyone lived there with a child during the relevant period," Sam said, once gain playing devil's advocate.

"What about the stuff that happened today?" interjected Tuwanda. "McDougall showed up at the old folks' home, an' Candy come out to warn him off, pro'bly because Kate an' Emily were there. Then, later, Candy comes to Kate's apartment and makes it clear she goin' for a ride and ain't comin' back."

"Who's Candy?" asked Sam. "Emily didn't mention anyone named Candy while we were at Paco's."

"Did she tell you about Kate haulin' her out of the old folks' ASAP when a real big guy came into Heiler's room?"

Sam nodded.

"Tha's Candy. He don't look like no Candy, but tha's who Webber said he was."

"From what Emily told us about the goings on in that Home, it could be that Candy and McDougall were afraid that Kate would blow the whistle on what sounds like a racket—getting big bucks out of patients and the state in exchange for very few services," said Sam. "Don't get me wrong, that sucks, but it's a separate issue and has nothing to do with our skeleton."

Sam's point was valid. I sighed and threw up my hands in a helpless gesture. Then something started nagging at me. Something Emily had told me. I shut my eyes tightly and tried to remember what it was.

It had something to do with Emily's review of the census records. *That's it! According to the 1950 census, a*

woman named Marci or Marcia Ratomski had lived in our
building. Emily said the handwritten report was hard to read,
though. Could the name actually be Marni Radowsky?

I explained my theory to Sam and Tuwanda.

Sam conceded that the names were close and promised to take a look at the census records again that afternoon.

"You got lots of interestin' facts," said Tuwanda, "an' McDougall seems to have a connection to most of 'em. It's unlikely he'd come out an' admit he done somethin' bad. But if we talk to him we might pick up on somethin' from his body language.

"We offer seminars at Pole Polishers on body language. Knowin' that stuff comes in real handy when you tryin' to figure out if a person's a potential client or a cop."

"You're right," I acknowledged. "We can't put off talking to McDougall anymore. We've exhausted all of our non-McDougall resources. The trick is to get information out of him without tipping him off as to why we're asking."

"That's exactly what Emily said at lunch."

I had a chilling thought.

"You don't think Emily would try to talk to McDougall on her own, do you?" I asked.

"I have no idea," Sam answered with a shake of his head. "MJ told her that, since he is a client of the firm, we could probably find a reason to set up a meeting with him on our turf. But then, anything he said to us would be subject to the attorney-client privilege, and unless there was a clear admission of guilt, we couldn't use anything we learned against him."

"That's when Beth mentioned where he lived, and everyone jumped in with silly ideas on how we could trick him into an admission. MJ wanted to dress up as a Girl Scout selling cookies. Apparently a Girl Scout uniform is part of her permanent costume collection."

"Are you sure Emily understood you were joking around?" I asked nervously.

"She seemed to. She joined in and said she was the only one of us who could come close to passing as a Girl Scout," said Sam. "Oh God, you don't think she was serious, do you?"

I patted his hand. "I don't think she would do something like that. She's a smart girl. Plus, where would she find transportation to McDougall's house?"

"She found a way to get from Goodwill Industries to your condo, and since you think she might go back to the Goodwill, you obviously think she's capable of getting around," Sam pointed out.

"Okay. So we stake out McDougall's house too. You take one location, and I'll take the other."

"I'll ride with you, Kate," offered Tuwanda.

"Ride or sleep?" I asked suspiciously.

"With any damn luck, one'll lead to the other," said Tuwanda.

I stuffed the last half of my solitary enchilada into my mouth. Tuwanda had already finished her much-larger meal and was polishing off the taco chips.

"I should take the Goodwill Industries gig since I have connections there," I said. "Maybe we should take a drive by McDougall's house now to get the lay of the land. Plus, while I don't think she would have gone there directly, it won't hurt to check."

"Wait. You have connections at the Goodwill?" asked Tuwanda. "You don' look like the Goodwill shoppin' type."

"Not *at* the store. *Behind* the store," I clarified. Then I explained about meeting Basil and Beth's godson, Duane.

"You got a strange collection of acquaintances," she commented.

"Present company excepted?" I asked, smiling.

"Uh-uh. Present company included an' pro'bly takin' the top spot on the weird people list. Sam here's a close second."

"Speak for yourself, Tuwanda," he said. "The only reason I hang around you, Kate, and MJ is it makes me feel relatively normal by comparison."

Again my father's logic popped into my mind, only he would say, "you want to appear sane? Hang around with nuts."

There was definitely something going on with Tuwanda and her self-image, though. I didn't want to put her on the spot in front of Sam, but when we were alone we needed to talk. The fact that Tuwanda didn't offer so much as a "harrumph" in response to Sam's snipe only added to my concern.

I wiped my mouth carefully with my napkin. I remembered that Sam hadn't yet told what else he'd learned about Maria's stepbrother. I reminded him of that fact.

"Remember Beth told you that Maria had left everything to the Foster Care Association in her will?" Sam waited for me to nod before continuing. "He's contesting it. He claims that the will the police found in her safe was superseded by a subsequent agreement by Maria to leave the restaurant to him in exchange for a $50,000 operating loan from Mario. Until the suit is resolved, he's been appointed as the trust asset manager, and since the Foster Care Association is a charity, they don't have a lot of money to fight this thing."

"They're not going to need it," I said through gritted teeth. "They don't know it yet, but they just found an attorney willing to represent them *pro bono*."

Sam groaned. "At some point, Kate, we will have to expand our client base to include paying clients you don't suspect of murder."

I went into the ladies room to clean myself up while Sam paid the bill. Unfortunately, the bathroom sink was too small for much of a clean-up effort, but I at least managed to wipe down all the parts that weren't covered by the suit. The way it turned out, a more thorough cleaning would have been a waste of time anyway.

Chapter 24

Sam was parked outside the entrance with the engine running and the AC on by the time I got out of the ladies room. For those of you who have never sat down in a car that has been baking in the Phoenix sun, the experience can be compared to sitting on a hot stove. (This, of course, assumes that sitting on a hot stove is a more common experience. I hope this isn't true.) Pre-cooling your car for your passengers is the height of courtesy in Phoenix. Throwing a cape over a muddy gutter does not even come close.

I borrowed Sam's phone again, this time to call Duane and tell him to watch for Emily. His shift didn't start until the store closed, but he promised to call me if she showed up during his watch. He said he'd put Basil on notice, too, but Basil's monthly sci-fi film festival started tonight, so he wasn't sure how much attention Basil would be willing to give to the matter.

After I ended the call, Sam gave me McDougall's address, and I acted as navigator with Tuwanda participating as navigation consultant. I knew Phoenix pretty well by now, but Tuwanda was the hands-down expert when it came to the city's nooks and crannies.

McDougall lived a couple blocks west of the North Central Avenue Mansion Row, in what I would describe as the even-bigger-mansion cul-de-sac. We grew quiet as we approached his home. Sam parked across the street so we had a good view of the front of the Tudor-style mansion. Our position also gave us an excellent view of the electronic entry gate, the iron-bar fence surrounding the property, and the security cameras attached to the fence posts at regular intervals.

Sam gave a low whistle. "That guy is either seriously paranoid or he's had a bad experience with burglars."

Tuwanda, who was leaning forward between the two front seats to see, said, "It looks like the kinda' place where they don' like to be bothered by people sellin' things. Hell, it looks like the kind of place where they don' like people period. So it ain't likely he'd let Emily in, no matter what she dresses up in."

"You are assuming that McDougall is trying to keep people out," I muttered. "Maybe he's trying to keep them in. Maybe he's a sexual predator who likes his victims to stay put."

"You got a sick mind, Kate," said Tuwanda. "I'm the one leadin' a life of sin, here. If anyone should be cynical and un-trustin', it should be me. You an educated, middle-class white woman with a legitimate job. What bid'ness do you have bein' so neg'tive?"

"I've been practicing criminal law for over fifteen years," I countered. "You don't see many positives in my line of work."

"Shhhh. Get down!" ordered Sam, as McDougall's front gates started to slowly swing open. Before he too dived down, he angled the rearview mirror so we could watch without lifting our heads into the discovery zone.

The same black car I had seen McDougall get into at the funeral slid out.

"Tha's the old fart's car," hissed Tuwanda.

It stopped outside the gate, and a man who looked like a bouncer got out of the driver's side. He left the door open as he unlocked a post box standing outside the gate and removed a stack of mail.

"The man can't even walk to the damn mailbox," whispered Tuwanda disgustedly.

I was trying to see into the car's interior, though. I couldn't care less about the man's level of activity.

I couldn't see through the dark-tinted passenger side window into the backseat. But what I saw in the front seat was enough to make my blood run cold: a froth of black and white net peeked out of the top of a paper grocery bag.

"Emily," I whispered frantically.

"Do you see her in the car?" Sam asked softly.

"The bag in the front seat. That's her tutu." I pictured her lying in the backseat or, God forbid, in the trunk.

"She ain't in the car," Tuwanda whispered.

"How can you tell?" I asked, hoping she was right.

"'Cuz he ain't actin' like he's got a bo … um, passenger in the car. He don't seem like he's in any kinda hurry, and he ain't checkin anythin' in the backseat. People got somethin' to hide, they don't take their time like that, an' if Emily's in that car, she ain't there willin'ly, so she'd be somethin' to hide."

"She must be in the house," I said, going for the door handle.

"Stop," hissed Sam. "Let's wait to see if he goes back in. If he does, maybe we can slip in before the gate closes."

But he didn't. He drove off instead.

"He's trying to dispose of evidence," I moaned. "It may be too late."

"Uh-uh," said Tuwanda. "It ain't too late. I jus' know it."

"But …"

"Now ain't the time to express your neg'tivism," she growled. "We gotta get in that house."

I swallowed the lump in my throat. "We should call the police," I said.

"In the time it would take us to explain what's goin' on an' convince one of Phoenix's bravest that one of the city's most upstandin' citizens is a freak, we could already be in there.

"Or maybe you think we should skip the police an' call your friend Bryan for help."

"Let's go," I said.

But now it was Sam's turn to demur.

"Are you *sure* it was her tutu?" asked Sam as he hauled a Glock out from under his seat.

Despite a flash of doubt, I nodded. "Yes."

"Then I'm going in," he said.

"No *you* are not. *We* are," I said.

"If 'we' includes me, I agree with Kate," said Tuwanda in a tone that did not invite dispute.

"I've only got one other gun—a thirty-eight I keep in the trunk," said Sam, probably hoping this would make one of us back off.

"Tuwanda can have the gun," I said. "I've never used one so I wouldn't know what to do with it anyway."

"It's real easy," Tuwanda assured me. "You point and pull. Thirty-eights don't got no safety to worry about. 'Course it's got twice the kick of that Glock," she said, looking enviously at the gun in Sam's hand."

"Oh for God's sake," he muttered. "I'll take the thirty-eight. Tuwanda, you take the Glock. Kate, you stay behind us."

"You got a knife or somethin' for bashin' she can carry jus' so she don't feel naked, weapon-wise?" asked Tuwanda.

"I've got a tire iron. That's about it," said Sam.

"I'll take it," I said. I really didn't want to haul a heavy tire iron along with me on an illegal entry that was likely to involve a fair amount of physical exertion, but I didn't want to hold things up.

Tuwanda and I got out on the curb side and stayed

down while Sam went around to the trunk, popped it open, and removed the additional weaponry. He pretended to examine one of the tires for the benefit of anyone who might be watching. However, since the houses were set back far from the street and bougainvillea and oleander screened us from view, it was unlikely that we had an audience. Even someone in McDougall's house would have to stand in the middle of the driveway to have a clear view of us.

Sam handed the Glock to Tuwanda and the tire iron to me.

"Where do I put this if we have to climb over a fence?" I grumbled.

"Toss it over first," Sam answered promptly. "Try not to hit anything that could clang or yell when you do."

"Got it: thump okay, clang or scream not." I wasn't sure I agreed with, or even completely understood, these guidelines, but I didn't want to waste time nitpicking.

"Follow me," ordered Sam, giving us the "let's go" command with a wave of his gun.

Running in a half–crouch, Sam skirted the cul-de-sac, keeping a row of oleanders between himself and McDougall's house. Tuwanda and I followed, inches from his heels. Instead of heading for the gate, he went down a small alley running between McDougall's fence and the neighbor's. Oleander lining both sides of the alley made it seem as if we were fighting our way through a Guatemalan jungle.

We were moving in single file now, with Sam in

the lead and me at the rear. It was clear that Sam and Tuwanda had never been in the Scouts, because they didn't comply with the hiking rules of courtesy: don't let branches snap back and whap the person behind you. Oleander branches are especially elastic, and after a couple of slingshot rebounds to the head, I dropped back and maintained a safe distance.

Every so often, Sam would stop to scrutinize the fence. I had no idea what he was looking for. Breaks in the bars maybe? If so, he wasn't finding any. Finally, after we'd rounded the corner of the fence and were behind the house, he found a gap in the oleanders and grunted in satisfaction.

I didn't see what was so special about this particular spot, but Sam seemed pleased.

Through the bars, I could see the windowless back of a shed built out of the same red brick as the house. Sam took the tire iron from me and shoved it through the bars to the other side. He did the same thing with the guns. Making a sling out of his hands, he motioned for Tuwanda to step up for a boost. She shook her head, joined her hands to make a sling, and motioned for Sam to go for it. Tuwanda is no dummy. She wanted Sam on the other side to catch her when it was her turn to vault over.

Sam rolled his eyes, but he put one foot into Tuwanda's hands and grasped the bars as high up as he could. She boosted him up, exhibiting a level of strength you would never guess someone with her physique possessed. Sam pulled himself up and managed to get one leg over the fence. The tops of the bars dug into his upper thigh, and I could tell by the look on his face how much it hurt. He stoically flipped his other leg over, so now the top of the bar had full-on contact with his groin. He let out a puff of air and moaned. Tuwanda and I grimaced in sympathy. He then dropped to the ground and lay in a fetal position. After some muted groaning, he managed to uncurl and stand up, although his face was still ashen.

After a brief, wordless argument during which we each urged the other to go next, I boosted Tuwanda and she went over like an Olympic gymnast. Sam caught her around the waist on the other side and lowered her gently to the ground.

It was my turn. There was no one left to give me a boost, so I moved over to an oleander and tested its lower branches with my foot. It wasn't one of my finer moments, but I had once before climbed over a high stone wall with the assistance of an oleander. It had taken me a couple of tries, and I ended up with a lot of cuts and bruises, but I'd managed to pull it off. This prior experience did not make me a pro, but it had taught me a few dos and don'ts — mostly the latter.

I planted my right foot on the base of a promising-looking branch and started to climb, making it a little over three feet off the ground before the oleander started to dip under my weight.

Sheesh. Maybe I have *gained some weight,* I thought. But then my highly developed system of rationalization kicked in, and I blamed the plant for being a wimp.

The fence was about eight feet tall. I managed to get high enough to grab the cross bar, but the rest of the operation was a no-go. The only way I was going to make it over was head first.

Because I am distrustful both by nature and profession, I fully expected to land on my head, and I mentally prepared for another concussion. It didn't happen that way, though. When I pushed up and went into a dive, Tuwanda and Sam caught me by the shoulders and lowered me to the ground. Tears of emotion stung my eyes.

"Are you hurt?" mouthed Tuwanda.

I shook my head. I was not hurt. I was touched.

We picked up our assigned weapons, and, with Sam taking the lead again, crept along the side wall of the shed toward the house.

I scanned the back of the house with dismay. Climbing over the fence was hard. Going through the narrow, barred windows on the first floor looked impossible. Not only were the bars formidable, but if the owner was as security-conscious as he seemed, you could bet an alarm system had been installed as well.

Sam and Tuwanda seem to share my sense of futility, because neither made a move toward the back of the house.

A second-story window began to slowly open. It moved in the short jerks indicative of a rarely-used mechanism. We reflexively shrank back into the shadow of the shed.

Emily's head emerged, her eyes wide with panic. She

ducked back inside and a kneesock-clad leg appeared over the sill.

"My God, she's going to jump," I whispered hysterically. Sam grabbed my arm before I had a chance to bolt to the side of the house to catch her. He snatched up a piece of gravel with his free hand and hurled it at Emily's leg. It missed, but the soft sound it made when it hit the wall made her look up, and she searched the yard uneasily. Sam took aim with another pebble while Tuwanda and I waved frantically to get her attention. When she didn't see us, I took a step out of the shed's shadow and continued to wave. Sam hauled me back, but not until she'd seen me. Her face lit up with hope. She pulled her leg back in and leaned out to see us better. She was wearing a pink flower-print dress with lace around the neck and smocking over the bodice. I shivered. Maybe I was imagining it, but the material looked similar in design and color to the cloth remnants clinging to the bones of our skeleton.

"What's taking so long, girl?" called out a querulous voice. The panic returned to Emily's face, and she recoiled as if she'd been slapped.

"We gotta storm the house," Tuwanda whispered urgently.

"No. We've got to get Emily out of there before we do anything. I don't want to give him a chance to get to her before we can get to him," I whispered with equal urgency.

"Who him?" asked Tuwanda.

"McDougall," I said, looking at Sam for verification.

Sam nodded. "That sounded like him," he confirmed. "We need to distract him until we can get Emily out."

"One of us should go ring the doorbell," I suggested.

"What if he don't answer?" countered Tuwanda.

"Then you bang on the front door until he does," I said, shrugging helplessly. I couldn't think of what else to do.

"It can't be you. He sees you out there dressed like the jolly green giant, ain't no way he's gonna answer the door."

"I'll do it," whispered Sam. "He knows me. I'll tell him I dropped by with some papers he needs to sign for his case. I'll say the chauffeur let me through the gate on his way out."

Before we could argue him out of it, Sam began working his way around the perimeter of the yard toward the front of the house.

We could hear loud banging inside the house. McDougall was probably pounding on the door to Emily's hideout.

"How we gonna get her out of that window?" whispered Tuwanda.

I smiled grimly. "She's done it before. She knows what to do."

After climbing down from the third floor of the Pearly Gates, a second-story window should be a piece of cake for her.

We motioned to Emily to stay put for the time being. It wasn't long before we heard the stentorian sound of an old-fashioned doorbell. McDougall's door pounding stopped. The bell rang again, and then again and again, until the noise became a continuous string of loud gongs. I could barely stand it. I couldn't see how McDougall, for whom it had to be much louder, could take it. Apparently he couldn't, because the ringing stopped.

Tuwanda and I raced across the yard and stood beneath the window. I set down my tire iron and Tuwanda tucked the Glock into her waistband, and we stretched our arms upward, leaning against the side of the house for stability. Right on cue, Emily flipped her legs over the sill and lowered herself until she was hanging by her fingers from the window frame. She was a few inches above grasping level.

"Let go, Emily," I whispered. She did and we caught her between us and lowered her to the ground. Once she was safely down, I put my arms around her and held her. She was shivering even though the temperature was still in the nineties.

"Why you dressed like that?" hissed Tuwanda. "You look like you in grade school."

"He made me," said Emily in a small, scared voice.

"Let's get Sam and get out of here," I said, no longer caring about lowering my voice. We had Emily. Nothing bad could happen now.

We headed for the front yard with Tuwanda in the lead. She stopped short after she'd just rounded the corner of the house and quickly backed up.

"The driver's back," she hissed. "An' he got a gun on Sam."

Sam had his phone with him, so now I had no way to call in the cavalry.

I motioned for Tuwanda to take Emily into the backyard, then I took a few steps forward until I was even with the house's facade, but still hidden.

I heard a punch and an "ooph" followed by a thump against the wall.

"You are overreacting, Mr. McDougall," Sam said, gasping for breath. "Tell your guy to put the gun down. I left the papers in my trunk in case you weren't home. If you come out to my car with me, I'll get them. It's parked right outside, at 413 E. Wagon Wheel."

Why was Sam making a point out of reciting the house's address? Did he think McDougall wasn't clear about what "right outside" meant?

"He said you let him in the gate, Lester," said McDougall, sounding amused.

"No sir. I did not." Lester had a surprisingly high voice for such a large man.

"Check him for a gun," ordered McDougall.

There was a pause, and then Sam giggled.

"What the hell," yelped Lester. "Are you some kinda fruit?"

I assumed the question was directed to Sam, because it's hardly the type of thing to ask your employer.

"This freak is enjoyin' this," spat Lester.

"I've had better," said Sam.

Another pause.

"All's he got is this lady-gun," said Lester, using a

sarcasm-laden, high, prissy voice when he got to the "lady gun," part. (Although, in my opinion, he didn't need to bump his voice up an octave to sound feminine.)

I gathered that Lester had found Sam's thirty-eight.

"Here's his BlackBerry. I didn't know they made these things in pink."

He'd found Sam's cell phone, too.

"Is he alone?" asked McDougall.

"Why don't you ask me?" Sam piped up. "I'm standing right here."

I heard what sounded like a slap.

"I looked inside his car when I got here. Looks like he was alone," said Lester. "Actually, it looks like it had never been ridden in. The damn car is spotless."

"Check around anyway," ordered McDougall. "Give me his gun, and I'll watch him while you search.

I backed up toward the rear of the house, frantically looking for a place to hide. McDougall must be a believer in minimalist landscaping; except for the pool, the backyard was mostly gravel with the occasional small ground plant. I dismissed the shed as a possibility when I saw the padlock on its door.

I motioned for Tuwanda and Emily to follow me as Lester started his search on the other side of the house. We hurried to the opposite side, and I positioned myself at the back corner with my tire iron raised. Tuwanda pointed her Glock in the same direction, but I motioned for her to put it down. I was afraid that, if McDougall heard a shot, he'd fire at Sam. I only hoped that my tire iron was faster than Lester's trigger finger. At least I had the element of surprise on my side.

I heard the crunch of footsteps on gravel as he neared our corner of the house. My knuckles whitened as I gripped the tire iron. The footsteps hesitated, and then the barrel of a gun appeared. I stepped forward and brought the tire iron down as hard as I could. I knocked the gun out of his hand, but he caught the tire iron neatly with his other hand before I could strike again. I struggled with him briefly and then Tuwanda slid out from behind me and cold cocked him between the eyes with the butt of the Glock.

"White girls," she muttered.

I squatted on my haunches and picked up Lester's gun, which had landed too close to Lester's supine body for comfort in the event he came to.

I needn't have worried, though. When Tuwanda knocks someone out, she goes for broke (or, perhaps more accurately, "for broken").

I motioned to Tuwanda and Emily to stay put. Holding Lester's gun in front of me in a two-handed grip, the way I'd seen Detective Benson do it in *Law and Order: SVU*, I moved quietly toward the front of the house, hesitating at the corner to gingerly peek around and check things out in the front yard.

McDougall saw me almost immediately. Keeping his gun trained on Sam, he gazed at me imperiously, exhibiting neither surprise nor fear. "Who are you?" he asked distastefully.

I stepped around the corner and smiled brightly. (A good lawyer can smile brightly—or assume any facial expression for that matter—on command. When the apocalypse comes, while everyone else is screaming and running for their lives, the attorneys will merely exhibit controlled concern while they discuss matters of causation and allocation of liability.)

"I am Kate Williams," I said. "Your attorney."

It is hard to pull off professionalism when you are wearing a green lizard suit. (I had given up on the frog characterization because it invited too much debate.)

"Ah, yes," he said, delightedly, as if that explained everything.

"Mr. McDougall, why are you holding a gun on my investigator?" I asked, trying to maintain a businesslike tone.

He would be justified in asking me why I was holding a gun on *him*, but he didn't. Instead, he appeared to spot something over my shoulder and his eyes softened.

"Lily," he whispered.

I glanced back and saw that Emily had come up behind me.

"My name is Emily, not Lily," she said in a strained, yet firm, voice.

"No, Lily. Remember? I saw you at the house—the house on Third Street." He spoke in the sweet, singsong voice people tend to use around small children.

"You saw Emily at my office," I corrected wondering when and how this creeper had watched us.

"Marni wouldn't tell me where you were," he said, ignoring me.

"Marni, your secretary?" I asked sharply.

McDougall continued to address Emily as if I wasn't there. "She was jealous of you, you know—because I loved you, not her."

Emily moved closer to me, and I could feel her breath on my neck.

"Where is Marni?" I asked. When he didn't respond, I whispered to Emily, "Ask him where she is."

"Where is Marni?" asked Emily.

McDougall shrugged. "I don't know. Adolph took her someplace. She wouldn't tell me where you were. I tried everything I could to persuade her, but she said she was going to the police, and they would take you away from me. But I hadn't *done* anything," he said, his tone becoming peevish. "All I did was take care of you and the other children; I looked after all your best interests.

"Of course, you are the one I wanted, Lily. I've been with girls since, but they all turned out to be little flirts who couldn't handle real intimacy.

He paused and looked at Emily thoughtfully and then smiled crookedly. "I guess you could say you're the 'one who got away.'"

Until that moment I had never before felt anger, fear, repulsion, and nausea simultaneously.

His thoughtful expression suddenly morphed into one of anger. "But those other children—Adolph and I found the ungrateful little colored bastards good, honest work.

They'd be thieves or worse if we hadn't. How dare that girl Maria complain."

His emotional pendulum took another swing. "You are different though, Lily," he said softly. "You are beautiful."

Sam had been standing like a statue throughout this exchange which, since the barrel of a gun was pressed against his temple, was about all he could do. Throughout his ramblings and despite his roller-coaster emotions, McDougall had kept his finger on the trigger and watched Sam out of the corner of his eye.

Suddenly we heard a commotion at the gate. While McDougall was momentarily distracted by the noise, Sam made his move and grabbed for the gun. The gun went off, and Sam slumped to the ground. McDougall raised the gun to fire again and then I—the one who hates guns, hates weapons of all kinds for that matter, and has never fired so much as a slingshot in her entire life—aimed to kill and pulled the trigger.

McDougall flew backward. There was a neat hole in his forehead. From a distance, it could have passed for a mole you might want a doctor to take a look at. But that illusion was shattered once you noticed that the back of his head was missing.

Duane came running up the driveway, gun drawn. "Duane?" I asked weakly. The sight of him should have shocked me, but since I was already in shock, that particular emotion was already in use.

He glanced at McDougall, and, no doubt realizing he

was a lost cause, knelt down and felt Sam's neck for a pulse and then thumb-punched three numbers into his cell phone. Nobody had to tell me which ones they were.

Once the 911 operator was on the line, he explained the situation and gave our location with great precision and minimal verbiage.

I had dropped the Glock and wrapped my arms around Emily as soon as I realized that McDougall was out of action. I squeezed my eyes shut tightly, afraid, so afraid, to look at Sam. I heard Tuwanda call out, and I managed to tell Duane about Lester. A different male voice joined the conversation.

"I'll stay with him," he said. "You go help the black lady."

I slit one eye open and immediately recognized the speaker. It was Basil, the old man who lived under the loading dock at Goodwill Industries. He had flipped Sam over and was holding a plastic grocery bag over a wound in his chest. The portion of the bag over the wound moved in and out slightly with an erratic rhythm.

I managed to get out, "Basil, it's me, Kate."

"Yes, I know," he said in the same clipped and cultured voice I remembered.

I worked up my courage, and asked, "How is my friend?"

I didn't hear his answer, though, because the sound of sirens drowned it out.

The usual crowd showed up: first the police, with the EMTs hard on their heels, and then the news vans. The police quickly disabled the gate's mechanism, and the yard filled with emergency and police vehicles. The news vans stayed out on the street, but the photographers and reporters did not.

Emily hid her face in my shoulder. Tuwanda joined us and wrapped her arms around us both. We crab-walked as one toward the exit. I wasn't sure where we were going. I only knew I had to get Emily away from there, fast.

I felt a hand on my shoulder. "Come with me," Webber whispered urgently. Since we didn't have a lot of other options, we did, keeping Emily cocooned among the three of us.

Webber's Crown Vic was parked near the entrance, its front wheels resting in a bed of geraniums.

With surprising gentleness, he guided us into the backseat, pausing briefly to hug Emily and gruffly whisper, "I'm sorry."

Emily, who had initially recoiled from her father's touch, sagged into him and started to cry.

"Sam!" I yelled. I shoved my foot in the door before Webber could close it all the way.

"They're taking him to St. Benedict's," Webber said not unkindly. "It's up to the docs now."

When I kept my foot on the door, he added, "I'll take you there as soon as we're through downtown." Webber's voice had a gentleness I thought him incapable of.

I relented and pulled in my foot.

Webber slapped a bubble light on top of the car, and,

after yielding for an ambulance, took off with the blue light flashing.

As Emily sobbed, I stroked her head, repeating, "It's okay, baby—you're safe," over and over.

Chapter 25

Emily's mother was waiting at the police station, and mother and daughter were hugging and crying when Tuwanda and I were led off to separate interview rooms.

A young, attractive detective named Sharon Delong brought me a Diet Coke and then took my statement, which I delivered in starts and stops between sobs and hiccups. She asked me several times during the interview if I needed anything. I got the feeling she wasn't talking about more Diet Coke, but something more along the lines of Xanax or Valium. I was pretty upset.

When I was done, Detective Delong led me out to a waiting area and deposited me into a surprisingly comfy armchair. Tuwanda was already in the room, lying on a puke-green couch with her eyes closed.

I begged Delong for information about Sam, and she promised to get me an update on his status.

As soon as Delong left the room, Tuwanda, without opening her eyes, said, "This was some kinda day."

I smiled grimly in response to her incredible understatement.

She opened her eyes and looked at me. "You did good, Kate," she said softly.

"I shot a man," I said miserably. The surge of determination and focus I'd felt as I faced McDougall had disappeared as soon as I fired the gun, and shock had set in and prevented what was happening from sinking in. Now, the shock had worn off, and I was left with the despair of realization.

"You had a damn good reason to do what you did," said Tuwanda, sitting up and swinging her feet to the floor. Her eyes were filled with concern.

Detective Delong made a brief appearance to tell us that Sam was in surgery, but other than that, there was no report on his status.

"He's in surgery," Tuwanda repeated. "Tha's a good thing, Kate. They only operate on live people."

Delong appeared a few seconds later to tell us an officer would take us home, but neither of us felt much like going home. We asked him to drop us off at St. Benedict's instead.

MJ, Beth, and a nice-looking man named Craig were already in the hospital waiting area when we arrived. The fact that they failed to comment on my lizard suit was evidence of their level of concern about Sam.

For the next eight hours, we waited. To my surprise, Bryan joined our little vigil sometime during the night.

Conversation was limited to the occasional inquiry as to whether anyone wanted something to eat or drink. No one felt much like eating. Instead, we survived on coffee.

At last, we got the news that Sam had made it out of surgery and was in the ICU. Permission was given for one of us to see him. The others insisted that I go in. This prompted me to let loose with a fresh batch of tears which, amazingly, were not coffee brown but were the regular, clear color.

The nurse cautioned me to stay behind the clear plastic curtain surrounding Sam's bed. She explained that he'd suffered a collapsed lung, and the danger of infection remained high. He was hooked up to the usual IV and blood pressure monitors, but tubes running out of his nose and chest indicated that something more than a bad case of the flu was going on.

His eyes were closed, and his face looked gray. I looked at the nurse nervously. "Will he be okay?" I whispered.

"We'll know better in twelve hours, but the fact that he made it through surgery is a good sign."

Twelve hours seemed like a long time. I wasn't sure I could hold up that long. Then I looked at Sam's gray face, and I knew if he could hang in there, so, by God, could I.

"I'm so sorry, Sam," I whispered. "This is my fault."

The room was quiet except for the whooshing of the oxygen machine and the rhythmic blipping of the monitors. I would have given anything to hear one of Sam's sarcastic comebacks.

The nurse urged us to go home and get something to eat, and maybe take a shower and get some sleep. (She looked directly at me when she made the shower suggestion.) Although we were reluctant to leave, each of us realized the outcome would be the same regardless of whether we stayed.

Beth, who had driven MJ over, volunteered to take Tuwanda as well as MJ home. After an awkward pause, Bryan said he would drive me to my condo.

Once we were in his car, I asked him flat-out what was wrong. I was too tired and too emotionally wrung-out to play games.

After an uncomfortable silence, he cleared his throat and gently said, "It's not working between us, Kate. You know that as well as I. We're too … different."

It sounded like a line from *Days of Our Lives*—dramatically trite. I didn't have the energy to muster a response, though, so I simply nodded. The good part was that my heart had already broken when Sam was shot, so nothing Bryan said could hurt me. I was already numb. I guess you could say I needed to be on emotional life support.

That support came in the form of the tiny Jewish lady who met me at the door, led me into my bedroom, and ordered me to shed the lizard skin, take a shower, and get in bed while she whipped up a little snack for me. I was grateful for Macy's bossiness, because it kept me from having to think. All I needed to do was follow orders.

Ralph and Walter were subdued and exhibited that

amazing empathy pets are capable of. Both of them climbed into bed with me after I took my shower, comforting me with their warm bodies pressed against my side. The depth of their understanding and discretion was underlined when Macy came in with a bed tray—no doubt hers, because I owned no such thing—laden with Macy's version of a snack and neither dog made a food-grab. However, Ralph did begin drooling. I forgave him, since this was an automatic response over which he had no control. Macy got both dogs off the bed and gave them treats of their own.

It was almost noon on Friday, and I had not had anything to eat for more than twenty-four hours. So for someone who didn't feel like eating, I packed away a fair amount of chicken soup, tuna and egg salad sandwiches, and chocolate-chip cookies that were still warm from the oven.

Macy removed the tray when I was done and returned with a bottle of water.

"Thank you for everything," I said.

She acknowledged my thank you with a smile. "Sleep," she said.

A tear slid down the side of my face. "I don't think I can."

"Would it help to talk about it?" she asked, her forehead wrinkling with concern. "Sometimes talkin' gets the bad thoughts out of your head so you can concentrate on sleep thoughts."

"I put Emily in terrible danger, and she'll be traumatized for the rest of her life; I got Sam shot; and I killed a man."

Macy looked at me thoughtfully. "So, you lined up three people; made one of them shoot the guy next to him while the third one watched; and then shot the shooter, to even out the body count—and you forced Emily to watch the whole thing? Somehow, I don't think that's what happened," she said softly. "You aren't responsible for what other people choose to do."

Macy brushed my hair out of my eyes. "I know you, Katy, an' you got a good heart. There isn't an evil bone in your body. Plus you're smart. But you think way too much of yourself."

I looked at her in surprise. The last part didn't seem all that supportive or sympathetic.

"You think if you can be perfect, everything else will be perfect too. Like it's all up to you. But that's not how it works. It's not all about you."

Sheesh. I'm a selfish control freak on top *of being a catalyst for catastrophe,* I thought. Tuwanda was right; I needed therapy.

Macy took my silence as a positive sign and patted my hand. "You get some sleep, sweetie," she said.

She took the dogs with her when she left the room, but Ralph made a nuisance of himself by whimpering and scratching on the door, so I got up and let him back in a few minutes later. I wasn't annoyed, though. I welcomed his non-judgmental doggy presence.

A few hours later, I still hadn't slept. I gave up on the napping idea and turned on the television in time to hear the mid-day news announcer say, "Prominent philanthropist Roy McDougall was found dead in the front yard of his home. The preliminary police report states he died of a gunshot wound to the head. According to the police, all persons of interest were interviewed and released."

No mention was made of the fact that the prominent philanthropist had shot a fine man and was revving up for another volley of gunfire before he was killed.

I told myself I should be happy the announcer hadn't given the names of any of the "persons of interest."

But then the camera cut to a shot of me in my lizard suit. Emily was standing next to me, but her head was buried in my shoulder, so her face was not visible. Mine was, and it looked terrible. Further, despite the partial camouflage provided by the multi-directional frog/lizard scales, it was clear that I needed to knock off a few pounds. The voiceover informed the audience that, "the woman in the furry green suit (*Great; now it was furry?*) was identified by police as Kate Williams, a local criminal attorney."

"Criminal *defense* attorney," I muttered.

The phone rang, and I beat Macy to the pick-up. "Hello," I said, half-afraid it was bad news.

"Damn," said Tuwanda. "I'm thinkin' you should hire a public relations firm. You got a knack for embarrassin' yourself in front of the media."

"What was I supposed to do? Dash away to freshen up and prepare a speech before the news trucks showed up?"

"Thas' stupid an' you know it," she harrumphed. "I'm talkin' 'bout someone who can deal with the press on your behalf an' explain all the shit you get into in a way that don't make you look so damn weird."

She had a good point. I just might follow up on her suggestion. But right now, I had other priorities. "Have you heard anything more about Sam?"

"Uh-uh. I did find out somethin' else, though." She continued. "I ran into Duane when we was leavin' the hospital an' he was comin'' in. I thanked him for helpin' us the way he did, but I said I was curious as to what made him and his raggedy friend decide to come out to McDougall's place.

"He said he'd gone over to the Goodwill before his shift to watch out for Emily, an' while he was there talkin' to … Basel, I think he said his name was … he got a call from Sam's phone. He thought it might be from you, 'cuz you jus' called him from that number. But all he heard when he picked up was Sam talkin' to some guy, an' from what he was sayin', it didn't sound good. Then Sam makes a point of givin' the address of where he was. So he headed over ASAP with that Basel dude …"

"Basil," I corrected.

"I don' care if his name was Rosemary, that ain't the point. Anyways, as I was sayin, he heads over with the other guy an' you know how it went down after that."

"How is that possible? Sam couldn't have called Duane; he didn't have his phone in his hand when McDougall's chauffeur came up. The chauffeur only found Sam's gun and phone after he searched him. I listened to the whole thing," I said, thoroughly mystified.

Tuwanda was silent for a while, then started to chuckle. "He butt called," she said.

"What?" I asked, thinking I hadn't heard her right.

"When Sam ain't wearin' a suit coat, he puts that phone in his back pocket, don't he?"

"Yes," I said, not seeing where she was going with this.

"So you never sat on your phone or bumped against something and accidently called someone?"

"No."

"Tha's cuz' you got a flip phone. Sam, he's got a BlackBerry like me. I call people all the time by mistake when I get careless an' forget to put my phone in the side pocket of my purse, an' it bumps up against like my lipstick or somethin'. Sam's butt coulda' pushed the redial button when that Lester guy was shovin' him around."

"I guess it could have happened that way," I said reluctantly. Even though Tuwanda's logic was a bit sketchy, I couldn't think of any other explanation.

"I was thinkin' a headin' back to the hospital," said Tuwanda, moving on from the butt-call topic. "You want me to swing by an' pick you up?"

"Yes," I said without hesitation.

"Gimme 'bout thirty minutes. I'll call you when I'm outside."

Because we were delayed by uncooperative traffic and a poorly timed road construction project, we didn't get to the hospital until over an hour later. But the news was good when we arrived. Sam's condition had improved steadily, and the doctor thought he could be moved into a regular room as early as the next day. I called Beth and MJ with the good news, and Beth promised to pass the message on to Craig, who, it turned out, had been Sam's steady boyfriend for over a month. Sam never talked about his romantic interests, so I hadn't known about Craig. Beth knew about him because she ran into them shopping couple weeks ago, but Sam had sworn her to secrecy.

Chapter 26

Sam was staying at my condo for the duration of his convalescence, which meant, three weeks later, that I was sleeping on the couch and looking at the homes for sale ads in the paper every day. I had finally realized that neither my lifestyle nor those of my friends could be accommodated by a one-bedroom apartment.

Sam claimed he was still too weak to go back to work, but, after I came home from grocery shopping one day and found him vacuuming, I suspected him of malingering. The furniture looked suspiciously well dusted as well, and he had arranged everything in my kitchen cupboards and bathroom cabinets in alphabetical order.

Sam's friend Craig, who turned out to be his contact in the Department of Health Services, offered to share his room at his mother's house, but Sam made it clear he wished to burden me. Still, Craig is a frequent visitor—and a welcome one, since it turns out he is almost as good a cook as Macy.

Sam confirmed that, when McDougall's chauffeur first confronted him, he had indeed tried to make a butt call. He figured he had done it so many times before by accident, he should be able to pull it off intentionally for once. When Lester slammed him against the wall he had successfully hit redial, but at the time he had no idea if it had worked, and, if so, whose number he had called. Since Duane's had been the last number dialed, Duane got the butt-call. Thank God he didn't hang up but listened instead. He sized up the situation quickly and got moving as soon as he heard Sam's loud recitation of McDougall's address. I remembered thinking that had been an odd thing for Sam to emphasize.

I went to the Goodwill Industries distribution center to thank Duane and Basil, and, after oohing and ahhing over Basil's plastic bag collection, I took them both to dinner at El Barrio, which is now under new management

I see Tuwanda quite a bit, since she is on a temporary hiatus from her job and spends hours visiting with Sam and Craig and philosophizing about life's purpose.

There have been several interesting developments in McDougall's case. With their boss dead, Bunny, Lester, and Candy became extremely cooperative and provided information tying McDougall and Maria's stepbrother, Mario, to her death.

Apparently, Maria had tracked down Heiler and had come to the Pearly Gates to talk to him. Heiler was right about the walls having ears: Candy and Bunny had listened over the intercom to their conversation. Maria told Heiler that she suspected the skeleton was that of a foster child placed in the care of a woman who had lived at that address. Apparently, Maria had met the girl while she was in foster care and recognized her at the Third Street house after she was removed her from their group home. Maria said she had been fascinated by the pretty child who had been taken away by the rich, handsome man, and from time to time, she had sneaked out of the group home to watch the Third Street house. She was surprised to see a woman living there with the little girl, but when she saw McDougall visit the house several times, she thought maybe the lady was his fiancée or even his wife. One evening, while Maria watched the house, McDougall's car pulled into the drive, and both Heiler and McDougall got out. Heiler stayed by the car, while McDougall walked toward the house. The lady came out and met him on the front walk.

She seemed angry, and she and McDougall argued. At one point, she slapped him. He grabbed her, and it had appeared to Maria as though he was hugging her, and Maria thought they'd made up. The woman had slumped forward, which Maria's young imagination interpreted as a romantic swoon—something she saw herself doing if someone as handsome as McDougall held *her*. Heiler had helped McDougall carry the lady into the car. But then Heiler left with the woman, and McDougall went into the house. The lights went on inside, and she could see him through the windows going from room to room, searching for something.

Maria told Heiler she had been afraid that her absence at the foster home would be discovered, so she didn't wait to see if he found what he was looking for. As she hurried home, though, she saw McDougall's car heading back toward the Third Street house.

Candy had immediately called McDougall and told him about the conversation between Maria and Heiler. McDougall said he would send Mario over to handle things, and he instructed Candy to keep Maria at the home until Mario got there. Apparently, Mario's family had a longstanding relationship with the McDougall family and had done favors for McDougall in the past, in exchange for a constant supply of cheap labor. McDougall knew there was no love lost between Mario and his stepsister and he resented her success as a businesswoman. The fact that he thought he had a good chance of inheriting her business if she died provided additional incentive.

I suggested that perhaps Mario had also feared that Maria would tell people about his family's abuse of the foster care system, but Craig, who was a licensed social worker, said any such fear on Mario's part would be unjustified. He went on to explain that people, and young children in particular, subjected to the kind of treatment to which Maria had been subjected typically suffer from a sense of despair and learned helplessness and a belief that they deserve whatever treatment they got. As such, they are unlikely to report their abuse to the authorities.

The police believed that Mario came to the Home and either Maria left with him willingly or was forced to leave. However it happened, they ended up in the alley in back of the Pearly Gates, where he shot her, put her in her own car, and drove her to where we found her body. He had set things up to make it look as if she had been alone in the car.

Of course, as soon as the police brought him in for questioning, Mario lawyered up and shut up, but the discovery of blood spatter in the alleyway behind the Home that matched Maria's blood and partial thumbprints on a metal fence post in the alley and on the driver's wheel of Maria's car that matched his gave the police enough to get a warrant and search his house. Once the police found blood—Maria's blood—on the bottom of a pair of Mario's shoes, they arrested Mario and charged him with first-degree murder.

Another mystery was solved when Lester told the police that after reading the newspaper article about our discovery of the skeleton, McDougall had became unhinged. In his muddled mind, he believed that the skeleton was Marni. Lester confirmed that McDougall was obsessed with a young girl named Lily and was convinced that she still lived at the house. He believed that they could be alone now that Marni was out of the way. Lester claimed he had no idea that McDougall's Lily would be in her sixties by now. McDougall had hired our firm on the pretext of needing representation in a lien dispute in order to gain access to the house to search for Lily.

Candy told police that McDougall had sicced him on me after he learned, courtesy of Bunny-the-spy, that

I had talked to both Heiler and Madam K. Candy, like Lester, testified that McDougall was obsessed with a girl he referred to as Lily, and that he had seemed to lose his already tenuous grip on reality when he heard about the discovery of our skeleton. Candy also told us that McDougall had planted a transmitter in our office the day he had met with Sam on his fabricated case. Then, on McDougall's instruction, Candy had driven to our neighborhood in the middle of the night and placed a surveillance camera in our eucalyptus tree. Apparently, when McDougall saw video of Emily, he was convinced that she was his Lily and we had made her dye her hair in an attempt to hide her from him.

As to how Emily got to McDougall's house, it turned out that she didn't go there to talk to McDougall, but she had been snatched outside my condo building by Lester when she ran out after her father had confronted her. Of course, Lester claimed that she went with him willingly, but Emily set everyone straight on that issue. (I believe her exact words were, "Eeeeeeuuuw. Why would I ever get into a car with an old creeper like that? He's gotta be, like, *forty*.")

We couldn't prove that McDougall had, in fact, killed the woman at the Third Street house or that Heiler had disposed of her body, and we still had no answer as to why a child had been imprisoned under the floor of my office. Had McDougall found the child in the house and—intentionally or unintentionally—injured her, and, thinking she was dead, then placed her in the space beneath the floor? If so, why did he still think she was alive?

The police tried to interview Heiler, but Heiler had taken a permanent vacation to fantasy land, and none of his ramblings made sense. I suspected that part of it was an act, because Heiler had visited planet earth for at least a while when he had talked to Maria and then to Emily and me a few days before.

As a chilling aside, Lester also confirmed that he had brought young girls to McDougall's house in the past. At the end of the day, he would pick them up and drop them off in busy, public areas. Lester claimed that all the little girls came with him willingly and the possibility that McDougall was a sexual pervert had never occurred to him. He thought he was just a lonely old man who never had children of his own and liked the company of young girls. He pointed out that each of the girls had left with a new doll and a cupcake, and they had never seemed any worse for the experience.

Perhaps we would never know what actually had happened in my office building all those years ago. Past events have a way of affecting the future, though, and in this case, they had resulted in the murder of a good woman and the near-death of a good man. I also had a suspicion that Emily had suffered more at the hands of McDougall than she let on, but she refused to talk about what happened in McDougall's house except to say Mr. McDougall made her put on the pink-flowered, smocked dress she was wearing when we found her.

One good thing to come out of the whole mess was that, after the Arizona Department of Health Services inspected the premises, all the residents of the Pearly Gates Home were transferred to different facilities and the Home was shut down. The McDougall Family Trust had been using the home to collect fees and state funds that had all gone directly into the McDougall family's pockets.

Most of the home's residents were retired employees of various McDougall enterprises with no family in the area, and they had signed their Social Security checks and other assets over to the Home. The funds from the checks and sale of their assets, together with grants, charitable contributions, and funds from the state and federal governments, made for quite a tidy income—especially since the "high-end specialized elderly care" the Home advertised consisted of a bed, one television per floor, lousy food, and an untrained staff who doubled as McDougall's household help and security staff.

The facility had passed state inspections due to the cooperation of certain employees of the state's oversight agency who were also on McDougall's payroll. Those who were not on McDougall's payroll had been coerced into going along with the plan by Roger McDougall, Roy's nephew, who had threatened to use his power and influence to get them fired if they didn't. As soon as news of McDougall's death broke, many of these people beat a path to the police station, and with their statements, together with the information Emily and I had given the police about conditions in the Home, McDougall's scheme collapsed. There would be no more pictures of the McDougall family in the society section of the Phoenix newspapers. They were now front-page news.

Chapter 27

The police had found Madam K.'s puffin tutu in a dumpster about a half-mile away from Roy McDougall's house. They agreed to release it to me, and I picked it up and dropped it and the lizard suit off at the cleaners. Today, I would return them to Madam K., who had been transferred to a legitimate elder-care facility in west Phoenix.

I hadn't seen Emily since the incident at McDougall's house, but I had called her house several times and spoken to her mom, whose name was, in fact, Missy, about how she was doing. Missy told me that, after a nasty confrontation between Miss Dresky and Webber, they had agreed to Emily's request to transfer her to a public school next year. Apparently, Webber called to set up a meeting with the principal, Sister Mary Grace, to discuss Emily's classmates' online behavior. Miss Dresky, upon hearing the subject of the meeting, made a comment about girls being girls. Then, she suggested that he take what Emily told him with a grain of salt because she was probably making it up as an excuse for getting caught with the other girl's backpack.

She didn't realize, of course, that I had given Emily's parents a printout of the Facebook comments about Emily. I like to think that Webber would have taken his daughter's side anyway and laid into Miss Dresky without the evidence.

I mentioned my plans to visit Madam K. to Missy during one of our conversations, and she'd apparently passed the information on to Emily, because Emily had called me and insisted that I take her with me. I told her she could go only if her parents approved. After everything that had happened, I wasn't exactly on their list of acceptable companions.

Missy got on the line and said she had discussed the matter with her daughter and husband—and they were fine with it, subject to certain restrictions, all of which were undoubtedly the result of Webber's input. First, I was to take Emily to visit Madam K., period. No side trips. Not even a stop for gas. Second, Emily needed to be home within one hour of her departure.

I agreed to the stipulations, and, this morning, after making sure Sam had plenty of water, soda, and snacks within reach and presenting him with the copies of *Elle*, *Vogue*, *Cosmo*, and *Gentlemen's Quarterly* I'd purchased the day before at the drugstore, I picked up the tutu and lizard suit at the cleaners and drove to Emily's house. I spotted

Webber's Crown Vic in the driveway, but Emily was sitting on the front steps, which relieved me from having to ring the bell and suffer through the awkwardness of talking to Webber. Although I had talked to Missy several times since the incident, I had yet to speak with Webber. I did see him at the courthouse last week, but when we passed in the hallway, he had only growled in response to my polite greeting.

Emily seemed pleased to see me. As we drove to west Phoenix, she chattered excitedly about a recent visit to her new school, where she had shadowed a girl with whom she immediately bonded. She didn't mention the events at McDougall's house.

Madam K.'s new home was a large, modern facility next to a lovely park, where several people with walkers and several more in wheelchairs were enjoying the outdoors.

I carried the costumes, while Emily took charge of a framed, autographed photo of Gillian Murphy of the American Ballet Theater dancing the part of Odette. I'd found the picture on eBay and thought it would be a perfect gift for Madam K.

The inside of the facility was clean, light, and bright. The receptionist had our names on her visitors list and immediately buzzed Madam K. to let her know we arrived. A young woman wearing a badge that identified her as a volunteer materialized at the desk and offered to serve as our guide to Madam K.'s room.

We took the elevator to the third floor, where I glanced into several of the rooms as we walked down a wide hallway. Each resident had a television, and, although all the rooms were similar in size, each was decorated with personal items that reflected the character of its occupant.

Madam K. was in a corner room, so she had not one, but two large windows that looked out onto the park. No bars were in evidence.

She was gazing out of one of the windows when we walked in, but she spun her wheelchair around so she could face us when she heard the polite knock at her door.

I wasn't sure she would remember us. Madam K. had seemed to have a better grip on reality than Heiler, but I knew that things can change quickly at her age.

She immediately dispelled my fears. "Kate, Emily—my two shy performers—how good to see you."

I smiled and held up the dry-cleaning bag. "We've come to return your Swan Lake costumes."

"Ah, yes. Did the performance go well?"

"Very well, thanks to your help," I said with genuine warmth.

She nodded graciously. "One does what one can for the *corps de ballet*."

"Would you like me to hang them up for you?" I asked, still holding up the dry-cleaning bag.

"Please. But first, may I see them? I am sure you are returning them in excellent condition; it's just that I don't get to see any of my wonderful costumes very often. It's so difficult to get anything out of the closet, you see."

I understood. I remembered how hard it was for me

to pry the costumes out of the packed closet at the Pearly Gates, and although this room was much cheerier than her previous one, the closet looked like it might be smaller.

I slipped off the dry-cleaning bag, and laid the tutu and frog suit on her lap. She stroked the tutu lovingly and then lifted it to look at the far-less-elegant frog suit.

"Oh dear," she said.

"Is there a tear?" I asked anxiously. For having been worn for a day of wall and fence climbing, I thought the costumes looked pretty good.

"No, dear," she said. "It's in fine condition. But you took the wrong costume. This is for the snake performance in *Le Beyadere*. Frogs don't have scales, silly girl."

I was glad I hadn't known. A smiley-faced snake would be even harder to explain than a frog.

"Look what Kate found for you, Madam K.," said Emily. Then, catching her presumption, she added, "I hope it's okay if I call you Madam K."

"Of course, dear. That's what everyone used to call me at the studio. It saves on syllables, you know," she said.

Emily held up the photo for Madam to see.

She gasped in delight and held her hands out for the picture. Emily passed it to her, and she held it close to her eyes to scrutinize it. She seemed transfixed by the image of the graceful ballerina.

"I never stopped, you know," she said dreamily. "Even after I went to work for Mr. McDougall. I danced in every production put on by the Tip Toe School of Dance, and when I could no longer dance, I sewed costumes."

That explained the collection in her closet.

"That's where I first met Marni." A note of disgust crept into her voice.

Emily and I exchanged meaningful glances.

"At the dance school?" I prompted.

"Yes. She was already working for Mr. McDougall when we met." The note of disgust was now more like a chord. "She came to my class once in a while. She had certain … natural talent. But she was not serious about her art. She did not put in the hours of practice required to be a ballerina."

"Did Marni get you your job in Mr. McDougall's office?" asked Emily.

Madam K sniffed. "She *told* me about the job as her assistant. But I *got* the position because I was qualified."

I waited a few beats before asking the next question. "I remember you telling us she babysat for children Mr. McDougall took in. Did you ever meet any of them?"

"Only one of them. I went to Marni's house to pick up some papers once. Mr. McDougall was allowing her to stay in one of the houses he owned, and, in exchange, she was to watch a young girl." Madam K's expression softened. "The girl met me at the door. I have to admit, she was a lovely child." Her expression hardened again. "But Marni made her dress in clothes more appropriate for a girl half her age. She looked at least twelve, and here she was wearing a frilly little smocked affair with white lace socks and Mary Janes."

"Do you remember her name?" I asked, trying to

sound casual, as if I were merely curious. In fact I was fighting to control an urge to lean forward and fire questions point blank.

Madam K. shook her head and looked back at the photo in her hands. She was getting that fuzzy look again. I was losing her.

"Madam," I said sharply. Out of the corner of my eye, I saw Emily start.

Madam K seemed to cringe, but then her eyes cleared.

"The girl you saw at Marni's house. Do you know what happened to her?"

Madam K. straightened her back but said nothing.

"You said Marni left. Did she take the child with her?" I prodded, softening my tone.

"She said she was crazy about that child," Madam said. Her answer was unresponsive, but at least she was talking again. "I think she really only used the child as leverage, though, because she knew how much McDougall liked the little girl.

"One day I left to eat my lunch—I usually brought a sandwich and an apple from home—but I ran into some of the other secretaries who worked in the building, and they asked me to go out to lunch with them. So I went back to my desk to get my billfold. When I walked in, I heard Mr. McDougall and Marni talking in his office. I didn't think anything of it until Mr. McDougall raised his voice and told her he intended to pick up the child— Lily, that was her name, it just came to me. Anyway, he was going to come and get Lily, that night. Marni started to cry, and I couldn't hear what he said to her next, but I could tell he was angry. Marni quieted down for a while, but then she started yelling. She said she'd stayed quiet about his visits to the little girl because he'd promised to marry her, Marni, and now he was breaking his promise. She pronounced 'visits' like it was a dirty word.

"Mr. McDougall said he didn't know what she was talking about, and he doubted anyone else would either. Then she said she was going to hide the child in a place he would never find her. Her voice sounded like pure hate.

"I didn't hear the rest of what they said. I was afraid they would find me outside listening, so I left. I'm sure neither of them realized I'd overheard."

"Did you later ask Marni what it was about?"

"I didn't have a chance that afternoon, and she didn't show up for work the next day—or any day after that."

"Didn't you wonder what happened to Lily?" asked Emily.

Madam shrugged. "At first, I thought Marni must have taken her with her when she left. But when the police officer came to talk to Mr. McDougall about Marni's disappearance, Mr. McDougall explained that Mr. Heiler had taken Lily to her new family the day before. He said that's probably why Marni had left—because she had wanted to adopt the child herself and was upset."

"You knew Mr. Heiler?" I asked.

"Not personally, but he came to our office quite a bit because he was the head of an agency that helped out children whose families couldn't take care of them, and Mr. McDougall, God bless him, was a huge contributor to the program." Madam K.'s voice reflected pride in her boss's philanthropic efforts.

"You never talked to the police about the conversation you overheard between Marni and Mr. McDougall?" I asked, trying not to sound—or look—incredulous.

Madam K. looked at me in bewilderment. "Why would I? Mr. McDougall had already explained everything."

I wondered if Madam K. knew that McDougall was dead. Even if she did, I doubted she knew that I was the one who had killed him. I didn't think she'd talk to me if she did. She spoke his name with reverence, as if he were still her boss. It was clear that she hadn't considered that he might be a child molester and a crook.

I looked at Emily to see how she was handling the conversation. I suspected that she knew more about McDougall's dark side than any of us.

She did not meet my gaze, however. Instead, after taking the photograph and costumes from Madam K and placing them on the bed, she squatted next to the wheelchair and held one of the elderly woman's thin, blue-veined hands between hers.

"You like Mr. McDougall, don't you?" I noticed that Emily was using the present tense. She, too, had picked up on the possibility that Madam K. had not yet heard about his death.

Tears appeared in Madam K.'s eyes. "Yes, of course," she said softly. "He did right by his friends and employees.

I didn't have the money to pay for a place like the Pearly Gates, and I doubt that Mr. Heiler did either. Mr. McDougall let both of us stay there for a fraction of what it should have cost. He let other retired employees stay there as well—ones who, like poor Mr. Heiler, were mentally incapacitated."

How very wise of McDougall to select residents either too out of it or, in Madam K.'s case, too loyal to complain, I thought cynically.

Madam K. paused to look around the room. "I expect I'll have to leave here soon because I can't afford to pay for it."

That bastard still has her fooled, I thought.

"Don't worry about that," I assured her. "The state has a program for subsidizing those kinds of costs. You'll be fine." I didn't mention that the McDougall Family Trust would, in fact, be picking up the tab.

Madam K. looked at me hopefully. "Will you explain that to the people at the front desk before you go? I want to make sure they know."

"Of course," I said, smiling. "But I'm sure they know already."

Emily and I stayed a while longer, wedging the costumes into the closet and hanging the picture, and then we said good-bye, assuring Madame K. as we left that we would be back to visit again soon.

I stopped at the front desk on our way out and asked that a staff member reassure Madam K. that she would not be kicked out of the home. The woman who had greeted us when we arrived smiled sympathetically and said she would talk to her.

Emily and I were quiet as we drove back to her house. But when I turned onto her street, she asked, "Could we go for coffee? I don't think I can go home yet."

I slowed and pulled over to the curb. "First, you heard your parents' rules, which included both a time constraint and a prohibition against side trips. Second, since when do you drink coffee? You're thirteen. The stuff is supposed to make you gag at thirteeen."

Emily ignored my agitation, and I detected a glint of mischief in her eyes. "Addressing your second concern first," she started out (I couldn't decide if she sounded more like me or her father), "you grew up in the old days, before vanilla lattes. Second, we still have fifteen minutes left on my curfew, and my parents won't know we stopped for coffee unless you tell them."

"You want me to *lie* to your parents?" I asked, knowing full well that if I did, it wouldn't be the first time.

"No. I don't want you to *tell* them," she said. I must have looked like I wasn't convinced—and I *wasn't*—because she added in that wheedling "pleeeease" voice teenagers are so good at, "There's a Starbuck's two blocks away. Seriously. It will be okay. I want to talk to you. I haven't seen you in so long."

Her final appeal got to me. We had spoken to each other very little after the event at McDougall's house, and I hadn't even had a chance to tell her how well she had handled it and what a remarkable girl she was. I had hesitated to raise the subject because I didn't want to remind her of the trauma of that day. However, if *she* was ready to talk about it, I was more than willing to listen.

"Fifteen minutes," I said, throwing my car into gear. I made a quick U-turn and headed back to the main drag. I had never noticed a Starbucks on the corner, but then, in Phoenix, it's a safe bet that there is a Starbucks on every corner.

Sure enough, hiding behind a drive-through bank was a small shop with the ubiquitous green signage—the Golden Arches of the twenty-first century.

We both ordered Iced Chai Grandes, mine low-fat, Emily's with cream, and sat at a small table by the front window where we had a lovely view of the bank's ATM.

I looked at Emily expectantly. This had been her idea, so she had the burden of starting the conversation. She seemed inordinately absorbed in removing the paper from her straw, however.

I cleared my throat and looked pointedly at my watch. "You've got ten minutes," I said.

She looked at me intently and her eyes filled with tears. "He touched me," she said.

She didn't have to say who "he" was.

"He made me change into that dumb dress, and he watched, then he ... I told him I had to go to the bathroom. I wasn't lying. I wanted to throw up. As soon as I got into the bathroom I locked the door and went to the window. I don't think he thought I could get out because we were on the second floor." She smiled shakily and said, "He didn't know I had been trained by a pro."

Tears stung my eyes as well, and I reached out and covered her hand with mine.

"I'm so sorry, Emily. So very sorry."

Her brief smile disappeared. "It's my fault this happened. I should have tried harder to get away when that guy grabbed me and pushed me in the car."

A long-ago scene flashed into my mind, and just as quickly, I pushed it away.

I squeezed Emily's hand. "No!" I said it so loudly that the businessman working on his laptop at the next table nervously picked up his computer and moved away.

"None of this was your fault. People like McDougall are … evil," I said. "You are not the first young woman he abused, and he would have done the same thing to others if he wasn't stopped. You are the bravest person I've ever seen. You stood up to him."

I was so angry at McDougall for what he did to Emily I think I could have killed him all over again. Some of the feelings of guilt I had been suffering over taking the life of another human lifted.

"Do you think that's what he did to Lily? The little girl who died in your office?" asked Emily.

This possibility had occurred to me more than once, and after hearing what Emily had to say, I was now sure it was true. I nodded sadly.

"Do you think she was hiding from him? That maybe that's why she was under the floor?"

"It might be," I said thoughtfully, "but if she got in, why couldn't she get out?"

I thought back to what we had seen when the floorboards first broke. I remembered seeing the outline of a hatch, but it had been nailed shut, and years of re-varnishing had filled in its outline.

I had a glimmer of an idea. I ran it over in my mind, testing it against what we had learned from our research, the interviews with Madam K. and Heiler, and the confessions of Candy, Lester, and Bunny. The glimmer became a glare.

"Do you remember what Madam K. said about Marni threatening to put Lily someplace McDougall could never find her?"

Emily nodded and then her eyes lit with realization. "You mean Marni had her hide under the floor when she found out McDougall and Heiler were coming to get her?"

"Yes, but Marni didn't know she was going to get killed, and there was no way for Lily to get out." The final piece fell into place. My stomach lurched, and I regretted chugging the Chai. "Lily didn't call out for help while McDougall was looking for her because she was afraid of him. She didn't want him to find her. And he must not have known about the floor hatch."

"And after a while, she died," Emily said miserably.

The thought of the little girl slowly dying alone under the floor with a Betsy Wetsy doll as her only source of comfort was heartbreaking.

Now Emily was doing the hand-holding as she clutched my limp hand in hers. "In a way, McDougall killed her," she said. "We avenged Lily's death—and Marni's too."

"And Maria's," I said. Tears were now freely flowing down both our faces. The man with the laptop shot us another nervous look, then packed up and left—or, from his point of view, escaped.

I snuffled some more and then the left side of my brain—the logical lawyer side—prompted me to say, "We don't have any proof—I mean about what happened to Lily."

"It's what happened though. You know it is," Emily said calmly.